CODENAME:

UBIQUITY

Wendy Devore

ISBN: 9781710118919

First printing edition 2019.

wendydevore.com

ACKNOWLEDGMENTS

Words can't express my gratitude to Douglas DeVore, my number one beta-reader, most excellent husband, and partner in crime. Doug wouldn't let a single technical detail go unexplained and astutely pointed out all my hairbrained plot twists. Barbara Feist's stream-of-consciousness analysis reminded me to let Kate's inner voice shine. Stacey Anderson's unvarnished critique pushed me to work harder to find the right words. Thank you to Tricia Castellan for her review, encouragement, and invaluable assistance drinking rosé champagne.

Abundant thanks to Anna Jean Hughes, who ripped this story apart and helped me pick up the pieces in the best possible way. Working with AJ was a fantastic opportunity and an extraordinary pleasure. Big thanks to Sandra Ogle for not one, but two excellent and insightful copyedits. Cover design comes courtesy of the very talented Cherie Chapman.

Finally, a big shout out to all the extraordinarily innovative, passionate, and intelligent people who are my friends and co-workers. You are the home where a geeky girl can thrive. You're an amazing bunch, and I am lucky to know you.

CODENAME: UBIQUITY

CHAPTER 1

KATE

September 9

For a moment, I'm disoriented. Where am I? I blink again, hard. Under the dark belly of low-hanging clouds, salt-scented waves lap against the rocky shore just feet from the jogging path where I stand. To my right, in the distance, I see a small, rocky island dominated by an imposing fortress. Alcatraz. To my left, I glimpse that famous orange-vermillion suspension bridge—the Golden Gate. The tops of its lofty towers are lost in the forbidding cloud cover. The disorientation passes immediately—I'm in San Francisco. I wrap my bare arms around my chest and shiver. I'm spared the fog that normally blankets this part of the city, but without any sun, the breeze coming off the water is frigid.

A wiry cyclist in skin-tight shorts and a colorful race jersey whizzes by on a high-end road bike, and I leap out of his way onto the grassy median.

I decide I will be warmer if I'm out of the wind. I jog across the parking area and the neatly trimmed lawn of Marina Green. The dew soaks through my worn black Converse, and the icy chill invades the tips of my toes.

The morning commute has already clogged Marina Avenue. I cross at Fillmore and wander aimlessly down the wide, tree-lined sidewalk, watching cars inch along. The homes I pass are in the classic Marina District style—stacked shoulder to shoulder, two stories of living space

1

squatting atop a first-story entryway and single-car garage. A product of the roaring twenties, the charming stucco structures are clad in sage or cream or gray and evoke the unexpected marriage of Mediterranean and art deco architecture. Every home has an expansive wall of jauntily perched bay windows or gracefully arched panes overlooking the street.

I hear it before I feel it—the rumble that vibrates through the earth sounds like a freight train, but there are no railroad tracks here. The sidewalk jolts violently and my heartbeat quickens. I clutch the nearest tree in a death grip. Above me, the leaves tremble as if shaken by a giant's invisible hand. I'm suddenly conscious of a new note to the cacophony—the sound of a hundred windows rattling in their panes.

I stare down the street and watch as cars screech to a halt, shuddering violently, as if locked in some sinister dance. Those parked along the street shake too, and one by one their car alarms are triggered, adding their shrill wails to the dissonance.

I'm breathing fast, wondering how long this will last, when suddenly the deep rumble subsides. The car alarms screech in an otherwise eerily silent city.

I release the tree trunk and close my eyes, calming my breath. The earthquake was terrifying, but the damage seems minimal. A few dazed souls emerge from their doorways, and traffic begins to slowly creep ahead once more.

I've taken a few tentative steps when I hear a loud crack, and the rumble resumes, more tumultuous than before. The intense shaking of the earth is so deafening it drowns out even the car alarms. Three more sharp jolts in quick succession, much more violent now, actually knock me to the ground.

Somewhere behind me, someone screams. I clench my eyes and grip the pavement as if this can somehow save me from the convulsing earth, but it can't block out the fearsome groan of the buildings as they heave and contort. Across the street, an ear-shattering crash reverberates through the air. The lower story of one of the houses has partially collapsed, the garage corner now resting on the still-shaking ground. A *gray cloud of dust and debris billows from its wreckage. A huge crack opens up in the concrete near my left hand, and I stare in fascination as the chunks of sidewalk on either side shift independently as if the very earth were breathing. I raise my eyes and catch my breath as I see Fillmore Street begin to undulate. The pavement twists and deforms as the seismic waves slam through the surface. Trees pitch manically from side to side in its wake. The motion of the earth knocks the standing cars into one another. The sickening waves just keep coming, strong enough to make me nauseous. Behind me, the bottom story of every home on the block begins to shift. Windows shatter and great sheets of glass crash to the sidewalk as the structures across the street collapse like a row of dominoes.*

I stare at the home to my left in abject horror as it jolts and rattles, but somehow continues to hold. Great patches of plaster fall to the ground and splinter all around me. As I scuttle away from the falling debris, I see a woman clutching the doorframe in the covered entryway. The structure gives a mighty tremor as she lurches toward me, but without any warning, the entire ground level gives way and the house deflates like a fallen soufflé.

The woman's silenced scream is echoed by my own frantic wail as I reach ineffectively toward her through the mushrooming cloud of dust, my heart hammering hard enough to burst from my chest.

"Earthquake!" I shrieked, bolting upright in my bed and struggling wildly in the tangled mass of sheets. Sweat poured from my forehead and plastered my auburn tresses to my scalp.

"Kate, stop!" my sister insisted, her strong arms encircling my trembling body.

"The building fell and—oh God! She's dead!" I panted, pushing hard against her shoulder.

My pulse was racing; my body tensed, poised to jump into action at the slightest hint of another tremblor. "It's the big one! We have to get outside, before the building collapses!" I urged.

The terrible groan of the earth in motion still roared in my ears.

"There wasn't an earthquake, Kate," Michelle insisted. She gingerly released me.

And then suddenly, the roaring ceased. The sudden quiet was almost as unnerving as the powerful re-experienced echo of the night terror. I peeled open one eye, ignoring the growing blurry disk directly in my field of vision. My sister perched on the edge of my bed, her dark curls disheveled and her face weary. A quick glance around the room showed photos hanging perfectly horizontally on the wall and my ceramic lamp still perched precariously on the edge of my bedside table.

Michelle was right. There hadn't been an earthquake. I slumped in my bed and felt the warm relief flood through my body. It was replaced by a massive wave of nausea, and I cradled my head in my arms. A deep throbbing radiated from the base of my skull.

Michelle laid a cool hand on my forehead and murmured in her low, soothing alto, as she'd done countless times before. "I couldn't wake you. Are the nightmares back?"

"Yeah," I sighed, gathering my drenched hair with a shaking hand. My stomach lurched. The blurry aura grew larger and more vivid—brilliant purple and red, shimmering at its edges.

"I heard. Actually, I'm pretty sure the whole building heard. You want to talk about it?"

"Definitely *not!*" I shuddered. I closed my eyes, and the vision of the woman crushed by her home came rushing back, so real that the dust from the debris triggered a hacking cough. I could still feel the jagged concrete beneath my palms and relived the abject terror in her scream. I forced a deep, slow breath, then another, and the vision faded, but already I could feel the familiar tightening sensation around the crown of my head. A sickening dread formed in the pit of my stomach that had nothing to do with the blossoming migraine.

"I can't believe they're back. It's been over a year since I've had one; I was doing so well."

Michelle sounded exhausted, and I knew it wasn't just that I'd woken her from a sound sleep. "That fellowship interview is totally stressing you out. Should I call Dr. Daniels?" She rubbed her hand across my shoulders.

I pushed my clenched fists hard into my eye sockets. "No, I'll be okay. I'll see him later today."

"Maybe you should meditate?" she suggested.

I blinked hard against the onslaught of multicolored orbs dancing through my field of vision. My head was throbbing so incessantly it was difficult to think.

"No time. I need to get ready. For the interview."

Interview day—the mere thought brought on heart palpitations. Today I was interviewing for the prestigious Breckinridge Fellowship. As a graduate student on scholarship, I was required to do the grunt work for my adviser's research and act as teaching assistant for his undergraduate classes. But this fellowship would provide three years of exorbitant funding to pursue my own research instead. And the project I would work on was an easy choice. If I could study these night terrors, perhaps I could finally be rid of them.

"At least let me get your meds," Michelle insisted. "You can't shine like the code-writing, science-geek superstar that you are if you can't even see straight."

I gave her a weak smile and the slightest of nods. The eletriptan sometimes made me drowsy, but I didn't have hours to meditate this attack away. I'd have to take the chance.

I clasped my sister's elbow as she rose. "Hey, Shell? I know you would rather have a normal roommate. And I was so hopeful that would happen soon."

Michelle began to protest, but I held up my hand. "I know it's no fun living with this. Babysitting your older sister..." I cringed.

"But I just want you to know, I appreciate it."

Michelle smiled, but I could see the frustration swirling in the blue-green eddies of her eyes.

An hour later, the meds, some strong coffee, and a hot shower had done a credible job of restoring me to a functional human being.

I bustled to my postage-stamp of a room and pawed frantically through the tiny closet, though I had no idea what I hoped I'd find there. My entire wardrobe hung neatly in color-coded clusters, but the pickings were slim. No magical clothing fairy had left me the perfect sophisticated business outfit while I slept. I shimmied into my most comfortable black jeans, shoved my feet into a pair of simple ballet flats, and grabbed a navy button-down shirt.

In the bathroom, I self-consciously pulled my shoulder-length auburn hair into a messy bun and snapped an elastic around it. A critical examination of my ashen face didn't inspire any of the confidence I'd need to make it through the day. I slathered a layer of foundation under my eyes to hide the deep purple bags that always appeared the morning after one of my episodes. I'd just finished applying the slightest hint of eyeliner and a touch of mascara when Michelle sauntered in, steaming coffee mug in hand. She took one look at me and wrinkled her nose.

"Is *that* what you're wearing? This fellowship is a *big deal*. You need to nail this. You want to borrow that cute little black dress I picked up on super-clearance last month?"

I stopped a moment to consider. Maybe I *should* dress up for the interview.

Michelle produced the dress. I frowned. Was a little black dress appropriately conservative? I picked at the plastic button on the sleeve of my shirt, and without warning, it popped off and rolled behind the toilet.

"See," she said, grinning. "You can't wear that old thing—take the dress. Put it on!"

The dress wasn't me, but I couldn't shake the thought that I'd need to be better, smarter, and more compelling if I wanted to ace the interview. I tried it on. It fit like a glove but fell conspicuously above the knee. I tugged at the hem.

"Are you sure this isn't too short?"

"You look great. Just take your hair out of that silly bun. It makes your face look pinched. Put on some lipstick. And you need some heels, shorty."

At five-foot-eight, my sister towered over me by half a foot. The scientific literature concluded that sleep deficiency wasn't to blame for my stature, but studies *did* note that short women are perceived as less competent. I sighed and shook my head.

"I don't *have* any heels," I replied, desperately wishing I could ditch the dress, retrieve my jeans, and slide into my vintage, perfectly broken-in Converse Chuck Taylors.

Michelle returned with a pair of black kitten heels. "Wear these."

I slid them on; there were benefits to having a sister who shared my size and actually bought dressy clothes—on purpose. I guess if you have somewhere to go other than to class… I thanked the bargain-bin shopping gods that the heels on Michelle's shoes were short and that I could walk in them without teetering.

My hair, released from the elastic, fell in limp waves over my shoulders. I wished fervently for a style with sassy, swingy layers, but no haircut fairy appeared, either. Instead I slapped on a layer of what I hoped was a conservative neutral lipstick from a tube so old I couldn't remember when I'd purchased it. It looked awfully shiny to me.

Michelle eyed me critically. "The lipstick is good, but you still look…drab. Why don't you let me do your eyes?"

I frowned impatiently. "Okay, but don't do theater makeup on me. It's an interview, not an audition."

She feigned insult as she pulled out her caddy of tools and brushes. "I'm just going to give you a little brown and gold, which will perfectly complement those hazel eyes. Don't worry. I'll be subtle."

When she was finished, I hardly recognized myself. I looked so...girly.

"Perfect. Now, go ace that interview!" Michelle's radiant smile lit up her eyes and wrinkled her nose, which made her freckles stand out.

On my way out the door, I threw a packet of ramen noodles and a snack pack of peanuts into my battered canvas bag and dashed out of our miniscule apartment. I headed to the corner of Emerson and Churchill as quickly as my little heels would allow.

It was another perfect morning in California. Though the calendar was inching toward fall, Mother Nature refused to relinquish her seemingly endless summer in the college town of Palo Alto. Our sunny days were reliably perfect, yet just an hour's drive north would land us in San Francisco's famous chilly fog. The cloudless sky was an eye-popping blue that stretched all the way to the foothills. I loved living near the coast; the air here felt silky, like satin on my skin, and always smelled fresh with a hint of the sea.

The farmlands of central Illinois where Michelle and I were raised were known for their charming agricultural odors of livestock and corn pollen and I couldn't wait to introduce my parents to my adopted state. They were expecting a fantastic harvest this year, and we hoped they would visit us soon. It would be their first visit in the six years since we'd moved to California.

The bus arrived right on schedule, and we puttered past block after block lined with multimillion-dollar homes before turning onto University Avenue. We veered past Stanford Shopping Center, where my sister's gig as a singing waitress at Max's Opera

Café kept us in groceries. I shifted uncomfortably in my seat—Michelle was a great vocalist and a talented actor. Her gifts were wasted serving Reubens and warbling show tunes. She should be trying to make her way in LA or New York, but instead, she'd patiently endured years of my episodes, with no end in sight.

I pulled out my phone for a quick email check. The only new message was from Mom—a link to an article suggesting that vitamin B-12 supplements might improve my focus. By this she meant keep my debilitating night terrors at bay. The miles between us didn't decrease my mother's concern about my condition one bit. She and I both knew a bottle of vitamins couldn't cure my disorder, but she'd never stop trying to find something that would. I wanted to curl up in her lap and cry over the latest horrors I'd witnessed, like I had as a child. But I was an adult now, and she lived half a continent away. Instead of adding to her anxiety by confessing I'd relapsed, I replied to her email with a smiley face and the three-z's sleep emoji.

I put away my phone and reached into my bag for this month's copy of *Vogue,* my one guilty pleasure. Though my lack of personal style in no way reflected it, I adored the art and symmetry of high fashion. Never mind that I'd never in a thousand years be able to afford that kind of luxury.

The trees that lined Palm Drive stood like sentinels standing watch over Stanford University's iconic Quad. I took the first campus stop, right at the end of the lushly landscaped green oval. It was a longer walk, but I liked to stroll through the Quad, its inspiring sandstone arches perfectly framing the Romanesque splendor of Memorial Church.

I headed toward the building housing the Cognitive Imaging Systems Research Lab where I shared a small office with three other graduate students. The lab was under the joint direction of the departments of electrical engineering, computer science, and medicine, and I was extremely fortunate to work for the lab's founder, Dr. Christopher Daniels. I'd actually met Dr. Daniels a dozen years before, when he was still a post-doc at the University of Illinois, and I was a dangerously sleep-deprived child suffering from years of untreatable, debilitating night terrors. My entire college career had been leading up to this singular goal: I was my own built-in research project, and if I could only secure the funding to free up my time and get unrestricted access to an fMRI machine, then I could finally understand how to fix my broken brain. When Dr. Daniels found the call for applications to the Breckinridge Fellowship in last month's *Journal of Sleep Research*, I knew I had to apply.

I poked my head into Dr. Daniels's office on my way to the grad student office. He was busy reshelving texts from the stack on his desk

"You look very nice today," he remarked.

I felt a little self-conscious but smiled in return. "Thanks," I said.

"You look a bit fatigued. Are you having trouble sleeping? Experiencing any—"

The nightmarish groans of the earthquake roared fiercely in my ears, drowning out the sound of his voice. I closed my eyes and took another deep breath.

"What did you say, Dr. Daniels?"

He paused for a moment, cocked his head, and narrowed his eyes. "I asked if you had experienced any night terrors or other disturbances?"

If I told him about the relapse, he'd send me home to rest for a week. I'd miss my interview. This was *not* going to happen.

I straightened my spine and looked him directly in the eye.

"I'm fine. Just stayed up a bit too late. What's up?"

Dr. Daniels gave me a wary look but seemed to dismiss his misgivings. "I need those results on the EEG parasomnia data by end-of-day today," he mentioned, shoving the last book into place.

"No problem. I've almost got the bugs worked out of the code," I assured him. "Anything else?"

"I've done some digging into the Breckinridge Fellowship," he said, stroking the neat black beard on his chin as he always did just before he was about to impart some wisdom. "It's a new grant program, so there's very little information regarding the types of students or research pathways that they're interested in funding. However, word through the grapevine is that Breckinridge's company is expanding his biomedical devices program. So definitely play up your role in our EEG research."

I frowned. "Then why would they advertise the call for applications in the *Journal of Sleep Research*?"

Dr. Daniels shrugged, but his smile was warm and encouraging. "Beats me, but it's definitely right up your alley. With a grant of that size, we'd definitely be able to free you up to get started on your pet project. You'd be able to spend all the time in the fMRI that you could handle."

"You think I stand a chance?"

He patted my shoulder. "If anyone around here does, it's you."

The grad student office was windowless, cramped, impersonal, and completely devoid of other grad students. Four simple veneer-topped tables pushed into a cluster in the middle of the room defined the space, and roll-away office drawers sat below each workspace. My tidy desk stood in stark contrast to the piles of paperwork, sticky notes, computer peripherals, and general disorder cluttering the workspaces of my officemates. Atop a particularly chaotic heap of spider-lined EEG traces on Yoshi's desk sat a wooden sign that read "A cluttered desk is a sign of genius."

I snorted at the thought and dropped my bag on the desk before waking my laptop. I intended to take full advantage of the quiet to check out the latest version of the code we were developing. I hoped that this deadline would take my mind off the impending doom that overwhelmed me every time I imagined standing in front of the interview panel.

I stared blankly at the screen, trying unsuccessfully to squash the stubborn bug that was breaking my code. I rubbed the back of my neck, stood up, and stretched. Despite my best efforts, the looming interview was making it impossible to concentrate. At that moment, Jeff, Silvan, and Yoshi strolled in, locked in animated conversation.

I hunched over immediately, concerned about my almost-too-short hemline.

"Whoa!" Jeff called, taking an exaggerated step back. "Who the hell let a *girl* in here? She's dressed up like a country bride," he hooted.

"Dressed to impress for the interview?" Yoshi's knowing nod was equally irritating.

I glared at Jeff and slid back into my seat, tugging at the bottom of the dress. Hoping my agitation wasn't showing, I affected my coolest stare as I stuck in my earbuds, called up a techno instrumental mix, and dove back into the code.

Even with the techno blasting, it was easy to overhear their conversation.

Yoshi leaned back in his office chair and hucked a squishy stress ball toward the ceiling. Jeff caught it easily on the rebound, passing it hand to hand and kneading it in a way that somehow struck me as salacious.

"Ashley invited me to dinner to meet her parents," Yoshi complained, motioning for the ball and cupping his hands.

Jeff whipped it back to him. "Ho-boy. I'll tell you what," Jeff suggested, propping his massive, well-worn cowboy boots on his desk. "Let's head out for a beer tonight and talk about the reasons why you should immediately break up with that crazy chick!"

Silvan chuckled. "Sounds like another office hours session at the Dutch Goose."

Yoshi shook his head. "No way, man. She'll *kill* me if she knows I've been hanging out at a dive bar with you two."

"Nah," Jeff drawled with his big Texan grin. "Just tell her it's a lab celebration—we'll say it's Katie's birthday. Say we're all going, and you can't say no."

I nearly did a double take. I *never* went out with the other grad students. Actually, I never went out—with anyone. I bit my lip and scrutinized Jeff and Yoshi, racking my brain for an excuse to beg off a night of drinking.

Yoshi shrugged. "Okay, well, then...the Goose it is. Ashley never needs to know that it's a boys' night out."

I dropped my gaze deliberately to my keyboard, blinking hard. The slight stung more than I'd expected. But I suppose it was just as well. A night out drinking with "the boys" was really not something that fit into my regimen for avoiding debilitating night terrors—or, at least, I suspected it wouldn't be wise, if in fact I had ever actually tried it. I took a deep breath, cranked up the music, and sank back into the safety of my work, determined to focus.

Jeff's tap on my shoulder was so unexpected I nearly jumped out of my skin.

"It's interview time, girlie-o!" he sang, giving me a completely inappropriate wink.

My palms immediately went clammy. This was it; now or never. I closed my laptop, slid my feet back into the kitten heels I'd kicked off under the desk, and tried to rise gracefully from my chair without showing too much leg. I noticed that Jeff waited to follow me out of the room, and I hoped he wasn't staring at my ass.

As we headed to the seminar room where the panel interviews

were to be held, the cold sweat spread.

Jeff was up first, so I sat outside the room and agonized while I waited. I popped open my laptop, thinking I'd fill the time by finishing some work, but instead I stared vacantly at the blinking cursor, my mind simultaneously racing yet blank. Pools of sweat formed beneath my armpits. I had a feeling Michelle was going to regret loaning me her dress.

It seemed like ages before Jeff finally strode out of the room, completely relaxed and with a mammoth smirk on his face.

"No worries, little lady, they're a bunch of pussycats. We spent most of the time shootin' the breeze. Those boys sure have a thing or two to say about the women's basketball team. Good luck. See you back at the ranch."

He winked at me again. If he wore a ten-gallon hat, he would have tipped it toward me. I hated that guy sometimes.

I took a deep breath, dry-swallowed, gathered my laptop, and marched into the room, trying to look more confident than I felt.

Three conference tables were arranged in a semicircle, and I quickly counted ten interviewers. All of them were men, all of them were over sixty, and all of them were wearing dark suits. Not my kind of crowd.

I sat in a chair in the center of the tables and waited. The longer I sat, the shorter and less confident I felt. It was as if I'd time traveled to the Spanish Inquisition.

The interviewers shuffled stacks of papers and glanced at one another, but no one spoke and no one would look me in the eye.

Just when I thought I'd have to begin the interview myself, the door flew open, and a tall, gaunt man with a mane of silver hair strode purposefully into the room. His piercing, glacial gaze conveyed complete authority. His exquisitely tailored, crisply pressed navy sharkskin suit gave him the air of an aged, menacing James Bond. He was clearly older than my parents, yet his flinty expression radiated a vitality that was equal parts mesmerizing and intimidating. The force of his personality was so great that his presence alone filled the room with a palpable sense of gravity. I felt my shoulder muscles form an instant knot, and I fought the urge to shrink back into a dark corner. The interviewers uniformly straightened in their seats but maintained total deferential silence.

The newcomer stood between me and the rest of the panel, leaned against the table, and snatched my application from the lead interviewer's hands. He paged quickly through the document.

"Good afternoon, Ms. Rathman, I'm Andric Breckinridge. Let's just get a few preliminary questions out the way."

I gulped and nodded, spine ramrod straight and bare knees glued together. I clenched my clammy palms and tried to breathe slowly.

Andric Breckinridge stared at me with his cold aquamarine eyes.

"Tell me about your undergrad work."

I struggled to maintain eye contact. The sound of my own heartbeat pounding in my ears made thinking impossible. I looked away and composed myself. "Well, sir, I've been a student at Stanford for the last six years. I did my undergrad in electrical engineering here. My master's is in computer science. I am currently pursuing my PhD with Dr. Daniels."

He frowned and glanced at my application. "You didn't start your undergraduate program immediately after graduating from high school?"

"I was actually homeschooled. I had some, uh, medical issues that prevented me from starting college immediately."

"And this means your age is…" Breckinridge probed.

This seemed like a completely inappropriate question.

I glanced nervously around the room. Was my age a problem? "Sir, I'm twenty-eight."

Breckinridge cast a withering look in my direction. "You're no child prodigy, then. Perhaps your social isolation explains why you chose to wear a cocktail dress to an interview instead of appropriate business attire."

I shrank in my seat.

"Do enlighten us, Ms. Rathman—how is it that you find yourself working with Dr. Daniels?"

I took a deep, centering breath and tried to keep the tremor out of my voice. "Well, sir, I have been a patient of Dr. Daniels for many years. When Dr. Daniels came to Stanford to lead the Cognitive Imaging Systems Research Lab, he invited me to participate in his PhD program. Under his guidance, I have been writing algorithms to analyze electrophysiology for a variety of projects and trials."

"Certainly not the standard method of admission."

"There's no favoritism," I stuttered. "I work hard, just like all the other grad students."

Breckinridge pursed his lips and shuffled through my application again. "I'm not hoping to fund 'all the other grad students.' I'm seeking an exceptional candidate. What makes you a worthy investment?"

I clutched my shaking hands together tightly, blinked hard, and composed my thoughts.

"I understand your company is developing new biomedical devices. My current project uses a combination of fMRI and electroencephalography—EEG, of course—to further understand the biology of parasomnias—that is, sleepwalking, nightmares, night terrors, etcetera. Using the two technologies together presents some interesting problems, since the strong magnetic field of the MRI introduces artifacts which generally render the EEG unreadable, but after several months of trial and error, I've managed to write some algorithms that can filter out many of the artifacts so that a clearer picture of the patient's neurological status can emerge."

"You've written algorithms. Do you mean that you've implemented Christopher Daniels's algorithms?"

Had I misspoken? I rubbed my sweaty palms together and licked my dry, cracking lips. "No, sir. *I* developed several algorithms to define the data."

He segued into seemingly endless grilling, as Breckinridge asked me to explain the logic of each of my algorithms on the whiteboard. That was followed by multiple requests to write sample code in several different programming languages. Finally, he demanded a detailed explanation of the inner workings of functional magnetic resonance imaging and the complex statistical procedures that are used to cut through noise corruption to extract the underlying signal. None of the ten other interviewers in the room spoke a single word.

Breckinridge paced as I left the whiteboard and dropped heavily into to my seat. The cold sweat had drenched my body, and the tips of my fingers and toes had gone numb from the strain of trying to withstand the formidable disapproval of this man.

"One final question." His long pause unnerved me. What incredibly complicated subject could he possibly broach now?

"What research will you pursue if you are the recipient of this grant?"

For the first time since I entered the room, I managed a genuine smile. That simple act was enough to flood my body with endorphins. My heartbeat slowed and my body relaxed, just enough to allow me to look him in the eye with some real confidence.

"I suffer from a rare sleep condition—extreme night terrors that present with an unusual REM pattern in EEG. I would like to further understand the source of my disorder, which I believe I can do by monitoring the dreams using fMRI. Ultimately, I want to find a cure."

Breckinridge stiffened and slightly cocked his head. His

newfound interest was somehow even more disconcerting than his presumption that I was clueless, and my self-assurance withered.

"What is the content and structure of these night terrors?"

I unconsciously clutched at the hem of my dress and twisted the silky fabric in my fist. "They are extremely vivid sensory experiences, sir, firmly rooted in realism."

His chin jutted forward and he took a step closer. "Do you experience bizarre or hallucinatory images? Imaginary creatures? Do you fall or fly?"

I breathed in sharply; the horrible sight of the woman screaming as her home crashed upon her replayed before me. The musty scent of plaster dust overtook my senses, and the reverberation of crashing glass windowpanes rang through the room. I closed my eyes tightly and took two slow, deep breaths, waiting for the vision to subside.

"Ms. Rathman, are you unwell?" His callous tone contradicted the concern in his words.

I pried open my eyes, thankful that the only sound I detected was the hiss of the room's ventilation.

"Yes, sir. I'm fine. The answer to your question is no; these night terrors are not, in fact, dreamlike in any way. The normal laws of physics and time always apply. There are never any magical creatures or superpowers." *Which is why they are so damn terrifying,* I thought, making the conscious effort to quiet my mind so that last night's carnage wouldn't creep back in.

Andric Breckinridge's aloof expression had suddenly morphed into something even more unsettling. His keen eyes gleamed with laser-sharp interest.

"Show me the abnormal EEG."

I lifted my laptop from under my chair and typed my password with quaking fingers. My nervous tremor was completely obvious as I handed the machine to him.

He paged through various scans, completely absorbed in the data.

"Fascinating," he murmured

Back in my seat, I sat in silence, doing all I could to suppress the urge to vomit from sheer, unfettered anxiety.

Finally, he stood and handed me the laptop. "Email copies of these EEG traces to me."

"I'll send them by end-of-day."

His frown made the entire room seem darker. "Send them now."

I shrunk back a bit more in my seat but immediately complied.

"The recipient of the fellowship will be announced in January," he said in his clipped and precise manner. Without another word, he turned and left the room.

When I returned to the grad student office, I was mentally exhausted and sweating like a pig.

Jeff looked up from his desk. "You've been gone a good long while, darlin'. How'd it go?"

I clenched my teeth but let the "darlin'" roll off me. "That was pure hell!" I snorted, plopping into my chair. "Breckinridge gave me the third degree. It was like he couldn't possibly believe I had any idea what I was talking about."

Jeff blinked hard and leaned forward in his chair. "Breckinridge was in the room?"

"Breckinridge ran the entire interview."

His incredulous look spoke volumes. "For *your* interview?"

My witty reply was preempted by my stomach's loud groan.

"I am absolutely starving." I rooted around in my bag for my ramen.

Jeff shook his head as he rose from his desk. "Sorry, darlin', the grub'll have to sit till later. There's a gaggle of undergrads waiting for us."

"Shit!" I sputtered. "I totally forgot!" I grabbed my canvas bag and a pile of graded quizzes from the bottom drawer of my desk and hurried after him. Jeff and I were the teaching assistants for Dr. Daniels's BioEngineering 204L Diagnostic Devices class, and we were going to be late.

Nineteen students were shifting restlessly in their seats as we rushed into the room.

A petite woman in a clingy pink sundress flipped her shoulder-length blonde hair and smiled sweetly at Jeff as we began to return the quizzes.

"You just made it, cowboy," she teased as he slid her paper onto her desk. "Another three minutes we'd have taken off." She winked.

I elbowed him as I passed. "She's a student!" I whispered.

No one winked at me as I returned exams.

After the test review, I trudged up to the whiteboard to begin covering the assigned topic for the day: Intro to EEG.

"EEG, or electroencephalogram, is a test that detects postsynaptic dendritic currents from cortical pyramidal cells in the brain using small metal electrodes placed on the scalp," I explained. I looked up and realized that most of the students were staring intently at Jeff instead of me.

"What Katie means…" Jeff interrupted.

"Kate!" I growled under my breath.

"…is that the EEG will detect and chart electrical impulses of the brain."

I sighed as Jeff rambled on, mansplaining the lesson. After a few minutes, it became obvious that he was going to teach the lecture without any input from me. I plunked down in a chair at the back of the room, swept my unruly hair back over my shoulders, tugged at my hemline, and pulled the peanuts from my bag. I munched through the first food I'd eaten since breakfast and resolved that tomorrow I would go back to dressing like just another one of the boys.

The afternoon turned to evening, but there was no rest for the weary graduate student. While "the boys" headed off to the Dutch Goose, I spent hours pouring over my code until the EEG parasomnia analysis for Dr. Daniels was complete. Exhausted, I finally headed home; it was well after eight. When I arrived, Michelle was planted on the sofa, watching an episode of reality TV and singing vocal exercises as she fast-forwarded through the commercials.

"Shell," I admonished. "You have the voice of an angel, but the neighbors are gonna wring your neck. The walls here are like paper."

She flashed her most mischievous pixie grin. "Are you kidding? I have the voice of Amy Winehouse, and no one's going to complain. It's Friday night, live a little! The guys in 2E are having a giant bash. Matt stopped over and said we should come by. They got a keg. Don't you have something to celebrate? How'd the interview go?"

I kicked off my sister's pumps and flexed my sore feet. "Not well. It was like they didn't believe a word I said—about *anything*. All I want is to change into some yoga pants, pronto. You go. I'm exhausted."

"Mmmm-hmmm. Maybe I'll go over there for a little while. You should come."

"I'm really tired. It's been such a long day. And I don't party. And I don't drink…"

"You're going to have to get out there and interact with the rest of the world sometime. Why not tonight?"

I pinched the bridge of my nose, hard, then pressed my fingers into my temples. Neither action relieved the sensation that my head was filled with concrete. "You know I can't! If I stay up too late, I dream. If I drink, I dream. If I don't meditate for an hour before bed, I dream."

"I wish it didn't make you such a stick-in-the-mud," Michelle sighed, her levity deflating into weariness. "I suppose I could just party for you."

I sighed and plopped next to her on our overly soft, overly beige Goodwill sofa. "Please don't drink too much. You know I hate lying to Mom about that stuff. And Matt is kind of...well, handsy."

Michelle turned off the television and slipped on the kitten heels I'd so recently abandoned. "Sis," she said, striking a pouty pose. "That's exactly what I'm counting on."

"Michelle!"

She rolled her eyes but gave me a sly smile. "Just because you can't have anyone in your bed doesn't mean I shouldn't find someone to snuggle up to in mine."

I snorted and buried my forehead in my palm. "Oh, my God—you are such a horndog!"

Michelle rested her hand on my shoulder, and I reached up to give it a squeeze. "Seriously, though, you just had an episode," she said. "Are you sure you'll be all right without me?"

I nodded and motioned for her to go.

She blew me a kiss as she skipped out the door.

Without the din of the television and Michelle's arpeggios, I could easily discern the bass pumping through the complex from our neighbor's raging kegger. I sighed and shook my head. The truth was, I *wanted* to go to Matt's party. I wanted to drink with my sister until I grew giggly and uninhibited and happy. While I didn't need Matt in my bed, someone to hold hands with would be nice. Someone who would ask about my day, take me on an evening walk, or delight me with a homemade meal. And maybe, one day, there would be more. But what man in his right mind would choose to wake up next to a screaming lunatic who might punch him in the face because she's having a violent night terror?

Retreating to my bedroom, I closed the door and withdrew to

the corner. A faded and badly flattened oversize patchwork pillow served as my trusty meditation mat. My mother had sewn it for me when I was ten, and I caressed its faded pink and purple calico squares before lowering myself to the floor. I crossed my legs and placed my hands in my lap, palms turned upward, and took a deep breath.

"With this practice, may I be safe from harm," I whispered.

I thought, *Peace*. I inhaled again and added *light*. I paused before I added *love*.

I cleared my mind and focused all my attention on the sensation of my breath. As fragments of today's calamities arose in my mind, I gently encouraged each to wing away like a little bird into the ether. For as long as it took, I would do nothing more than simply be.

CHAPTER 2

ANDREW

September 17

Andrew opened his eyes, then immediately clenched them as the vertigo set in. He took several deep breaths before the nausea passed.

Lily's shaky voice was filled with awe. "Sweet mother of God, are you seeing this?"

And then, suddenly, he was seeing it. A moment ago, they had been reclining on hospital gurneys. Now, they were sprawled on the dirt floor of an immense warehouse, surrounded by hulking piles of scrap metal. The smell of engine oil hung heavy in the air.

"I can't believe this worked," Lily whispered, hauling herself from the floor and dusting off her jeans. "We are definitely not in Kansas anymore. I can hardly believe this is still Palo Alto." Despite the ramshackle surroundings, her astonished grin stretched from ear to ear.

She offered Andrew her hand, and she pulled him to his feet, even though he easily outweighed her and dwarfed her by a foot. Her long, dark ponytail swung like a pendulum.

"You never told me what Andric's big breakthrough was. How did he work out a method for getting us this far out?" She crept around the edge of the nearest pile of junk and motioned for him to follow.

"He said he acquired some EEG traces of a novel REM state," Andrew replied, creeping after the diminutive Filipino woman. "But you know Andric—everything's strictly 'need to know.'" Andrew's laugh was bitter. "Despite the fact that this is my project, he decided I didn't need to know. Amir reverse-engineered the readings and integrated them into our signal, and here we are...wherever this is."

"Any idea how long it'll be before we converge?" Lily asked.

Andrew shook his head. "Your guess is as good as mine. This is a brave new world."

Lily peered down the aisle of the warehouse. Nothing but silence. She straightened and took another cautious step. "Then I suppose we should get out there and explore it."

It was near sunrise, but the ashen morning light was dismal and gloomy. An unpleasantly warm wind swirled the choking, smog-tinged air through the nearly deserted streets, but Andrew suspected it wouldn't be long before the area was bustling with activity. The smog was so thick that he could barely see the outline of the adjacent building in the sprawling industrial landscape. A discarded sheet of paper flapped against a lamppost marred with graffiti, and a monstrous rat scurried around the corner. In the distance, he could hear the low rumbling of heavy morning commute traffic.

"What is with this insane pollution?" Lily coughed. "Did we somehow land in the middle of Beijing?"

"You know that's not possible. No...this is Palo Alto. It's just not our Palo Alto."

They wandered along the streets in the complex, dodging a flatbed as it rumbled toward the warehouse laden with scrap metal, until they reached a six-foot fence topped with razor wire. The rush of traffic grew louder. The gate that protected the compound was secured with a heavy padlocked chain, but Lily easily slid through the gap, waiting impatiently for Andrew to cram himself through.

The broken concrete sidewalk snaked through an anemic wall of shrubs that obscured the roadway. Six lanes of traffic were clogged with bumper-to-bumper traffic. It seemed that every other vehicle was a imposing, lumbering block of metal, incongruously painted in bright primary colors. Most of them belched noxious black exhaust.

"People here sure love their Humvees," Lily said. "No wonder there's so much smog—those behemoths get terrible gas mileage."

They trudged along the roadway for at least a mile. Andrew's sandy blond hair stuck to the film of sweat on his forehead, and his irritated eyes watered constantly. "None of this looks familiar at all, and the fact that the smog obscures everything isn't helping." He'd been outdoors for only an hour, but already his voice was raspy.

"We need to get out of this junk before we end up with contact emphysema," Lily wheezed.

The sidewalk dipped into an underpass beneath a wide set of train tracks, and at last downtown Palo Alto came into view.

Andrew stopped in his tracks. Instead of familiar bistros, cafés, and trendy clothing shops, University Avenue was illuminated like a small-scale version of Times Square. Where he expected low-rise buildings, he instead found seven-story towers, their exterior faces sheathed with screens flashing a never-ending parade of brightly colored logos that illuminated the smog with an eerie, rainbow-tinged glow. The onslaught of advertising was overwhelming. And here too, like on the main thoroughfare, the traffic snarl proceeded at a crawl, generating a low-hanging cloud of fumes.

A lone pedestrian approached them. As the figure emerged from the gloom, Andrew noted his purple-brown flared pants and short-sleeved shirt with a wide collar in a raucous pattern that reminded him of a skinned pink giraffe. The man stared openly at their tight jeans and solid-color T-shirts as he passed.

Lily elbowed him in the ribs and snorted. "Something tells me we're going to need to try a little harder to blend in. And I can't wait to see you in puce bell-bottoms."

She pointed to the left, and they ducked through the door beneath the glowing crimson Salvation Army sign.

On the store's main floor, he strode casually into the men's section. He selected the least objectionably patterned button-down shirt he could find and a rust-colored pair of slacks. He cringed at the feel of the unidentifiable synthetic fabric. With a glance over his shoulder to ensure the lone employee's attention was elsewhere, he strolled casually into the fitting room.

The clothes fit well enough, looked comfortably worn, and so would do nicely; but he was carrying no cash.

He pulled the tags from his new attire and hung his old clothing, carefully sandwiching them between other items still hanging haphazardly in the fitting room. Without a glance toward the unsuspecting clerk, he strode nonchalantly out of the store. Lily was waiting for him, now sporting a checked coatdress in yellow and toast tan. Fawn vinyl boots completed the look. She slid a totally unnecessary pair of round Jackie O. sunglasses down her nose and peered over the frames.

"You look ridiculous," she said, chuckling.

He gave her a playful shove. "Thanks a lot. I'm starving. Why don't you break out your black ops training and find us something to eat?"

"Yes, sir, mission leader, sir," she replied in a mocking tone. "Seriously, though, a market would be perfect. Everybody needs groceries, right?"

They roamed multiple blocks before locating a promising storefront. When Lily emerged, she had an oversize paisley-patterned hobo bag slung over her shoulder. She reached inside and handed him a sack of jerky.

He ripped the bag open and bit into a chewy chunk with gusto. "What? No eggs Florentine?"

"Next time I'll infiltrate an upscale restaurant and take the sous chef hostage. But in all seriousness, there were surprisingly few options. I don't know what these people eat if there's next to nothing in the market. But in any case, I suggest we keep moving; someone's likely to notice that her purse has gone missing."

They roamed the length of University Avenue, ducking into shops when they could. The quality of the air indoors was drastically better than outside.

When they reached the end of the street, Lily reached into her bag and shuffled through the contents. "We're three hours in, and we still haven't converged. While this place is definitely polluted as hell, it doesn't seem especially dangerous. I suggest we split up and learn as much as we can using whatever time we have left. Keep the jerky. And here..." She handed him a wad of pale-blue currency engraved with a somber portrait of J.D. Rockefeller.

Andrew shoved the bills in his pocket.

"Think you'll be okay on your own?" Lily asked.

"I can handle myself," he scoffed.

"Good," she said, grinning. "If we don't converge first, meet back here at five. We may need to make arrangements for overnight accommodations."

Five o'clock had long since passed. Lily glared at Andrew impatiently as he approached the rendezvous. She held out two keycards to the Cardinal Hotel.

"You're late. Fifteen minutes prior to fifteen minutes prior."

"At ease, soldier. This is a civilian operation. Leave the marines-speak at home." He flashed his most charming grin and selected a keycard. "Thanks for taking care of this. How did you manage it?"

Lily's face relaxed into an impish smirk. "Justifiable appropriation. Better you don't know the details. What have you learned?"

Andrew pulled a folded newspaper from under his arm.

"That's it?" she scoffed.

"What? You have something better?"

"Oh, yeah." She nodded, punching his arm and pointing toward the doorway to a modest café. "You're gonna love this..."

In a booth at the back of the restaurant, he flipped through a menu that was easily thirty pages long.

"What's the most complicated dish on this menu?" she asked.

Andrew pointed. "The beef Wellington."

"Perfect. Now order it with shaved white truffles. And ask them for Kobe beef."

Andrew shook his head. "These tabletops are plastic. The silverware's mismatched. What are you trying to do? Get me thrown out?"

Her smug smile was infuriating. When a harried waitress in a sunshine-yellow uniform arrived to take their order, Lily kicked Andrew under the table. He clenched his teeth and ordered beef Wellington, with Kobe beef, topped in shaved truffles. The waitress didn't even bat an eye. Lily asked for the same.

Andrew eyed Lily suspiciously. "What's your game here?"

"Just wait..."

Three minutes later, the waitress returned with two plastic plates laden with puff-pastry-wrapped tenderloin, topped by thin shaves of truffle.

Andrew took a bite. "Astonishing. This is the most tender beef I've ever tasted. Perfectly cooked. With fine ingredients...served in mere minutes."

Lily beamed. "I know, right?"

"But how?"

"Molecular 3-D printing. For food. It's like a magic microwave."

His jaw dropped. "For food? Impossible! The technology is in its infancy. It's capable of manufacturing a few molecules, at best. And even if it were possible to rebuild an entire meal, using it this way would be an extravagant waste of energy."

"Yeah, well—no one here seems to be concerned about energy use. Haven't you noticed? The enormous cars...the choking smog...the biggest oil magnate of all time staring at us from the currency?"

He stared thoughtfully at his meal, then took another bite.

"So what did you find?" she asked.

Andrew lowered his fork and raised the thick tabloid to the table. He flicked past the categorically absurd "Hedgehog with Human Head Found in Albuquerque" to the more believable "Record-breaking Wildfire Season Claims More Lives" and "Shifting Climate Extends Atlantic Hurricane Season into January." He slid the paper toward Lily and pointed to a brief article buried in the back pages.

PALO ALTO, Calif., Sept. 17—Psychologist Dr. Kathryn Rathman believes her study of the effects of meditation on the brain physiology of Hindu monks may hold the keys to unlocking alternate realities. Her research suggests that the monks' ability to achieve a state of nonduality, or oneness with the universe, may correspond to multiverses as referenced in the Hindu Puranic literature.

Rathman's own sleep disorder led her to meditation at an early age. "I was shocked to discover that the brain patterns of the meditating monks looked similar to readings taken during my nightmares." Is Rathman planning to voyage to an alternate dimension anytime soon? The young doctor hasn't dismissed the idea. "Creation is vast and mysterious, so why not?"

Lily sat in silence, staring at the newspaper.

"Well, damn," she said. "I guess you win."

Andrew's self-satisfied grin never failed to irritate her. "You were right. The beef *is* excellent. However, we have just found someone who thinks her brain structure may allow her to traverse the multiverse. It's almost too good to be true. I want to know what she knows; perhaps it can further our own investigation. Maybe she can slice without the Bug? If she can get in whenever she wants, maybe she can get out, too. The strategy for tomorrow will be to find that research."

The late-afternoon sun beat down through the haze, cooking the smog into a toxic ozone soup. His pace was purposeful, but given the poor air quality, he did not drive to exertion. He circled the concrete municipal building, moving toward the slight figure that slipped out from a side door.

Lily fell into step beside him, her long black hair knotted into a severe bun.

"Where have you been?" she hissed. "There's no telling how much longer before we converge. You're wasting time."

"I took a little field trip to Woodside."

Lily's features transitioned from annoyed to concerned. "You were looking for your mother."

Andrew nodded, his expression grim. She didn't need to ask to know that he hadn't found her.

"Did you locate the research?" he asked.

Though her stride was easy, her pursed lips betrayed the fact that she had returned empty-handed. Lily was not accustomed to failure, and it left a bitter taste in her mouth.

"Negative. Data here is locked down tight. If you want access to research, there are just three ways to get it—you're the originating scientist, you're a bigwig politician, or you own one of those damn multinational corporations spewing out this toxic crap we're breathing." She waved her hand in front of her face, as if the action could cut through the noxious smog choking the skyline.

"You can't get access to anything? Pick some locks? Hack some network?"

Lily shook her head. "Nothing that won't get me arrested." She frowned. "Seriously, these people lock up their scientific data like we lock up nukes. I wasn't able to access any research at all, let alone your gal's paper. These people seem terrified of the free exchange of scientific ideas. It's obvious that corporations run the show here, and protecting intellectual property is priority one. Credentials to access the data are impossible to fake. They use biometrics extensively. So unless you want to cut off someone's finger or pluck out their eye…"

He raised an eyebrow. "Is there any good news?"

"I couldn't find your research, but I did find your girl; data is hard to come by, but it seems it's just as easy to access personal records here as it is at home. I have an address. I think there is potential for…compromise." She handed him a small slip of paper.

Andrew glanced at the slip, nodded, and crumpled it in his hand. "How should we approach the subject?"

"Are you in the mood for a little assault and battery with a side of petty theft?" she suggested, with the slightest of smiles.

He nodded once with determination. "If that's what it takes."

Lily stretched into a lunge, took a deep breath, and coughed. A bead of sweat trickled down her brow. "Are we ever going to converge? It's over forty-eight hours—I don't know if I can handle much more bad air." She raised her hand to her left eye and rubbed vigorously.

"Something wrong with your eye?" he asked.

"It's been twitching all morning," she complained, blinking rapidly.

"Let's just focus on the mission."

She raised her chin and nodded. "Roger that."

The midday sun tried in vain to pierce the haze, enhancing the sickly orange glow; the smog obscured even the closest of the foothills. The short cab ride to the Stanford campus took mere minutes. As the taxi traveled down an uncharacteristically darkened and foreboding Palm Drive, he was shocked to see a nine-foot brick wall topped with razor wire stretching around the campus perimeter. Andrew and Lily feigned animated conversation as they fell in behind a group of students who strolled through the gates.

Inside, the campus looked as he expected—an oasis of familiarity in a Palo Alto gone horribly wrong. Even the air seemed lighter, which he realized was due to a series of enormous humming ionizer towers littered throughout the Quad, purifying the choking air.

"According to her schedule, she'll be heading this way for lunch anytime now," Lily said, her voice low. "Get into position."

He nodded and slowed his pace, trailing well behind. Within minutes, he caught sight of Lily tailing her mark, and he was careful to avoid detection. When he saw her dart into a trash-strewn parking lot behind a coffee shop, he knew it was time.

He ducked behind a row of hedges and watched as Lily sprinted toward the pretty auburn-haired woman with the bobbed haircut and hazel eyes. With practiced moves and feline grace, Lily grabbed the woman's large tote bag, wrenching it from her shoulder.

The woman was initially startled but was not going to surrender without a fight. She grabbed the heavy bag's strap, using her superior weight to swing both the bag and her attacker around. The target balled the fingers of her left hand into a fist and caught Lily in the chin with a clean uppercut. Andrew flinched at the sound of knuckle on bone. He had to admit, it was a good punch.

Lily snorted in pain but refused to loosen her grasp on the bag. She stood just out of range as the woman kicked and scratched in an attempt to regain her belongings. Lily ducked low, swung around quickly, and in a flash was behind the woman. She lashed out at the kidneys, then smashed her foot into the back of her target's knees, propelling the woman to the rough and broken pavement.

The victim let out a sharp cry as gravel dug into her hands and knees. Lily pushed her down once more, then tugged violently at the tote. As it finally loosened from the woman's grasp, the bag sprang open, and its contents scattered around the parking lot.

Watching intently from behind the hedge, he knew his cue and was not about to miss it. He burst through the foliage and ran toward the scene, shouting at the top of his lungs.

"Hey!" he yelled. "What's going on here? Miss, are you all right?"

Lily looked up and glared; then she dropped the bag, turned on her heels, and ran.

He dropped to his knee and reached for the woman's shoulder. "Are you okay?"

Kathryn Rathman looked up from the ground, tears rimming her eyes, breath quick and ragged. Despite the heat of the day, she was trembling.

"Can you stand?" he asked, offering a hand.

She nodded, accepted his arm, and rose slowly.

"Your things—let me help."

She stood, nursing her wounds as he scurried around, collecting her books, pens, a tablet device, and a large sheath of papers, now smudged and creased. He placed the items carefully back into the bag, which he threw casually over his shoulder.

"You're bleeding," he said. "Let me see your hands."

Kathryn turned over her palms and winced as she realized her elbows were casualties as well.

"You're going to need to get these washed up. And you should report this..."

"No," she pleaded, her eyes wide. "If the authorities get involved, I'll just sound...careless." She sighed and pointed to her bag. "Nothing lost except my pride." She looked up with a weak smile. "Thanks to you."

"Still, you're in pretty bad shape," he observed.

She gingerly limped a step, then another. "I think I'll live. Though I'm sure I'll have some cringe-worthy bruises tomorrow."

"Can I help you get cleaned up? You could use some bandages, at least."

She pointed to the back alley door of the café. "I'm a regular. I can wash up in there, and I'm sure the barista won't mind if I raid her first aid cabinet."

Kathryn hobbled gingerly toward the coffee shop. Once inside, the barista took one look at her, gasped, then shepherded the injured woman directly to the back room.

Andrew ambled to a small table near the back of the nearly empty café, far from the windows. He allowed the bag to settle to the ground near his feet, and with a furtive glance to ensure he was positioned out of sight, he reached inside. He pulled the sheaf of paper onto his lap and paged through it deliberately, spending only seconds on each page. When he reached the end of the document, he slid it carefully back into the bag and moved to a well-worn brown leather armchair near the front of the shop.

Kathryn emerged from behind the counter wrapped in bandages and beginning to regain her composure. She sank down into the adjacent armchair. The barista brought her a cup of steaming mint tea.

He sat quietly as she sipped.

When she finally spoke, her eyes were downcast, and her shoulders remained slumped. "I should thank you, but I don't even know your name."

A sincere and confident smile spread across his face as he handed her the tote. "I'm Andrew. No need to thank me; it's what anyone would do." He extended his arm and enfolded her bandaged hand in a gentle handshake with a precisely calibrated amount of pressure. Keeping her hand pressed within his own, he fixed his gaze directly on her face until she finally looked up. Her shy smile was exactly the response he was hoping for.

"I'm pleased to meet you, Andrew. I'm Kathryn. I really am grateful; I can't begin to explain what kind of complication it would cause if I'd lost this." She instinctively gripped the bag tighter.

He allowed a look of recognition to blossom in his eyes. "Hey—your picture was in the paper! You're studying the brains of Hindu monks."

She straightened and looked at him curiously. "I can't believe you saw that. It was buried on page sixty-three. But yes, the results of my study have just been published."

"The article said you are the youngest fellow in the psychology department."

She blushed, but nodded and beamed with pride.

He smiled even more warmly and nodded toward her bag.

"Your paper is in there?"

"Yes," she sighed, looking at her bandaged hand as it cradled the steaming beverage.

A moment passed in silence. She sipped more tea. A bittersweet love song played in the background, and she tapped her foot to the rhythm, but she said nothing.

As the song ended, he sighed, turning his steady, intense gaze toward her, confident that she would not detect his subterfuge.

"My father was a scientist. He always thought that there was infinite potential locked inside the human brain. Too bad he didn't live to see your discovery. He would have been thrilled to read about it."

She raised her head and met his gaze directly, scanning his features for any hint of insult. Finding none, she waved a hand dismissively. "If he was a scientist, I'm sure he would have scoffed at my research. Psychology is a soft science, you know."

He tilted his head and arched an eyebrow. Time to take a calculated gamble. "I'm not so sure. According to the work of Hugh Everett—"

Kathryn pursed her lips in an attempt to suppress a smile. "Are you a physicist?"

Andrew allowed the slightest of smiles and gave a halfhearted shrug.

She leaned forward slightly and self-consciously rubbed the bandages on her left hand. "Then you know that Everett's many worlds theory of quantum mechanics was discredited. I believe he was described as 'indescribably stupid' by his contemporaries."

"You're familiar with Everett's work?" Too late, Andrew realized he'd momentarily lost control of his careful mask.

Her eyes sparkled; she'd caught his fleeting moment of surprise. "Why? Because I'm a psychologist? That sensationalist rag implied I'm off my rocker, but I'm no random whack job. I've done my homework. String theory, quantum theory...the scientific community is a tough nut to crack, but from the inside, I have access to a great deal of information."

Andrew felt his pulse quicken. He lowered his voice and shifted his weight almost imperceptibly toward her. "What would you say if I told you that I believe Hugh Everett's theories, and that I'm incredibly interested in knowing more about how they apply to your work?"

She snorted and shook her head. "I would say I have never met any physicist quite like you."

"No," he replied, in a moment of unguarded candor that surprised even himself. "I doubt you have."

She considered him for a long time, eyes searching for even a hint of derision. In the end, she didn't find it.

"Would you have another drink with me?" she finally asked, smiling shyly. "If we're going to have a deep and meaningful conversation about the nature of the multiverse, something a bit stronger is in order."

His genuine grin illuminated his vivid blue eyes. "I can honestly say I'd like nothing better." He stood and offered her his hand.

She accepted his gesture but startled him when she kept firm hold of him as she slung her bag over her shoulder. Hand in hand, they headed toward a trendy wine bar three doors down. As soon as they settled into a booth, she requested an expensive bottle of Heidsieck rosé champagne.

"Now, Kathryn," he said, folding his hands and giving her his most earnest smile. "Tell me more about your musings on multidimensional travel..."

CHAPTER 3

JANINE

September 19

The darkened hospital room sat at the end of a long, desolate hallway. Isolated from the bustle of doctors and nurses, the space radiated an unnatural silence. The man in the rumpled white coat standing guard outside was the only indication that the corridor wasn't completely abandoned. He might have been a medical resident, except for the military-style buzz cut, his hard, chiseled features, and the presence of a poorly concealed sidearm.

Within the dimly lit room, two identical hospital beds flanked a utilitarian plastic chair. In the bed on the right, an unconscious male form nestled beneath the loft of a silver Mylar warming blanket, his breathing rapid and uneven. A thick umbilicus of wire snaked from a dense web of sensors intermingled with his sandy blond hair. EKG leads covered his chest, and an oxygen sensor was clipped to his finger. A metallic device, three inches tall, balanced on spindly legs on the back of his right hand. Under darkened lids, his eyes flickered erratically and unceasingly. Monitors recorded the wild spikes in heart rate and brain activity, and relentless beeping permeated the gloom.

The other hospital bed was occupied by a slight woman, her long black hair wrapped around a matching set of leads, sensors, and wires. An identical silver device rested on her right hand. The machines monitoring her recorded similar readings, suggesting an identical malady.

At vigil beside the patients, visibly uncomfortable in the unyielding plastic chair, sat a woman in her mid-fifties. Dr. Janine Mori's slight frame was dwarfed by an immaculately pressed white doctor's coat. Under a helmet of short, stylish salt-and-pepper hair, her obsidian eyes bore a look of weary resignation.

In the adjacent bed, the young man gasped and convulsed; the doctor leaned forward in expectation and frowned before cautiously gripping the patient's arm. There was no response.

The door to the room swung wide, revealing the towering, lank silhouette of Andric Breckinridge. Intensity radiated from his gaze, and he looked ready to pounce at any moment, despite the deep circles beneath his icy blue eyes. When he spoke, it was with authority; his voice was cold, succinct, and imperious.

"Well, Janine?" He didn't bother to fully enter the room, his features etched into a permanent scowl.

"Hello, Dr. Breckinridge," Dr. Mori replied curtly, removing her tortoiseshell glasses and rubbing her eyes. "Neither Andrew nor Lily is responsive. Abnormal REM sleep patterns continue unabated. Brain activity is off the charts. Cortisone levels read through the roof. But neither have awakened."

"And the vitals?"

Dr. Mori picked up a tablet and swiped through a series of charts and reports.

"Elevated temperature, pulse, and breathing. Andrew's white blood cell count is unexpectedly high, and increasing. Lily's last MRI has uncovered an unsettling swelling of the brain stem." Dr. Mori sighed, shaking her head. "I don't know how much longer they can hang on."

Andric Breckinridge took two long strides into the room and snatched the latest round of test results from her hands. She stood deathly still as he flipped through the scans on the tablet.

She shook her head and breathed heavily. "It's been over two days. With every passing hour, it's more likely they won't converge. We can't allow this to continue." She regarded Andric expectantly. "It's destroying them, from the inside out."

Andric scowled and vehemently shook his head. "I refuse to throw away four years of R and D. The experiment continues."

Dr. Mori's frown deepened. "If you don't end this, you will kill them both!" Despite the rising volume of their argument, neither patient showed any sign of consciousness.

"For your sake, I hope you've bought them enough time," Andric hissed as he pressed the call button for the nursing station and the intercom sprang to life. "I want the anesthesiologist in here immediately. It's time to medically induce coma." Andric stared pointedly at Janine. "This had better work," he growled, "because if it doesn't, we'll be doing some recruiting."

The anesthesiologist bustled into the room pushing a cart containing a pair of computer-controlled propofol pumps. He efficiently connected the first machine to Lily's IV, depressed a flurry of buttons, and checked the patient's vitals. With a satisfied nod, he turned his attention to Andrew and began a similar procedure.

"I expect a call when they awaken," Andric barked. He charged from the room without a further glance at either patient. As the door hissed closed on its pneumatic hinges, Janine Mori clenched her jaw, cursing under her breath in Japanese. She glared in the direction of the departed CEO, anger clouding her voice. "Isabel always warned me you were not to be trusted."

CHAPTER 4

ANDREW

September 19

The brilliant kaleidoscope of color generated by the video panels plastered on every building in sight counterbalanced the sallow gloom of dusk when Andrew stepped into the lobby of the Cardinal Hotel. His quick scan of the space confirmed that Lily wasn't there, so he headed directly to the second floor.

When he reached his room, Lily was slumped on the floor in front of the door. He moved quickly to her side and reached for her chin.

Lily snapped to attention and slapped his hand away, hard. "Where have you been?" she hissed. "You're hours late."

He rocked back onto his heels and scrutinized her features. Her eyes were swollen and slightly bloodshot, and her forehead was damp with a sheen of sweat.

He frowned and stood, offering her a hand. "I've been gathering information."

She blinked rapidly, rubbed her left eye vigorously, and allowed him to help her up. He noted with rising concern that her grip was uncharacteristically weak.

"Why aren't you waiting in your room?" he asked. He reached for her arm as she stumbled.

"Something's wrong…" Lily listed noticeably to the left, and her voice held an uncharacteristic tremor.

Andrew fumbled with the keycard and managed to open the door without dropping Lily. He moved her carefully to an armchair and lifted her wrist to check her pulse. Her arm began to quiver. At that moment, he felt a stabbing pain in his left eye.

"What are your symptoms?" He pressed his palm into his left eye.

Lily took a ragged breath. "I've lost vision in my left eye. My left arm has been convulsing on and off for the last hour."

He moved closer and gently lifted her left eyelid, then her right, ignoring the small, dense hole forming in his own field of vision.

"Dilated pupils, clammy skin…" he muttered.

Lily's body suddenly went rigid, her head twisting to the side as her eyes stared blankly into space. Then she began to convulse, her body jerking over and over. Her breathing became ragged and irregular, and her skin grew pale.

"Lily!" Andrew shouted, cushioning her head.

As quickly as it started, the seizure was over. Lily turned to him, a look of terror in her eyes.

"Andrew! What the hell is happening to me?"

He opened his mouth to reply, but then she blinked—and he had vanished.

Lily gasped; her eyes grew wild. She attempted to calm her breathing, forcing herself to inhale and exhale as time slowed to a crawl. Fifteen minutes passed, then thirty. Hot tears ran down her cheeks as she raised her uncontrollably shaking arm before her face. With a guttural sob, Lily slipped from the armchair to the floor and curled into a fetal position. "Please," she implored in a voice now hoarse and raspy, "don't leave me here." When the next seizure began, there was no one there to bear witness.

CHAPTER 5

ANDREW

September 19

Janine had sent the text mere minutes ago, and the CEO had responded instantly. Andric Breckinridge's menacing step toward the cowering anesthesiologist was interrupted when the urgent pulsing of the monitors abruptly slowed to a steady, regular pace. The jagged peaks and troughs on Andrew's EEG shifted; the erratic pattern suddenly stabilized. The deviation in sound from the tangle of machines stopped Andric midstride, and he turned toward the gurney. Beneath the warming blanket, Andrew shifted once, then again. His eyes fluttered, then opened.

In a hoarse voice, he whispered, "Lily. Did she make it back?"

Janine shifted her gaze to the flatlined graph of the EEG monitor beside Lily's motionless body and shook her head.

Andrew closed his eyes once more and breathed a single ragged sob.

In the hospital bed beside him, the slight Filipino woman lay pale and lifeless.

The distraught anesthesiologist stood, solemnly disconnecting Lily's propofol pump. "I'm terribly sorry, but there's nothing more I can do for her."

Janine inclined her head and laid a hand on his shoulder.

"Thank you. I know how hard it is to lose a patient," she murmured.

Andric glowered at the medic as he gathered his equipment and rolled it from the room.

The moment the space was cleared, Andric snapped open a laptop and shoved it roughly onto Andrew's lap. His face remained pale and his breathing was uneven, but Andrew's eyes fluttered and opened.

"Write it down," Andric barked, gesturing impatiently toward the computer. "Everything you saw. Every word you read."

Andrew reached gingerly across the laptop and instead gathered up the small, silver device resting on the back of his right hand.

Janine gently removed the object from Andrew's shaking grasp and took a step that placed her firmly between Andric and her patient. She squared her shoulders and affected a fierce stare.

"What he needs right now is rest," she countered.

Andric scowled threateningly at the device, then over Janine's shoulder at Andrew. "I expect your full report by tomorrow morning. No exceptions!"

Andric pulled sharply at the lapels of his fine suit jacket and abruptly spun on his heels. He charged briskly from the room.

Janine slumped into the chair between the two gurneys, crumpling as if all the air had gone out of her. At best she'd been able to snatch sleep in twenty-minute intervals over the past three days; she was exhausted in every sense of the word. Yet despite all her effort, the results had been disastrous.

She gently squeezed Lily's unresponsive arm and tenderly removed an identical small, silver device from her hand. She cradled both objects, but her musing was interrupted by the tentative staccato clacking of the keyboard.

"Andrew, stop. Rest. It can wait," she pleaded.

His lips were pinched in a firm, thin line. "No," he said,

pausing long enough to unclip the EEG cap from beneath his chin and casting aside the web of sensors. Andrew turned his attention back to the laptop. "He can go to hell, but I owe it to Lily to salvage what I can from this disaster."

Janine stared at him in disbelief. "Salvage what? We've lost Lily—that's devastating. I nearly lost you as well. This procedure is just too risky. There's no choice. We have to shut it down."

Andrew's typing abruptly ceased, and he turned his hard stare to Janine.

"You're right—this is dangerous. Now we know that we won't converge unassisted. We can't use the propofol protocol again. But we don't have to abandon everything. I may have found our silver bullet."

Janine snorted. "You can't be serious. I won't endorse another medically induced coma."

Andrew's gaze never faltered. "If I'm right, you won't need to. It's not a procedure I need. It's a person. Keep this as quiet as you can, but find me a woman named Kathryn Rathman."

CHAPTER 6

KATE

September 21

I sink heavily into a plush, almost buttery black leather sofa in a spacious modern condo high above Lake Shore Drive. The wall of windows showcases a panoramic view of Lake Michigan down to Navy Pier. The strong, nutty scent of expensive coffee permeates the space as it brews. It is near daybreak, and I casually follow the headlights of the early morning traffic as it flows along the thoroughfare below. A fit and vital man in his early sixties wearing a brown silk bathrobe shuffles in and meets an attractive woman with bobbed gray hair and white satin pajamas in the kitchen. She reaches for a waffle iron and shuffles through her kitchen cabinets. They share a kiss, and he pours her a cup of coffee before preparing his own.

The tranquility of the morning is suddenly disrupted by the droning wail of the tornado siren. The man's forehead wrinkles as he walks to the windows, his confusion intensifying as he notes there's not a cloud in the sky. He fumbles for the remote control and flips on the morning news.

The first rays of the sun erupt over the lake, and I catch the glint from a silver object soaring through the sky. It grows larger much too quickly, and my pulse quickens as I realize it's a wide-bodied plane.

As the man and his wife listen in shock, the newscast is replaced by a bright blue screen and a high-pitched warning tone accompanied by a prerecorded message—"This is not a test. This is an actual emergency. Please read and comply with instructions on the screen." White text on the blue screen urges residents of Chicago to evacuate immediately. An air threat is imminent. A mounting feeling of dread turns my mouth to sandpaper, and I'm left with a sickening metallic taste at the back of my tongue.

"Harry, what's going on?" the woman asks, her voice heavy with confusion. Harry is still staring at the television, silently mouthing the emergency information.

"This is bad…this is bad…" I chant. Something horrific is going to happen, any minute. I struggle to rise from the cushiony depth of the sofa. "YOU HAVE TO GET OUT OF HERE!" I shout.

Harry and his wife cannot hear me.

Agitated, I move to the wall of windows, willing the aircraft to swerve. The glorious sunrise intensifies above the sparkling blue waters of the lake, and the plane grows even larger. The speed and trajectory of the aircraft are undeniable; it's headed directly toward us.

Harry finally looks up from the television and notices the plane. He drops his coffee; the stoneware cup explodes into a hundred shards on the travertine tile, and a pool of dark brown liquid spreads across the floor. He urges his wife into the bedroom, and I hear dresser drawers slamming and closet doors hastily pulled open. I wring my hands and pace. Why don't they escape? They're running out of time! They dash from their bedroom, haphazardly clothed, heading toward the flat's entranceway. I know I should go too, but it's as if I'm frozen in place. The dread burrows deeper in my chest, but I'm unable to follow.

The plane draws so near that I can see the elaborate crest of a two-headed eagle painted on the side, and I fear that this will be another 9-11 terrorist catastrophe—that the plane will impact the building. But at the last second, it pulls sharply upward. An oblong silver canister, sleek and aerodynamic, is released from its belly and begins its glide toward the earth.

The woman turns, uncertain, and rushes back to the sideboard, where she snatches a heavy glass-framed photo. It's their wedding portrait. In an instant, the room is awash in a blinding flash of searing white light, and I sense heat intense enough to melt my flesh. The pain I should feel is instead supplanted by a terror so complete that my entire body trembles violently. My breath comes in short, ragged gasps, but I stay rooted to the spot, as if paralyzed. I watch as the woman's face twists in horror, and her skin begins to burn and peel like newsprint in a fire, yet I cannot look away. I hear her husband's earsplitting scream from the hall as the glass frame of the photo melts away and the picture turns to dust.

"IT'S A DREAM!" I shriek as loudly as I can. "IT'S A DREAM! IT'S A DREAM! IT'S A DREAM!"

I crawled out of my bed and stumbled to my mat, struggling to breathe. The violent afterimage of the detonation still burned my retinas. Stabbing pain pulsed behind my left eye. I smashed my hand hard against my skull.

I clutched the cushion to my chest, my trembling body still racked with spasms. Focusing on its familiar scent, I fought for each gasping breath for what seemed like an eternity. Eventually, the tremors stopped, and my chest relaxed. I released my pillow to the ground and gradually settled myself. I needed to begin meditation practice immediately or the blossoming migraine might knock me out for the next week. I forced open one eye to check the clock: four thirty in the morning. Two nightmares in two days? There was no doubt that this was very, very bad.

I rested on the mat, eyes closed, palms up, thumbs touching middle fingers. "With this practice, may I be safe from harm," I chanted in a ragged whisper, and then I compelled myself to breathe deeply and with intention. I forced all my attention on the sensation of my breath. Slowly, slowly, with each passing inhalation, I let every terrifying thought, every grisly image, every horrible tendril of the nightmare slip from my mind's eye until I was left with nothing at all.

It took a long time, but the migraine was circumvented, and the dread and nausea had nearly passed. Sleep was not an option, so I headed to the shower and let the hot water do the rest of the work. When I emerged it was nearly seven. The last golden rays of sunrise stretched across the sky and birds chirped in the tree outside our sparse living room. I plopped onto our lumpy secondhand sofa and thanked all that was good in the world that no planes were flying anywhere near our building today.

My thankful musing was interrupted when my phone rang. I fumbled around until I found it, on the floor, and yanked it from its charging cable.

The photo that appeared on the phone's lock screen showed a beaming eight-year-old girl side by side with her mother. Their joined hands cradled four darling little balls of fur. A wan smile crept over my lips. That was the year Mom and I had raised rabbits for my 4-H project.

"Hi, Mom."

"Katie, I'm sorry I called so early. Did I wake you?"

I knew my mom rose with the sun, and in central standard time, she had already been up for hours by now.

"No, you didn't wake me."

"Well, I was just thinking about you. How did the interview for the fellowship go?"

I groaned. "It was a total disaster. The CEO of the company showed up and grilled me. There's no chance I'm going to get that grant."

"Oh, honey, you're always too hard on yourself."

"Just realistic, Mom," I interrupted. "And to make matters worse, the nightmares are back."

"Oh, no!" she gasped. "And you were doing so well! Are you okay? Is Michelle there? I should talk to her—"

"No, she's still asleep. I'm fine; I didn't get much of a headache.

I'll be okay."

"Well, you should call Dr. Daniels right away. Maybe he would want you to go back on the medication."

"No way!" I protested. "That stuff made me a waking zombie. If I hadn't been on those drugs, maybe I could have gone to high school—like a normal kid. And the drugs didn't work, anyway."

"Well, yes, that was unfortunate. But you thrived in homeschooling."

Except for my social life, I thought. Time to change the subject. "So...how are you and Dad?"

"Oh, we are doing fine," she said in the traditional Midwestern way. "Your dad is just starting the corn harvest now, but that old combine harvester keeps breaking down. It's lucky he has such a fine mechanical mind. It would cost us a small fortune to get that old thing repaired every time it decided to conk out."

"Are you and Dad still planning to visit once the harvest is in?"

"It doesn't look good," Mom said dejectedly. "We had the twelve weeks of drought early in the summer, and then all the flooding in August—half the crop's ruined. Thank goodness for the farm subsidy, but your dad still isn't sure how we're going to make ends meet."

I closed my eyes against an unexpected wave of vertigo and pressed my fingers hard against my temple. For a second, I really thought my parents were coming to visit soon. I chalked it up to the aftereffects of the near-miss migraine, but this wasn't a normal symptom of my weird nightmares. I'd have to mention it to Dr. Daniels.

"But you guys are okay, right?" I pressed.

"I hope we'll scrape by."

My heart sank. The weather had been weirder than usual across most of the country this year, but for some reason, I'd been certain that my parents were expecting a bumper crop. I hadn't realized that my family's fortunes were in such bad shape.

"Oh, Mom—I wish there was something I could do."

"The best thing you can do is study hard and take care of yourself. Well, you should get started with your day, love," Mom suggested. "You sure you can't put Michelle on the phone?"

"I hate to wake her—you know how she's always taking care of me. Let her sleep."

"You know, it was her decision. We didn't ask her to do it."

"I know," I replied. "But I feel so guilty. She shouldn't have to babysit me. She deserves her own life."

"Well, let's just take things one step at a time," Mom advised. "You just go see the doctor. Your dad and I love you, kiddo."

"I love you too," I replied. I disconnected, missing her more than I wanted to admit.

I was just about to set the phone aside when an email notification flashed on my screen. When I read the subject line, an uncontrollable yelp burst from my lungs.

"Ohmygod, ohmygod, ohmygod!" I squealed.

Michelle dashed from her room, her rumpled black hair askew. "Kate! What's wrong? Did you have another nightmare? Should I call—" She stopped short when she saw the enormous shit-eating grin plastered on my face.

"I got an email from Albaion—it's Breckinridge's company."

"Is it about the grant? I thought you said the selection is in January…"

"They want to offer me an internship for the semester!" I flicked the display to read more.

"That's amazing!" Michelle beamed, plopping down on the sofa beside me and reading over my shoulder.

As I scanned the screen, my brow furrowed. "They've set up an appointment for me to meet the team at Stanford this afternoon."

Michelle read the next line. "Due to the secure nature of our facility, you cannot be admitted prior to completion of a thorough background check and the submission of a signed nondisclosure agreement."

I flicked again, scanning the text. "They want me to start immediately."

"But what about the rest of this term?"

"I'll talk to Dr. Daniels. Maybe one of the other grad students can cover for me."

Michelle reached over to swipe the screen. "Holy shit! Look at that salary!"

My hand flew to my mouth. "That's four times my annual stipend. For one semester of work? That's insane."

"Oh, Katie, this is amazing."

"There's one more line here—'Successful completion of this internship will advance your application for the Breckinridge Fellowship. Please confirm your interest by replying to this message.'"

Michelle was actually bouncing as she urged me on. "Reply. Reply immediately."

I thumbed a quick acceptance message and hit Send.

Michelle wrapped her arms around me. "This is it, Kate. Your big break. I couldn't be happier for you."

It seemed so perfect. So why did I suddenly feel so uneasy?

Dr. Daniels's reaction to my news was less enthusiastic than I'd hoped.

He sat back from his desk and frowned. "It's highly unusual for a corporation to propose an internship that starts immediately, especially when the term is already in progress."

"Yes, I know, but it's such an excellent opportunity…"

"I know you've been in remission for over a year, but do you think it's wise to make such a drastic change?"

I clenched my hands and stared down at my feet. "About that…"

"Kate, have you relapsed?"

I nodded.

"I'm not so sure this is a good idea. The stress alone is almost certainly a trigger."

I wanted to plead but tried my best to sound convincing instead. "Please, Dr. Daniels—they suggested that taking this internship will help me get the grant. I need to do this."

Dr. Daniels pinched his lips and shook his head.

"Okay, Kate. If it's really what you want, we can make it work."

The rest of my day at the lab was singularly unproductive. The hours crept by at a snail's pace as I waited for the meeting with Albaion. I found my mind wandering as I graded student homework, read through a few new research papers, and tried unsuccessfully to refactor some poorly structured code. At four thirty, I headed upstairs to the conference room, steeling myself for another interview-style grilling.

To my profound relief, only three people were waiting for me in the room, and none of them were old men in suits.

A trim, earnest woman wearing a smart black blazer rose from the conference table and extended her hand. Her graying shoulder-length hair framed dark, sincere eyes behind her thick-rimmed glasses. "You must be Kate. I've heard so much about you. I'm Dr. Janine Mori, vice president of the research division at Albaion."

I swallowed hard. Since when did big companies send their VPs to interview interns? Her grip was firm, but her palm was warm and soft. "It's so nice to meet you, Dr. Mori," I replied, trying to quell my nerves.

"Please," she said, smiling. "Call me Janine." The hit of anxiety I felt when she introduced herself ratcheted down a notch. She gestured to the two men who had also risen from the table. "These are the project's head architects, Amir and Andrew."

"'S'up, Kate?" Amir asked, with a nod that tossed his dark, wavy hair. His olive skin, day-old growth of beard, and Middle Eastern name did not at all jive with his southern California accent, or with the maroon T-shirt that was emblazoned with big, white letters spelling out "Code Monkey." He was barely taller than I was, but one look at his build made it obvious that he knew his way around a set of weights.

Andrew seemed mildly surprised, but for only a moment. He ran a hand through his slightly unruly, tousled sandy blond hair. A slow smile crept across his face, but it never reached his eyes— eyes that were the most startling shade of blue. That smile transformed his pleasant but blandly handsome features into something decidedly more...mesmerizing.

He was lanky and wiry and loomed over me by nearly a foot; but unlike most engineers I knew, he was impeccably dressed in skinny Tom Ford jeans and a crisp, pale blue button-down shirt with the little polo pony on its breast. *Ralph Lauren*, I thought, and suddenly felt an unexpected wave of vertigo. For a moment, I thought I recognized him from somewhere. Maybe Stanford? But then the sensation passed.

"Hello, Kathryn." His deep voice was pleasant, but I couldn't get a read on his expression at all, and the way he refused to look away was disconcerting. "I'm Andrew," he said, extending his hand. A bulky bandage covered the back of it.

"It's Kate," I said apologetically. I noticed that he held the handshake a moment longer than was really necessary.

Janine placed a hand on my shoulder and shepherded me toward the table. "Please, sit."

I chose a chair, and Janine sat beside me. Andrew seated himself directly opposite, continuing to scrutinize me. I fought the urge to squirm in my seat, uncomfortably reminded of the phrase "under a microscope."

I turned toward Janine as she spoke, intentionally avoiding

Andrew's penetrating stare.

"You've indicated your acceptance of this internship, but there are a few details I'd like to go over with you before we proceed."

I nodded and clasped my hands tightly in my lap. This *had* to go well. I couldn't afford to lose this opportunity.

"Your application for the Breckinridge Fellowship is exceptionally strong, and I am certain that your participation in the internship program will boost your standing when it's time to select a recipient."

I beamed, releasing a breath I hadn't even realized I'd been holding. Exactly what I wanted to hear. My hands relaxed, just a bit.

"As you may know, we work in a secure facility located just outside of town. The reason we are meeting with you here today is that outside visitors are prohibited, even prospective hires. Your background check has been expedited, and you're cleared to participate. However, you and everyone in your household needs to sign a nondisclosure agreement before you can begin."

My eyebrows knit together. The request seemed a bit extreme, but I was just a lowly grad student, so what did I know? Maybe that's the way big tech companies worked these days. "I can do that. My sister is my only roommate."

"Excellent. We'll have those NDAs drawn up for you and Michelle and delivered first thing tomorrow morning."

I stiffened. "How do you know Michelle?" How had she collected this much of my personal information in one day?

"From your background check."

Of course they would know about my sister from the background check. Her name was also on our lease. I forced my shoulders to relax. Surely my frayed nerves were causing me to overreact.

"Because of the sensitive nature of our work, staff is expected to live on-site in corporate housing for the duration of the project."

I cringed and clamped my eyes tightly as the blinding flash from last night's nuclear detonation replayed in horrifying detail in my field of vision. With great effort, I relaxed my hands, softened my eyelids, and very intentionally drew two long breaths. Thankfully, the apparition receded. I returned my attention to Janine, hoping my momentary lapse hadn't ruined any chance I had for securing this internship.

"I'm not sure I can do that…"

Janine looked at me curiously, as if weighing whether my fleeting hesitation was worth mentioning. I followed her swift glance to Andrew, who cocked his head in a nearly imperceptible nod.

"It's a firm requirement," she explained with a hint of apology. "I can assure you that the accommodations are reasonably comfortable. And finally, our work is extremely time sensitive. We need you to begin your assignment first thing tomorrow."

Tomorrow? I was starting to think that Dr. Daniels's hesitation may have been well founded. This was moving way too fast. "But I can't just…disappear," I objected. "I'm a student and a teaching assistant. I have a job and classes to go to. The university…"

"The university is going to be quite happy to grant you a leave of absence to pursue an excellent opportunity for outside study," Andrew insisted with noticeable impatience. "In fact, they are already quite pleased to have done so."

I stared at him blankly, trying to digest this latest turn of events, quietly troubled that my life could be upended so quickly. How had they managed to push through university bureaucracy in less than a day? The proposition of working at the secretive facility definitely rang all kinds of warning bells.

It felt like I was shriveling under Andrew's intense stare. I deliberately returned my attention to Janine. "And will I be working for you, Janine?"

"Within my division, but not for me directly. Andrew is the lead on this project."

I drew in a sharp breath and glanced at him in my peripheral vision. Sweat began to pool below my armpits. Janine seemed like she'd be an incredible mentor, but simply sitting in the same room with Andrew sapped every ounce of my confidence. I reminded myself that it was only for a semester. Even if I never managed to overcome my intimidation, the assignment would last only a few months. This was the closest I'd ever come to finding a cure for my disorder. For a chance at that incredible grant, I could grin and bear it—whatever *it* was.

I turned to Janine and forced a pleasant smile. "Sounds amazing. Thanks so much for the opportunity. I can't wait to begin."

A sharp knock on the door put an abrupt end to the meeting. Conference space in our building was in high demand, and we were kicked out of our room by a group of impatient associate professors.

Janine lingered in the hallway. "It's nearly dinner. Kate, what would you say to a bite to eat?"

I eyed Andrew, but he was listening to voice mail on his phone.

I wasn't sure how I'd manage to force down a meal if Andrew stared at me as I ate it, but it seemed rude to turn her down. "Uh, how about Max's?"

"That sounds perfect. I have a soft spot for their pastrami on rye. Amir?"

"That joint is dope. I'm in."

Andrew lowered the phone, his face grim. "I'm afraid I'm needed at the hospital."

Janine reached over and placed a hand on his forearm. "Of course. We'll catch up later."

Andrew turned and fixed his piercing blue eyes in my direction. Like Alice after drinking her potion, I felt the unpleasant sensation of shrinking under his unyielding gaze.

"Tomorrow, then," he said, frowning.

And then, to my tremendous relief, he was gone.

It was too early for the dinner crowd, and the restaurant was dead. The deep-black leatherette booths were mostly empty, and the pianist doodled an impromptu mash-up of show tunes. My sister and another waitress sang two-part harmony for an ancient gentleman wearing a paisley-patterned silk scarf and a natty fedora who was trying unsuccessfully to consume an enormous piece of chocolate cake.

The hostess seated us in Michelle's section, and my sister waltzed over.

"Hi," she said. "I'm Kate's sister, Michelle."

Janine rose and shook Michelle's hand. "I'm so pleased to meet you, Michelle. I can't tell you how eager I am to get to know your sister."

Michelle leaned against the back of my chair. "Yeah, she's pretty great." She turned to Amir and gave him a little wave. "Hello..."

He stood and leaned across the table to offer her an awkward handshake. "Amir Tahami, at your service."

Michelle's grinned. "I'm the waiter here. I'm actually at *your* service. I like your shirt, by the way."

Amir beamed as he took his seat. I wasn't entirely sure, but I think he may have been blushing.

Michelle took our orders, and Janine related a story about her college days in the '80s, when she was the only woman enrolled in the chemistry program and her organic chem professor's final exam involved synthesizing the odor of flatulence. Halfway through the tale, Amir excused himself. When I peeked over Janine's shoulder, I saw him huddled with Michelle in the corner by the kitchen. Whatever he said caused her to double over in a fit of giggles.

I shook my head, suppressed a smirk, and returned my attention to Janine. Too bad for my sister that her latest crush would soon be sequestered within a high-security facility in an undisclosed location.

CHAPTER 7

ANDREW

September 21

Andrew's silent vigil beside Lily's prone body was stretching into its second hour. The rhythmic hiss and thump of the ventilator lulled him like some hypnotic chant as it forced air into her lungs. It kept her alive; but he knew the end game. Her heartbeat was regular, but the montage from her EEG trace showed no variation at all. Her body was here. But the spark that had been his friend and colleague? That was long gone.

When Janine entered the room, he didn't bother to look up.

"Have you eaten?" Janine asked, presenting a cardboard carton. "I have half a pastrami on rye."

Andrew shook his head. Pedestrian concerns such as eating meals hardly seemed important.

Janine set her leftovers aside and took a seat on the opposite side of Lily's gurney.

"What do you think about Kate Rathman?" she asked, force of habit driving her to review the bank of medical monitors that surrounded the patient.

Andrew finally raised his eyes and frowned. "She's very green."

"How likely is it that she'll be suitable?"

He shrugged and rubbed his chin absently. "Based solely on the fact that she has nightmares while in an unconventional REM pattern, I'd say encouraging. Combined with similar conclusions drawn by the Kathryn in the far-slice, I'd say the odds are beyond very good." He paused and focused his intense gaze on Janine. "Based on the fact that an alternate Kathryn spontaneously materialized in the lab this morning right out of thin air, I'd say she's almost certainly capable."

Janine laughed, but quickly suppressed her mirth given the seriousness of Lily's condition. "You should have informed me that an alternate Kate paid us a visit."

Andrew's expression softened into a weak smile. "I've encountered her dozens of times in other slices over the last week, but until she manifested here, it was impossible to be certain."

"That *is* a very good indication. So you're confident she'll perform well?"

Andrew lowered his gaze. "She's *very* green. And there's no telling how the variances in this Kathryn's brain structure will affect the outcome."

"Are you saying we shouldn't use her? Andric won't tolerate delays forever, and we're completely lacking other options."

Andrew pushed back his chair and paced the length of the small room.

"She's nothing like the Kathryn Rathman that I was expecting. She's inexperienced—immature. Almost ridiculously naive. I always knew that Lily had my back. We could go anywhere, anytime, and she was always equipped to handle the situation."

Janine rose and joined him, resting her hand on his shoulder in a maternal gesture. "I think you need to give Kate time. She's overcome a great deal of adversity, and that shows the girl's got some spunk. Besides—" Janine grasped both of Andrew's shoulders and looked him square in the face. "We've already lost so much. If there's even a small chance this could work, we can't give up now."

Andrew cast a mournful glance toward Lily. No. Ending the program now would mean her sacrifice was meaningless. The experiment must be allowed to continue, and Kathryn Rathman was the key.

CHAPTER 8

KATE

September 22

I was nervously slurping down my second cup of coffee when my sister shuffled into the kitchen. I pushed an empty mug in her direction. "Good morning, sunshine. What happened to you last night? I didn't hear you come in."

"To me?" she replied with a yawn. "Nothing happened to me. I finished my shift, then hung out with your new boss's little buddy, Amir. You know, the short dude? Writes code? Oh, I know his whole life story now. His dad was a theoretical mathematician in the 'old country' but turned a single dry cleaner in Encino into a Los Angeles hotel and restaurant empire. Junior is a boy genius who wanted to be a stand-up comedian, but instead he ended up with a PhD in math from Berkeley. So he's a total nerd, but he sounds like a surfer from SoCal. He's freakin' hilarious—even for a geek. And he has really dreamy eyes." Michelle winked at me. "After I got off work, we went to this dive bar and sat around playing poker for hours. Look—I won eighty bucks!"

She flashed me a grin and pulled four crumpled twenties from her pocket, slapping them triumphantly on the table.

"Is there any guy you won't flirt with?" I chided, but I couldn't help but return her grin.

She poured herself a cup of coffee and joined me at the table. "So about that new boss—what's he like?"

I pursed my lips. "He's kind of a jerk. He won't call me Kate, and he treats me like I'm some kind of airhead newbie. He's got this stare—every time he looks at me, my scalp goes all prickly and I want to crawl under a desk and cry. So, yeah—I'm not really getting that 'welcome to the team' vibe."

"At least Janine seemed nice, and Amir's cool. I was surprised when he told me you agreed to move to the facility, though. Do you really think you're ready for that?"

I shuddered. "No, I don't think I'm ready. I'm terrified. What if I keep having nightmares? But it's nonnegotiable."

Michelle set her mug on the table and grew serious. "You don't have to take the internship, you know. You haven't signed anything yet."

I straightened my shoulders and tossed my head, preemptively psyching myself up for battle. "I gave them a verbal agreement, and if I give up on this gig, there's no way they'll keep me in the running for the fellowship. I *need* to figure out what's causing these night terrors so I can stop them. And the money's crazy-good. So good that it'll more than cover rent *and* leave extra to send to Mom and Dad."

The doorbell buzzed, and Michelle rose to answer it. "Speak of the devil…"

She returned with a two-inch-thick FedEx overnight envelope with my name on it.

The package bore two copies of a sixty-page nondisclosure agreement—one with my name and one with hers. Michelle flipped through the pages and grimaced. "Okay, I get why *you* get the third degree, but why do I have to sign this?"

I scanned the legalese, trying to discern what I was actually agreeing to, but my eyes quickly glazed over. I frowned, flipping to the signature page. "This does all seem over the top for an internship, doesn't it?"

Michelle shrugged, turned to her signature page, and picked up a pen. "I'm not crazy about this plan. It's weird to ask you to stay shut up in their facility for months. It's like you're joining some sort of techno-geek monastery—or some weird science cult. Not to mention that it's going to be totally lonely here without you around. But you know I'll always be your biggest cheerleader." She signed and dated the page, then handed me the pen. "Go. Impress the hell out of those guys."

I took a deep breath and signed the document.

Amir arrived to drive me to Albaion clad in leather flip-flops and driving a dusty, unmarked white pickup. He hadn't shaved since yesterday, and his black T-shirt read "404 Error: Beer Not Found."

"Hey, Kate. You've signed your NDAs, right?" he asked.

I handed him the FedEx envelope. He tucked it under his arm and hoisted up my meager duffel bag and rolled-up meditation mat.

"Perfect-o. Hey, M-shell!" he called over my shoulder to my sister. "We need a rematch. You gotta give me a chance to win back my beer money." He grinned.

"You know where to find me," Michelle retorted with a coy smile.

I cast a curious sidelong glance at Amir before I turned to give her a tight hug.

"Text me or call me," she said. "At least every couple of days, okay? I want to be sure you're all right."

"I'll be fine. It's an internship; it's not like I'm moving to Tibet."

"Be good, then." She returned the squeeze, using the phrase our father always spoke in farewell.

"I will."

It was still early enough in the morning that rush hour traffic was not yet in full swing. I shifted uncomfortably in the passenger seat as Amir barreled down Highway 280 away from town and toward the rolling grassland hills, veering and swerving from one lane to another to pass slower moving motorists.

I grabbed the door handle in a death grip as he swerved and narrowly avoided hitting a white minivan that had slammed on its brakes.

"My other ride is a Tesla roadster—with racing stripes," he said, chuckling. His dark eyes sparkled with mischief. "We'll be back at the mother ship in no time!"

"That explains your need for speed," I mumbled. I screwed my eyes shut but that just made his driving even more terrifying.

"Where is the office exactly?" I asked through clenched teeth. My foot slammed on an invisible brake as Amir took a curve at a questionably high speed.

"It's hella off the grid. This setup puts the 'black' in ultra-black."

"But Janine said it's just outside of town," I protested.

"Oh, it is," Amir assured me, slamming on the brakes, then gunning the gas. "But let's just say that no one ever accidentally pulls into our parking lot."

When he took a hard right onto a dirt road, the rear tires spun out and I was sure we were both about to die.

"What the hell, Amir!" I protested as my seat belt locked up hard against my collarbone and I struggled to remain upright. "You're not even on a road!"

His eyes twinkled above his mischievous grin. "Roads?" he quipped. "Where we're going we don't need roads..."

Amir was forced to lower his speed as we bumped along a rural gravel path surrounded by tall, golden grass, gnarled oak trees, and shrubby Pacific madrones. At a fork, we veered left and followed progressively smaller dirt tracks; it was difficult to discern if any of them had been recently traveled by a vehicle.

Below us, almost obscured by a stand of trees, sat a compact white building. There were no signs of life, no parking lot, and no identifying features. The walls were blank slabs of concrete, except for a row of narrow windows that ran along the eave of the roof.

As we swung along the side of the structure, Amir triggered a set of huge roll-up garage doors. I glanced around nervously as he deftly wedged the pickup between six other identical vehicles in the building's industrial garage. Amir used his badge to open a cabinet near the door and hung the truck's key on a hook inside. He badged us into the hallway. Our footsteps echoed off the polished concrete floor, and the plain white walls were an ominous indication of what lay ahead. This was not the "welcome the intern" greeting I was expecting.

Janine met us in the hall. She flashed a reassuring smile. "Thanks, Amir—I'll take her from here. Breakfast?"

My stomach growled audibly.

Amir chuckled. "I'll make sure your things end up in your room. Later, Kate."

Janine's warm welcome was a balm in an otherwise overwhelming morning. In her familiar presence, I noticed a minute release of tension in my neck and shoulders.

"I'm so pleased to see you," she said, gesturing down the long, spartan hallway. I walked beside her, the deafening echo of her footsteps against the polished concrete interspersed with the squeaks from my Converse. We stopped before a looming unmarked door. She handed me a badge bearing my name and photo. I examined the badge critically, surprised to see the photo from my student ID staring back at me. How had they managed to get campus Card Services to release such sensitive information? Though I guess by now I shouldn't be surprised. This company seemed to value its deep secrets, but apparently everyone else's personal data was fair game.

Janine gestured toward the small raised box mounted on the doorjamb. "I know this is all very disconcerting, but don't worry; I know you'll catch on quickly."

I held my ID to the trim black card reader, and the door clicked open to reveal an institutional break room on steroids. The bland white space was vast, scattered with plain tables and modern-looking chairs that didn't look at all comfortable. A high-end stainless refrigerator and microwave on a long counter lined one long wall. Next to the sink sat a complicated-looking Italian espresso machine. Janine opened an enormous industrial freezer to reveal a wall of tightly packed, white wax-coated boxes on the shelf.

"How about some breakfast? Sorry it's not fresh," she said, looking genuinely sheepish. "But the prepackaged meals are gourmet, and I guarantee that it'll heat up well. What's your pleasure?"

My jangling nerves meant I wasn't the least bit hungry, but I was running on nothing but coffee. I shrugged. "Anything is fine."

She selected a carton and slipped a white cardboard tray from the box, placed it in the microwave, and punched the reheat button.

I slid my phone from my pocket to check the time.

"I should mention—there's no mobile signal in here," Janine warned. "You'll need to connect to the corporate network. And even then, you'll want to be careful about your communications. Big Brother will be watching."

I eyed her curiously. Why would any corporation need to eavesdrop on a lowly intern?

The microwave chimed, and Janine placed a steaming plate of French toast artfully draped with blueberry compote before me.

I could feel her observing me carefully as I nudged the

admittedly beautiful meal with the edge of a fork. "Please, enjoy," she urged. "It's our best breakfast selection, by far."

Janine nodded toward a gleaming industrial espresso machine. "I'd make you coffee, but Amir is our ace barista. Last time I attempted it, I backed milk up the steamer, and they haven't let me touch that monstrosity since."

I chuckled despite the butterflies dive-bombing my stomach. If we had a fancy espresso machine at home, I'd be equally likely to be banned from using it. "It's okay." I smiled. "I've already had two cups today."

Janine tapped her watch and frowned. "I'm afraid I can't stay, but the cavalry will arrive soon. Enjoy your breakfast. And good luck."

Her warmth was palpable and infectious and had apparently generated a force-field bubble of calm, because as soon as she departed, my first-day panic returned. I took a few bites of decadent brioche toast and closed my eyes in a moment of bliss as the blueberries melted on my tongue, but the events of the last twenty-four hours kept churning through my memory. My shoulders immediately tensed; breakfast no longer seemed so appetizing.

The mechanical sound of the door release startled me. Andrew burst into the kitchen, with a purposeful stride and an intense set to his jaw.

"Good morning, Kathryn. It's time to get started."

I dumped the rest of my uneaten breakfast into the trash. "Please call me Kate," I suggested with a hopeful smile.

Andrew's piercing gaze settled on me, and I tried hard not to squirm. "I prefer you as Kathryn."

I trailed behind Andrew into a cavernous white room, easily as large as a standard lecture hall. Industrial LED fixtures hanging from the exposed metal beams lining the ceiling emitted a subtle electronic hum that only served to set me further on edge. Despite the vast square footage of the space, it was almost unoccupied. A modest conference table sat to one side of the room, flanked by just two very cushy-looking black leather office chairs. Several black server racks packed with what looked like medical sensors towered over the table. Next to them sat a full height filing cabinet, drawers secured by electronic keypad locks. Desk-height counters lined the perimeter, supporting the occasional spectrometer or tabletop centrifuge. Another wall held a number of unfamiliar machines, though one of them resembled a much more high-tech version of my dad's old wood lathe. The final wall's desk space was equipped with multiple top-of-the-line computers.

Amir was already hard at work, installed before one of the workstations. He looked up from his computer, lowered his headphones, and spun his chair around to give me a welcoming wave. Under those bushy black eyebrows, his brown eyes projected a look of anticipation.

"Hey, Kate."

Andrew arched an eyebrow. Amir grinned and turned back to his keyboard. Andrew shifted his attention to me; his focus was so intense that I fought to avoid squirming. "About your assignment here. The man who runs our facility has a certain...vision. This facility is pursuing some truly groundbreaking projects. Game-changing work." He stared earnestly into my eyes, without wavering. "Modified-REM dimensional shift."

I blinked hard. "What?"

"Shifting dimensions—that's what we do here. We're going to knock you out of your own plane of existence. You are about to experience an alternate reality."

A nervous laugh escaped me; was this some prank they played on all the interns? But Andrew showed no sign that he was joking. I looked from Andrew to Amir. He wasn't laughing, either.

"Bullshit!" It was out before I could help it. "I don't believe you. I know I'm new, but you can't spout this kind of sci-fi nonsense and expect me to believe you."

"Then let me show you."

I followed apprehensively as Andrew approached the heavy-duty gray file cabinet and entered a long code into the keypad. Then he slid out a heavy drawer, reached inside, and pulled out a small device.

The little gadget was composed of a silver-colored substance, about three inches high. Its hexagonal pyramid-topped bulb sat atop a long stem supported by six jointed, spindly, insectlike legs. He held it carefully in the palm of his hand, as if it were a cherished pet. It reminded me of a model I'd seen before—the T4 bacteriophage, the classic virus included in every first-year biology textbook.

"Sit," he instructed, pointing toward the closest leather chair at the small conference table. Display screens glowed on medical monitors behind me.

I shrugged and sat down.

"Take out your ponytail."

I gave him a curious look, but he didn't elaborate.

He carefully placed the spindly legged device on the table. With practiced movements, he pulled an umbilicus of wires ending in a twenty-four-sensor EEG cap from a small white bucket filled with saline solution and stretched it over my head, tightening the rig's chin strap under my neck. He glanced at a screen on the rack as he began wiggling sensors so that they snuggled closer to my scalp and the dots on the schematic turned from red to green. Small rivulets of saline solution ran down my neck.

"Give me your hand," Andrew demanded, looming over me.

"What?" I countered, confused about how his erector-set insect-virus model was going to clear up any of my questions.

"Your hand," he insisted.

I stuck out my right hand, palm side up. He grasped it impatiently, turning it over. He snatched the device from the table and balanced it on the center of the back of my hand. Though it appeared to be metal, it was feather-light; I guessed that it was constructed of some kind of polymer compound or composite material. The points of its spindly legs were sharp and put uncomfortable pressure on my skin. The device began to hum and vibrate.

My stomach lurched. "What is this thing? I didn't sign up to test prototype medical devices."

Andrew's gaze was cool. "Actually, you did. It's all in the NDA."

"Is it going to hurt?" I gulped, unable to suppress the tremor in my voice. My stomach dropped, and I was suddenly very sorry I had decided to take this internship.

A slender metal probe emerged from the body of the device and moved menacingly toward my skin, glinting in the clinical light. Andrew's bright, preternaturally blue eyes locked onto mine, but his expression was completely inscrutable.

"This *might* be uncomfortable," Andrew cautioned.

Without warning, the probe shot down from the underside of the device and pierced my skin, reaching deep into flesh and tendons. Undulating waves of pain raced up my arm as the device's radial extensions burrowed under and attached to my median and ulnar nerves. My free hand involuntarily clutched Andrew's as my vision began to swim.

The last thing I heard before the room dissolved into blackness was the banshee cry of my own piercing scream.

When I opened my eyes, I was sprawled clumsily on the cold, hard concrete floor of the lab. The back of my right hand bore an angry red welt, but the vile little silver device was gone. The only light illuminating the room was the dim glow from the screens attached to the medical monitors. The atmosphere was decidedly mad-scientist, and my pulse kicked into overdrive.

I massaged my temples in an attempt to dissipate the tension headache beating in my skull and realized my EEG cap had mysteriously vanished. I felt tremendously queasy, like I'd been riding backward along winding roads for hours. I took a few deep breaths to soothe my jangling nerves and steady my nausea. The lab was silent; Andrew and Amir had disappeared from the room. When minutes passed and still no one arrived, I pulled myself up and took an unsteady step toward the wall, searching for light switches. When I finally found them, I switched on the whole bank.

The newly illuminated room was much less sinister.

The pulsing in my brain had faded, but reason had completely failed me. I couldn't process the situation at all. Just how long *had* I been unconscious? And why had Andrew and Amir simply left me alone, in the dark?

I wandered around the lab and noticed small differences there as well. The conference table was in a different location. Workstations around the perimeter had been moved to a different counter and were powered down. My uneasy feeling intensified. Hadn't the two men been working here just minutes ago?

The inexplicable need to escape intensified; everything about this place felt wrong. Just as desperation began to set in, I heard a beep and a click, and the door to the lab swung open. Andrew strode in and flashed a satisfied smile.

"Ah, excellent. You're awake. And with no ill effects."

"What are you talking about? Where have you been?"

"Waiting for you to wake up."

"What the hell?" I demanded. "What did you inject me with? I want an explanation, and I want it now!"

"That went surprisingly well," he observed wryly. "It worked great for you. Most people can't manage it. The few of us who can don't wake up so quickly, at least not the first time. And most are a bit more unsteady on their feet."

"Answer my questions. Where's Amir? Where did that evil little device go? Where are my electrodes? Why did you move the computers around?"

"I didn't move anything. In this slice, that's where the machines have always been."

"In this *slice*?"

"Are you just going to repeat everything I say? Really, Kathryn, I expected more from you."

"It's Kate. And would you please lay off all the cloak-and-dagger and please just explain what is going on here?"

"I'll try to use small words." His smug expression made me want to punch him.

Instead I winced and squeezed my eyes shut as a new throbbing began, this time near the base of my skull. The intensity of the burgeoning headache rapidly increased.

Andrew grasped my arm. "Kathryn, you're turning a little green. How are you feeling? Not everyone responds well to this sort of thing."

"What sort of thing?" I mumbled, suddenly light-headed. The throbbing was getting worse and spreading up the sides of my skull like a series of ice picks plunged into my brain. I'd suffered a lot of migraines, but I'd never experienced one like this. My stomach whined and gurgled, and I pressed my fingertips hard against my temples. Intense glowing auras exploded before my eyes and blurred my vision. I blinked hard and took rapidly quickening breaths.

"Hold on!" Andrew sprang to action. "You're going to need

this."

He dashed toward me with an orange five-gallon bucket. Just in time, I kneeled down, closed my eyes, and lost my cookies.

When I finally finished heaving and raised my head, I was surprised to find that the orange bucket had disappeared, and I was keeled over in the black office chair, staring at the floor. Jackhammers still pounded my skull and the room was still spinning. With a shaking hand, I detached the cap-shaped matrix of electrodes and peeled them from my head, leaving my hair a tangled bird's nest, wet with saline. I slowly raised my head as Andrew, clad in his own web of EEG sensors, reached over and plucked the little silver device from the back of my hand.

"Deep breaths," Andrew instructed.

I tried to protest, but speaking was not possible. The pounding in my head was too debilitating.

"Hey, Boss," Amir called. "Kate's trace showed some unexpected peaks at the end, there."

Andrew removed his sensor cap and dropped it in the bucket of saline solution. "She'll be fine." He stood and loomed over me, pulling up each of my eyelids and examining my pupils as if he were checking for concussion. Each time the light penetrated my irises, a new stabbing jolt plunged through my brain. "You'll be fine. Your headache should abate within fifteen minutes. Close your eyes and stay still."

The migraine passed more quickly than I expected, right when he said it would. What remained was an annoying but completely bearable dull ache and a persistent, sharp twinge every time I flexed my right hand.

Andrew placed a glass of cold water before me on the conference table and took a seat.

I licked my dry, cracked lips and scowled. "What the hell was that? Did I just have some kind of seizure?" I carefully probed the painful welt on the back of my hand.

He spoke laboriously, as if he was instructing an especially dense child. "As I told you: modified-REM dimensional shift. You just survived a visit to an alternate slice."

I examined his face once again for any sign that this was an elaborate hoax. He returned my stare without even a hint of humor. It finally sunk in—he was completely serious. And I had just vomited my way through an alternate reality.

"Uh—" I faltered. " So which *slice* or whatever you call it am I in now?"

"Your native slice," Andrew replied.

"And how did I get back here, exactly?"

He folded his hands and leaned forward. "Slices—realities— they don't want to diverge. Slices that are similar tend toward convergence. The math says the universe doesn't want an infinite multiverse; it wants to simplify. So two slices that are nearly identical tend to converge, which is what you felt when you—"

I groaned. "Made my offering to the porcelain goddess?"

He smirked. "Yes. Most people routinely experience the result of slice convergence. They don't really understand what's happening, but they feel it, and they call it déjà vu. You've probably felt it too—like when you find yourself thinking about an old friend minutes before they call. Slices converging. Possibilities reducing—simplification. But you and I—we were in a reality where we didn't belong. So when the slices converged, we suffered a much more physical response than a minor déjà vu experience."

"So why didn't you blow chunks?"

"5-HT3 receptor antagonists. Anti-nausea drugs."

"Huh. You might have shared."

Andrew winced. "Yeah, about that. We weren't completely certain you'd be able to slice, and sometimes the receptor antagonists can interfere with the process."

This explanation almost made sense—except for the fact that it was completely and utterly impossible. The more I thought about it, the more my thoughts curled around in confounding and confusing loops. It was as if the synapses of my brain had been trapped in an M.C. Escher print.

I rubbed my forehead, wishing it would untangle my thoughts. "Explain again about the déjà vu?"

"Remember that closely synchronized slices collapse," Andrew explained.

I gave him a blank stare.

Andrew sighed and tried again.

"When two slices with slightly different historical data points collapse, the conflicts have to be resolved. You write code," he said. "It is just a merge."

I stared at him blankly. "It's a merge?"

I could see by his frown that I was trying his patience.

"In complicated software development, a team of developers all work on the same project at the same time. Many developers are writing or changing the codebase. To keep it all synced up, we submit it to a central repository. But sometimes two developers are working on the same section of code at the same time. When both commit their changes to the repository, there are conflicts. We have to resolve them, taking the best of each, and merge it into something coherent that still works."

I rolled my eyes. "I *know* what a code merge is." I paused, trying to fit the pieces together. "So, I remember both realities, but everyone else gets a new version of truth? Reality does *code merges*?" I echoed, wrinkling my nose. Reality was a big nerdy geek. I could get behind a universe like that.

"The end result is similar," Andrew confirmed. "Though we can't predict exactly *how* reality will resolve the divergent pieces. In other convergence events…"

"In other convergence events? You've done this before?

Hanging out in alternate realities?" I stammered incredulously, still struggling to grasp the enormity of the situation.

"Repeatedly. And now, so will you."

I gawked at him until I realized that my mouth was gaping open. I consciously closed it and tried again to understand.

"How many times?" I asked in a small and uncertain voice.

He sat back in his chair and stared at the ceiling, releasing a long, audible sigh.

I rubbed my arms and cowered slightly. It was obvious that I was a colossal disappointment. I wondered how common it was for an intern to get fired on her first day. I combed my fingers through my tangled mess of hair, self-conscious about my bedraggled appearance. I needed this internship because I needed the grant. I grasped desperately for a way to repair this train wreck of a conversation.

"Don't get me wrong—this is literally blowing my mind, but I was under the impression that the purpose of this internship was to vet my research for the grant."

Andrew clenched his jaw and frowned. "Ah, yes, the Breckinridge Fellowship. The fellowship *is* going to you—provided you complete this internship. So if you want to have any chance to begin your research in earnest," he said, staring at me pointedly, "you're going to have to do it here."

I gulped and nodded. "Yes, of course." I stuttered. "I will do my best."

Andrew's single nod didn't telegraph any great vote of confidence. "Congratulations. You are now part of the Albaion Corporation, and the newest member of Project Ubiquity. Welcome to the family."

"You mean, like the Addams family?" My own voice sounded thin and tinny, and I grimaced at my own sad attempt at a joke.

Amir's sardonic laugh projected from across the room. "Nope. More like the Corleone family."

CHAPTER 9

ANDREW

September 22

Janine Mori's lab was housed two stories underground. Even though upper floors of the facility were also covert and windowless, Andrew was always struck by the ambient change when he made his way down to her lair. An almost eerie tomblike silence accosted his ears whenever he descended into the depths of the building.

He badged himself into her large, well-stocked workroom and found her off in a corner, poring over a research article.

"Find anything interesting?" he asked.

She looked up from her journal and motioned for him to take a seat. "Turns out the field of single-cell transcriptomics is on the verge of uncovering what individual brain cell types actually do. But I'm sure that's not why you're here. How are things? Did Kate slice? How did it go?"

"The trial run succeeded. Kathryn successfully sliced. She regained consciousness quickly and showed few serious adverse reactions to the modified-REM state." He looked away and chuckled. "Except, of course, for the emesis—there was a prodigious amount of vomit."

Janine suppressed a smile and gave him a light smack on the

arm. "That's just mean. You should have given her anti-nausea."

His eyes glinted under his raised eyebrow. "Just limiting the variables in the experiment, Doctor."

"In all seriousness, though; does Kate understand the full weight of what we're asking of her?"

"She could barely wrap her head around the idea of slicing at all. She's resting now, but I think a visit to Lily is imperative."

Janine slapped her journal onto the lab bench, her face drawn in alarm. "Certainly not! You'll scare the crap out of her. There's no sense terrifying the poor girl. Why amp up the pressure any more than it already is?"

The set in his jaw told Janine that she would lose this argument. "It was you who said to give her a chance. And I will. But she has to understand what's at stake here."

Janine pressed her fingers against her forehead. "All right, if you insist. But I'm going with you—to make sure you don't chase her off. Without her, this whole project is dead in the water."

CHAPTER 10

KATE

September 22

Janine Mori and I sat jammed shoulder to shoulder in the front
seat of the dusty white pickup, her elbow jabbing me
uncomfortably as we bumped along the unpaved road leading out
of the hills. Andrew turned left when he reached smooth
pavement. No one had informed me of the purpose of this field
trip, but I was relieved that my bag wasn't in the bed of the truck.
I hoped this meant that they weren't kicking me out of the
program—at least, not yet.

It didn't take long to arrive at Stanford Medical Center. We
parked and made our way through the main entrance, past
reception, and into the elevator.

The intensive care unit was subdued, with few visitors and
occupied primarily by efficient nurses. Janine stayed at the front
desk to speak with one of them while we continued down the hall
until we reached a room guarded by a burly security guard poorly
disguised as a medical resident. He gave Andrew a familiar nod
and waved us in.

Inside the darkened room, one of two hospital beds was
occupied by a motionless Filipina woman. Slight and pallid, she
seemed dwarfed by the surrounding series of medical devices and

monitors. A respirator helped her breathe. A catheter snaked from beneath the covers. The web of EEG sensors woven into her long black hair looked uncomfortably familiar. I blinked in confusion as the repetitive mechanical whirring of machines permeated the uncomfortable silence.

Finally, Andrew spoke. "This is Lily." He moved toward the hospital bed and gently clasped her pale, limp hand. "She and I have worked together for a long time."

"What's wrong with her?" I whispered.

He patently ignored me, offering no further explanation. I tried to swallow the lump in my throat. The sounds emanating from the machines gave me the willies.

Janine appeared at my elbow and gently steered me away from the gurney. "He's too close to Lily. This tragedy has touched us all, but it's harder for him."

I couldn't wrap my head around why we were even here in the first place. "What happened?" I insisted. Even from a distance, watching the motionless woman made my hands break out in a cold sweat.

"Lily suffers from permanent widespread brain injury. She no longer has any measurable brain function."

I kept my voice as low as possible. "Janine, this sounds like a terrible tragedy, and I'm really sorry about what happened to her, but why did you bring me here?"

Janine looked directly at me, considering her response. "It was a very divergent slice," she said simply. "She never made it back."

My stomach dropped and I had to look away. This woman had been testing the Bug too, and now look at her. This was insane! I'd been attacked by a prototype medical device that could kill people. Slicing *had*, in fact, killed someone. Someone who was lying here, brain dead, right in front of me. I took a step away from Janine and eyed the door warily.

Janine closed the gap between us and clasped my elbow once

again. I suspected she sensed that I might bolt at any minute.

"I understand they've demonstrated slicing to you," Janine said, her gaze level and her voice composed.

"They have," I said with an involuntary shudder. "Wait—did you know? Dr. Mori!" I pulled my elbow free, anger rising. "Did you know this could have happened to me?"

Janine looked down for a moment, then met my eyes. "I'm sorry, Kate. We had no choice." Her apology did nothing to calm me.

"Dr. Mori," I muttered between clenched teeth, "I have been through a hell of a lot in the last twenty-four hours. What else haven't you told me? If you're going to put my life at risk, I deserve to know."

She sighed. "Where to start?"

I pursed my lips and gave her a hard stare. "Why don't you just start at the beginning?"

Janine ran a hand through her hair. "You've been introduced to the device. Its function, in a nutshell, is to goose the nervous system into an instant REM state. However, if that's all it did, the subject would simply fall asleep and dream. The REM pattern introduced by the gadget is highly abnormal. You've probably noticed"—Janine paused as she searched my face—"that this experience is far more than just a dream state. It allows the subject to shift from our version of reality. The theory is that this REM state allows the dreamer, for lack of a better word, to physically manifest in another parallel reality."

I stared at Andrew, still by Lily's side, then Janine. "I wouldn't have believed a word of this, even from you, had I not just experienced it for myself."

Janine's expression grew more pained. "You have also undoubtedly noticed that one returns from another slice when it converges with ours. However uncomfortable that may be, for those who are able to tolerate the device and the dimensional-

REM shift, it appears to leave the traveler with no lasting physical or mental damage beyond a vague feeling of disorientation along with a set of memories that don't quite coincide with the present reality. Until recently. Until Lily."

"So what changed?" I insisted. "And what's my role in this?"

Janine focused her eyes on the ceiling. "Dr. Breckinridge devised a method to adjust the REM-state brain wave even further. Two volunteers agreed to test the new protocol. Andrew was one, and Lily was the other."

"So what went wrong?" I repeated.

Janine frowned. "Andrew was revived, through administration of a risky medically induced coma, from which he emerged. Lily did not."

"There's no chance she'll recover?"

Andrew released Lily's hand and placed it carefully by her side. His expression was grim. "It's irreversible."

"Her brain function has completely shut down," Janine confirmed. "Her EEG shows complete and permanent loss of all brain and brain stem functions."

For a moment, everyone was silent.

"You asked why you?" Janine continued. "We've all read your file. Christopher Daniels's reports of your condition are fascinating. You have undergone extensive testing over the years."

I nodded, recalling every psychological evaluation and brain scan, all of which proved inconclusive.

"One thing that is unique about your condition is the quality of your dream states. After examining your EEG traces, we believe that your night terrors are something more than dreams. Your REM state, your brain patterns—they closely match what we see in Andrew, and in Lily, when they have sliced."

I gasped, and my eyes widened as I realized what she meant. "You mean to tell me that I'm not dreaming, I'm in another reality?" The dreadful image of the Chicago woman's flesh melting away from bone invaded my field of vision, and I clamped my eyes and forced deep breaths until it receded.

Janine laid a concerned hand on my shoulder, and I slowly opened my eyes, terrified the vision would return. I was unexpectedly comforted by her gesture, but I noticed the she looked utterly exhausted. All of this was taking a heavy toll on her as well. "Not exactly. Your brain patterns are similar, but they're not the *same*. I believe that you are not traveling to these other eventualities, but instead you experience a window into them."

"A window?" I repeated slowly, chewing my lip.

"Precisely. And if this theory is correct, this means you have a unique connection to these other realities."

I continued to force deep, even breaths, half expecting the sensation of quaking earth to overtake me. Nothing happened, and I sighed in relief.

"I'm sorry if I sound thick, but I still don't understand. You think I see distant alternate realities. And he"—I pointed to Andrew—"wants to *go* there? Let me tell you"—I shook my head—"you do *not* want to go there." I didn't want to think about the terrible destruction of my latest nightmares, and I *definitely* didn't want to believe that the horrors that I'd witnessed had really happened to someone. Someone real.

Andrew abruptly broke my concentration. "We can already go there. Going is not the issue." His impatience seemed to multiply the longer this conversation progressed. "The problem is that we need to be able to come *back*."

Janine threw Andrew a warning look and squeezed my shoulder. "The great Buddhist monk Bhante Gunaratana called meditation 'an awareness so intense, concentrated, and finely tuned that you will be able to pierce the inner workings of reality itself.' Not only are you able to spontaneously experience the altered REM state through your dreams, Kate, but because of your many years of training in meditation, you are also able to exit the state."

My forehead crinkled with incomprehension. "I can't believe the reason you offered me this internship is to teach meditation to Andrew."

Janine shook her head. "I'm afraid it's not that simple. Research has shown that people with long experience practicing meditation experience a change in their EEG patterns. I believe this is why your practice has decreased the frequency of your abnormal night terrors and made it possible for you to awaken yourself."

I nodded. "I'm aware of those studies. It's why Dr. Daniels was so adamant that I learn to meditate."

"But newer studies have revealed that long-term meditation also causes physical changes in the underlying structure of the brain. If we were to do an MRI on you right now, we'd find that your brain has a thicker than average insular cortex. The interesting thing about the insular cortex is that it's a very small lobe, and while it's not fully understood, it appears to have an astonishingly intricate connection to a wide number of functions. It's also very close structurally to the base and the back of the brain stem, which controls stages of sleep."

"So what you're telling me," I reasoned slowly, "is that Andrew needs *my* brain."

Janine leaned forward, lips pressed tight. "Yes," she sighed.

I turned to Andrew. "And if I help you understand this abnormal REM state, can you help me get rid of the nightmares?"

"At this point," Andrew admitted, "we're not completely certain. But we'll collaborate with you and Christopher Daniels to advance our collective understanding of these abnormal REM states. Your involvement in this project will vastly accelerate the pace of his research as well."

"But what about Lily? If I really can figure out how to get out of a slice, can't I go get her?"

Janine and Andrew exchanged a dark look. "I'm afraid that's not possible," she replied. "Lily has no measurable brain activity. The duration and the divergence of that slice put tremendous strain on her, both mentally and physically. The medically induced coma was supposed to give her a chance to recover, but rather then healing, her mind has simply shut down. We believe that if your brain stops functioning here, your manifestation in the other slice is no longer feasible. Sadly, in our best estimate, there is no 'Lily' left anywhere to retrieve."

I stared from Janine to Andrew, trying to ignore the troublesome metallic taste that had erupted at the back of my tongue. They were asking me to sign on to an experiment using an unproven technology that had fried this woman's brain. This was madness. No wonder they'd offered such an enormous paycheck. "What if I decide I don't want to continue with this assignment?"

A moment passed, then two, the silence becoming increasingly awkward. Andrew turned his intense gaze on me, and I suddenly had the uncomfortable sensation of standing alone in a searing hot spotlight.

"We won't force you to honor your commitment to this project," he said. The monotone inflection of his voice somehow magnified the insinuation of disappointment perfectly. Why did I suddenly feel so mortified for falling short of his obvious expectations?

Janine's apprehension couldn't hide behind her practiced calm. "Breckinridge has a long reach, so if you do decide to leave us, I would caution you never to reveal what you've just seen and heard. There's a real possibility that doing so would end your scientific career—permanently. And after all, who would believe it?"

I blinked hard. It didn't take a genius to see that Janine had huge reservations. I wondered exactly how long Breckinridge's reach could possibly be.

"And then there's your personal interest in the matter," Andrew continued, still studying me with uncomfortable scrutiny. "You're not going to find a faster—or better funded—way to understand what's happening to you."

I drew a long breath. The risks were mind-boggling, and any sane person would immediately run the other way. Unless, of course, she was burdened by soul-crushing night terrors that were apparently really happening to someone, in some reality. It was difficult to accept, but this experience had actually made my condition seem even worse.

In the end, my answer was inevitable. The nightmares needed to stop. A final backward glance at Lily cemented my resolve. "I guess I have no choice."

I stepped out of the room to call Michelle, eying the hulking security guard as I dialed. He stared directly ahead and ignored me completely. I couldn't explain any of this to my sister, but she needed to know that I could potentially be out of contact for days at a time. With any luck the long absences would be because I was "working" and not because I was incapacitated like Lily. I shuddered as I imagined myself lying lifeless on a gurney, and I hoped Michelle never needed to stand in this room and hear this diagnosis.

My call rolled over to voice mail, so I left Michelle the most reassuring message I could muster. I wished with all my heart that I could disappear down that hallway, leave this place, and forget all about this ill-advised undertaking. But it was not an option. I took a deep breath, squared my shoulders, and prepared myself to embark on my precarious assignment.

I eased the door to Lily's room open a few inches and realized that Andrew and Janine were in the middle of a heated exchange. Despite the hovering presence of the guard, I paused for a moment to eavesdrop.

Janine's tone was steady and maternal. "...everyone would understand."

"I need to be here for her. I can't let her go alone." His voice faltered, and my gut clenched in response to his obvious heartbreaking sadness. "Her family will be here tomorrow to say goodbye. I'll be here as well."

His phone's message alert chirped.

"What is it now?" Janine asked.

"He's demanding that Kate slice—immediately."

Janine sounded apprehensive. "Do you think she's ready? She's barely recovered from yesterday..."

I cleared my throat loudly and pushed the door fully open in time to catch a look of worry that passed between them.

Andrew focused his attention on me and frowned, every trace of the emotion I'd overheard wiped away completely. "We're finished here. Let's go."

As Andrew drove us back toward the hills, my mind was reeling. He kept his eyes trained on the road, his shoulders rigid and his expression slack. Wedged between him and Janine, I stared forward uncomfortably and tried to make myself as small as possible.

"We could delay a day or two, until everything at the hospital is resolved," Janine suggested.

His hands clenched the steering wheel even more tightly. "You know there can be no resolution."

"I'm just suggesting a minor postponement."

In my peripheral vision, I could see his pinched frown. I suspected that my presence was preventing a conversation that would have gone completely differently had I not been sitting between them. He took several breaths to compose himself before he replied.

"I need to see this through."

Janine nodded, and the rest of the ride was spent in silence.

My stomach lurched as we left paved roads for the gravel track back into the hills. I thought about Lily, and my whole body felt ponderous, like I was carrying the weight of the world packed into a tight ball within my chest. I had committed to a project with a fail state of death. It was only my second day and I was already in mortal peril.

When we reached the building, I followed Andrew to the lab. Amir was toiling away at his workstation. I wondered if he ever let up and then remembered that he'd managed that game of poker with Michelle.

Amir rose from his chair and flashed his lighthearted smile. "Ready to get to work?"

I sighed and nodded.

"Time for a little primer on multiverse travel," he said.

Andrew retrieved the two hand-stabbing devices, stroking their bulbous heads absentmindedly.

"We call these little guys Bugs. As you're already aware, they attach to your nervous system and transmit signals that do two things—trigger the brain stem to shift into the REM state, and induce the abnormal REM pattern that allows us to shift to another slice. They can be synced."

He handed the Bugs to Amir, who returned to his computer and attached a thin, black cable to each. From his workstation, Amir unleashed a fury of keystrokes.

"When two Bugs are synced, the travelers will shift to the same slice."

"Okay, I'm with you so far. But how do you set them up to tell them where you want to go?"

"That's the first problem. We can't actually tell them to go anywhere. When you shift to a different slice, you end up exactly where—and *when*—you started, only in another reality. So if I'm in this lab at ten thirty a.m. when I activate the Bug, in the slice I reach, it's ten thirty a.m. And I'd physically be right here, at the same coordinates in space."

"But you're still here, in this reality too?"

Andrew nodded. "Yes, you're still here, but in a unique state. You are not unconscious, but you can't be awakened. We routinely monitor with EEG while we are slicing."

Amir disconnected the Bugs and placed them carefully on the conference table.

"Let's get started," Andrew suggested, gesturing to the pair of the plush leather office chairs next to the rack of medical monitors. He pulled an EEG cap from a bucket of liquid and handed it to me.

"Think you could share some of those anti-nausea meds this time?"

Andrew tossed me a small pill bottle. I eyed the Bug sitting menacingly on the table.

"I don't suppose there is anything you can do about the massive, horrifying pain that thing causes?"

"Afraid not. I'd like to say you get used to it," he said as he sat down and slipped an identical sensor cap over his head and began wiggling leads. "But you never really do."

Andrew reached for his Bug. He rested his right hand on the table, positioned the device, and motioned for me to do the same.

"Does it have to go on my right hand?" I asked, thinking about how painful everything had been following yesterday's encounter with the device.

"Either hand will work," Andrew replied. "I'm just a lefty."

Ignoring the nervous sensation brewing in my stomach, I positioned the device on my left hand.

"Stoked for the trip?" Amir asked.

I grimaced. Andrew shrugged in a manner that was dismissive yet still telegraphed his irritation. Both Bugs began to hum. My chest tightened and I drew in a quick breath. I closed my eyes and waited for the scream.

When I opened my eyes, I was still sitting at the table, though during the trauma of the Bug's activation, I had again grasped Andrew's free hand. A sardonic half smile tugged at the corner of his mouth as I pulled quickly away. The Bug that had been affixed to my left hand had vanished, leaving the throbbing welt but no other evidence of its existence.

I looked around. The lab looked the same; we still sat at the table, and Amir was still typing away at the keyboard.

I took a deep breath, bracing for the nausea, but I felt fine.

"Did it work?" I asked.

Andrew ran his hand through his hair, which I noticed was now free of the EEG cap. I touched my chin. Mine was gone, too.

"No EEG, no Bugs," he replied, shaking out his right hand. "I intentionally asked Amir to configure us for a very near slice. We won't be here long."

"Hey, Amir," Andrew called.

Amir lowered a set of headphones that I didn't remember him wearing just a moment ago. "Did you sneak in or slice in?"

"Sliced in."

"Rad. Need anything?" Amir replied, still staring intently at his screen.

"We're fine."

I surveyed the room nervously. "If this reality is so similar to ours, why aren't the local versions of ourselves sitting here right now?"

"It's surprising how much variation there is, even in these similar slices. From time to time, I've encountered my local self, but it's fairly rare, unless I go looking for him."

The thought of a carbon copy of myself suddenly appearing before me out of thin air was mind-boggling. What would we even say to one another? I shook off the thought and tried to concentrate.

"How do you tell the Bug where to send you? I mean, how do you know which slice you'll end up in?" I grimaced. Talking about the multiverse made me sound like an idiot.

"We don't have fine control on how divergent the target slice is," Andrew replied. "We can distinguish between a slice that's likely to converge, and one that is so mathematically dissimilar it won't naturally collapse."

"And if the slice doesn't converge?"

"Then we can't get back. The procedure that Janine tried with Lily was risky. Really risky. We had no clear indication that it would work. And now we know it won't, at least half the time."

"My clothes haven't changed. I look the same. You look the same."

I took a closer glance at Amir. He was still wearing a faded T-shirt, but it was now blue rather than athletic gray. His hair seemed a little longer, and it was slicked back. No five o'clock shadow, but the same bemused eyes.

Andrew nodded. "You generally arrive with what you were wearing, and most of what was in your pockets comes, too. Except tech—watches, mobile phones, or cameras—for whatever reason, none of it makes the jump, there or back. Not even the Bug comes along."

I probed the angry red welt on my left hand. A tiny droplet of blood oozed from the pinpoint incision. I wiped it away, vowing to avoid traumatizing the injury any further.

"It's interesting that the slicing always lands you in the same physical location as where you started. That doesn't happen in my dreams."

"True, but your windows of travel, while not space-bound, do seem to be time-bound. Think back to the last one."

I felt a chill pass through my body as I fought the suggestion but allowed my mind to drift back to that horrible scene.

"What time was it when you dreamed?"

"Early morning," I replied. "Sunrise."

"And where were you?"

"'Chicago. I remember the traffic on Lake Shore Drive."

"What time did you wake up?"

"Four thirty."

"Two hour time difference," Andrew confirmed.

As I considered Andrew's theory on my alternate-reality windows, I stood up, walked around the room, and picked up a coffee-encrusted cup from the counter. Another slice difference. I held up the cup and examined it closely.

"This is also different than my dreams. During the nightmares, I can see, hear, and sometimes even smell what's around me. But I can't interact with anything. And I can't talk to anyone."

I set the cup down, walked over to Amir, and gave him a poke on the shoulder, just to be sure. He turned and gave me a thumbs-up. I waved my hand in front of my face, then pinched myself just for good measure. "How is it possible that I am actually here?"

"About ninety years ago, physicists discovered that subatomic particles can exist in two locations at the same time. This, of course, is the heart of quantum mechanics."

"I'm a bit bigger than an electron."

"The physics behind it is complicated. The truth is, the equations of quantum mechanics explain the universe of the very small. Einstein's equations explain the universe on a macro scale. But there is actually no theory that credibly connects the two. If you box a physicist into a corner, they will offer one of two theories. The earliest theory, the Copenhagen Interpretation, was proposed by Bohr and Heisenberg in the 1920s. They basically suggested that the act of observing a quantum effect fixes the possibility."

"Oh, that's Schrödinger's cat!" I replied, recalling my Physics 101. It felt encouraging to understand some part of this absurd conversation, if only for a moment.

"Right. A fine theory, but with no basis in mathematics or measurable observation. A more recent explanation was proposed by a Princeton doctoral student in the late fifties and is called the many worlds theory. Hugh Everett proposed that every possible quantum outcome actually exists in worlds parallel to our own."

"Thanks for the physics lesson, but none of these theories really explains how all this is possible." My head was spinning. It wasn't so hard to imagine the existence of parallel worlds, but to be *in* one?

"You've heard of Penrose, right?" Andrew asked.

"Ummm, nope."

"Seriously? I suppose I can't expect much from a school whose team mascot is a color."

I glared at him. "You know I'm not a physics major, right? Neuroscience. I'm interested in brains, not bosons."

Andrew breathed a long-suffering sigh. "Penrose postulated that our very consciousness is a product of quantum mechanical processes occurring in minute structures within our brain cells called microtubules."

"Really." I rubbed my temples. This was too much. "You're trying to tell me that *I think therefore I am* because subatomic particles exist in two places at the same time? And how on earth does an abnormal REM state translate into appearing in a completely different reality? Seriously," I said, "when are you going to tell me something I'll actually believe?"

"Perhaps you'd prefer this: in the late nineties, a theoretical physicist by the name of Juan Maldacena produced work on string theory and gravity that led to an audacious theory that the universe that we experience is actually a hologram—that everything you see is a mere projection of the events that take place."

I couldn't contain the snicker. "So, I'm actually a hologram right now?"

Andrew shrugged. "That's one interpretation. If we subscribe to Maldacena's theory, however, you'd always be a hologram, no matter what reality you're experiencing. It might help to use quantum teleportation as a model to explain it. Think of it this way; the Bug puts your brain into a state where it's possible to reimagine the exact state of your atoms in an identical time and place in another reality due to an existing quantum entanglement between the sending and receiving reality."

I paced across the room, trying in vain to fuse the unfamiliar theories into something coherent. "Okay, so you're telling me that I'm actually a photocopy? That's weird, but let's say I believe you. Why is it that I'm out like a light in my 'real' reality?"

Andrew looked amused. "The current operating theory is that our puny human brains can't deal with the cognitive dissonance of experiencing two realities at the same time."

"This all sounds like a steaming load of hand-wavy nonsense," I huffed.

Andrew raised an eyebrow. "Have you ever seen an electron?"

I stopped pacing and stared at him. "No, of course not. No one's ever seen an electron."

"But you believe they exist, right?"

"Yes..."

"You just accept it on blind faith?"

"I believe a hundred years' worth of experiments that suggest electrons are real."

His eyes gleamed with challenge. "And yet you don't believe the firsthand experiment you're conducting right now?"

Before I could refute his logic, I was interrupted by the distinct click of an access card triggering the lock. The door swung open, and I watched in fascination as I saw myself walk through. I stared at the other version of myself in shock, blinking hard. She was wearing the same outfit as I was, down to the scuffed Converse. I absentmindedly touched my straggling hair, half expecting to feel the messy bun I observed on my twin. It was exactly like looking in a huge, room-size mirror—with the mind-bending exception that my reflection was moving completely independently of me. I closed my eyes and opened them again, willing my brain to stop its futile attempt to reconcile her presence to my reality. In the second it took all this to occur, the light of comprehension flashed in my double's hazel eyes. A wave of dizziness washed over me, followed by overpowering nausea. I clutched my head in agony as the migraine exploded at the base of my skull, coming on faster and stronger than any episode I'd ever experienced. I blinked hard for a moment as the ground seemed to lurch below me, and when I opened my eyes, I found myself sitting once again in the comfortable leather chair, monitors beeping behind me, my right hand still desperately clasping Andrew's.

His self-satisfied smirk faded as I jerked my hand away and used it to pluck off my Bug. When I dropped the vicious little gadget on the table, it bounced once on its spindly legs and came to rest on its side. I pushed my fists hard into my eye sockets. The room was much too bright, and the migraine was unbelievably intense. The sudden ringing in my ears was so loud that I could barely hear myself think.

Amir sounded like he was speaking from the end of a long tunnel. "What's wrong with Kate?"

"Migraine. Horrific migraine," I groaned through gritted teeth.

Andrew's voice came from far away, layered with a funny echo that made it sound like there were three of him speaking simultaneously. "Did her EEG spike again?"

Amir's voice wavered. "Yeah, it did. Worse this time."

"This is definitely unexpected. I'm going to move her to the dormitory. Please contact Christopher Daniels. Tell him it's urgent."

CHAPTER 11

JANINE

September 22

Janine Mori pushed away from her perch at the lab bench and stretched. From her station, she could easily survey the entire room—her staff diligently at work. She glanced at the clock on the wall and was surprised to see that it was well after ten, and her growling stomach told her she'd forgotten to eat dinner—again.

She picked up a substantial pile of paperwork and paged through the research. She paused, added a few notes to the chart she was constructing on her laptop, then referenced the paper again.

She had concluded that her gnawing hunger could no longer be ignored when the lab door swung open and Andrew stepped in.

"Hiya, Doc."

"Hi yourself." Her affectionate smile quelled the fatigue lining her face. "How are things progressing?"

He took a deep, pained breath and sunk onto the stool beside her. "We've had a bit of a setback."

She pushed the laptop back and turned to him, resting an elbow on the bench. "What sort of setback?"

He leafed through the stack of research papers but failed to meet her gaze. "Kathryn saw herself for the first time while slicing, right when we converged, and she developed a massive migraine."

Janine's look of concern deepened. "Let me see the traces."

Andrew picked up her tablet and spent a few moments swiping and tapping before handing her the device. Janine examined the test results and frowned.

"Migraines aren't a side effect we've observed in you or Lily, or any of the other subjects that we have tested. I don't think the Bug is causing it."

"We know she has a history of migraines linked to her nightmares. And if our hypothesis is correct, her abnormal REM state is inexorably linked to the slice state. Perhaps we're closer than we think to a solution for far-slice exit."

Janine's eyebrows drew together. "What if she's already cracking under the pressure? We should proceed with caution—"

"What if it's simply necessary growing pains?"

Janine shook her head. "Why push her? We should take this slow, understand the risks..."

"I know she's capable of more."

Janine noticed a faint flush creep into his cheeks.

"Andrew, are you blushing?" Janine teased. "Perhaps you're not made of granite after all! You never did share the details— how exactly *did* you acquire the information about Kate from the far-slice?"

Andrew simply arched an eyebrow. "A gentleman never tells."

Janine blinked expectantly, hoping for elaboration.

Andrew met her pointed stare with an enigmatic smile. "Has our fearless leader asked for today's status update?"

"Not yet." But as she spoke there was a buzzing from her tablet and she frowned. Janine looked up at Andrew and his mouth tightened. He took a step away from her desk so that he was behind the tablet and out of the view of the video conference, and Janine answered the call.

On the screen there was a distressingly thin face, surrounded by thick silver hair falling in waves. His piercing gaze rested immediately on Janine Mori.

"Progress report," he demanded succinctly.

"Good evening, Dr. Breckinridge," Janine greeted him briskly. "Andrew is about to send you the latest summary on Kate's most recent slice. There has been a slight setback."

"What setback?" he barked.

As always, Janine felt uneasy beneath the stare of his ruthless blue eyes.

"Kate has had a bad reaction to the latest slice. Her EEG traces show some anomalies at the point of convergence. In addition, she developed a severe migraine. But we have brought in her physician, Chris Daniels, and with his help we hope to prepare her for another attempt in the next few days."

"She will slice tomorrow."

"Kate is unfit; we can begin the preparation in two days at the earliest," Janine said firmly. "We hope to have her ready for her first far-slice test by the end of next week."

"That is unacceptable," Breckinridge said in a low voice. "There's no time to waste. I want your people on this around the clock."

Janine looked to Andrew; his face was thunderous. She turned her attention back to the tablet. "I am not risking the life of another innocent. It is hard enough finding subjects that can slice. If we lose Kate, we lose the project—"

Without another word, Breckinridge reached up and the screen went black. Janine released an audible sigh of relief.

Andrew's voice was taut. "So now we know what we need to do."

Janine pulled in her stomach and stared at him. "There is no way you're slicing with Kate for the foreseeable future."

"You heard him. We have no choice."

"Andrew, this is insane. You are treating her like nothing more than a splayed frog. She's more than a science experiment—do you want another Lily on your hands?"

"Don't bring Lily into this. Don't even mention her name."

"If you push her too hard, Kate will die."

Andrew turned and marched out of the room.

Janine stared after him for a moment before reaching for her pile of paperwork. It was going to be another long night.

CHAPTER 12

KATE

September 23

I stand before the full-length mirror in a pale pink silk peignoir, holding a brush in my hand. The soft incandescent lights magnify the red highlights in my short, wavy locks. I feel my hand as it rises to plump my hair, then reaches for a tube of lip gloss. It tastes like strawberry and smells faintly of rosewater. As I purse my lips to distribute the gloss, I have the strange conflicting sensation of being out of body, while still perfectly attuned to each movement I make. I try to raise my left hand, but nothing happens.

For a moment I panic; I am trapped inside this body that I can't control. I think I should be hyperventilating, but I'm not. As I move, the silk slides sinuously over my breasts and my reflection smiles. It's a tremendously bizarre sensation, but I can feel her delight, mixed with something else. Anticipation. I turn away from the mirror, and my bare feet move across the cool tile floor. I flip the light switch and plunge the spalike bathroom into darkness. Cool tile gives way to soft, plush carpet.

I walk into a vast room; a kitchen clad in dark cabinets and sparkling white marble flows effortlessly into a comfortable sitting room. A warm fire crackles in a river-stone fireplace. I feel a lazy smile creep to my lips as I pass by the kitchen's breakfast bar and pluck a sparkling crystal glass filled with a generous pour of white wine. I raise the wine to my lips and sip; the buttery chardonnay slips down my throat. The taste is both strange and utterly familiar. I experience a sense of comfort and well-being—a warm feeling that begins in the pit of my stomach and radiates throughout my body.

There is rustling behind me, but before I can turn, hands encircle my waist. A warm breath on the back of my neck becomes a soft, lingering kiss that makes me catch my breath and close my eyes. Then there is another kiss, and another, as he works his way down my neck and across my shoulder. The peignoir falls to the floor, and the warm relaxation of the wine blossoms into the urgent thrill of desire.

My back arches as he presses his body against mine. His right hand moves to cup my breast while the other begins moving slowly downward over my belly. His tongue tickles my earlobe as his left hand finds its mark. Pure rapture radiates through my body, and when I can bear it no longer, I turn and raise my head. My lips brush his, warm and soft, and unbelievably gentle. This teasing kiss feels utterly familiar, and I fleetingly wonder who he is. But then I smile coyly, and my eyes drift closed. My lips fall open, and my world narrows to a tiny pinprick of sensation as his mouth finds mine. The kiss is passionate and urgent. Every fiber of my being aches to be with this man. I slowly raise my eyelids to find Andrew's startling blue eyes devouring me with an intensity and hunger I have never imagined.

I emerged from the dream suddenly, drenched in sweat, with an exquisite burst of pleasure radiating through my body accompanied by a loud and embarrassing moan.

Someone cleared their throat, and I turned in horror to find Dr. Daniels sitting beside my bed.

"I'm glad to see you've recovered," he quipped with a sternly disapproving frown.

My face blanched in mortification, and I involuntarily clutched my arms over my chest to cover myself—then realized that I was still wearing yesterday's jeans and tee. I opened my mouth, and my lips cracked, dry from the chill, sterile air. My jaw throbbed, and my eyes thrummed under the cold strip lighting that lined the walls, but there was no colorful aura. Astonishingly, my head felt fine.

Dr. Daniels stood and dimmed the lights.

My dormitory room was monastic and much quieter than my apartment. The silence was so dense, it was almost hard to concentrate. I inhaled a deep breath and tried to sit up.

"Take it easy, Kate."

I slid back beneath the blanket of my austere bed and closed my eyes, as much to hide my embarrassment as to ward off any impending migraine.

"Do you still have the headache?" Dr. Daniels asked, reaching for my wrist and checking my pulse.

"No," I murmured.

"And your nightmares?"

I forced open one eye; he made no effort to hide his reproach.

"Haven't had any," I lied.

Dr. Daniels's doubt was written all over his face.

"I spent several hours yesterday evening with Dr. Mori, and she reluctantly explained the parameters of this project. I stand by my earlier assessment—I think this internship is a terrible idea. The stress alone..."

I wrenched open my other eye, and still my vision stayed blessedly clear.

"Dr. Daniels, I appreciate your concern, but I can do this," I pleaded. "I promise, I'll spend every spare minute meditating; I'll minimize my stress, I'll—"

"I can see you won't be persuaded. I'll see to it that they're stocked with your migraine meds."

I managed a weak smile. "Thank you, Dr. Daniels."

His grim smile was less than encouraging. "I'm not leaving here until I'm sure you're up and about. Go—get ready."

I moved deliberately to the bathroom, brushed my teeth, then tackled the tangled mess of my hair.

"Oh! Ow...ow...son of a..." The hairbrush clattered to the ground, and I flexed my injured left hand. When I retrieved it, I made sure I held the brush in my uninjured hand. I brushed until my hair fell in loose auburn waves over my shoulders, but I frowned as I noted how sunken my eyes looked under the harsh fluorescent lights.

"Nothing like hideous lighting to make you look your worst after a long day skipping through alternate reality," I said to Dr. Daniels in mock cheerfulness.

"I have known you for a long time, Kate Rathman, and I know how determined you can be. But as your doctor—and your friend—I want you to understand how concerned I am for your health—and your safety. Please be careful."

"I will, Dr. Daniels. I promise."

When I arrived in the kitchen, the tables were full, and a quick scan of the room revealed that Andrew wasn't among the diners. I was immediately relieved. Amir whipped up a steaming latté on the complicated-looking Italian machine. He held it out to me with a broad grin.

"You're going to need this after your trip yesterday."

"Thanks, Amir."

"How're you doing?"

"Better than yesterday." I took the coffee and wandered over to a table where Janine was picking at the remains of a frittata.

"Hi, Janine," I said, sliding into a seat.

"Good morning," she said, welcoming as always. "How are

ı feeling, Kate?"

"Better, thanks."

It was easy to see the concern behind her smile. "Are you still periencing any symptoms? Any at all?"

"I'm fine—really."

I noticed the dark shadows beneath her eyes seemed more ominent than yesterday.

I placed my still-useless phone on the table. "Hey, can you help ɔnnect me to the corporate network? I really need to get ahold of ndrew."

Janine frowned, but after a moment's pause, she gestured for he device. I unlocked it and passed it to her. She tapped for a long ime; apparently the setup was complicated. Finally, she handed it ɔack to me and picked up her cup.

"I know I've said this before, but it's important," she said, staring down into her coffee. "Be very careful what you say via the network. In any case, you may have difficulty reaching Andrew today. He's at the hospital with Lily's family. They're pulling her life support. I don't expect he'll leave her until it's finished."

"Oh," I replied awkwardly. For reasons I couldn't explain, I was suddenly awash with disappointment, which I objectively knew was crazy. If he were here right now, I'd almost certainly feel like a total amateur imbecile.

"Is everything all right?" she asked. "Is there something I can help with?"

"It can wait," I said with more assurance than I felt. "I had another nightmare, but something was different, and I thought maybe he should know."

Janine was suddenly alert. "What happened? Are you okay? Do you want to talk about it?"

I sucked in a deep breath as I felt the brush of his lips on my neck and the quiver of my bare skin under his insistent touch. It was all I could do to hold back a gasp of pure, liquid ecstasy. Warmth flooded my body as blood rushed to my cheeks. I took a deep breath, then another, almost as desperate for the sensation to linger as I was for it to subside.

My hallucination abruptly faded when Janine laid a concerned hand on my forearm. "The subject matter's not important," I stuttered, forcing myself to focus. "But something really weird happened. I saw myself. Or, rather I was myself. That's never happened before."

"So," Janine said slowly with barely concealed excitement, "you were yourself? Could you actually interact with your environment?"

"No. I was me—I mean, I could see and feel everything that was happening." My skin began to tingle, and my cheeks grew increasingly flushed. I took several more deep breaths. "But I wasn't driving, if you know what I mean. There was only one me, I saw things from my own perspective, but she—the other me— was definitely running the show."

"Hmmm..." Janine replied, picking at a slice of red pepper in her eggs as she thought. "I wonder if it's random? Or if the slicing is starting to change your experience?"

After breakfast, I popped my head into the lab, but it was empty. Without anything to do, I returned to my room and called my sister.

"Oh, my God, Katie, what's going on? Are you okay?" Michelle demanded the moment she picked up the call.

"I'm okay. I had a massive migraine yesterday, and I'm still dreaming, but I'm better today."

"Wait, what—you had a migraine before you dreamed? Kate, are you sure you're all right?"

"I probably shouldn't share the details..."

"I signed that stupid NDA too, you know."

"Yeah, I know, but better safe than sorry."

"You could have called sooner," she said. "I've been glued to my phone since you left."

"I've only been gone two days," I chided, trying to be reassuring.

"They've been two really long days." She began to cough. "Hold on," she said, gasping, "I need my inhaler." I heard her set the phone down, then rustling and bumping. "Okay," she said a bit breathlessly. "Can you believe this stuff?"

"What are you talking about?"

"The smog. It's so weird."

I glanced up to see the filtered sunlight streaming through my high window. Now that she mentioned it, the light did have a funny orange cast that I hadn't noticed earlier.

"What is it, a heat wave? Smoke from a forest fire? I'm like the pet lab rat. They don't let me out."

"No, it's not the heat, and there aren't wildfires. There's something else going on. Some kind of weird atmospheric inversion or something the meteorologists can't seem to explain. We're on our third Spare-the-Air day. The unhealthy air quality levels are off the chart. It's as thick as pea soup out there. Seriously, I can hardly breathe."

"Really?" I scratched my head and wondered if my sister's inhaler was expired. She hadn't needed it in years. And I hadn't noticed any air quality issues the day before I'd started this job.

"They're saying it's worse than the smog during the seventies. I'm running the A/C twenty-four-seven just to try to filter the air to keep it breathable."

"Michelle! Our electric bill is going to be astronomical."

"Oh, don't worry about that," Michelle replied. I could

practically hear the enormous grin on her face. "There was a deposit in our joint checking account this week. Apparently from your new employer. They paid you nearly fifteen thousand dollars."

"Wow," I gasped. They were paying me for a month of work I'd yet to complete. And the amount was staggering—it would keep our bills paid for months. Hazard pay, I thought. "Have you told Mom about this?"

She hesitated before replying. "No. Mom's been going over the books, and this year's harvest is going to be a disaster for them. It's just been one weather catastrophe after another. They've never had such a bad year. I didn't want to pile on more worry."

"Yeah, me neither. Listen—I've been warned twice now that my communications are monitored, so I'm going to try my best not to use my phone. Don't worry if you don't hear from me often. Would you send a check to Mom and Dad? But until I know more about what's going on here, please don't say anything to them. I'm not sure how I would even begin to explain this...."

Our conversation was interrupted by a knock on the door.

"Gotta run," I whispered. "Duty calls. Or, at least it knocks."

"Okay," Michelle replied. "Be good. And, Kate? Be careful."

I opened the door of my room to Andrew waiting impatiently. His face was drawn and pale. "Hey," he said brusquely. "Ready? It's time to get started."

And then I made the mistake of glancing at his mouth.

The phantom feeling of his breath on my cheek—and those lips! I could actually feel them; the intense heat as they pressed urgently against mine, the familiar line of his teeth. The taste of his tongue. The rush of euphoria that overtook me was both alarming and rapturous. The sudden sensation of standing naked before him was so intense that for a moment, I was certain he could see it, too. I clutched the doorframe hard enough to turn my fingertips white and forced myself to breathe.

"Kathryn, are you well?"

Clinical and succinct, his actual voice was startling enough to break the spell. Blessedly, the physical echoes of my dream faded. I deliberately loosened my grip on the doorframe. Not a dream, I reminded myself. If they were right, I actually had been making out with my boss. Just not here.

I nodded and stepped out of the room, careful to look away. The residual buzz coursing through my body triggered merely by his proximity was nearly unbearable. I closed the door and followed him through the hallway, careful to stay a half step behind him. I kept my eyes glued to the floor, praying that this dream was one whose aftereffects would dull quickly.

"I heard about Lily," I said. "I'm sorry—"

"Amir has been attempting to analyze the EEG recording of our slice shift from yesterday," Andrew interrupted as if I hadn't even spoken. "We have been trying to separate common patterns that correspond to the shared experience, as well as understand the abnormality in your EEG during convergence. So far he hasn't been able to massage the data to pull out anything interesting at all. I think you should take a look at the readings to see if you can find anything. And then, we'll proceed to extraction."

I gulped uncomfortably. "You mean you need me to figure out how to intentionally remove myself from a slice? Today?"

"Yes, that's right."

My pulse quickened and I clenched my sweaty palms. I forced a few deep, calming breaths and tried not to panic.

"But I have no idea how to do that. Do you have a plan?"

"I think I know where to start," he said. "Once we have isolated the data that corresponds to the slice shift, the next step will be comparing that to your dream 'windows.'"

Amir set me up at my own workstation, which already contained the EEG recordings from my two sessions with Andrew, as well as reams of other paired brain wave sessions, presumably from Andrew and Lily. Amir helped me punch through the facility's formidable firewall to download a copy of my code from Stanford's repository, including the routines and algorithms I'd been working on for my PhD thesis. I began to analyze the data. As usual, once I became engrossed in my work, the hours flew by.

Amir delivered a plate of surprisingly tasty yellow chicken curry to my desk for lunch, and I scarfed it down in front of the computer.

I pushed away from my screen and rubbed my eyes. Across the room, Amir and Andrew looked up.

"Anything?" Andrew asked hopefully.

"Well, maybe…" I said.

He and Amir quickly hurried to my workstation. I punched a few keys and a graph animated onscreen.

"Here," I said, and pointed. "And here. There is definite spike at this point in these readings. I believe," I said with certainty, "this is what's keeping you in sync, and keeping you in the other reality."

"And did you compare the data recorded during your slices? Anything anomalous?" Andrew asked, clearly excited.

"No, not really," I said. "I don't really see how this will help."

"Your thesis research," Amir said, "your plan was always to analyze your own sleep disorder, right?"

I nodded.

"Well, can you compare this to readings taken during your dreams?" Amir suggested.

"I have some really early EEGs from when I was younger, but I don't have anything recent—not since I learned to wake myself up."

"Well, then," Andrew reasoned. "Seems like the next thing we need to understand is the nature of your dream states. Time to get on that."

"Uh, okay," I said with uncertainty. "You know I can't just turn them on, right?"

"But you have had success avoiding them?"

"Yes..."

"Then we'll just have to apply all your triggers, get you wired up, and put you to bed."

After spending most of my life trying to repress these nightmares, rolling out the red carpet to dreamland seemed like a spectacularly bad idea.

"Tonight?" I replied nervously.

"No time to waste!" Andrew insisted. "What do you do to keep the dreams at bay?"

"Well, obviously, meditation is the big gun. Stress and sleep deprivation seem to contribute. Oh, and alcohol. I don't drink."

Amir grinned, slapping his hand against the desktop. "Smokin'! But you know the old man's policies about bringing the sauce into the facility. How about we head to town and grab some brewskis and a couple of Paxti's deep-dish pies? Everyone loves Chicago pizza, right?"

I shuddered at the mere mention of Chicago.

Andrew's jaw was set. "I'll deal with any repercussions. Besides, I have something a little more clinical in mind."

Amir shut down his workstation and bounded out of his chair. "Then count me out. If we're taking a night off, I'll spend it jammin' on Warcraft without you two lame-os."

Amir's absence left the lab feeling conspicuously empty. "Can Janine sit in with us?" I asked hopefully.

"I'm afraid she's otherwise obligated."

I sighed. I'd been careful not to look directly at Andrew all day.

So far, I'd avoided any embarrassing flashbacks. I groaned inwardly at the irony—I was actually hoping for the imminent nightmare to be some horrible cataclysmic disaster, rather than endure another romantic interlude with my boss. I gulped and resigned myself to the experiment. The faster I could get this assignment completed, the faster it would get me out of this lunacy. And admittedly, the prospect of finally getting some more recent EEG readings during a dream was tantalizing.

I tried to ignore the clammy sensation under my armpits and picked at my cuticles to avoid looking at him. "So, we're doing this, then."

"We are doing this. Eat a light dinner, and don't meditate. I'll make a supply run and meet you back here in an hour. What do you drink?" he asked.

I shook my head. "I have no idea. I wasn't kidding. I really don't do alcohol."

Andrew rose and headed to the door. "I've got this covered."

I waited in the empty lab, rocking back and forth in one of the plush leather chairs. My dinner, which I'd barely tasted, refused to settle in my churning stomach. I pulled out my phone and tried to distract myself by reading net news. The headline article reported that the air quality index had reached the "very unhealthy" level, with recommendations to avoid outdoor exposure. Definitely not helping. I put away my phone.

At last, Andrew badged into the lab, dimming the lights as he entered the room. Two champagne flutes dangled from one hand and a pair of bottles nestled under his arm. I thought I'd feel relief, but instead tension descended over me like a thick, suffocating blanket.

My voice cracked when I spoke. "What are we drinking?"

He gave me another one of those inscrutable stares, and I

quickly dropped my gaze.

"Pink champagne. I have a feeling you'll take to this."

I tilted my head to the side, but he offered no explanation. He removed the foil and loosened the wire cage. The pop of the cork echoed in the empty lab. He poured a glass and set it before me. The bubbly pink liquid fizzed loudly in the near silence. I raised my glass and sniffed, startled by the distinct aroma of strawberries. The tiny bubbles tickled my nose, and I quickly suppressed a smile, vowing to remain all business.

Andrew touched his fingertips to his lips before hesitantly lifting his flute. "To...big things."

I risked a quick glance. His usual impassivity seemed to be cracking—his slack expression and slumped shoulders triggered a surge of sympathy. The man had watched his friend die today. I couldn't actually imagine how painful that must have been.

I clinked my glass somberly and took a tentative sip. I was prepared to hate it, but the wine had a pleasant flavor. It had none of the sweetness I expected, but instead brought to mind creamy baked custard and tart cherries. No one had ever told me that wine could taste like this.

The awkward silence continued, and I nervously gulped down the rest of the glass. I racked my brain for some neutral topic of conversation.

"The wine is good," I muttered.

He leaned back in his chair, staring intently at the tiny bubbles rising from the bottom of his glass. "I knew you'd like it."

I took another sip. "What is it, again?"

"Heidsieck rosé. It's nice, isn't it? A solid French champagne. The 2006 vintage runs about one hundred and fifty dollars a bottle."

I choked on my bubbly. "What? A hundred and fifty dollars for wine? That's more money than I spend on two weeks' groceries!"

Andrew smirked. "Then enjoy it while you can." He topped off my glass.

The growing tendrils of intoxication set in faster than I expected and created a pleasant floating sensation in my head. A warm haze of alcohol-fueled contentment washed over me, and my unease began to drift away on the wings of the effervescent pink bubbles. My shoulders relaxed and I took another swig of champagne. Without thinking, my gaze flickered toward him. A huge sigh of relief escaped me as I realized that he was no longer triggering any nightmare side effects.

"Other than your taste for pricey wine, I know almost nothing about you."

"I'm not sure that's entirely accurate," Andrew said obliquely.

I had no idea what he was talking about. I tried again.

"Have you always been interested in biomedicine?"

He finished his drink and poured another. "My bachelor's degree is in electrical and computer engineering from UC Berkeley, and my MD-PhD in medical engineering and medical physics is from MIT. You could say I have interests in multiple fields," Andrew answered.

I did the math as quickly as my already alcohol-impaired brain would allow. He'd likely been at Cal for four years, five or six at MIT. That course of study would have required at least ten years in college, plus a residency; that would put his age somewhere north of thirty.

The conversation petered out again, and I racked my brain for a safe topic. "What do you do for fun?"

His eyes locked on mine, and the intensity of his gaze made me want to squirm in my seat. I couldn't read his expression at all, and before he answered, he expertly refilled my glass. "I don't get out much," he finally confessed. "My work is my life, quite literally."

"Surely you have a hobby or a girlfriend or...something?"

The slightest hint of amusement flickered in his eyes. "That's a very forward question, Kathryn." He took another drink of wine, as if fortifying himself before answering. "Like everyone else, I live at Albaion; it keeps me closer to the things that interest me most." A dark shadow fell over his brow and he looked away. "I used to practice martial arts, though I've lost my best sparring partner."

I looked down too, knowing that I'd hit a nerve. I guessed his training partner had been Lily.

An hour ago, a social faux pas like this would have rendered me embarrassed and tongue-tied, but the delightful floaty feeling made my awkwardness seem somehow insignificant. I sipped more wine and tried to think of a question that had nothing to do with work or death.

"So...what is the craziest thing you have ever done?"

For a moment, I was certain he wouldn't answer. Then the corners of Andrew's eyes crinkled in a genuinely bemused grin. "You mean other than hanging out in alternate dimensions?" He chuckled. "The craziest thing I've ever done..." He thought for a moment. "When I was twenty, my mother and I went on safari to Africa."

"That is amazing," I replied. "But it doesn't sound crazy."

"My mother wanted to see the big silverback gorillas. She was an avid photographer, so we traveled to Uganda to track rare mountain gorillas."

"Again, cool, but not crazy..." I pointed out.

"Africa is an amazing place. Beautiful, but also wild in a way that feels distinctly dangerous. One day, after we had been trekking through the jungle for a couple of hours, I asked one of our guides if the AK-47 he was carrying was to protect us from the gorillas. Without even the hint of irony, he said that the weapons were to protect us from the guerrillas."

An icy shiver ran down my spine.

"We were fine; we eventually found the troupe and my mother shot some amazing photographs, one of which ended up in National Geographic. But two weeks later, in that same forest, a group of tourists were confronted by a mob of soldiers—Hutu rebels, the same crew that carried out mass killings in Rwanda. Eight tourists were murdered, including two of the Americans and all the Brits. If our trip had happened just a few weeks later—" Andrew paused.

I grimaced; I thought about how a near miss in this reality might not translate to such good fortune in other slices.

"Ah, but your glass is empty again," he remarked, pouring the last drops into my glass.

"Yours is, too," I pointed out.

"So it is," he mused. He reached for the second bottle, removed the foil with a flourish and deftly untwisted the wire cage. The cork blew off with incredible velocity, soaring straight upward. I watched in fascination as it ricocheted from the high ceiling and came tumbling back down, bouncing harmlessly off the top of Andrew's head.

An inadvertent giggle escaped my throat, and I quickly clamped my hand over my mouth. Andrew vigorously massaged his scalp, his expression careening toward furious. But then he looked up, blinked hard, and unleashed a jubilant laugh. The effect was transformative, and it took all my determination to stop staring. I hoped the flush I felt creeping into my cheeks was counteracted by the dim lighting of the room.

"Are you all right?" I giggled again.

"I think I'll live," he said, grinning.

A moment of vertigo overtook me. I stared down at the lively little pink bubbles. Maybe I needed to slow down. Or was it something else? I set my wineglass carefully on the table.

"You know, I can't quite put my finger on it, but I'm suddenly having the strongest sense of déjà vu."

Andrew barely stifled a laugh. "Seriously?" he replied, his tone mocking.

Normally I'm perturbed when I'm not in on the joke, but I found myself uncharacteristically giddy. Apparently laughter is contagious when wine is involved, even if it's at my expense.

"What's so funny?" I giggled in a largely unsuccessful effort to contain myself.

He drained his glass and appraised me with those disconcerting eyes. "The universe is funny. And the reason that this feels so familiar is that this is not the first drink we've shared together. It's not even the first time we've shared this wine."

After all the alcohol, it took a second, but then my eyes widened with comprehension. "No. Freakin'. Way." I narrowed my eyes. "That's why you keep calling me Kathryn." My mind conjured the thrill of his kiss, and I suffered a surge of irrational jealousy toward the other version of myself—which I knew was ridiculous. My dream wasn't this reality. And neither was that other Kate. I frowned. "So Janine and Amir must be yukking it up right now."

For a fleeting moment, Andrew actually looked hurt. Then before I could be sure, the expression had vanished. "No," he said quietly. "That detail I kept to myself. But you need to know that the reason I recruited you—the reason I knew we needed you—was because of your extraordinary work in the other slice."

I immediately felt like the biggest jerk in the entire world, a sentiment no doubt magnified by the ridiculous amount of champagne I'd consumed. My boozy state made my emotions swing wildly in a way that was extremely unfamiliar and altogether unwelcome.

I clenched my hands in my lap. "Sorry, I was out of line. I apologize. It's just—" I paused, trying to collect my swirling thoughts. "It's been a weird couple of days. I can barely tell what's real and what's not. Or at least, what's real here. My world is a little upside down."

"I know," he replied, rubbing his chin. "I'm asking a lot of you."

The silence between us intensified. But the bubbles were messing with my head; and it suddenly struck me as hilarious that I was having this deep heart-to-heart conversation with a man my brain patently disliked but that the rest of me viewed with lustful intrigue.

I narrowed my eyes and poked him in the arm. "Dude, you totally harshed my buzz."

The solemn expression disappeared, and his lips twitched as he tried not to smile. He raised the bottle. "Finally, something that's easy to fix."

I held out my glass, and when he poured, I noticed that his hand was the slightest bit unsteady. At least I wasn't getting sloshed alone.

"I've been dying to ask—how did you find yourself working as a mad scientist?"

"Personally, I prefer the term Crackpot Visionary."

I almost snorted up my wine. Did he actually have a sense of humor? "That doesn't answer the question."

"I guess you could say," he said with a thoughtful pause, "that it's my father's influence that brought me into the business of bucking reality."

"Well, there's an original answer," I groaned, rolling my eyes. "Whose parents don't mess with their heads? How about the answer to the question I actually asked? So tell me, what is your role here at Albaion, Doctor Crackpot Visionary?"

"Well, you might say I discovered a new species of insect," he replied evasively.

Despite my foggy mental state, I took note. The Bug was Andrew's baby—interesting.

Andrew rested both elbows on the table and leaned in. "There's something I've been dying to ask you. About your dreams…"

"Ah, yes, the nightmares," I said with an involuntary shudder, which Andrew promptly noticed.

"It's almost as if you're drawn to disaster. Or it's drawn to you."

I winced. "They're almost always something awful; and night after night I'm stuck in another scene from a postapocalyptic horror film."

"What's the worst?" he asked quietly.

"That would be the time when I watched my mother get raped by militant religious zealots," I confessed. "I was only four years old when that gem was visited upon me."

If this revelation made Andrew uncomfortable, he didn't show it. Nor did his enigmatic gaze stray.

"I honestly don't know how I'll bear it," I said, clenching my hands in my lap. "Now that I know it's not just my sorry excuse for a subconscious. Now that I know that somewhere, in someone's reality, these horrible things are actually happening. Thankfully, I wake up. The killer migraine that follows is a special parting gift."

"They're always nightmares?"

"Once in a blue moon, they're different." The sudden heat in my cheeks made me certain I was blushing again. If he noticed, he gave no indication. "Sometimes, they are actually quite nice. Once I dreamed about this couple," I sighed. "I think maybe they were in love." An echo of his touch fluttered over my belly and I inhaled sharply.

His eyes locked on mine; the intensity of his gaze made me catch my breath. It wasn't possible, but for a moment I was convinced he could read my mind.

"In that case, it is my wish that your travels tonight are auspicious." He raised his glass and tapped it gently against mine, his blue eyes luminous. "I'm reminded of something Yoko Ono once said: 'A dream you dream alone is only a dream. A dream you dream together is reality.'"

CHAPTER 13

KATE

September 25

The room is spacious, bright, and airy. A comfortable brown sofa faces a cozy flagstone fireplace. The soaring cathedral ceiling is knotty cedar and a large, vividly colored giclée print of Yosemite's iconic Half Dome in all its autumn splendor graces the wall. Beyond the picture windows stands a verdant forest of towering spruce trees that sway in the light mountain breeze. Somewhere nearby, a woodpecker's staccato stutter adds counterpoint to the wind song. It is early morning, but the sun has begun its ascent, and through the open French doors in the adjacent kitchen, I can smell the sweet, crisp scent of pines. I have never been to this place, yet in some inexplicable way, it smells like home.

A toddler girl, head bursting with strawberry-blonde curls, waddles into the room, giggling deliriously. She totters around in an unsteady twirl, the pink and purple tulle layers of her dress floating around her huggable, plump little body. I instinctively bend down as she darts toward me, ready to catch her in my arms, but she careens right past me. With an excited squeal, she pulls a throw pillow from the sofa to the floor and dives beneath it. From down the hall, I can hear a man's voice.

"I'm—gonna—get you!" he calls, causing the child to squeal again in delight.

From the darkened hall, the child's father begins to crawl toward her, making exaggerated thumping noises.

"Where is she? Where is my little doodle bug hiding?"

The child wiggles with uncontained delight and tries unsuccessfully to remain quiet. I am nearly overcome by a visceral urge to pick her up and snuggle her to my chest; to bury my nose in her curls; to feel the weight of her body in my arms.

When her father finally thumps around the corner, a powerful shock of recognition jolts my body. The man who is playing with this child is Andrew. My breath comes in shallow gasps, but he also brushes right past me, unaware of my existence.

When he finally lumbers to the toddler's hiding place, he reaches out a finger and gently tickles her tiny bare foot. She erupts into a cascade of giggles, throws aside the pillow, and launches herself into his arms. Warmth floods me like a gut punch to my soul, and for reasons I can't explain, bittersweet tears collect in the corners of my eyes.

"Dada!" she shouts, patting her chubby starfish hands against his face. I realize she shares his deep cobalt eyes. "Dada!"

He blows raspberries on her smooth, rosy cheek. The child breaks away and totters to a low shelf on the nearby bookcase. She clasps a small picture frame and races back to Andrew's arms.

She offers up the frame. It's covered in tiny fingerprint smudges. "Mama?"

A shadow darkens Andrew's face, and his sorrowful sigh makes his deep grief and loss plainly evident.

"No, sweetie. No Mama," he whispers quietly. "Mama can't be with us anymore. Mama's our special angel."

He gently removes the frame from her chubby little fingers. She furrows her little brow and stares hard at Andrew.

"Dada. Why twy?"

The little girl reaches a tiny, perfect finger to his face to catch the tear at the corner of his eye. He kisses her cheek, stands up, and replaces the photo. He sweeps the child up, and she wraps her small arms around his neck. She gently strokes his hair. It is obvious from his sad, sweet smile that he adores this child and longs for her mother. My chest constricts with the weight of his heartbreak, and also with some other sentiment. Some small part of me is deeply envious of this child's dead mother.

I move tentatively toward the bookshelf, intensely curious yet dreading the identity of this woman, my paradoxical rival. At first I'm not sure what I'm seeing. It's a woman, pale and drawn, in a hospital gown, holding a red, wrinkly newborn infant. The woman is me. Without warning, the floor lurches off kilter and a peculiar spinning sensation distorts my vision. My knees go weak, and I grasp the edge of the bookshelf for support. A sob catches in my throat, and the hot tears that I'd just barely contained pour down my cheeks.

The tsunami of sorrow threatens to overwhelm me, and I drop to the floor, close my eyes, and fight to calm my ragged breath. "This is not mine," I chant hoarsely. "This is not my reality." Time becomes unbounded, and I allow the swells of sadness to break over me until my concentration grows so great I can no longer hear the child, no longer hear her father, no longer smell the pines. At last, I allow my conscious mind to assert itself. I am not really here, I think to myself. I will not be here. I WILL NOT BE HERE.

When I awoke, I was half reclined in a leather office chair in the lab. Uneven gasps punctuated my breath, and my arms ached for the solid weight of my child. *No, not my child*, I reminded myself. I reached a hand to my face to wipe the tears from my swollen eyes and realized the EEG electrode cap was attached to my skull, but I had no clear memory of how it had gotten there. Taking deliberate, deep breaths, I struggled to sit up, but the familiar, forceful pounding on the right side my head was compounded by a sickening lurch in my stomach. I was expecting the migraine, but the nausea was new—thanks to all that stupid wine. I quickly sank lower and lay as still as I could. With a groan borne of churning stomach, headache, and aching heart, I laid my arm over my weary eyes. *How much more of this can I endure?* I desperately wished that I could rewind the clock, back to when my biggest worry was whether I'd finished grading student exams.

Moments later I heard a gentle knock on the door, then the click of the lock as someone badged in. I snuck an eye open and detected a shape through a glowing aquamarine aura.

"Who is it?" I mumbled.

"It's Janine," she whispered. "How are you feeling?"

"Not great. I can't really see—I have a hideous migraine right now."

"It might help if I lower the light and the temperature."

I could hear Janine tap her phone and the lights dimmed. I heard the soft hiss as cool air began flowing through the ceiling ducts.

I raised an eyelid halfway, then another. The cool darkness was soothing.

"Can you help me get this EEG cap off?" I asked. The web of sensors extended over my nose, past my cheeks, and fastened below my chin like a crazy sci-fi bonnet from hell. My voice was raspy, and it felt as if my teeth were covered in fur.

"Sure." She unsnapped the chin strap and gently extracted the sensors from my tangled hair. "Can you lean forward?"

"I think so…" I said, but as I raised my head, a monumental wave of nausea formed in the pit of my stomach and then surged quickly upward. Janine was more than prepared—she immediately produced a large plastic bag and positioned it deftly. It caught every bit of expensive pink champagne that erupted from my body.

"I can't believe he got you drunk," she muttered, rubbing my back as I coughed and sputtered.

When I had finally purged every last ounce of liquid from my gut, she whisked away the bag and returned with a cool washcloth, which she used to gently wipe my face.

"I'm so sorry," I coughed, closing my eyes and wincing

through the rhythmic pounding in my head. "I almost puked all over you..."

"It's okay," she assured me. I could hear the kind smile even though I couldn't see it. "But I'm going to have words with Andrew..."

Despite the throbbing in my skull, I managed a weak smile. I wrapped my arms around my body and shivered. The temperature in the room had already dropped, and I was covered in goose bumps.

"Let me try to make you a bit more comfortable." She gently enfolded me in a thick microfleece blanket.

"You rest for a while. Sleep if you can. It says in your medical records that you have had some success treating migraines with eletriptan?"

"Mmmmm-hmmmm..." I agreed, trying to nod. Bad idea. The pain was nearly unbearable.

"I'll get you a dose. And you're probably dehydrated as well; we'll get you some fluids. I'll be back soon, Kate."

The distant click of the door latch indicated Janine was gone.

I shifted slightly, adjusting my arms so that my palms faced upward. I certainly couldn't get into a full lotus position, so I would do the best I could, given the raging hangover. I took a deep breath and tried to relax my body.

I exhaled and thought, "Peace." I inhaled again and added, "Light." Finally, I added, "Love."

"Mommy is our special angel," I heard him say as clearly as if he was actually standing beside me. And then I felt the phantom brush of his breath against my neck; his mouth against my lips.

"Oh, no..." I whimpered, willfully compelling the hallucination to end. I took another deep breath, refocused, and tried again, abandoning my mantra and instead deliberately and vehemently pushing every conscious thought from my troubled mind.

Relief washed over me when Janine returned with a single orange pill and a cup of lukewarm peppermint tea.

Within an hour, the aura had abated, and my eyesight had been restored. The pounding in my head had subsided, and instead I was left with a consistent, but manageable dull ache. Despite the tea, I still felt queasy. After this experience, I promised myself that I was off alcohol—for good. I managed to stumble to the bathroom and splashed some water on my face, but the effort made me feel like walking death, so I shuffled to my dorm room, collapsed on the bed, and resumed meditation.

The incessant pressure in my head blended with the very real pounding on the outside of my door. I pulled my pillow over my head and rolled over. After what seemed like hours, the pounding stopped but was replaced by the familiar click of an access card releasing the lock.

"Kathryn?" Andrew called, poking his head into the room.

"Leave me alone!" I groaned, waving my arm clumsily to ward him off. "Haven't you ever heard of privacy? What did you do to me? "

"Did the meds work on the migraine?"

"Yes," I grumbled through the pillow. "But I still feel like shit."

"You're just hungover. Let's go." He grasped the pillow and yanked. I tried to swat his hand away but missed by a mile.

"You need some coffee, some vitamin B, and hydration. And then we need to get to work. We'll need to get started right away on the data analysis on your dream state."

Right—my dream state. I had to remind myself that while he knew about my nightmare, there was no way he could know its content. I shook off the thought with a shudder, sat up, pulled back my tousled hair, and smoothed my rumpled shirt.

The bed bounced slightly as he sat beside me. I warily eyed the small medical kit as he snapped it open and extracted a vial and a syringe.

"Time for the vitamin B."

I got the distinct impression that he was getting some perverse enjoyment out of this.

"Wait, what? I'm not letting you inject me! Where is Janine?"

"Don't be such a baby. Janine isn't the only one with an MD in this place. And unlike Janine, I actually *completed* my residency. Besides, it'll help with the headache—and the nausea."

I snatched the vial and examined the label; it looked like a legitimate B-complex dose. I closed my eyes against the dull ache in my head and handed it back, resigned to do whatever it took to ward off the aftereffects of my night of alcoholic indiscretion.

He inserted the needle into the vial and drew back a dose. "Let's take a look at that ass of yours."

I was in no condition to participate in witty repartee. I pushed up my left shirtsleeve. "Haha. Very funny."

A swipe with the alcohol swab and a quick stab and it was done. Andrew handed me a sizeable bottle of water.

"No time to hook you up to an IV like the professional drinkers. There's work to be done. Go eat something with protein in it, drink all this water, and have some strong coffee. I'll see you in the lab in twenty minutes."

I was thankful to discover that the prepackaged frozen chicken soup was excellent. The B-vitamins and a dose of industrial-strength espresso returned me to a nearly human state. I plodded down the hall to the lab and badged myself in to find Amir working alone at his workstation. He swung around in his office chair as I trudged through the door.

"Well, did it work?"

"Oh, yeah," I confirmed, "and I have the mother of all headaches to prove it!"

"You dreamed? And you were able to exit?"

I nodded.

"Great! That means we have a baseline reading of your dream

state *with* a self-determined exit," he said triumphantly. "I'm texting the A-man."

Amir whirled back toward the keyboard and typed furiously.

"Do you want me to get started on the analysis?" I mumbled unenthusiastically as I dropped carefully into the chair at the third workstation.

The lab door clicked open, and Andrew strode in carrying a thumb drive, which he handed to Amir.

"Amir will start on the new data, but what I really want is some hands-on results. Let's just get you in there and see if you can elicit an intentional exit. Just do whatever you did in the dream."

I stared at him with wide eyes, and my heart lurched against my rib cage. Did he expect me to exit the slice by accepting the reality that I was his dead wife? I blinked hard, reminding myself that there was no way he could know what I'd dreamed. My head still felt thick and my stomach still vaguely queasy, and I had just recovered from a monumental migraine. More pressing physical concerns supplanted my psychological trauma. What if the slice caused the migraine to come roaring back? What if the anti-nausea didn't work?

"Can't we at least wait until...later?" I begged, casting a worried glance toward the Bugs perched menacingly on the conference table.

"Fortune favors the brave, Kathryn. Catch."

The bottle of anti-nausea pills whizzed though the air, and I lurched out of my chair to catch it. Resigned, I shuffled toward the rack of medical devices and plopped down in the leather seat.

Andrew fished out the EEG electrode cap, wired me up, and positioned my Bug. Then he sat beside me and positioned his own set of electrodes.

"You're coming too?" I asked, trying to stifle my alarm. He was sitting too close to me; what if his mere presence provoked another flashback?

"I'll be here as a reference. We'll shoot for a near slice. You should try to return before it collapses. If you get back before I do, we'll know it worked."

The Bug's manic humming interrupted any further protests.

The hangover made the device's burrowing probe even more excruciating than usual, so I was relieved when I opened my eyes to find the horrid device had vanished.

"You know," I groaned, massaging my hand. "You could have built that thing so that it hurt less."

Andrew looked at me for a moment, then his face registered the tiniest hint of amusement. "The original prototype burrowed into the spinal cord at the base of the neck," he said. "Trust me, it hurts less."

I suppressed a shudder and glanced around at the nearly identical lab. Another slight wave of dizziness engulfed me, followed by the unnerving feeling that this had all happened before. I squeezed my eyes shut and swallowed hard.

"I think experiencing two different realities is messing with my head," I mumbled. The sensation passed and I opened my eyes. "Does this bizarre feeling of déjà vu ever go away?"

Andrew lounged sedately in the overstuffed leather office chair I'd come to think of as the first-class airline seats to an alternate universe. He didn't seem at all concerned. "Studies show that memory is not an accurate representation of reality. Memory is adaptive and flexible, designed to reshape itself to accommodate new situations. You're just experiencing a little bit of cognitive dissonance. The brain has strategies to handle contradictions; with a little practice, you'll find that blending your knowledge of realities becomes quite easy."

I was perfectly familiar with the idea of neuroplasticity and current research on memory consolidation. But understanding the science and personally experiencing these realities was a whole different matter. I wondered if holding dozens of conflicting realities in my head might actually drive me clinically insane.

Andrew tapped the table impatiently. "Well, you'd best get to it. Poof yourself out of here."

I cast a withering glance his way, then considered my surroundings. The hard concrete floor didn't look like an appealing place to break out a full lotus position. With few other options, I opted to remain in the cushy leather chair. I closed my eyes, relaxed my hands in my lap, and began to breathe.

I was concentrating deeply on my breath when I noticed the rhythmic thumping. I opened my eyes; Andrew sat staring at me, both toes tapping restlessly. I frowned in the most disapproving manner I could muster.

"Do you mind? I'm trying to concentrate here."

"Oh. Sorry," he replied sheepishly. "I'm not used to sitting idly by and waiting."

I scowled and tried to focus. As my concentration turned inward, I began to feel lighter. My breath calmed and my muscles turned slack. As my mind relaxed and focused, my conscious thoughts moved to the background. I thought, *I will not be here. I will not be here.*

Then, in a forceful voice, I stated, "I WILL NOT BE HERE!"

When I opened my eyes, Andrew was still sitting on the cushy leather chair. "You're still here," he said, eyeing me quizzically.

"Really?" I replied, dismayed. "Are you sure I'm still in the slice?"

"Yep. I've been watching you this whole time. You're still here."

"Damn," I spat. "I was really hoping that would work."

"That's how you do it? In the dreams?"

"Not exactly. I never have to work for it. You know, if it's bad—and it usually is—I can get out fast. Just stating my intention was enough to get me out last night."

"Well," Andrew said with a sigh, "I guess there are no shortcuts in science. As soon as we converge, you should sit down and take a look at last night's EEG readings."

"How long do you think it'll be?"

"Shouldn't be too long. You sat there for almost twenty minutes."

"So we just hang out here, and wait?"

"You know, I could use a little break. Why don't we go take a walk?"

My eyes widened. Freedom! "Won't you get in trouble for letting the lab rat out?"

"What they don't know won't hurt me." He grabbed my hand and practically yanked me out of my chair.

The moment we stepped outside, I wished we hadn't. Instead of the scent of dry grass, oak trees, and madrone, the hot, stale air was tinged with an unpleasant ozone odor. I took a deep breath and coughed. Before I could even suggest we return indoors, the familiar feeling of vertigo pulled me back into our native slice. As I opened my eyes, I sat motionless in my office chair for a moment, anticipating the crushing migraine, but it never materialized.

From his matching black office chair, Andrew blinked at me as he slowly came to. He looked ridiculous with the mesh of sensors stuck to his head. I imagined I looked equally as attractive.

"Well, not this time," he said, reaching to remove the Bug from the back of my hand.

I unfastened the chin strap on the EEG cap and peeled off the web of sensors.

"We'll try again tomorrow."

My head dropped forward, and I dug my fingers into the tense muscles of my neck. This was the whole reason I was here, and I couldn't manage to perform. Thanks to the anti-nausea, at least I wasn't puking, but the experiment was still just as exhausting as ever, especially on top of a hangover.

"You want to see these readings?" Amir called from across the room.

"Let's take a look," Andrew suggested, unhooking his EEG cap and dropping it in the bucket of saline solution that would keep the contacts ready for the next use.

Tired and defeated, I trudged to my workstation.

"Amir," I sighed, "can you point me toward my readings from last night? I have work to do."

After seven hours of staring intently at the screen, running algorithms, tweaking, and running them again, I hadn't learned anything. The resolution of the EEG readings just wasn't providing enough data.

"These results are useless," I grumbled, flinging my hands into the air. Andrew and Amir clustered around my workstation.

"Here is my EEG from today," I said, showing the data represented by a graph. "And here is the set of data that I believe is responsible for the slice shift." Some of the data fell away. "When I peel away the noise in the signal, the graph of my dream data looks remarkably similar." I displayed a second set of lines on the graph. "But when I overlay them, you'll see one big difference. Here." I pointed to a huge spike. The graph after the huge spike remained in sync with my slice EEG for a short while, then the line went flat.

Amir leaned in excitedly. "But that spike, that's it, right? Whoo-freakin'-hoo!"

"Well, yes...that spike indicates the exit. But it doesn't tell me anything."

"What do you mean?" Andrew said, staring intently at the graphs.

"There isn't enough data here. The EEG just doesn't provide enough resolution. We can't get what we need with these tools. Maybe I could do something with fMRI readings..."

"That's all you need? An fMRI machine?" Andrew asked.

"Uh, yeah. That's *all.*" I frowned. "It's the reason I'm even involved in this lunatic venture in the first place, remember? But it's not like you're just going to roll one in. They cost millions of dollars. They have requirements. You need a room that is specifically sized, that is shielded to eliminate fields of any kind, and has exact temperature ranges."

"Done and done," Andrew said in his usual infuriating matter-of-fact manner. "Until that's ready, any other ideas about what might be facilitating your exit from your dream state?"

I stared at him in disbelief. Was that all it took to get an fMRI at my beck and call?

Andrew returned my stare, impatiently waiting for an answer to his question. I shook off my shock and tried to focus. "When I'm dreaming, even though the quality of the dreams is different—vivid, intense, almost hyper-real—I don't really grasp that it's happening until I've been there for a little while. And even though the dreams are almost always really horrible, there is usually some event—some tipping point—that jolts me into action. Something so sad or terrible or shocking that I can't stand to stay a minute longer."

"An interesting observation." Andrew nodded, taking a step back and considering for a moment. "We'll have to figure out how replicate that state. First thing tomorrow."

I was closing down documents on my workstation when the phone rang. Andrew reached for the keypad and placed the call on speaker.

"Status!" the voice on the line bellowed.

Andrew stiffened. "Nothing yet. We need to install an fMRI."

I leaned in toward Amir. "Who is that?"

"Big boss man," he whispered.

"Andric Breckinridge?" I was unable to keep the awe out of my voice.

Amir nodded.

"Yes, yes," Breckinridge snapped dismissively, as if a million-dollar piece of medical equipment was no more a challenge to procure than a cup of fancy coffee. "But this is no time for games. We need this operation up and running and we need it now."

I could see the tension mounting in Andrew's posture, but he said nothing.

The caller dropped his voice, which only made him seem more menacing. "I expect nothing less than complete dedication from you. You know what is at stake. Complete the task. Immediately!"

Andrew narrowed his eyes. Though his tone was quiet and steady, his words had sharpened to a razor edge. "Yes, sir, *Doctor*."

Andrew picked up the receiver and slammed it into the cradle to end the call.

"We have a job to do, and we're not going to leave this room until we've accomplished it," Andrew snapped, turning to me with barely concealed fury. "Okay, it's time to test your theory. Suit up! We're going back in, and this time it's not going to be pretty."

He strode over to the cabinet containing the Bugs.

"What, right now?" I stammered, shrinking back into my chair. The thought of another exhausting encounter with the Bug made my hands tremble. "I thought tomorrow…"

"No time like the present!" Andrew barked, irritated.

I swallowed hard, rose, and nervously followed. Within minutes, we were ready.

The painful, lurching jerk into the alternate slice was as unpleasant as always, but I'd no more than caught my breath and struggled to my feet when Andrew pushed past me. As usual for a near-slice travel, we were in the lab, but without Amir or any other staff. Andrew proceeded directly to his workstation; beneath the counter stood a trio of desk drawers. He quickly yanked one open, rummaged around in it, and whipped around.

"Andrew?" I said, stepping back cautiously, "What's going on?"

Andrew advanced in my direction, eyes flashing with fury. When he reached me, he roughly grabbed my left hand. With frightening speed and surgical accuracy, he plunged a pair of office scissors deep into the center of my palm.

The pain was excruciating; I let out an anguished wail as I pulled away from him and stumbled backward. My eyes clenched and I cradled my bleeding hand to my chest.

"You are a total fucking psychopath!" I screamed.

I opened my eyes and tried to flee. My stomach was roiling and my head was pounding. My heart was beating a million miles a minute, but I couldn't escape because I was tangled in the thick cable attached to my EEG cap. I tore it off and stumbled away from my leather chair. Andrew appeared as if asleep, still wearing his sensors. I raised my quivering left hand and examined it closely. No mark was visible, except the expected welt from the Bug. I wiggled my fingers. The pain in my hand had vanished.

I looked up to see Amir staring at me, his jaw hanging open. "You did it!" he said, his voice thick with wonder. "Hot damn, woman, you did it." He grinned in amazement. "So...how'd you do it?"

I clenched my teeth and glowered at him. "You tell your deranged buddy over there that I am *done*," I spat, motioning to Andrew. I charged out of the room, leaving Amir standing there, mouth agape.

Full of righteous indignation and barely concealed anger, I strode down the hallway to the windowless facility door. I flung it open and stared out into the blackness; not a single light was visible for miles. There was no way I'd find my way back to town in the dark on foot, and I had no access to the fleet of pickups. I slammed the door shut and pounded it with my fist, barely feeling the pain of the impact on the steel-reinforced panels.

With no options remaining, I bellowed in frustration, spun on my heels, and marched back to my room. I launched myself onto the bed, grabbed the pillow, and pressed it over my face as I let out a long, frustrated howl. Then I hurled the pillow across the room, lay back, and fumed.

Twenty minutes later, my fury had only grown. The knock at the door was perfunctory, but there was no doubt it was Andrew. There was no way I was going to open that door. "What is it?" I growled through clenched teeth.

"Let me in," Andrew called flatly. "Now that you've done it, there's more work to do."

"I'm not letting you in!" I shrieked.

"Fine," he replied tersely. I heard the click as he used his keycard to unlock the door.

Before he set a single step beyond the threshold, I let out a rebel yell and launched myself at him, swinging, clawing, punching, hoping desperately to get him out. I had no training in self-defense and had never even been in a girl fight, but my anger and indignation provided the fuel for ferocity. None of my punches landed, but I was certain I managed a few good scratches.

He shoved me back toward the bed, and when I spun to reengage, he stepped quickly and efficiently outside the door. With another click I was again contained.

Utterly defeated, I collapsed on the bed and roared. Hot tears ran down my face. The thought crossed my mind that they were probably monitoring me, either with audio or video or both, but I couldn't douse the waterworks. The raw emotion layered atop fear had finally gotten the best of me.

After an hour, I had a red face, puffy eyes, and a prodigious pile of wadded-up industrial-grade tissues, but the fury was spent. In its place, a plan was forming.

I put my ear to the door and listened for several minutes. The floor outside was polished concrete, and the absence of footsteps assured me that the coast was clear. As quietly as I could, I opened the door and slipped out. I suspected they would soon realize I had left my room, so I had to work fast.

I quickly navigated the halls to the kitchen, where two men in white lab coats were finishing their dinner. I straightened my back, held my head high, and tried to look menacing. I strode purposefully over to their small table, placed my palms flat upon it, bent down, and stared darkly.

"You know who I am?" I asked, hoping that my reputation would proceed me.

The men eyed me warily. "Yes," the one on the left replied. "We know who you are."

"Take me to Janine," I demanded. I leaned in until I was just inches from his face and stared at him, unblinking, for one second, five seconds, ten long seconds. I wasn't sure this was going to work, but I needed to get out of that facility, and fast, before Andrew realized I was gone. Based on what had happened to Lily, I had no doubt that they would resort to medical intervention to achieve their goals, and I had no desire to be tranquilized.

I kept my gaze steely and refused to back down. The staffer blinked first.

"Okay," he said, shoving back his half-eaten dinner and rising from his seat. "I'll take you."

We marched along unfamiliar hallways and through another locked door. Then we descended a narrow concrete staircase to the basement level, which led to another hallway, lit with fluorescent bulbs and dotted with still more windowless steel doors. He knocked forcefully on the fifth door on the right. We waited a minute, maybe more, before another man in a white lab coat opened the door but barred us from entering.

"Please call Dr. Mori," my guide requested.

I stood, fidgeting, hoping my brash plan would succeed. My position was tenuous at best, and the longer this took, the less likely it was to work.

The door closed slowly with a quiet click, and we waited again. Minutes passed. I was getting antsy. Surely by now Andrew knew I had left my room.

"Why don't you just take me in?" I demanded impatiently.

"You can't go in there," he responded tersely. "I can't even go in there. These labs are need-to-know access only."

Finally, the door opened just wide enough for Janine to slip through. She was also wearing a white lab coat, over rumpled khakis and a black knit shirt. Her eyes were glazed and weary. When she saw me, her exhaustion quickly turned to concern.

She nodded to the lab coat at my elbow. "Thanks, Ken. I'll take it from here."

My hostage nodded and departed without hesitation.

Janine sighed, rubbing her forehead with her fingertips. "Kate…what is it? What's wrong?"

"Andrew," I said through clenched teeth. "He is a complete psychopath! He assaulted me; I can't go back in there. There's no one I can trust. You've got to get me out of this place."

With a sidelong glance back at her lab, Janine put her arm protectively around my shoulders. Despite my resolve to remain as intimidating as I possibly could, this motherly gesture caught me off guard.

"Okay, let's swing by my office. I'm going to grab a couple of things and we'll check out a car."

We walked deeper into the basement hallway maze, until we stood before another unmarked, windowless door.

"I'm sorry about this, but I can't allow you in this room, either. Just stay here. I won't be a minute."

Janine pressed her keycard to a reader, and the door clicked open. She slipped through and was gone, leaving me alone in the hall. I nervously swept my eyes across the length of the corridor, waiting for some burly men to drag me back to my room, but none materialized. After what seemed like an eternity, Janine emerged, sans lab coat.

We followed the hallway until we reached a bulky service elevator. We took it up to the first floor, where it opened directly into the large garage bay. Two of the facility's light-duty pickups were waiting. Janine used her keycard to unlock a panel on the wall, and she grabbed a set of keys.

As Janine carefully navigated the pickup through a large roll-up door, I caught a lungful of foul smog. I felt my throat constrict as I struggled to raise the open window.

Janine kept her eyes glued to the dirt track she was navigating more rapidly than was prudent. The headlights cast eerie shadows through the oaks as we bounced past.

"I'm sorry, Kate, but you should know—everyone is aware that I'm taking you out."

I felt a tiny stab of betrayal, which was alleviated by the fact that I was, at least, fleeing the facility. I was out—I was free. I pushed my distrust of Janine down deep and stared out the window.

When we reached the pavement, Janine relaxed her death grip on the wheel and glanced in my direction. "What did Andrew do?"

"He stabbed me. With a pair of scissors."

Janine breathed an exasperated snort. She sounded beyond tired, like she needed to sleep for a month.

"This is no excuse, but we're under enormous pressure. It's not easy to work for...our boss."

"Breckinridge, I know," I said flatly. "I met him."

"Well, then, you have some idea of the working conditions. He's incredibly illustrious. He's been named Entrepreneur of the Year, Innovator of the Year, and has been one of *Time Magazine's*

Top 100 Influential People. He's ranked seventh on the *Forbes* list of the World's Most Powerful People. He's wealthy, influential, brilliant, and driven. But the expectations on his staff are severe," she explained. "For many of us, the cost is extremely high."

She expertly navigated the traffic on the crowded residential streets. "You'll be home soon, but don't think that there aren't consequences. Whether you return is your choice. I want you to meet me in Dr. Daniels's office tomorrow afternoon. It's important you understand the gravity of this situation."

She offered nothing more, so I rode silently until we arrived at my apartment.

"Thanks," I muttered as I scurried out of the truck. She nodded once as I closed the door, and then she was gone.

I didn't have my house keys with me, so I pounded on the door, hoping Michelle was home.

The door flung open, and my sister enfolded me in a fierce hug. "Amir texted. He said you were on your way." She ushered me into the apartment and closed the door. "Are you hungry? I made spaghetti."

I realized I hadn't eaten since breakfast and stuffed down two big bowls full of warm carbs with Michelle's zesty homemade sauce before I even offered a word of explanation. Michelle shifted uneasily from the kitchen to the counter to our thrift-store dining table, barely containing her curiosity.

As we deposited our bowls in the kitchen sink, I leaned in close to my sister. "I think this place might be bugged," I whispered in her ear. "We have to get out of here."

"I'm so glad to see you!" Michelle countered loudly, nodding as she met my eyes. "Why don't you come out with me? You look like you've been cooped up far too long."

I was mentally and physically exhausted, but there was no time to rest. "Sure," I agreed, grabbing a sweater on my way to the door. "Let's go!"

We headed for Stanford's Green Library. Michelle had to use her inhaler twice during the few blocks we walked to reach the bus stop.

We arrived at the Green Library with only thirty minutes to spare. We'd have to work quickly.

"What's the plan?" Michelle asked as we made our way through the doors.

"The CEO of the Albaion Corporation is Andric Breckinridge. Everyone treats him like he's some sort of brainiac god, but I don't know anything about him or his company. I need to know what's really going on there." I made a beeline straight for the computer stations.

"Why are doing this at the library, instead of at home? You know we could have done this search on your phone, or your laptop," Michelle asked.

"I'm certain I'm being monitored, and I'll bet you are, too. I don't think I can securely use the computer from home, and I don't even think it's safe to search from any machine that that has any of my account information. Or my IP address. And just to be sure, power down your phone." I turned mine off and sat on it for good measure. At the public computer station, I typed in "Andric Breckinridge." Michelle sat at the machine next to me and did the same. I clicked rapidly through the links and skimmed each article.

"Oh, man... Janine was right; the man is dripping in awards and honors. He's got this incredibly long CV. Look at this... he won the genius grant in 1981 for a paper he published that changed the way people think about stock prices and economic growth. He has... wait, he has *a hundred and seventy-two* patents. He has founded eleven successful companies, seven of them within the last five years, in industries ranging from energy to biomedical to genetics to privately funded space travel. Albaion flies under the radar, but the subsidiaries... he owns a successful company in every hot market segment out there."

"Oh, Kate, this is weird," Michelle interjected. "Breckinridge is a big-time donor to several prominent universities, and one of his biggest pet projects is sleep research."

I frowned. "Well, that explains the Breckinridge Fellowship and his interest in my condition."

"Your Dr. Breckinridge comes from money, too. His grandfather was a big shot in the timber industry at the turn of the century, and his father was a financier. Did a lot of speculating in oil and gas. His current personal net worth is estimated at seventeen-point-one billion."

There was too much to read, and we needed more time, but the lights dimmed and the impatient frowns from the librarian finally forced us out. What was glaringly obvious was that Breckinridge was a bona fide genius. His work was multidisciplinary, his success rate was extraordinary, and his ventures were incredibly lucrative.

As we left the library, I caught Michelle's elbow and steered her toward the oversize sculptural fountain just outside the east entrance. We sat down on the big concrete step beside it. I hoped I was just paranoid, but trusted the roaring of the fountain would drown out any sort of listening device.

"Shell, I'm in trouble. It's clear that Breckinridge is not only obscenely wealthy but also incredibly powerful. I'm still not entirely sure why his organization needs me, specifically...or why they let me go."

"Why *did* you leave?" Michelle wheezed, pulling out her inhaler.

I scowled and held up my hand.

"That ass Andrew stabbed me."

Michelle eyed me quizzically. "Your boss stabbed you? Where? Are you injured? Do we need to go to the ER?"

I threw my hands up in exasperation. "Ugh...too complicated to explain. I'm fine. No lasting injury. But he's proven he's dangerous, and probably mentally unstable, and definitely untrustworthy. But it gets worse."

"What could be worse than being stabbed?"

"I'm dreaming about him."

"Dreaming? Or *dreaming*?" she asked.

"*Dreaming*. More than once. Sometimes...uh, well...erotically. In one of them, I was his wife. Though I *was* dead in that one..."

She looked concerned. "Do you have feelings for him or something?"

I closed my eyes and took a deep breath, trying to logically inventory my emotions. I felt disgust, then fear, then something else. I never wanted to see Andrew again, yet I couldn't get his damn face out of my mind.

"Yeah, I have a feeling—that he's an arrogant ass!" I grunted. "But make no mistake—someone as powerful and driven as Breckinridge doesn't just give up, take his toys, and go home. Apparently he needs me, and I doubt he will simply let me out. Not knowing what I know."

"So, now what? What will you do?" Michelle insisted as we headed to the bus stop.

I cleared my throat and coughed, feeling an acrid burn in the back of my sinuses. I hoped the bus would arrive quickly. "Today was pure hell. Right now, more than anything I need to sleep. Tomorrow, I'll go see Dr. Daniels."

CHAPTER 14

ANDREW

September 28, 2002

Andrew had taken a wrong turn on his way to the rec sports facility and now he was late for his first tae kwon do sparring practice. The relief that he'd finally found the assigned room was quickly extinguished when he realized that the only other student without a partner was a slight Asian woman wearing a worn Cal Bears T-shirt and sweats. Her long, black hair was pulled neatly into a braid and it hung to the side as she stretched. He sized her up instantly; she was easily forty pounds lighter than he was and a full head shorter.

She greeted him with a confident smile. "Hi, I'm Lily." She extended her hand, and he noted that she had a startlingly firm handshake—for a girl.

Within the first three minutes, she'd knocked him to the floor twice.

"You must be new at this. You're a freshman, right?" she taunted. She bounded around him on the pads of her feet as she waited for him to peel himself off the mat.

"I've studied tae kwon do for years!"

Lily took him down again.

"Need a break?" As she bounced foot to foot, her long braid swung rhythmically. She wasn't even winded.

"No way!" he panted. "I want you to know, I'm not going to take it easy on you just because you're a girl."

"I'm a woman," she countered, dancing about the mat. "And you know I'm a black belt, right?"

By way of answer, he threw another punch and followed with a kick, which she easily avoided.

"You're telegraphing," she goaded him as she dodged. "I can see you coming a mile away!"

He gritted his teeth and launched a new assault.

She spun around and threw all her weight behind a well-paced kick high above her head. The strike caught him under the chin and knocked him flat on his ass. Blood began to stream down his neck.

"What the hell?" he yelped, clutching his chin.

"Don't freak out, but I think my toenail caught you on the way down. Stay still!" she commanded. Without a hint of hesitation, she pulled off her shirt and pressed it firmly to the wound to staunch the bleeding, revealing a camo-patterned sports bra and dog tags.

"Get that sweaty piece of crap off me!" he shouted angrily, attempting unsuccessfully to swat her away. "You're going to give me gangrene!"

Lily literally slapped him upside the head. "Stop being such a baby, frosh. I'm taking you to the Tang Center. You probably need stitches."

December 4, 2004

A typical Northern California winter storm had turned the night cold and rainy. Lily spent more time than usual stuffing her workout clothes into her gym bag, and he noticed that she repeatedly cast sidelong glances his way. He was surprised. Sometimes she was brash, bold, and forceful; sometimes she was calm, cool, and collected. The uncertainty was new.

She intently examined the end of her long braid as she spoke. "So...I know this is last minute and all, but the battalion does this formal every year, the Tri-Service Ball. Who knows how long this military action in Afghanistan is going to drag on? There's no doubt I'll be deployed there as soon as I graduate." Lily tried to sound flippant, but he could read between the lines. "It may be the last real party I see for a while. And I don't want to go alone."

"Are you asking me...on a date?" he replied incredulously.

"Don't be such an enormous dorkwad!" she insisted, punching him in the arm—hard. "There is no way I'd ever date you! For one thing, you don't have tits..."

"Ouch!" he protested, rubbing his arm. "That's yet another bruise I'll be sporting for the next week, thanks to you. You're a psych major. Can't you use your words rather than resorting to violence?"

She grinned. "Forcefulness is my strong suit."

"There ought to be some rule about seniors beating up underclassmen," he grumbled.

"So are you going to help out a friend here, or not?"

"For my most endearing—and brutal—martial arts foe? Yes, of course I'll go."

Lily nodded, zipping up her duffel. "I sure hope you can dance better than you fight."

"Yes, ma'am, I can dance," Andrew smirked. "And I clean up real nice, too."

"Good. And no wacky-ass ties printed with secret messages in binary. I know how you code monkeys are with your nerd humor."

Andrew pretended to be insulted.

That evening he took the BART train to San Francisco to visit the Nordstrom men's department. He left with an overpriced black tie made of Italian silk and the attractive, petite, blonde, and somewhat vacuous young saleswomen who spent the evening persuading him to purchase it.

May 8, 2006

He had been holed up in his apartment for the past forty hours, working feverishly to perfect the speech he would present at commencement. A loud knock interrupted his progress.

"Hey, Mr. University Medal! Just two days until the biggest smarty-pants I know addresses the graduating class of 2006!" Lily grinned as she burst through the door.

Andrew immediately wrapped her in a warm embrace. "I can't believe you're here!" His smile was broad and genuine. "When did you get back?"

"Yesterday," she replied. He ushered her into the apartment. "I'll spend a couple of weeks leave with my family, then it's back to the base for a round of gear repair and mission training."

He reached into the fridge for a pair of cold IPAs, twisted the cap from the first, and handed it to her. She took a long drag of beer, crossed the open layout of the spacious and well-appointed apartment, and dropped down on the tawny leather sofa.

"Oh God, I love this sofa!" Lily moaned, caressing its soft, supple surface. "How I have missed this sofa. I have dreams about this sofa!" She leaned forward and ran a finger along the top of the sculptural glass-topped coffee table. "There isn't a speck of dust in this place. Didn't you just finish finals? How do you have time to keep this place spotless? Is your mother still sending her cleaning lady?"

His expression ricocheted from elation to despondence. He sat down carefully on the matching leather armchair, but his normally inscrutable face showed the strain of exhaustion.

Lily's demeanor suddenly became serious. "What happened? Is it your mom? I thought she was in remission."

"Yeah, so did I." Andrew sighed, downing more beer but staring into space.

"Hey, man, I'm sorry. I was out of line." She stared down at her hands, picking at a nail. "What's the prognosis?"

"It's not good. She's back in the hospital. They wanted to do another round of chemo but her kidneys are failing. She won't be out in time for graduation."

Lily winced, grasping the implication. She took a pull from the longneck bottle in her hand. "But your dad's coming, right? You are literally the most distinguished scholar on campus right now."

A dark look crossed his eyes, but his gaze was still far away. "He's in Luxembourg, setting up some new subsidiary. He won't be back anytime soon. In fact, ever since she's been sick, he's gone more than ever."

"But he must be proud…"

Andrew scowled. "He's never forgiven me for turning down Princeton."

The light glinting on the chronometer on his left wrist caught her eye. She nodded toward it. "You started wearing a watch."

"Mom had it couriered over last night." He gently ran a finger across the smooth sapphire crystal of the timepiece. "She's dying, yet she still somehow managed to make sure I received my graduation gift."

Lily reached across the sofa and grasped his arm. "I'm so sorry."

Andrew's eyes regained focus and settled on his friend. "You always did have a ridiculously firm grip—for a girl."

Lily's eyes were sad, and tender. "For a woman," she corrected, but gently and with genuine affection. She gave his arm an extra squeeze. "Forcefulness was always my forte."

June 30, 2015

He was working another marathon shift at the neurology clinic when he saw her at the admitting desk.

"I'm looking for Andrew. He's a resident," she asked politely.

He frowned at the uncharacteristic tremor in her voice.

"Lily?" he asked, tapping her on the shoulder. She swung around to face him, and her red-rimmed eyes screamed that something was very, very wrong.

She slowly rotated the titanium band on the ring finger of her left hand. "It's Maddie," she stammered. "There was a roadside IED and her convoy caught it and now she's gone." She stared at him with forlorn eyes, brimming with tears.

He immediately folded her into his arms. Her mascara left a dark smudge on the lapel of his white coat. After a long moment, he guided her to the patient lounge flanking the admitting desk.

She dug a tissue from her black leather handbag and wiped her eyes with efficiency.

"Sorry," she sniffed. "All this emotional crap; this isn't me. Right now I need...I need to decide if I'm going to stay in the corps, and I really need someone to talk to. Now that she's gone, everything feels...wrong."

"Listen, I'm off in about an hour. Can you meet me across the street for coffee?"

She nodded, composing herself and squaring her shoulders.

"My residency ends in a couple of weeks, and I'm not planning to stay in neurology practice. I'm going to work at Albaion, and I think you should come with me."

She eyed him quizzically. "You and your dad are like oil and water. Why on earth would you agree to work for him?"

He leaned in toward Lily so that he wouldn't be overheard.

"I'm building a prototype for a medical device. Right now it's just me and this hotshot programmer I rescued from the math department at Berkeley. Amir and I have been meeting with venture capitalists for over a year, but no one will bite. I've got something—something big. But no one wants to take on the risk. The irony is not lost on me, but he's the only person who will give me a chance—and the seed money."

"But I don't have any skills that would make me useful at a biotechnology company," she protested.

Andrew smiled. "Oh, I think you'd be surprised."

September 26, Present

Andrew drew the sharp blade of the razor along his neck and winced as he nicked the edge of a barely discernible scar just below his jawline. He touched his finger to the cut and pulled it away, gazing absentmindedly at the single scarlet droplet.

He lifted the collar of his starched and crisply pressed white Armani dress shirt and draped an Italian silk tie over his neck. He crossed the ends of the smooth, dark fabric and drew the end through the knot, which he cinched into a perfect half-Windsor.

He pulled on his black Brioni suit jacket and was halfway out the door when he grasped his left wrist and realized he'd forgotten his watch. He dug through the rumpled pile of workout clothes, random computer hardware peripherals, and scraps of paper uncharacteristically strewn atop the sleek maple bureau. With a sigh of relief, he extracted the platinum Patek Philippe timepiece. He cradled it gently in his hands, running his finger over the words engraved on the back: "Reality is merely an illusion." A quote from Einstein.

Andrew opened the passenger door of the dusty white pickup and offered his hand to Janine Mori, who slithered from the seat in a practiced way, despite her black skirt and heels. A layer of fog had pushed in overnight, painting the sky gray and turning the fall morning moist and chilly. The marine layer had pushed the smog inland, and the salt-tinged air was a welcome respite from the pollution—at least until the fog burned off. Janine pulled her black sweater tighter as they walked the three blocks from their parking spot to the gothic Victorian facade of St. Thomas Church. Andrew held the heavy wooden door open for Janine as she stepped inside. The interior of the church was white, bright, and airy—a stark contrast to the black-clad mourners who filed quietly inside and filled the pews.

Andrew unbuttoned his suit jacket as he and Janine found seats near the rear of the church. The priest recited the funeral mass; prayers and hymns were followed by a solemn reading from the Old Testament. Then a distinguished soldier in a marine corps uniform strode forward to deliver the reading:

"So let our sister receive the abundant grace of Jesus Christ,
Yet through one transgression
Condemnation came upon all,
So too, through one virtuous act,
Absolution and life came to all."

As the organist began another hymn, Janine glanced to her left.

Andrew was rhythmically clenching his jaw. She reached over and placed her hand gently on his arm.

"Her one transgression was her faithfulness to the cause. Our cause," he murmured.

Janine shook her head and squeezed his arm. "Don't be so hard on yourself."

"I can't believe she's gone. And that transgression *did* cause a condemnation — it's a curse on this reality."

"We'll correct it," Janine assured him. "We'll get this right."

Following the service, the congregation filed from the church and walked quietly to their vehicles. Half an hour later, in the lingering mist, Andrew and Janine stood among the mourners at Queen of Angles Cemetery as the hearse rolled to a stop. Six somber young Filipino-American men guided the white casket draped in the American flag from the back of the vehicle and carried it solemnly to the gravesite. The bereaved marched somberly behind.

The priest stood silently as the mourners assembled. "We gather here to commend our sister Lily Salonga to God our Father and to commit her body to the earth. In the spirit of faith in the resurrection of Jesus Christ from the dead, let us offer our prayers."

As the congregation silently prayed, the low clouds began to part and a ray of sunlight fell upon the assembly. The marine came forward to read a eulogy.

"Major Lily Salonga," he began, "served with distinction with the US Marine Female Engagement Team in Afghanistan. During her tours of duty she received a Navy and Marine Corps Commendation Medal for sustained acts of heroism. I was proud to know her and proud to serve with her.

"Those of us who have had the privilege of serving in the

marine corps value our experience as among the most precious of our lives. Major Salonga was proud of her corps and believed it to be second to none. She was loyal to her friends and to the marine corps, adhering always to the motto *semper fidelis*—always faithful."

Janine reached for Andrew's hand and clasped it firmly while the bugler played "Taps." The honor guard folded the flag draping the coffin into a precise and tidy triangle and handed it to Lily's weeping mother.

As the service ended, Andrew and Janine slipped away.

"He didn't even bother to pay his respects," Andrew lamented bitterly as he helped Janine into the dusty white pickup.

"You didn't really expect the illustrious Dr. Breckinridge to attend, did you?" Janine admonished as he drove listlessly toward the facility in the hills.

"She had faith in me, and I failed her. She gave her life because of his unreasonable demands. For his avarice!" Andrew shouted, pounding the dashboard with his fist. "And he didn't even have the decency to come to her funeral."

"Well, if I had to admit one thing," Janine remarked wryly, "it's that your father never was one for decency."

CHAPTER 15

KATE

September 26

At three, I stepped into the Stanford Sleep Research Clinic. The homey front office with its cozy, warm lighting was a stark contrast to the hazy afternoon that was rapidly becoming another unseasonably hot day. The receptionist's smile was unusually strained. Without any hesitation, I was ushered into an exam room, and an unfamiliar nurse recorded my vitals. The swollen red welt on the back of my left hand caused a raised eyebrow, but she didn't ask, and I didn't volunteer an explanation. The nurse made some notes in my chart and simply instructed me to follow.

She deposited me in the hallway at the rear of the clinic. The door to Dr. Daniels's clinic office was closed, so I knocked and let myself in. Dr. Daniels sat pensively behind his desk, fingers pressed together, eyes closed, slowly rocking in his office chair. The office was small and cramped, so it wasn't until I closed the door that I noticed Janine perched in one of the guest chairs.

Her fatigue was unmistakable. Her face, drawn and pale, offset the dark circles under her eyes. She was wearing dark, uncharacteristically dressy clothes and heels. I realized she must have come directly from Lily's funeral.

I lowered myself into the only other available seat. The slicing, the migraines, the hangover, and the apprehension I felt every time I relived the incident with Andrew and those scissors were definitely taking their toll. My brain was twisted with deep fatigue of my own. I took a few deep breaths and tried to temper the mental exhaustion. Uncomfortable minutes passed before Dr. Daniels finally opened his eyes and leaned forward. He heaved a heavy sigh as he finally spoke, his voice unbelievably sad.

"I wouldn't have blamed you if you hadn't come here today. I take full responsibility for getting you into this mess. If I had never mentioned that fellowship..."

"It really isn't your fault, Dr. Daniels." My eyes flashed at Janine. "It's hers."

She refused to meet my stare.

Janine sighed, "You may not believe me when I say I'm truly sorry for betraying your trust, for letting you fall into harm's way..."

Her tone made it obvious that she really *was* feeling tortured. My anger faded to a lighter shade of indignation.

Janine continued. "I never thought this would be the outcome of our research. But I'm afraid the parties involved are too influential, too powerful..."

"I know about Andric Breckinridge," I interrupted, unable to conceal the defiance.

"You know the *public* Andric Breckinridge," Janine corrected. "What you don't know is the depths to which he'll go to get what he wants." She clutched her hands together in her lap.

Daniels shook his head. "It's a mess. It's a tangled web, and I'm caught in it, and Dr. Mori's caught in it, and now you're caught in it, too."

"Well, I'm getting out."

"I'm afraid it's not as easy as walking away." Janine's words were sharp, but her eyes reflected sorrow.

"I know I signed a nondisclosure agreement, but what can he

do to me if I walk? As long as I don't talk about his little laboratory of horrors, there's nothing he can legally do."

"It's not the legal recrimination you need to worry about," Janine replied ominously.

Dr. Daniels reached across his desk and grasped my arm. "Kate, you have to go back to the compound."

"No!" I shouted, pulling away. Dread burgeoned in my gut. "I do *not* have to go back!"

"If you don't go back, Breckinridge will take action," Janine pleaded. "He *will* have you ejected from your graduate program. You will find yourself the object of some very public, very plausible rumors that will make it difficult, if not impossible, for you to find another professor who will be willing to take you on. Your career will be finished."

Bile rose in my throat and I swallowed hard to contain it. "I'm not a one-trick pony. Dr. Daniels can vouch for me. And Jeff! We've been teaching classes together for a year and a half. They'll back me up."

Janine shook her head. Her eyes never left mine as she asked, "Have you heard from Jeff? Any of your students?"

"No," I admitted, shriveling under her steely gaze. "But I can do something else. I'll find another field." My chin jutted out defiantly.

"You don't comprehend the enormity of his reach!" Janine insisted, eyes pleading. "He's a multi-billionaire; his resources are vast and so is his fury. He will completely and fully discredit you—almost certainly by engineering a smear campaign that will be far-reaching, public, and will follow you for the rest of your life. He'll start obscene rumors about your father's inappropriate involvement with preteen boys. Your mother will be accused of embezzling funds. Your parents will lose their farm, and your sister will lose her job, too. And he will go after anyone you've ever cared about, personally and professionally. Starting with

Christopher Daniels."

Despite my best efforts, my righteous indignation dissolved into pure, white-hot frustration. I stared at Dr. Daniels, in hopes that he would refute what she said, but his lined, tired eyes were downcast.

"No," I said, turning to Janine. "I don't believe you. You work for him. You have every reason to lie to me, to twist my emotions and my loyalty to get me to go back and work with that whack job Andrew."

Janine heaved another long sigh. She motioned to the laptop sitting on Dr. Daniels's desk.

"Can I borrow that?"

He nodded, disconnected it from its power supply, and handed it to her. Janine opened a terminal and began typing, tapping the keys with determination, her lips squeezed into a grim line. When she finished, she pivoted the computer on her lap, and I was able to see clear, sharp color security footage, with a time stamp burned on the upper right corner indicating that the footage was taken last month.

Six men and a woman sat uncomfortably around a conference table. Each one noticeably stiffened when Andric Breckinridge stormed into the room. Although there was no audio to accompany the video, the man's rage was evident. He seemed to focus all his ire on the woman, who seemed to collapse inward on herself as he continued to fume. The rant went on for five minutes before the woman collapsed in tears and darted from the room.

"Who is she?" I asked, unable to tear my eyes from the video.

"She was a Rhodes scholar. Top in her class at Harvard. She'd been working for Albaion for five years. Now she's unemployable."

My throat tightened until I couldn't breathe, and Janine snapped the laptop shut.

"Why?" I croaked, my throat tightening.

"The outcome of the research wasn't what he expected," Janine replied curtly.

I stared at her dumbly. The outcome wasn't what he expected?

"Why do you stay?" I whispered, turning to the exhausted woman. My mind reeled. All the secrecy, all the lies, made me question every word of her story, but my heart believed her.

"I made a promise to Andrew's mother."

"But I'm afraid of Andrew," I whispered, my rage now completely replaced by cold dread.

"I'm not excusing his actions," Janine replied. "Despite his behavior, I can assure you that he is not, in fact, psychopathic, nor is he prone to unnecessary violence. He is, however, under extraordinary pressure. And he's grieving."

"You've done a psych evaluation on him too?" I retorted.

"We've all been evaluated," Janine murmured. "For suitability. For stamina. For the likelihood that under incredible strain, we won't crack. It's like joining the armed forces—except your tour of duty only ends when Breckinridge is finished with you."

"But why? Why me? I mean, I get that not everyone can shift out of a slice, but surely there are other people who could learn? You know, Buddhist monks or something. I mean, I'm into mindfulness and I'm a good student, and I know my way around a compiler, but I'm hardly genius material. Why does he want me so badly?"

"Kate, don't you know?" Janine spoke with surprise. "Not everyone can slice shift. In fact, almost no one can. In our whole facility, it's just you and Andrew. You should have seen how ecstatic Andrew and Amir were when they determined that Lily could slice. He'd never admit it, but having a partner along for the ride turned every investigation into an adventure." Her dark eyes saddened. "And now Lily is gone."

"What makes me so unique?" I replied, confused.

"We don't know," Janine replied. "You can bet Breckinridge

wants more than anything to determine how to find more like you. But without criteria to guess who might be a candidate, there's no way to tell except to expose them to the Bug and let the chips fall as they may."

Janine stared at me hard. "And if you try to slice but can't there are side effects. Some of us suffered from uncontrollable eye tics and erratic large-muscle spasms for a few weeks after the test. We were the lucky ones. A few went temporarily blind; several now have an ongoing seizure disorder similar to epilepsy. One person lost the use of his legs for four months. The unluckiest of us experienced cerebral hemorrhage serious enough to require emergency surgery. Three researchers who tried have never recovered." Janine stared at me hard. "So you can see why, having found you, Breckinridge is extremely loathe to let you slip through his grasp."

"So I was in danger right from the start," I shuddered, thankful that my first rendezvous with Andrew's sinister creation had not turned my brain into gray-matter soup. I couldn't know for sure whether what they said was true. Maybe Breckinridge was just your garden variety power-hungry megalomaniac CEO. Then I remembered the feeling of complete and utter inferiority I felt the moment he entered the room, and I believed them. I believed that Andric Breckinridge would destroy me, my family, and anyone I had ever counted on.

I bit my trembling lower lip as I stared first at Dr. Daniels, then at Janine. I drew the only conclusion that was possible.

"I'll go," I said with much more conviction than I felt. "I'll go back to Albaion."

Janine nodded gravely, sinking back in her chair with relief. "Go home. It's not much, but take the evening to recover. We'll pick you up first thing tomorrow morning."

CHAPTER 16

ANDREW

September 26

Exhausted, Andrew retreated to his office. The windowless room was sparse, with soothing gray walls and a Scandinavian desk of maple in a simple natural finish—all hard lines and angles. It was free from clutter and distraction, and nearly silent except for the faint hiss of the ventilation.

No diplomas or photographs or awards were displayed. Not even a whiteboard marred the unbroken uniformity of the walls, which were bare except for a scale reproduction of a triptych of paintings by the Spanish modernist Joan Miró fittingly entitled *Blue I*, *Blue II*, and *Blue III*. Invariably when Andrew's mind ran unchecked, he would pace in his office and gaze at the large canvases' azure fields punctuated by a few simple black dots or an effortless slash of red paint. The paintings usually calmed him; the work of Miró was said to convey the artist's dreams and subconscious. But the symbolism of the artwork now struck too close to home—Kate's dreams, her subconscious—these were the key to the puzzle. And he had thrown out the key in a burst of anger.

In frustration, he stopped pacing and dropped heavily into his padded leather office chair. He should have been studying the data from Kate's remarkable slice extraction, but he couldn't concentrate. Instead he stared blankly at his laptop screen, at the terminal window with its blinking cursor, until his eyes glazed over. The minutes passed, and yet he sat, unmoving, unable to will his intellect to overcome his growing regret.

Andrew's brooding was interrupted abruptly when his heavy maple door swung violently open, smashing into the wall behind it. Andric Breckinridge stormed into the small room and slammed a tablet onto the desk with such force that the sturdy table shuddered. It was a small miracle the device remained undamaged.

"Where have you been?" he snapped. "I've been looking all over this damn building for you. Have you seen this?"

He glared menacingly, pointing to the browser window open to front page of the *New York Times*. The headlines for the day indicated that the extreme seven-year drought in the Midwest could cause Lincoln, Nebraska to begin water rationing in as little as three weeks.

"Where have I been?" Andrew asked incredulously. "I've been at Lily's funeral." He bowed his head in sudden exhaustion. "You should have been there, too. After all she sacrificed..."

Breckinridge waved his hand dismissively. "I have no time for sentimentality. The administration has convinced Congress to ratify the new Reykjavik Climate Change Accord. *In its entirety!* And they somehow got the Chinese to agree, all of the European Union, even South America is on board. India is expected to fall in line right behind them. Pollution has become so unbearable and the pace of global warming is now so extreme that no one, not even the flat-earth lunatic fringe, wants us to delay the drastic curbing of carbon emissions. The agreement calls for a complete phase out of all petroleum production and a total shift to renewables within a year. One year!"

Andrew leaned back in his chair, taking the measure of the man before him. "That sounds like an imminently responsible plan to me, given the state of affairs."

Breckinridge glowered. "Do you or do you not recall that your grandfather tied up a massive amount of our family's wealth in oil and gas?"

Andrew's face darkened. "I know you can't remember this," he hissed, "but I can. This ecological train wreck was a major concern *before* Lily and I raided that slice. But now?" He paused, returning the older man's steely gaze. "Now it's a crisis! You know what wasn't a problem two weeks ago? US cities in imminent danger of running out of water. Coastal Louisiana experiencing a 'hundred-year flood' for the third time in as many years. Clinically dangerous levels of toxic air pollution in this very valley. We brought back this problem, confounded tenfold!"

Breckinridge scowled. "A problem that Albaion Corporation would be able to address, with spectacular profit margins, if only your project would make any forward progress whatsoever. The solution is in all probability ready and waiting in that slice we extracted you from."

"You know it doesn't work that way." Andrew sighed, speaking slowly as if explaining to a petulant child. "We can't go back there. There's no signpost. No map! There are literally an infinite number of other possible permutations for this shitty existence we call reality. Without someone anchoring the Bug on the other side, there's an infinitesimal chance we could *ever* find that slice again, even if they did have a snowball's chance of forming a viable solution."

Breckinridge frowned, brow furrowed. In a sudden reversal as menacing as his fury, he adopted a calm, measured tone. "Surely you have considered this dilemma?" Breckinridge cajoled. "You must have some idea how to uncover an alternate slice that has fielded a solution?"

Andrew ignored the change of tactic. "Even if there are hundreds of slices where we might find a solution, long-range slice travel killed Lily. Likely *would* have killed me if I'd stayed in there much longer. Without a partner, and without a reliable way out, how can I even attempt it? The next funeral will be mine."

"I need progress, and I need it now," Breckinridge barked.

"You need to give us more time."

"Your time has run out," Breckinridge snarled. "Need I remind you I've been funding your little venture for years?"

"Forever in service of the almighty dollar, aren't we?" Andrew's snide words rung out like a challenge.

"Need I remind you," the elder growled, his tone suddenly lower and somehow even more menacing. "The almighty dollar generated by this corporation maintains thirty thousand employees in thirteen countries. It paid for your damn doctorates. And it funds your research. Need I remind you about your abysmal attempt at venture capital funding for your improbable technology schemes? Your plan was deemed a farce by every investor you spoke with. Except for me. And I am in no mood to argue with you."

Andrew's glare was steely. "Need I remind *you*, that improbable tech is the reason we're having this conversation right now? It's nascent at best. It's a fool's errand to attempt another far-slice until we have a reliable way back, and we still don't know for sure if Kathryn is even capable of extracting herself," Andrew lied. "And even if she can do it, she's no operative. We have no idea how she will hold up in the field. Lily was an ex-marine; she lived and breathed black ops, and was completely on board with your questionable methods. Lily was a fully committed soldier. There's no guarantee that Kathryn can perform at that level, even if you are able to convince her to take part in your plan."

"She *will* take part," Breckinridge predicted, "because I will use whatever leverage is required to secure her cooperation. Ms. Rathman's EEG patterns were the key to unlocking far-slice travel, and I am convinced that scrutinizing her will yield further advances. You had better prepare her quickly because further delays *will not be tolerated*."

The director emphasized each word with a slap to the table. Then he snatched his tablet and turned on his heels, stomping from the room and slamming the door behind him.

Andrew slumped in his office chair with an air of defeat. The pieces fell together flawlessly; of course Kathryn's dreams made the far-slice possible. He cursed under his breath; he should have guessed. And yet the thought that Andric considered Kathryn little more than a lab rat left a sour taste in his mouth. He sat there, unmoving, eyes closed, forcing himself to breathe slowly and methodically minute after minute. *Is it pride?* he wondered. *Is it just that he hates to be denied anything? Or, is there something more? How did he become such a power-hungry tyrant? And why does he need this so badly?*

The company's stock was doing well—in fact, it was up nearly 20 percent year-over-year. He had seen the company's financials; he listened attentively at each quarterly finance call and actually read each dense, nearly incomprehensible prospectus that was released to investors. Several of the subsidiaries were regular media darlings, praised as innovative and forward-thinking. There should be no reason for this panic.

Andrew suddenly sat bolt upright in his seat. He pulled his laptop closer, and with a few deft keystrokes, he connected to the finance department's server using a back door he'd installed into the operating system a year earlier. Unraveling the data that formed the financial structure of Breckinridge's vast private holdings was not going to be easy, but Andrew was determined and brilliant—and every bit as tenacious as his old man when it came to acquiring something he wanted.

CHAPTER 17

KATE

September 27

I trudge toward the entrance of the hospital, but something is terribly wrong. The streetlights are ominously dark, and so is the crimson sign over the door marked "EMERGENCY." The sliding entryway door sits wedged open by a wooden bench. As I walk past an abandoned reception desk and through a pair of swinging doors, a mounting feeling of dread consumes me. The power flickers constantly, alternating between bright fluorescent light and eerie green emergency backup illumination. The place reminds me of a scene from a horror film.

The sound of intermittent moans and wails reaches my ears from somewhere inside the building. As I draw deeper, I become aware of increasing disorder. The detritus of modern medicine is thrown haphazardly everywhere I look.

A bulky orange plastic bag emblazoned with the biohazard symbol lies open on the floor, spilling plastic gloves and towels darkened with what I can only guess is some sort of bodily fluid. As I peer down the hall, I see more bags strewn about. It's then that I notice the smell—metallic and putrid, like meat gone bad. I know instinctively it's blood.

I pass an abandoned gurney and wonder where all the doctors and nurses have gone. I pause to peer through the glass pane on one of the doors lining the corridor. It is lined with spiderweb cracks. I expect a modern hospital suite with one or two beds, but instead the room is cavernous, lined on each side with rudimentary pallets just a foot apart. Each bed contains a patient, but instead of hospital gowns, they wear their street clothes. The patients are staring, glassy-eyed and hopeless, at the ceiling.

I shudder and continue to move down the hall. A figure bursts forth from a door on the left, clothed from head to toe in a puffy white suit and wearing thick blue gloves. His face is completely obscured by a heavy-duty particle mask and safety goggles. As the suited apparition brushes past me, I feel the slipstream of fetid air that follows in his wake.

The next chamber I approach is nothing more than a series of cubicles constructed of draped plastic. A hand-printed sign on a small whiteboard propped near the entrance warns, "HEMMHORAGIC FEVER—HIGH RISK AREA" in thick red letters. An arrow points left next to the word "Confirmed" and another points right for "Suspected."

I leap out of the way as another white-suited orderly rushes past wheeling a creaking gurney. The unmoving shape beneath its white sheet makes my hands go clammy. Consumed with morbid fascination, I trail behind the gurney into the room as if in a trance, swinging left with it as it travels toward "Confirmed."

We turn a corner, pushing through more curtains of opaque plastic, and I suddenly find myself surrounded by a sea of makeshift hospital beds. As I focus on the closest patient, my stomach clenches into tense knots. An African-American man with close-shaved gray hair is lying on one of the makeshift pallets. Both of his arms are teeming with oozing black pustules. As his eyes turn to me, I shrink back in revulsion—his irises float in a sea of red. Blood, so much blood. Its scent hangs in the air. There are trails of it on the bedding. It seeps from the patients. Their blood, my blood—I'm suddenly acutely conscious of the blood coursing through my own veins and through my furiously palpating heart. The patient's bloodred eyes dilate as he gazes past my left shoulder; then abruptly they are focused, his eyes locked on mine.

"I am not here," I murmur to myself, each inhalation coming in

short, ragged gasps. "It's a dream, I'm not here, I will not be here..."

"Help me—" the patient moans.

I squint over my shoulder to see whom the man is addressing. There is no one else. Just me.

"Help me!" the man implores, extending his disease-riddled arm toward me.

I suddenly find I can't catch my breath. How can he see me?

Then his ruined hand brushes my arm. "Help..." he groans.

At the touch of his hand, I scream.

"Kate!" Michelle yelled, shaking me violently by the shoulders. I shoved away the man's oozing arm before I realized that it was Michelle that I'd roughly thrust away.

"Stop screaming! Wake up!" she shouted.

I sat up in a panic. The room was dark, but I could already see bright rhythmic flashes forming in front of my eyes. Cue the migraine.

"I was dreaming..." I panted. The gnarled knob of tension in my stomach rested like a lead weight in my gut. All those people, dying...

"No kidding," my sister interrupted. "You've been screaming for the last five minutes! What was it this time?"

"I think it was Ebola," I mumbled, struggling to catch my breath and leaning back into my pillow. "Or Marburg. Some sort of hemorrhagic fever. I think it was here, in the States, but the hospital looked so decrepit. All those sick people—there was one man—he knew he was dying, Shell." I clutched my blanket tightly around my neck, sweat streaming from my temples.

"Wow," Michelle said quietly. She gently placed her hand on my forehead. It reminded me of my childhood; all the times my mom had done exactly the same thing. "That sounds horrible."

"Something really terrifying happened," I confessed, my voice still quaking. "The sick man in the dream could *see* me. No one has ever seen me in a nightmare before. There's never been any interaction at all—until now."

"What do you think it means?"

"I don't know. But that poor man? He *touched* me." An icy chill scuttled down my spine.

"That's not good, right?"

"I doubt it," I replied, closing my eyes. The flashes had receded, but I could feel pulsing on the right side of my head, behind my eye. Before long it would morph into stabbing, debilitating pain. I blinked furiously and began to regulate my breath. "Something has changed, and it's not for the better. The nightmares are more frequent. People there can see and interact with me. And worst of all, Andrew and Janine have convinced me that I'm not even dreaming. I think these horrible places are actually *real*." Michelle gasped. In the dim light of the room, I couldn't see my sister, but I felt her concern.

I sat up and hugged her. "Thanks for trying to bail me out of there," I said with more bravery than I felt. "Go back to sleep. I'm going to meditate for a while, and we'll talk more in a few hours."

"I still don't think you should go back!" Michelle insisted as I scraped the last delicious remnants of her homemade muesli from the bottom of my cereal bowl.

"Shell, you are my rock. Every moment I'm away, I miss you. And I am so, so thankful that you have postponed your entire life to babysit me as I try to figure out what the hell is wrong with my stupid brain."

"Oh, Kate..." she replied, but I held my hand up to silence her protest.

"Something has changed. The frequency of my dreams is increasing, and now I'm present in these terrible situations in a way that was never imaginable before. Dr. Daniels is right. I need to go back. This is the best opportunity I have to understand these nightmares—and stop them."

Anxiety-tinged guilt prompted me to omit the important fact that if I didn't return, she and my parents would be ruined. It wasn't clear what action they could take to protect themselves, and I didn't want her to worry any more than she already did.

"Tell Mom and Dad I'm doing fine," I mumbled lamely. "Tell them I love them, and we'll talk soon." My resolve was wobbly enough. I was certain I could not maintain my facade of confidence in the face of my parents' questions and concern.

I was considering how long it would take me to walk back to the facility hidden in the hills when a knock sounded at the door. "I'll get it," I said, hoping for Janine but dreading the sight of Andrew.

"'Sup?" Amir greeted me, ripping a huge bite from a fast-food breakfast burrito.

"Uh, you have some egg on your cheek."

Amir swiped his cheek with the back of his hand and pushed his black curls back from his forehead. He was wearing a black T-shirt emblazoned with the words "/*NO COMMENT*/."

Michelle drew up behind me, peering over my shoulder. She gave Amir a stern frown. "I need you to promise me you'll watch out for my sister."

Amir traced an invisible x over his heart and raised his right hand. "I'll do my best."

She nodded, then wrapped me in a fierce hug. "You know what I'm going to say," she whispered.

"I'll be careful," I promised. With a final glance in her direction, I closed the door behind me and followed Amir to the familiar dust-covered pickup.

It was still early enough in the morning that rush hour traffic was not yet in full swing. I sat silently in the passenger seat as Amir barreled down Page Mill Road toward the hills, burrito in one hand, steering wheel in the other, veering and swerving from one lane to another to pass slower-moving motorists. I slumped in the passenger seat with my arms crossed, casting withering glances at my driver and honing my passive aggression. When he finally finished wolfing down his breakfast, he crumpled up the wrapper and dropped it on the floor beside him.

Amir glanced over at me as he accelerated, swerving once again into the left lane. "Looks like you're still pissed."

"I don't ever want to see that maniac Andrew again."

"Yeah, he's definitely an asshat. But he's a *brilliant* asshat. I know he stabbed you and all, but he knew that you wouldn't be injured back here in the real world. And if there's anyone who can help you figure out what's happening in that funky melon of yours, it's the A-man."

I thought back to the suffering Ebola patient. I thought back to the touch of his cold, diseased hand. I thought about Michelle, who had given up so much of her life to take care of me. I thought about my parents and their tenuous hold on their barely middle-class existence and of the big white farmhouse with the ancient oak tree—the place I felt safest in the world. I knew I wouldn't be safe there now; not from Breckinridge and not even from myself. I knew that going back to the lab was the right decision, but I hated it with every fiber of my being.

"Why do you even work there?" I felt petulant, and the question came out a bit whiny. "The long hours, the isolation, the demanding jerk of a boss, and the psychopathic coworkers don't seem all that appealing."

The pickup sped past the last of the commuters and Amir took the sharp turn onto the unmarked dirt road, and we were headed at last into the hills.

Amir took a sharp right onto a dirt road and fishtailed as he abruptly slowed the truck to a crawl.

As we bumped over the potholes, Amir expertly guided the wheel but gave me a long, hard look. He broke into a wry grin and shrugged. "Where else can I do work that literally changes the world?"

I thought back to the déjà vu, the tiny differences that impacted our world when a slice collapsed. "It doesn't seem like much of a change to me."

Amir cast a sidelong glance my way. "You'd be surprised."

My stomach dropped as Amir deftly wedged the pickup between six other identical vehicles in the garage. I was sure it wasn't Amir's breakneck driving that was the cause. I was silent as he badged us into the hallway.

Amir whirled around, walking backward. "Hey, you wanna see something?" His expression was conspiratorial.

"Uh, sure," I reluctantly agreed. The thought of confronting Andrew filled me with dread, and I was eager to do anything that would help me avoid the lab.

"Follow me," Amir instructed, leading the way through a series of unfamiliar corridors. Another series of turns down similarly indistinct and dimly lit hallways led to a wide, heavy, windowless door. Amir badged in and motioned for me to follow.

We walked into an expansive room, about twenty-five feet by fifteen feet. The ceiling was high, at least ten feet tall. Several of the sections of the wall were missing on one side, and on the opposite side, I could see the glass panels of a control room. A team of at least ten contractors was busy at work, installing huge sheets of galvanized steel.

"Welcome to your shiny new fMRI suite," Amir revealed, throwing his arms wide.

I furrowed my brow. "Already? It usually takes months of planning to get an fMRI installed."

"The contractors are making record time installing the RF shielding, which is convenient because your machine will arrive in three days. Breckinridge may be a slave driver, but he's an even bigger pain in the ass to his vendors than he is to his employees."

I glanced around the room again, feeling both giddy anticipation and lingering dread. We'd have the best tool there is for brain imaging, short of probes wired directly into my skull. I might finally be able to get some answers. The foreman, perched on top of a tall ladder, lowered his power drill, nodded toward Amir, and tapped his watch impatiently.

"We should let these guys finish," Amir suggested, motioning to the door. "You have a freakin' gnarly project to tackle, too. Time's a-wasting!"

I reluctantly followed Amir to the Bug lab but was relieved when I discovered that Andrew was nowhere to be seen.

"Time to suit up," Amir prompted, heading toward the sensor rack and dropping a single electrode cap into a bucket of saline solution to soak.

"Where is he?" I asked nervously.

Amir shrugged. "Andrew? I'm sure he's around here somewhere. But that hardly matters. What we need from you are sustained, accurate, intentional exits. So let's get you back on that horse," he suggested cheerfully, unlocking the cabinet where the Bug was stored and extracting it from its drawer.

"I'm going by myself?" I asked hopefully. The longer I could avoid my boss, the better.

"Well, I'm not going," Amir replied with a sidelong glance toward the Bug. "The one time I let that thing touch me, the entire left side of my body was paralyzed for a week. You're not freaked out, are you?"

I vigorously shook my head, but then a series of troubling thoughts tumbled through my mind. Should I be freaked out? What if I landed someplace horrible? What if I found myself in some grisly hellscape, like one of my nightmares? Without knowing whether I could escape?

Amir took one look at me and grinned. "You're freaked. No

worries, Kate. I'm not going to send you to the Twilight Zone. You'll hit another version of this room, guaranteed. Nothing to worry about."

With a sigh, I found the bottle of anti-nausea meds and popped one. I glanced at the back of my left hand, where the welt from previous Bug experiences was just beginning to heal. I suspected that my time at Albaion would leave me scarred for life, both literally and figuratively.

I yanked the elastic from my hair and shook out the messy bun. Amir helped me position the electrodes of the EEG cap, and I snapped it firmly under my chin.

"I'm going to configure this baby to put you slightly farther out. Not much farther; it should give you about an hour to work with. You'll still collapse naturally if your bail doesn't fly. You think that'll be enough time?"

"Honestly, I have no idea."

Amir positioned the bug and I closed my eyes. The painful stab and lurching in my gut was actually starting to feel familiar, which in itself was disturbing. I opened my eyes to a lab that was painted robin's-egg blue. Amir was tapping away at his keyboard.

"Uh, hey, Amir...."

"Oh, hi, Kate," he responded, without raising his eyes from his screen. Apparently it wasn't unusual for people to randomly appear in his workspace in this slice, either. "Did you just badge in or did you come through the back door?"

I looked around, searching for another entrance. "Uh, the back door?"

"So literal. I know you. You know the Bug. We're all good here." He chuckled. He swiveled around in his chair, and his impish grin was familiar and comforting, though his T-shirt was a new one: "Eat. Sleep. Code."

"How many ironic programming shirts do you have, anyway?"

Amir snorted. "Dude, there *are* an infinite number of

universes."

I spent the next hour meditating in an attempt to generate an intentional exit, but the slice collapsed without any success.

"Are you ready to go again?" Amir asked.

I could tell he was trying hard to contain his disappointment. I took a pained breath and closed my eyes. I knew that I was the reason that the project was on hold. My whole body was tense; I reminded myself to try to relax.

"Any chance you would make me a coffee? I could use a break."

"Sure." He stretched and left the lab, his flip-flops echoing against the concrete floor of the hall.

I unlatched the chin strap on the EEG cap and untangled the probes from my hair. I was trying to rub out the tight knots in my shoulders when I experienced the truly bizarre sensation of hearing my own voice ask, "Kate?" I looked up and came face-to-face with myself. Same long, auburn hair; same eyes. Same sneakers. My eyes as big as saucers, I waited for the migraine to kick in, and to find myself snapped back. Then I remembered I already *was* back.

"Uh, hi," she said warily. She kept her distance. "I figured this would happen eventually, but this is weird. I mean, *really* weird."

"Yeah, it's definitely loony bin material," I agreed, purposefully looking away. It was extremely unnerving to look at her; as cringe-worthy as watching videos of myself, but ten times worse. "Are you all right? The first time this happened to me, the headache was pretty extreme." I glanced nervously around the room, wondering what would happen if Amir returned to two of me.

"I'm fine, but I'm just going to sit…"

She lowered herself carefully into Andrew's usual leather chair.

"Is there some protocol for talking to yourself? Are we going to cause the collapse of the space-time continuum or anything?" I asked, eying the doorway again. Now I was almost hoping for an interruption. Anything to make this less weird.

She laughed nervously, averting her eyes. Clearly this was as disconcerting for her as it was for me. "I don't think so. The guys tell me it has happened to Andrew a few times, with no ill effects."

"That's a relief." I snuck a look at her. Why was it so unbelievably strange to have a conversation with myself? Even the sound of my own voice seemed foreign.

She caught my eye and looked away, too. "Andrew says this freaks us out because human features are not exactly symmetrical, and we're finely attuned to our mirror image. The change in perspective is slight, but our brains have an extremely hard time dealing with the difference, however small."

My breath caught in my throat. Could she read my mind, too? She was right, though. She was exactly like me, but...not.

"So...I guess you know about the Bug?"

"Obviously," she replied, grimacing.

"You don't happen to know how to intentionally exit one of these little trips, do you?" Would I find I was envious of myself if she had already managed to solve the problem?

"Damn, I was going to ask you the same thing. I've tried everything I can think of, but nothing works. Have you ever actually managed it?"

"Once. Completely by accident," I said.

"Really? How did you do it?"

I scowled and clenched my fist; but the phantom twinge of pain I felt was nothing more than a memory of yesterday's assault. "Well, Andrew stabbed me. With a pair of scissors."

She gasped and covered her mouth. "Are you serious? He *did* that?"

I nodded. "Yeah. Thankfully the injury didn't carry back over to my native slice, but basically I never want to see that asshole again."

She looked troubled. "I can't believe he actually hurt you."

"Well, he did. Damned thing, though, is that it worked. I keep trying to meditate my way out of this, but nothing works. I'm so frustrated."

"Do you think it's the trauma that got you out? That's how it works with the dreams, right?"

"You make a good point," I agreed, still finding it disorienting to look at her as we spoke.

"Do you think you should..."

"Oh, come on!" I protested. "Please don't ask me to stab you. That can't be the right answer. I can't do this if I have to intentionally injure myself every time I need to get back to reality."

"Maybe it doesn't have to be assault," she suggested, "at least not per se. Did you know there's a workout room in this place? Maybe you just really need some other kind of pain?"

"What did you have in mind?"

"Well, there is a prototype for a virtual reality rig there that you really should try. The graphics are actually pretty realistic, and I'm guessing you also share my fear of heights?"

I tilted my head thoughtfully, about to ask another question, when she disappeared. I shook my head and rubbed my eyes; it was incredibly unsettling to blink and find that a person you'd just been speaking to had vanished.

Amir badged in carrying a steaming cappuccino.

"Kate, you look pasty. Everything okay?"

I reached for the coffee and inhaled its comforting, bitter aroma. "Yeah," I said, closing my eyes and sipping the strong brew. "I'm fine. I'll finish this and then I can go again."

When I opened my eyes for my second reality-bending experience of the day, I awoke to an empty room. This time I was ready. I ditched the lab, headed down the hall, and rounded the corner. I found it just beyond to the dormitory wing. The gym was minimalist but well appointed, just like the rest of the facility. Several treadmills, elliptical machines, and spin bikes lined one wall but sat completely unused, which was not surprising considering this enterprise was staffed by workaholics. Free weights sat in one corner, and the opposite corner housed a man-size punching bag suspended over a padded floor. In the far corner sat a pretty basic-looking exercise bike next to an imposing-looking headset wired to a state-of-the-art computer tower. With a shrug, I mounted the bike, pulled on the headset, and prepared to feel the burn.

It wasn't difficult to get the simulation started, and the faster I pedaled the bike, the more rapidly I flew across the virtual countryside. I was panting and soaked in sweat, but I finally finished my level and was presented with some options for round two. Of all the choices, the simulation that looked the most intimidating involved riding the bike as if it were a zip line course. I gulped, selected the route, and pedaled with all my might.

I spent a terrifying and vertigo-inducing forty-five minutes fearing I would plunge to my death at any moment. Then, one minute I was pedaling for my life, and the next I was sitting in the black leather chair, panting, still strapped into the uncomfortable EEG cap.

"You okay?" Amir called as he tapped a few final keystrokes and sauntered over.

I noticed that I wasn't at all sweaty, and that the panting I'd been doing seemed much more like a mental appendage than a physical need. And while I was quite tired, I was not, in fact, winded at all.

"How long was I gone?"

"An hour and seven minutes," Amir confirmed.

My shoulders hunched over as exhaled. I hadn't been frightened out of the slice at all—I had simply timed out.

"Kate, why are you breathing so hard?" Amir asked, looking concerned.

"I tried to trigger my fear of heights using the VR in the gym."

"VR workout rig." He nodded thoughtfully. "That is a rad idea."

"Too bad it didn't work. Can you help me out of these electrodes? I think I need a giant glass of water. Or three..."

The slice shifts were really starting to take it out of me, and a break was long overdue. An hour later, fortified by massive hydration and a meal of incredibly tasty butter chicken over rice, I headed back to the lab for another round of alternate reality torture courtesy of the Bug.

"Third time's the charm," I grumbled to myself, grimacing through the Bug's agonizing stab and the accompanying lurch of nausea. I opened my eyes to the familiar white lab. Amir was still perched in his chair, coding away. I cleared my throat and he turned toward me. This reality's black shirt read "Declare Variables—Not War."

"Oh, hi, it's you," he said, all business. "Do you need anything?"

"No," I sighed. "Well, maybe I do need a little change of scenery. Do you think that since I don't really belong here, it's okay if I break out of jail?"

Amir grinned. "That's thinking outside the box. Can't let you take the truck. Don't want to have to go find it when you poof outta here. But if you just want a hike, then why not?"

It was a short walk from the lab to the heavy, windowless double doors of the entryway, and I encountered no one along the way.

The unexpected wave of dry heat that struck me as I stepped across the threshold gave me pause; the temperature differential from the air-conditioned lab felt like thirty degrees, but the evening light was golden, even through the thick, polluted haze. As usual for late in the day, a light wind had picked up out of the northwest, which helped alleviate the unnatural heat.

The gusts whipped my hair into my face; I cursed the fact that my hair elastic was on a table in an alternate reality. Impatiently gathering the tangled strands with my hand, I headed out toward a rise, walking briskly until I could no longer see the building below. I stomped down a small circle of knee-high vegetation and sat down in a half-lotus position, facing the setting sun in the west. I was far from the trails, and the only sound was the whisper of the wind in the dry grass and the cheerful chirping of grasshoppers, making it easier to push the Albaion Corporation and all it stood for far from my mind.

My practice was interrupted by a rustling in the grass. Startled, I stumbled to my feet. I anticipated a deer or possibly a dog off-leash, but instead it was Andrew. My shoulders immediately tensed and I dropped gracelessly into a crouch.

"Do not come near me!" I shouted, backing into the shelter of the wind-whipped grass. I scanned the field, but with a sinking feeling of dismay, I confirmed that I was otherwise alone. I considered a mad dash back to the building but quickly abandoned the idea—he was directly in my path.

My eyes narrowed in an accusatory glare. "Which Andrew are you?"

"I'm from your slice." Of course he was the psychopathic, intern-assaulting lunatic from my slice. Just my luck.

He took another tentative step closer. "Kathryn, I'm really sorry," he shouted into the wind. A strong rogue gust whipped my hair into my eyes and I retreated another step.

"That is *not* going to cut it!" I yelled. "And how did you know I was even out here?"

"Amir told me," he replied, still moving in my direction, albeit slowly.

I silently cursed myself—of course Amir would squeal. It was naive to think I could sneak out unnoticed.

"Listen," I yelled, "I'm only going to be here for another thirty minutes before this slice collapses; why don't you just go away and let me work?"

He had reached the edge of my clearing and stopped. I retreated another step.

"Look, I really am sorry," he repeated, sweeping my face with those intense blue eyes. "I betrayed your trust. That was wrong, and really damaging."

"Damn straight!"

I bent my knees and shifted my weight farther back onto my heels, ready to spring past him if he came at me with any sharp objects.

"You were never in any danger."

I eyed him warily as he held up two empty hands.

"Not at any time. A day before your you arrived, an alternate Kathryn sliced into the lab. It was obvious you'd be able to withstand the Bug without side effects. And I was totally wrong to attack you. That was never the plan; that man knows exactly how to push my buttons. But that's no excuse," he corrected quickly, never breaking contact with my eyes. "I also knew that injuries sustained in a slice don't propagate back when the slice collapses. The trauma was never supposed to be permanent."

"Well, what about the emotional trauma?"

He grimaced. "That's fair. If I could take it back, I would, in a heartbeat. But here we are. I know you've been trying to get out of a slice all afternoon, and I know that nothing has worked."

I looked at him, startled. "I came in alone; how'd you get here?"

"The Bugs can be synced, remember? Once one is activated, the second one can be used to bring in another traveler."

I groaned. "So you found me. Now what?"

"It was important to find you, to apologize." He raised his eyebrows and tried a crooked grin. "But hey, as long as I'm here, maybe I could zap you with a taser or something."

I felt a sudden flash of fury. "If that is your idea of a joke, no one's laughing."

"I don't have a taser," he admitted, reaching his outstretched hands farther as he slowly advanced. "Come back to the lab."

As quickly as it had appeared, my fury transformed into the bitter flavor of defeat. I threw my hands up in the air.

"No! Besides, I don't think this is going to work. You all thought I could do some magic here, but I can't. Nothing works. I don't think I'm the right person for this job."

"You couldn't be more wrong. Don't you see?" He took a step closer. His gaze was so intense and earnest that I had to bite my lip to keep from looking away. As if this unnerving moment of intimacy had flipped some switch inside me, I could feel my resolve draining away. He tentatively reached his hand toward me, as if I were a timid animal that might bolt at any moment. A single step more, and now he was near enough to smooth my wildly flying hair. He delicately gathered the tangled mass and gave it a gentle twist. I tensed as his hand fell toward his pocket, but he merely produced an elastic hair band, which he expertly snapped around my newly subdued tresses. His hands fell to my shoulders, resting lightly. My muscles tensed even more, and my gaze shifted restlessly from his chin to the magnetic blue of his eyes, wary and searching for a clue to what he'd do next.

"Andric fessed up. *Your* EEG traces allowed us to crack the far-slice problem. Your ability and this experiment are profoundly entwined. You are the key to everything."

I stood transfixed in the deepening golden light, and time

seemed to slow to a halt as he gently cradled my face in his hands. His thumb caressed my cheek, and an unexpected wave of disorienting bliss washed over me. My heart pounded in my chest and my breath turned shallow; had I turned into some ridiculous giddy schoolgirl or was I simply hyperventilating? He was so close; and my focus narrowed to those striking eyes—the astonishing sapphire of the iris edge framing lighter cerulean ripples. It was easy to lose myself in these tiny galaxies that seemed to bore directly into my soul. The pure liquid hatred I had felt for him was unexpectedly erased. Was he drawing still nearer? The earth's axis seemed to tilt precariously, and I feared that gravity might fail me completely. I closed my eyes to fight the vertigo but instead breathed in the scent of him—linen and spice and lust. Without another moment of hesitation, I inhaled sharply and leaned my face forward.

The instant his lips met mine, a powerful jolt left me breathless. Points of light blazed behind my eyelids like the flash of a thousand cameras, and I suddenly couldn't feel any sensation in my body at all. Had I just suffered some kind of aneurism? Bewildered, I snapped open my eyes. The rush of the wind had been replaced by the sound of rapid typing. I was back in the lab, seated in my chair, and bound by the cumbersome EEG cap.

"Hey, hey, hey!" Amir called, jumping out of his seat across the room. "You did it again! That's our girl," he crowed, bounding across the room.

I glanced across the table and realized that Andrew was awake as well, staring at me intently. Before Amir could reach the rack of monitors, Andrew unclasped his EEG cap and dropped it deliberately into its bucket.

"Excuse me," he said, his voice completely devoid of any emotion. Without another word, he left the room. The door's click as it closed seemed to echo in the lab.

"What's *his* problem?" Amir asked, staring at the door. "Wait a minute." Amir's eyes widened with dawning realization. "You didn't just get yourself out. You *both* got out! Now we're talkin'! So...how'd you do it?"

I sighed, carefully unhooking my own EEG cap and peeling it from my skull. The pounding headache was back. I should have been elated to have finally achieved my goal, but instead I wrestled with crushing exhaustion and almost paralyzing confusion.

"Listen," I said, dropping my electrodes into the bucket of saline solution. "I'm dead on my feet, and my head is killing me. I need to rest. Let's break this down later, okay?"

"All right," he agreed, stepping aside and nodding. "You're the boss...."

If only, I thought.

CHAPTER 18

ANDREW

September 27

The gym was empty except for a lone figure throwing an aggressive series of carefully choreographed punches and kicks against a double-angled heavy bag suspended from the ceiling. As soon as the pattern of attack was complete, Andrew released a grunt of frustration and repeated the series of strikes anew.

He heard the click of the lock disengaging as the door to the gym swung open with terrible force, but it didn't break his concentration. He continued with the series of strikes, rivulets of sweat streaming down his cheeks. Andric Breckenridge strode across the room, livid with anger, to the mat where his son trained.

"We have lost control of this project," Breckinridge shouted, grabbing Andrew by the shoulder and spinning him around midpunch.

Andrew lowered his taped knuckles and panted, swiping away the sweat from his brow. As he struggled to catch his breath, his frustration focused into an intense beam of aversion.

Breckinridge clutched his son's shoulder and violently shook him. "Laurent Fournier at the École Polytechnique has held a press conference, announcing his research regarding a revolutionary study involving the brain physiology of Hindu monks."

Andrew knocked away the older man's grasp, but Andric just carried on. "To add insult to injury, that French bastard has insinuated monks' possible connection to the multiverse could be triggered by a physical device. Our patent lawyers have not yet finished drafting their first round of documents on your prototype. We have released *nothing* publicly. What I want to know from you," the man growled, moving even closer to his son's flushed face, "is how our technology has been developed by Fournier? In France?"

Andrew scowled. "Are you suggesting we have a leak? We don't leak. Our people never leave. You monitor all electronic communications in and out of this building. We don't work with others in the scientific community. We work for you. There is no leak."

Breckenridge's upper lip curled into a snarl. "Then explain why I have devoted massive resources to your research when the outcome of all this expenditure is that *someone else reaps the benefits*?" the man bellowed, his tone rising at every syllable.

Andrew broke away from the elder's overbearing presence and gave the heavy bag another pointed strike.

"Need I remind you that *you* named your empire A. L. B. Aion, literally slapping your initials in front of the Greek god of immortality? Hell, my own name is nothing more than an English bastardization of yours. At best, my work is merely the extension of *your* colossal ego. You know as well as I do that I cannot predict what aspects of alternative slices merge back down into our own. In that slice Lily and I infiltrated, Kathryn produced that study. It's no surprise it's been discovered here as well. You have always known that the risk of unanticipated cross-contamination is there. You deemed that risk acceptable before, but now that someone else has gotten the jump on you, maybe you can finally see how dangerous this whole scheme has become."

"What I have finally seen," Breckinridge replied, his eyes cold, "is that I have coddled you and it's made you soft. You are to take that young woman with you, get out there, and resolve the issues with this technology, or..."

"Or what?" Andrew challenged, meeting the elder's icy gaze.

"Just do it!" Breckinridge snapped, turned on his heels, and stormed from the room.

As soon as the door slammed, Andrew released a volley of powerful punches against the bag. One after another, the blows flew, and he didn't even notice when Janine Mori entered the room. As the door closed again, Andrew wheeled around with a look of fury in his eyes.

"Rough day?" Janine asked, raising an eyebrow.

Andrew unloaded another few halfhearted punches on the bag before dropping his fists, but said nothing.

"I suppose you've already heard about Laurent Fournier."

Andrew sat down on a weight bench, breathing heavily. "I heard. The boss made it quite clear that it's my fault."

"I figured. I passed Andric as he stormed out of here." She sat down on a mat on the floor. "I know how he pushes your buttons, but he was just here moments ago, and you look like you've been abusing that bag for at least an hour. What's going on?"

Andrew carefully studied his taped knuckles. "I don't know what you mean."

"I was looking for you in your lab. Amir said Kate's been successful. And not only did she pull herself out, she brought you with her. That's the breakthrough you've been looking for, isn't it? I thought you'd be ecstatic."

Andrew grunted and frowned but avoided her eyes. Janine stared at him thoughtfully as she began a stretch.

"It's Kate, isn't it?" Janine probed suggestively, giving him a sidelong glance as her nose met her knee. "You have feelings for her."

Andrew stared at her with a blank expression.

"Oh, please!" Janine scoffed. "I've known you for far too long for that to work on me. It's not surprising, you know. She's smart, and full of spunk. You and she share that special little gene that's so useful for bending reality. I can see why you like her."

Andrew sighed. "She was the source of the EEG trace that made far-slice travel possible. And while I was there... well, let's just say her research was compelling."

Janine smiled triumphantly. "I knew it! You seduced her to get into her plans, didn't you?"

"Not entirely..."

Janine threw him a stern look.

"Well, maybe a little," he admitted. "But that's not the whole story. Ever since this endeavor began, we keep crossing paths."

"Maybe it's fate."

"I don't believe in fate—I believe in quantifiable facts."

"Well, then," Janine said, smiling. "Maybe it's statistics. Either way, there's nothing wrong with being attracted to her."

Andrew slammed his taped fist against the bench. "Everything is wrong with it! She has no idea what I've done. What I'm capable of. After all, like father, like son."

"Your father is a formidable man, but I knew your mother. And you're more like her than you're willing to admit. But I will tell you one thing. If you care about Kate, you need to lay it all bare. Tell her everything. Tell her about Andric, and Lily, and the leaking slices."

He dropped his head into his hands. "How can I do that?"

Janine extended her fingertips past her toes and held the stretch.

"You may need to do it sooner than you think. I've been

mulling over your hypothesis that the far-slice trip you took with Lily has leaked into our reality and has adversely impacted our climate situation. While you were in here beating the crap out of that bag, I came across a troubling weather report."

Andrew looked up, instantly tensing. "What kind of troubling weather?"

"The Center for Global Weather Forecasts in Reading, England is tracking a weather disturbance over the Atlantic, about eleven hundred miles west of Africa. Currently it's still a disorganized collection of thunderstorms, but there's an eighty-seven percent chance that it will develop into an extreme weather event."

Andrew frowned thoughtfully. "They accurately predicted the devastating path of Hurricane Sandy in 2012."

"That's right. Don't you know someone at the National Hurricane Center?"

"I know a guy. We worked the Sandy hack-a-thon together while I was at MIT; at least until she knocked out power to most of the eastern seaboard. He's a weather geek; there's nothing he likes discussing more." Andrew retrieved his mobile from under a crumpled, sweaty towel. He quickly unlocked the device and with a few deft swipes placed it on speaker and waited while it rang.

A tinny voice rang out from the device. "Charles Brannon here."

"Charlie! It's Andy. Andy Breckinridge." Andrew attempted joviality, but the edge in his voice remained.

"Andy! How long's it been, man?"

"Too long," Andrew replied, pacing the mat. "I'm guessing you're suddenly busy over there; I hear there's some weather brewing?"

"That's an understatement. We're tracking something, something big. I'm talking a five-hundred-year event. Some kind of superstorm. She's just about big enough to get a name, and when she does, Ophelia is going to be colossal. The mass of thunderstorms is intensifying fast. The storm path models look suspiciously similar to that of Sandy. Similar factors seem to be at work. The surface temperature offshore is crazy-warm. Currently five degrees Celsius above normal, so the storm is apt to remain tropical for longer than usual. And rather than turning out to the Atlantic like most storms, an upper level low forecast for the eastern US is likely to turn the storm inward."

"Five degrees?" Andrew muttered to himself, rubbing his chin. How could that be right? The normal variance was maybe one degree Celsius, max. "Might the storm just peter out?"

"I don't think so," Charles replied. "Wind shear is lower than normal over the western Caribbean right now, and it's the shear which would normally tear apart the storm before it had time to intensify. It gives us high confidence that this system is going to grow into a monster."

"What intensity do the models predict the storm will reach?" Andrew asked cautiously.

"It's a little early to be certain, but as of now, it looks bad—like, catastrophically bad. If the models are correct, we anticipate that Ophelia may reach well beyond hurricane category five status as it passes over the Caribbean, likely to strike Jamaica, Cuba, or Haiti. With a system this intense, it's hard to tell how accurate the storm track will be. There has never been a storm that surpassed category five, which adds to the uncertainty. If Ophelia takes the path the model predicts, it will then swing back over the eastern Caribbean Sea, picking up even more moisture. Worst case, the storm could remain a Category Five until it veers back toward the east coast."

"Category Five, or worse," Andrew repeated, shaking his head. "Where do the models estimate second landfall?"

"Right now the runs are showing really troubling

consistency—approximately the same path as Sandy. Somewhere north of Atlantic City, most likely. The storm surge will be intense through Boston and New York. If the storm strikes when the tides are up, New York in particular will be devastated. Coastal New York can't handle much inundation. You know with the current sea level rise—which is nearly thirty-one inches—that the city is already extremely prone to flooding."

Andrew looked at Janine in alarm. That number seemed terribly wrong.

"Are emergency plans deployed yet?" Andrew asked.

"Not yet," Charles reported, his frustration obvious to Janine and Andrew. "My bosses are taking a wait-and-see approach so they don't start a panic, but I personally think the safest plan would be to issue mandatory evacuation immediately. When Sandy hit, New York felt a storm surge nearly fourteen feet high. This storm runs the risk of flooding most of lower Manhattan. All up and down the coast, cities will flood, people will lose power, buildings will be destroyed—and if the evacuation order doesn't happen in time, there's no telling how many lives will be lost."

Andrew drew in a quick breath. "And you're telling me that this superstorm Ophelia is going to be three times worse than Sandy?"

"That *is* what I'm telling you," Charles confirmed.

"How much time do we have?"

"The European model estimates three days until Hurricane Ophelia makes landfall in the Caribbean and seven or eight until it strikes the east coast. The GSF model is in near agreement."

Andrew drew in a sharp breath. "Thanks, man. Stay safe?"

"You bet," Charles replied.

Andrew ended the call.

Andrew cradled the device in his hands for a moment, then turned to a silent and thoughtful Janine.

"Charlie said that the non-storm sea level rise in New York is thirty-one inches? And that the east coast's ocean surface temperature is five degrees Celsius above normal?"

Janine nodded. "That is what he said."

Andrew rubbed his temple with his palm. "That can't be right. New York's sea level has only risen about thirteen inches since 1900. And even an extraordinarily warm ocean surface temp should only be up about three degrees Celsius."

"How do you..." Janine started, then smiled wryly. "Right. Photographic memory. Well, maybe before you traveled, that was the case. But now the facts have changed. Your leaky slice accelerated climate change, and that can't happen in the blink of an eye. It took a rewrite of history. You may remember it differently, but this is the reality now."

Andrew uttered a grunt of frustration. "When Sandy hit Atlantic City, it wasn't even a hurricane anymore. At its most destructive it was only a category two, and still it impacted over sixty thousand people. This will be worse. Much, *much* worse."

"A lot of people are going to lose their lives," Janine observed quietly.

Andrew stood up abruptly and ripped the tape from his knuckles, casting it forcefully to the floor.

He spoke with determination. "There's no time to waste. I've got to do something. I've got to try." Without another word, he was gone.

CHAPTER 19

KATE

September 27

No one else was in the kitchen, and I relished the silence as I intentionally procrastinated. My head ached, my eyes were strained, and I didn't even want to anticipate what was coming next. At least the food was excellent. I was finishing the last bites of delicious reheated chicken piccata with garlic mashed potatoes when Andrew burst into the room, clad in worn gray gym shorts and drenched in sweat. He dropped heavily into the chair opposite mine.

"We need to prep for far-slice travel immediately."

"Uh, hello to you too," I replied wearily, wrinkling both my brow and my nose.

"It's urgent," he insisted.

I was just too exhausted to deal with the cloak-and-dagger. I glanced around the room to make sure we were alone.

"What the hell is wrong with you? First you stab me, then you kiss me, then you run off as if I've got the plague. Now you insist we do something dangerous enough to kill us both? I'm not ready! I don't know if I can reliably get us out. We need more time with the data. We need to wait until the fMRI is up and running, and I can get more resolution—"

"There's no time," he reiterated, his voice low and calm but firm. "We've done something—I've done something—and I have to try to stop it."

He grasped my left hand, which was still throbbing and tender from the day's multiple encounters with the Bug. He gently outlined the hot red welt on the back of my hand with the tip of his finger, fixing my gaze with his intense stare. Intense shivers radiated down my spine and the remembered sensation of his hands on my skin from that unfortunate dream echoed throughout my traitorous body. I impatiently pushed the unwelcome thought from my mind and pulled my hand away.

"What? What have you done *now*?"

Andrew flinched. Had I touched a nerve? But then, before I could be sure, it was gone.

"The last slice that Lily and I infiltrated was in the midst of an ecological disaster. Ever since I've been back, I can see the effects—the heat wave, the choking smog, the nearly constant Spare-the-Air days. But the situation just grew more urgent. There's a monster hurricane developing—a superstorm—and it's bearing down on the east coast. If it's as big as they say, and if the path of the storm really follows the projection, most of coastal New Jersey and New York City will be destroyed. Tens of thousands could die. And between the winds and flooding, who knows how many homes will be destroyed. Hurricane Katrina displaced more than a million people. This storm could be much, much worse."

I shrugged and shook my head. "Isn't that a little melodramatic? It's just a weather forecast. They change all the time. And what makes you so certain that you caused this? Or that you can do anything at all to change it?"

"The surface water temperature of the Atlantic off the eastern seaboard is much warmer than it should be. Warmer than it ever had been before, by several degrees. And the starting sea level in

New York harbor is thirty-one inches above 1900s level—but last month I know that the sea level rise in that city was only thirteen inches. My travel rewrote history, and I need to fix it." He stared at me intently. "I can't do it alone, Kathryn. If I attempt it, I might not make it back at all."

An invisible band around my chest tightened. We weren't ready. I wasn't ready. "What do you propose?" I asked cautiously.

"We need to find a far-slice where the environment is not already massively damaged," he replied. "And we need to stay there long enough so that some eco-goodness can leak back into this reality. With any luck, we can turn back the tide, just a little. Just enough to avoid the carnage this storm is going to cause."

"I'm not ready," I protested again, but without any real conviction.

"I know," he admitted, casting his eyes down. "We have at most eight days before the storm is expected to make landfall somewhere near Atlantic City. Go look it up—within hours it will likely become Tropical Storm Ophelia. The media hasn't picked up the story yet, but you can bet the news will break any time. We need to move on this as soon as possible."

I nodded nervously.

He returned my nod, staring a minute longer as if convincing himself that I would comply. "We slice tomorrow. Early." He rose and strode from the room, nearly visible eddies of purposeful resolve trailing in his wake.

My head was spinning, and my stomach churned. The few bites on my plate suddenly seemed intensely unappetizing, so I dumped the remainder into the compost bin and trudged back to the lab. When I badged into the room, I could see Amir still seated at his workstation, slice of pizza in hand and a Dr Pepper within easy grasp, completely engrossed in some graphically intense roll-playing game. I poked him in the shoulder, and he pulled off his headphones.

"All hail the conquering hero!" A huge grin spread across his face. "Now that you're fed and rested, you gonna let me in on the secret?"

"No time. Your boss just accosted me in the cafeteria. Apparently, we're heading out again as soon as possible—and this time we're going way, way out."

"What?" Amir asked, confused. "We're not ready…"

"That's what I said. But he insists that New York City is going to be destroyed and that he's the cause. He's convinced he can somehow fix it."

Amir's confusion turned to concern. "Oh, man, that's the big times." He swiveled back to his workstation, killed the game, and relaunched the software development environment, opening files and typing furiously. "If the last round is any indication, we're not going to be able to do this here in the lab. You'd better go catch some Z's right now because what's coming is going to be intense."

"No," I replied firmly. "If I'm staring down death, I need to see my sister."

Amir shook his head, never taking his eyes off the screen or his fingers off the keys. "I can't take you. There's too much to do here…"

I put my hands on my hips and stood my ground. "I *can* drive, you know."

"Hold on a sec," he said, switching to his messaging app, fingers flying. "It looks like Janine can take you."

"Fine, whatever. Tell her I'll meet her at the garage bay in fifteen minutes."

I stopped in my room to retrieve my phone and texted Michelle that I'd be home in half an hour, then headed to the garage. Janine met me at the door.

"So, are you in on this mysterious plan that Andrew has concocted?" I asked her as she retrieved a set of keys and activated the huge roll-up garage door. We climbed into the vehicle closest to the exit.

Janine looked at me sadly as she started the truck. "I'm so sorry, Kate—I really wish there was some other way."

Something about her mournful expression made me drop my guard. "Do you think it will work? And do you think we'll survive?"

The truck crested a small hill and bumped over the dirt track, the headlights casting ominous shadows in the darkness as we headed toward civilization.

"I honestly don't know if it will work. I hope so, for our sake. And for Andrew's. But as to whether you'll survive—I'm afraid that *you're* the key to that. How do you feel about your ability to extract?"

"Well, we've moved on from abject violence," I admitted, feeling my cheeks flush. "But we know next to nothing about how it works. I'm terrified I won't be able to get back myself, let alone bring him back with me."

Janine pursed her lips as she turned onto the paved road and headed toward town. "The timing is not ideal. But if you two can achieve Andrew's goal, you will have prevented a considerable amount of death and destruction. I hope you believe it's worth the risk. And I hope you know that I'll do everything in my power to protect you. And so will Andrew."

"Andrew?" I replied quizzically. "He couldn't care less about me. I'm just a cog, just some function in his great experiment. I'm nothing more than his ticket out."

Janine approached my apartment building and threw the pickup into park.

"Don't be so sure of that." She fixed me with her maternal gaze. "I'll be back to pick you up in half an hour. You *are* going to need rest. I expect you'll have a very early morning."

With a wave, she was gone, and I let myself into our

apartment.

Michelle leaped from our shabby sofa, vaulted across the room, and enveloped me in a fierce embrace.

"Katie!" she mumbled into my neck. "It's nearly midnight. Are you okay? I've been so worried. Are you back to stay? Are you done at that place?"

I hugged her back, like it might be the last time. "No such luck. This is but a temporary reprieve."

In her excitement, the asthma kicked in and she began to wheeze. She put up a finger, dashed to the end table, and took a hit from her inhaler. She took a deep breath before she continued. "Why are you back? Is something wrong? Did that asshat stab you again?" She eyed me quizzically.

It was then I noticed the television. A news bulletin had just interrupted the programming to alert the audience that a disturbance headed toward the western Caribbean had just strengthened into Tropical Storm Ophelia. I stared at the screen and felt my mouth go dry. It was happening, just like he predicted.

"Kate? What is it?" Michelle asked, turning to the television.

"This storm is not supposed to happen. Or so he says. He says that messing with the multiverse has made our reality worse, and that this storm will turn into an extreme weather event—a hurricane like no one has ever seen, and that it will kill a lot of people and destroy a lot of homes."

I clapped a hand over my mouth. Michelle didn't know any of these details—was I even allowed to say "multiverse?"

Michelle pursed her lips and shook her head. "It's okay. I know about the slicing. And the Bug. Amir's been keeping me updated. I signed the NDA too, remember?"

I released a long sigh of relief.

"But who is 'he'? Is it Andrew? Katie, this is really messed up. I don't think you should go back there. Maybe we can pack up and get on a flight back home. Lay low for a while."

I sighed. She had no idea how much I wished that were possible.

"Andrew thinks he can fix it. But he needs me. It's going to be dangerous. The kind of dangerous where I might not actually survive."

"They can't ask you to do that!" my sister replied incredulously, her big eyes widening even farther. "You're not going to do it, right?"

"I think I have to do it." I studied our familiar worn, gray Berber carpeting. I kicked at the weird stain in the shape of a rabbit that had been there since our very first day. I was nearly thrown to the ground by my sister's unanticipated bear hug.

"I can't lose you. Don't go."

My throat constricted and my stomach tightened. I closed my eyes and tried to remain calm. "Over a million people are in harm's way. And it was my EEG trace that allowed them to reach the slice that caused this mess. I didn't ask to be involved in any of this, but if there is a way to undo the damage, I need to try."

My sister released me again and dropped heavily onto the sofa.

"Can you even do it? Can you actually make it out of there alive?"

When she looked at me, I could see tears welling in the corners of her eyes. My chest tightened, and my breath caught in my throat, but I fought to keep my own waterworks under control.

"I hope so. I did it again today. I managed to exit a slice."

"How?" Michelle demanded, sniffling and wiping her nose with the back of her palm.

"I haven't told anyone," I mumbled, "but it happened when Andrew kissed me."

"Wait, what did you just say? He *kissed* you? What did he say? What did you say?"

I plopped onto the sofa next to her. "Yeah, he did. And then we weren't there anymore. We were back in the lab. Both of us. And then he ripped off his electrodes and bolted out of the room. It was the last I saw of him until he interrupted my dinner by demanding that we far-slice travel immediately."

A Mona Lisa smile spread over my sister's face as she sniffled and wiped away a tear. "Hell of a way to behave at your first job!"

I could feel my cheeks flush. "This is not my first job. I shoveled horse manure for Mr. Franklin for an entire summer when I was thirteen."

Michelle eyed me doubtfully. "Kathryn, cut the crap. Why don't you tell me what is really going on?"

The heat in my cheeks grew more intense, and I tried to suppress an unwelcome feeling of shame.

"If we are going to have this conversation, you are going to have to pour me something strong."

She eyed me suspiciously and shook her head. "I leave you alone for a week and you get a boyfriend and become a boozehound?" she teased. But to my relief, she rose from the sofa and headed to the kitchen. She popped open a can of Coke and rummaged around in the cabinet. In no time she'd poured a pair of rum and Cokes that were heavy on the rum and light on the Coke. I attempted to compose myself, and when she handed me the glass, I immediately gulped down half of it, grimacing at the strong, sticky-sweet taste of the drink.

"I don't have a boyfriend, and this is pretty much my second drink ever."

Michelle snorted and tapped her foot. "Spill it. Now."

It didn't take long for the rum to do its job. Lightweight that I am, the one strong drink was all it took to ease my confession. But I still found it difficult to look my sister in the eye.

"I don't understand what's happening to me. When he kissed me, every fiber of my being cried out 'No! No! No!' Then suddenly all I felt was 'Yes! Yes! Yes!' Honestly, I don't understand any of this. I don't want it. I wish I could stay here with you instead of going back. If I go back—*when* I go back—it's going to happen again."

My sister gave me an impish grin. "Would that be so bad?"

I frowned. "I doubt that Andrew cares about anyone, including me, except as his ticket back to civilization, or whatever we call this messed-up reality."

"So, he's using you. But you're afraid you're falling for him?"

"No!" I snapped. "Definitely not. Well, maybe. I don't know!" I scowled. "I feel drawn to him. But he's a total enigma. I know next to nothing about him, or this whole disastrous scheme. I always imagined that some day I would get this stupid sleep disorder under control—find a boyfriend, do some awesome science, get married. Maybe have some kids. You know, lead a normal life. But dammit, Michelle, I'm twenty-eight years old and I've never been in love! I have no idea what it's supposed to feel like. I don't even know myself well enough to know if I *am* falling for him. I'm no closer to understanding or controlling my messed-up brain, I've ditched my college career, I'm working with a whack job at a black-ops facility, and doing some insane sci-fi experiment that frankly shouldn't even be possible. This is not what I want. This is not how it's supposed to be!"

Michelle shook her head, and the look in her eyes suddenly made her seem decades older than she was. "Nothing is ever like it's supposed to be. You've told me how you want things to be. Now tell me how they are. Be real, Kate; this is me you're talking to."

I took a deep breath and considered my sister's request. She was right. She deserved the truth, no matter how much I didn't want to speak it.

"When he's not around, I wonder where he is. When he *is* around, my palms sweat and I feel like every word I say makes me sound like an idiot. When I imagine his face, I feel..." I faltered, searching for the right word. "I feel completely and utterly undone."

"Undone," she repeated, giving me a hard stare. "That sounds serious."

I placed my empty glass on the table and leaned my head against my little sister. My heart ached with the weight of my predicament.

"This whole situation is serious, in so many ways. I love you, Shell. Thank you for...well, listening to me. For protecting me. For sacrificing your whole life for me. If I don't make it back, please make sure Mom and Dad know that I love them, too."

At that moment, through the living room window, I could see the glow of headlights as a pickup truck slowed to a stop outside our building. I turned to Michelle and gave her one final squeeze. "I love you," I assured her, and I darted through the door, before I lost my resolve—or my nerve.

Janine carefully maneuvered the pickup back into the garage bay. "You're to be at Stanford Medical Center no later than six in the morning for prep."

"Prep?" I gulped. "Like for surgery?"

Janine smiled reassuringly. "We'll draw blood, place an IV, that sort of thing. Someone will be by at five thirty to collect you, so you have a little under five hours to rest. Don't eat anything. You should try to sleep, if you can. Oh, and wear comfortable shoes. And clothes you're not too attached to."

I reached for her arm. "Janine, can you...can you drive me? I could use all the moral support I can get."

Janine smiled warmly, unfastened her seat belt, and reached across the console to fold me into her arms. I closed my eyes, and for a moment, it was my own mother's comforting embrace.

"I know you're going to be okay," she whispered.

Back in my room, I threw caution to the wind and hit the sheets without bothering to meditate. I was exhausted, and I was going to eke out the most rest possible given the few hours I had.

The nighttime air is deliciously warm and sweet with the scent of jasmine. I am perched on a smooth teak bench in a beautiful courtyard surrounded by the most elegant example of Spanish Moorish architecture I have ever seen. In the center of the courtyard sits a grand fountain, water melodiously trickling from a large central chalice and falling playfully into the pool below. Four stately palm trees guard a gracefully arched double door leading into the home. My eyes follow their spindly trunks up past the terra cotta tiles of the roof up, up to the cloudless, inky sky where I can see the glow of the waning crescent moon and a sprinkle of stars. I feel completely at ease in this place, as if I've known it forever, and I never want to leave. I close my eyes and breathe deeply, and no thoughts trouble my mind at all. This place isn't just conducive to meditation; it is peace personified.

I am sitting quietly, at one with the gentle patter of the fountain and the rhythmic chirping of crickets, when the door under the arch swings open. Despite the fact that this has happened before, I am still momentarily stunned to observe myself walking out of the door. She is holding two steaming mugs. As the other Kate crosses the threshold, she passes under the sconce on the wall, and I can see that her auburn hair is cut quite short and is streaked with golden highlights. She pushes the door closed with her foot, and I notice she is wearing black leather Mojari shoes from India bedecked with elaborate gold embroidery and sequins. She crosses the courtyard to where I am sitting, and it is as if she can actually see me. It seems appropriate to stand to greet her.

She welcomes me with a wide and genuine grin.

"Hi. Do you want the mint tea or the green tea?" She holds out the matching pair of brown and green pottery mugs.

I am dumbfounded. She can see me. She can speak to me. And apparently I can share a pleasant teatime with a version of myself. I recall how disconcerting it was to meet my double in the lab, but for some reason I can't explain, talking to this version of myself puts me oddly at ease. I consider her offer and remember my five thirty a.m. call time. I reach for the mint tea, though it seems unlikely that caffeine in a dream would affect my waking life.

She sits beside me and takes a sip.

"I had a feeling I would find you out here. How's your tea?" Now that she's close, I eye her aquamarine kurta tunic and white linen shorts. I marvel that I suddenly know what Mojari shoes and kurta tunics are.

I think back to the patient in the biohazard ward. It feels both strange and totally expected that we are having this conversation, and that I can interact with her world.

I try my tea. It's amazing. "This is literally the best tea I have ever tasted in my life."

"Fresh mint. Grown here, right in this courtyard. Makes all the difference." The other Kate smiles.

"Where am I?"

"My home," she replies. "In Bel Air. You're in Los Angeles."

"You live here? This place looks like a mansion!"

She nods, tucking a lock of her beautifully styled hair behind her ear. I make a mental note to find a salon that can replicate Other Kate's hair, just as soon as I graduate and get a job. Then I remember Albaion's exorbitant paychecks, and think…maybe next week.

"The home is a little extravagant," she admits, while still somehow projecting an air of modesty and self-composure that I am astonished emanates from me—or at least a version of me. "But it's also a sanctuary. A place where I can refine my practice. Do you want to go inside?" she asks with gentle wave of her hand. "I can give you the tour."

"No," I reply quickly, already overwhelmed. "Is it okay if we stay out here and talk for a bit?"

"Sure." She smiles. "I've got all night."

I wish that I did, too.

I take another sip of tea and inventory the numerous questions I'm dying to ask. "I feel stupid asking you this, but I can't think of any other way to begin. Who are you? And how does the daughter of two farmers from central Illinois come to live in a Mediterranean palace in Bel Air?"

She throws back her head and releases a burst of laughter, a sound that fills my heart with pure joy. I realize that I cannot recall ever laughing with such abandon.

"Well, clearly you dream," she replies with a smile so wide that crinkles the corners of her hazel eyes, so like my own. "And your travels have brought you here, so you must have something to learn. So let me tell you my story.

"My parents aren't farmers; at least, they haven't been for many, many years. They moved to Los Angeles before I was born, and in fact, they still live in a quaint little Craftsman bungalow in Pasadena. Dad is almost ready to retire from NASA's Jet Propulsion Laboratory, where he has been engineering components for space flight for most of his career. He went to work there right after completing his degrees in electrical engineering from the University of Illinois."

I nod. I always suspected that my dad harbored a secret regret that he chose to maintain the family farm, but now I understand why he is so good at keeping the old farm machinery in perfect working order.

"When I was four years old, I started having these night terrors, and the dreams were terrifying."

"I know..." I murmur.

"My parents found that my pediatrician was of absolutely no help at all, nor were any of the psychologists. One day one of the scientists my dad worked with recommended we visit a friend of his. My parents were desperate; they were willing to try anything. That friend turned out to be my Gurudevi."

"What is a Gurudevi?" I ask, perplexed and intrigued.

She laughed with delight. "Not a what, a who. She is a sannyasini—a Hindu monk—my meditation teacher," she responded. "At first it seemed like she was just my caretaker. My visits to her home seemed like unusual day care where all the other children's parents were from India. But later, as I aged, I understood that she was actually teaching her students yoga and the meditative practices of Ananda Marga, which translates loosely into 'The Path of Bliss.'"

I nod. "Meditation is the only thing that helps me, too. But for me it was just a technique; a mental exercise."

"For me, it was a deep and expansive study. Through my discipleship with Gurudevi, I learned that the dreams are not some horrible mental defect, but a sacred and precious gift."

I snorted and nearly choked on my tea. "A precious gift? How can debilitating nightmares be considered anything other than a vile curse?"

Her lopsided grin reminds me of my mother. Our mother, I guess. "First I learned how to leave them. Then I learned how to become engaged with them. And finally, I learned to harness them. Your dreams don't have to be nightmares, you know. In dreams, as in life, you tend to find what you're looking for. You expect disaster, so that's what you find in your travels. But trust me when I say there's more to your gift than you know."

"What on earth does that mean? And how does any of this translate to living in a mansion?"

She smiles again. How could she be so self-assured when I am such a basket case?

"Now I decide where I go and when I dream. I have the most amazing job in the world. Whenever I choose, I meet exceptional people living extraordinary lives, in places that are like this yet vastly different. I visit them as often as I like, until they become my friends and confidants and then I write their stories."

"Wait, you're a writer?"

She nods. "Though I think of myself more as a scribe, or a chronicler. The first novel was published when I was nineteen. I'm working on my seventh book now. They're quite successful." Again that beatific smile, tempered with genuine modesty.

"Can you tell me how you do it?" I ask breathlessly. This may be the *most important question I've ever asked in my entire life.*

"You simply follow the path to bliss," she replies cryptically. "Sit with me for a while, here in the garden. It will help."

She and I sit in companionable silence for some time; with any other person and in any other place and time this would seem awkward, but despite these shocking revelations, I am at peace here in a way I've never felt before. It is like basking in the best parts of myself. I wish I could stay here with her indefinitely; I wish I could meet her Gurudevi, and I wish more than anything I could attain the inner peace that seems to radiate from her like rays from the sun.

As we sit, I seem to lose time; I have no idea how long we have been breathing the sweet scent of star jasmine on the warm night air. But then another figure appears at the grand door beneath the arch.

The door swings open, and someone speaks.

"Come in, love, it's late." The figure steps out beneath the light of the big iron sconce. Although by now I shouldn't be, I am in fact shocked that the person standing illuminated in the pool of light is Andrew.

And then I wake up.

CHAPTER 20

KATE

September 28

It was just before six when Janine and I sailed through the corridors of Stanford Medical Center. She navigated the byzantine passages without hesitation, and I followed nervously, hopelessly lost after a half-dozen twists and turns. As instructed, I had not eaten breakfast, but I was dreading the day so completely that my empty stomach was the furthest thing from my mind. Finally we arrived at a large patient room in an otherwise unmarked ward. I was immeasurably relieved to find Dr. Daniels waiting for us.

"I'm so glad you're here," I sighed, giving him a quick hug.

"I've cleared my schedule. I can't say I support this procedure, but I will monitor you until it's over," Dr. Daniels replied curtly as he patted my arm and gestured for me to take a seat on the teal-green institutionally upholstered sofa.

I glanced around the room nervously. "Where is, uh, everyone else?"

"Andrew will be here shortly," Janine replied. She pressed a call button on the wall.

I took the opportunity to look around the room. When I realized it was the place where Lily had died, my mouth went dry. I took deep breaths to fight the alarming surge of dread that swept up from my gut.

The two hospital beds were separated by only a few feet and divided by a small table. The EEG caps waiting in their containers of saline solution were almost comforting, as were the monitors, but there were also stacks of other unfamiliar medical consoles looming over the gurneys. A server rack packed with electronics was bolted securely to the floor to the left of the beds.

"I'm going to have the nurse draw some blood," Janine explained. "We need baseline levels for liver and kidney function. Our nurse will also insert an IV. You may be unconscious for some time, and it will allow us to keep you hydrated. The IV will also allow us to administer any medications, should intervention be required. We will monitor your EEG, cardiac function, heart rate, respiration, oxygen—all the usual stats."

"How will I...eat?"

"We'll insert a nasogastric feeding tube, which is a narrow plastic tube that is inserted through your nostril, down your esophagus, and into your stomach."

I shuddered. "That sounds fun..."

"Don't worry. We can place the NG tube after you're asleep," Janine assured me.

"Do I need to change into a hospital gown?" I asked, fidgeting on the sofa.

"Not unless you want to go exploring with your ass hanging out," Andrew suggested as he pushed through the door into the room. He was carrying a large, heavy-duty, shockproof plastic case. Amir was right behind him, looking drained and wearing a rumpled navy T-shirt that read "If you don't understand recursion read this shirt again."

Andrew had ditched his usual well-tailored button-down shirt in favor of a washed-out jersey tee, and his jeans were faded and ripped at the left knee. I'd never seen him dressed with so little care, but the thin cotton of the shirt hugged his well-defined torso, and my gaze lingered. I caught myself ogling and quickly looked away, shutting down this line of thought before it could pile any further tension on my already overwrought psyche.

"I see you brought your walking shoes," Andrew remarked. "Leave them on. You're going to need them. It may take us a few attempts before we find the right slice."

He placed the case on a bed, snapped open the clasps, and almost reverently removed the two Bugs that were nestled securely in the contoured foam. Amir attached the devices to cables snaking from the back of the rack-mounted computer, pulled out a keyboard tray, and began typing with quick, efficient keystrokes.

The nurse Janine had summoned arrived and adjusted a hospital bed into its reclining position. She motioned for me to sit and clipped an oxygen sensor onto my finger, then inserted an IV into the vein in the middle of my forearm and carefully taped it down. I was no fan of needles, but after the constant invasive burrowing of the Bug, the IV seemed like a walk in the park. As the nurse proceeded to draw three vials of blood, I mused about how particularly unnerving it was to lie in bed fully dressed and with my shoes on. I pulled my hair out of its messy bun and slid the elastic into my pocket. Janine helped me attach the EEG cap while the nurse explained that she would be attaching EKG leads under my shirt to monitor cardiac function. I glanced nervously at Andrew as the nurse snaked the leads and contacts under my fitted cotton T-shirt, but she was discreet and he was completely engrossed in programming the Bugs.

Amir detached the Bugs and placed them carefully on the small table between the beds. With a practiced air, Andrew adjusted his hospital bed to recline and climbed in. The nurse moved to his side and prepped his arm for the blood draw.

"Give us three hours once we've sliced," Andrew instructed Janine. "That should be long enough to assess our location. If we're not back, assume we've found the slice we're looking for and take the necessary steps."

"Uh, what are the necessary steps?" I asked nervously.

"We'll need to determine quickly if the slice we hit is the slice we want. If it's not, we need to get out quickly. We can't risk any additional cross-contamination, and we have no time to waste. If it *is* the slice we want...we'll need to park ourselves there long enough to get some cross-pollination."

"How long is long enough?"

"We can stay as long as we're free of symptoms, but we definitely need to be out before we reach the sixty-hour mark," Andrew responded. The nurse had finished placing his IV and had just drawn her final vial of blood.

I bit my lip and released a ragged breath. "What happens at sixty hours?" I asked.

"Your mind begins to shut down due to the strain," Janine explained gently.

Andrew's businesslike tone counteracted Janine's reassurance. "No sense sugar-coating it. Your eyesight goes, you develop tics, then it's convulsions. If you don't exit, then death."

"Right, no pressure then..." I mumbled.

I turned to Janine, unsure how to phrase my next question. "Uh, how will we...uh...take bathroom breaks?"

She smiled reassuringly. "Once we have determined that you'll be out for the long haul, we'll remove your clothing, place a catheter and the NG, and gown you."

This is not going to be fun, I thought. I was thankful that I wouldn't be conscious for most of the unpleasant poking and prodding.

I had the sudden and unnerving image of my shirt morphing into a flapping hospital gown. "My clothes won't suddenly disappear in the slice, then, will they?" I asked nervously.

"Your instance in the slice is unaffected by your outward appearance in this reality, beyond your initial emergence," Andrew replied.

Sensing my unease, Janine walked over to my bed and reached around all of the cables and leads to give me a warm and comforting hug. "You'll be okay," she whispered in my ear. "I'll be here the whole time, rooting for you. I know you can do this."

The best I could do was reply with a nervous nod, which she returned with her reassuring smile.

Andrew finished attaching his EEG cap. "Let's get moving. There's no time to waste."

Dr. Daniels handed me the anti-nausea pill and a small cup of water. Andrew popped his meds dry.

With his free right hand, Andrew reached for a Bug and handed it to Janine. Andrew grabbed the second device and deftly positioned it even though his left hand was hampered by an IV line and an oxygen sensor.

"Unless our vitals drop, or it's been longer than sixty hours, don't administer the propofol," Andrew instructed.

Janine's lips turned down in a frown, but she nodded her assent.

Amir gave a thumbs-up. "Lock and load!"

Andrew activated his Bug.

Here we go, I thought. I took a deep, centering breath and clenched my teeth as the needlelike protrusion buried itself deep under my skin.

I opened my eyes, saw the world lurch wildly, and tried to hold back dry heaves.

"The anti-nausea isn't working..." I complained thorough clenched teeth.

"Take a few deep breaths," Andrew advised, "then open your eyes—slowly."

I breathed as instructed, and when I slowly opened my right, then my left eye, the world stayed situated on its proper axis. I was sitting on the dusty floor of a storage room that looked like a graveyard for dead medical devices.

"Shake a leg," Andrew suggested, already on his feet. "We need to assess the situation quickly." He grasped my hand and pulled me up. After the first few unsteady steps, I felt fine.

"So, what's your plan?"

"We need to do a little quick reconnaissance. If we can get a feel for the average water temperature and ocean rise statistics, we can decide if we've landed someplace worthwhile."

"Okay," I agreed, dusting off my backside. With no idea what to expect, I crept quietly behind Andrew as he strode purposefully through the storeroom door.

It was obvious that we were still in the hospital. We roamed the corridors, following the signs to the cafeteria.

Andrew began to walk casually around the seating area. He weaved between tables as if he were meeting a friend he couldn't quite locate.

"What are you doing?" I whispered.

"Keep up," he insisted, the tilt of his head indicating that I should follow.

We heard a loud clatter; the entire dining area turned its attention toward the dish return station where an employee had dropped a large pile of plastic trays.

Andrew grabbed my arm and pulled me quickly along, toward

the entrance.

"Here, hold this." He shoved a women's handbag underneath my arm.

I stared dumbly at the black leather mass. "Where did you get that? Did you just steal some woman's purse?"

He explained, as if I was a dull child. "Right now we're in survival mode. Now, go stand over by that refrigerator case and rummage around in the bag so we know what we have to work with."

I'd never cheated on a test, lied to my parents, or even stolen so much as a breath mint. I felt a wave of guilt wash over me as I dug through the stranger's purse. Perhaps more troubling was the unexpected rush of heady elation that displaced it when I found her wallet. I plucked out a bill that appeared to be made from reflective Mylar.

"Whoa, look. Shiny! And holograms." I held the sheet up and turned it in the light, watching a hologram of the Statue of Liberty rotate.

Andrew snatched it out of my hand. "Don't be so obvious."

I kept my hand low in the bag and counted the rest. "Looks like twenty-seven dollars. And a mobile phone," I whispered.

"Hand me the cash, her ID, and the mobile."

I nodded and handed him the loot. He pocketed the mobile and took a quick glance at the ID before handing it back to me.

"Head to the women's restroom. Leave the bag there."

I shrugged but followed his instructions, where I left the bag conspicuously on the restroom counter. I pulled my loose hair back from my shoulders, twirled it up into a messy bun, and pulled the elastic band from my pocket. I took a moment to check the mirror. Dark circles gave my eyes a hollowed cast. I may have felt a bit like a secret agent, but I looked like a tired twentysomething in grungy clothes who had indulged in too many late nights.

Andrew checked the time on the pilfered mobile phone. "It's just seven; everything will still be closed," he said. "Are you ready for a walk?"

"Sure," I agreed.

We left the hospital, Andrew his usual cool self and me trying to conjure a casual facade. The early morning sun cut through the haze in the gray sky. So far this slice didn't seem so different from our own. As we headed down Campus Drive, Andrew pulled the stolen mobile from his pocket and began trying unlock codes.

"Where are we headed?" I asked.

"You know the Rodin sculpture garden?"

"Of course. Do you think it will actually be there?"

Andrew continued trying passcodes, and we walked on among the sparse early morning traffic. "No way to know except to go."

We'd just come into view of the building I knew as the Cantor Center for the Arts when Andrew exclaimed, "Got it!"

I looked at him with wide eyes. "How'd you do that?" I made a conscious note not to let him near my mobile phone.

"Keen understanding of human nature," he quipped. "She used her birthdate in reverse as her lock code."

As he tapped at the phone, he headed purposefully toward the iconic Rodin bronze called *The Thinker*. It was a very quiet morning in the garden; no other visitors were in sight.

My growing optimism that this mission would be accomplished quickly was trampled by the dark look that crossed Andrew's face as he scrolled and scanned the stolen device.

"This slice is not going to help us. The ecological damage here is not quite as severe as what we're dealing with in our own reality, but it's too close for comfort. We need to get out of here before anything leaks and try again."

Andrew set the phone gently on the steps to the Cantor Center and turned to me expectantly. I found I suddenly had trouble swallowing. This was it—this was the part where my boss expected me to plant one on him. I couldn't even begin to quantify the ways in which this was all just wrong. Completely against my will, the sensation of his breath against my neck resurfaced from my nightmare, and my mutinous body began to hum in a way that was awkwardly pleasant but relentlessly confusing. I pointedly looked away and gave in to an irresistible urge to pace.

"Kathryn, I'm not going to stab you," Andrew chuckled, with a slightly bemused expression. "I'm not going to surprise you, assault you, or injure you in any way. I'm not even going to stand within your personal space." He took a step backward. "This has to be your choice."

"Well, that's something new," I grumbled, using all my willpower to root myself in one spot without fidgeting. "And it's Kate," I corrected with a withering glance. But inside my chest, my heart pounded as if it were trying to escape the confines of my rib cage. I tried to conjure an air of outward cool, but inside I felt seriously nauseated. I was already drenched in cold sweat. Seconds passed, then one minute, then another as he stared at me and I squirmed.

"I don't know how to do this!" I finally protested. "I barely know you and I'm not even sure I like you."

"Am I really so repulsive?" he asked, cocking his head and cracking the smile that made other women swoon. He extended his hand. "For the sake of thousands of lives?"

Of course he was not repulsive. That was a big part of the problem.

Heart now pounding like a runaway freight train, I stepped toward him, wiped my sweaty palm on my jeans, and awkwardly took his outstretched hand. Nothing happened. We just stood there, holding hands. My heart continued to thump at an alarming speed, and my stomach lurched upward into the vicinity of my trachea. Then I did what I always do in times of crisis; I closed my eyes, focused on my breath, and began to empty my mind.

It took forever, but finally my breathing returned to normal. Andrew stood so stock-still that I forgot about his hand; I forgot about my hand; I forgot about the slice of alternate reality. My heartbeat slowed, and my breathing became calm and measured. When I finally opened my eyes, I found him silent and transfixed, gazing at me with the same inscrutable expression as always.

Before my newly restored inner peace could be disturbed, I took a sudden step toward him, reached my arms up to encircle his neck, and drew him toward me. In one quick motion, I closed my eyes and met his lips. In an instant his hands were caressing the small of my back, his body pressed close to mine. My hesitance was met with his startling passion and the kiss deepened. The sensation took my breath away; legions of bright white fireworks exploded behind my eyelids. I had the alarming sensation of falling, floating, soaring—then a bittersweet yearning so intense that it nearly knocked me off my feet.

I was confused for a moment when I opened my eyes and observed the slew of medical machines all humming and whirring. I was back in the hospital room; we were back in the hospital room, still reclining in our beds but fully awake and still dressed in our street clothes.

"Not the right slice, but a perfectly executed exit," Andrew remarked calmly, glancing pointedly in my direction. A glimpse at the monitors revealed that my heart rate was quite elevated. Through the vestiges of euphoria, I could sense the beginning of a migraine behind my right eye.

Dr. Daniels examined me with an arched eyebrow.

"Everything okay?" he asked.

"Uh, yeah..." I replied, avoiding his scrutiny. "The headache is coming on, though."

"Nurse," Dr. Daniels called. "Ten milligrams IV metoclopramide, please."

I again found myself sprawled unceremoniously on the hard linoleum floor, but this time I took a couple of deep breaths before opening one eye. A quick glance around confirmed I was in a patient room at the hospital. I sat up quickly and was relieved to find the room was unoccupied. Andrew pulled himself up on the other side of the bed. "Let's get going."

I struggled shakily to my feet. "More petty larceny? Or can we just go to the library this time?"

Andrew grinned and checked the time. "It's eight ten. Maybe we can get on the net at the Green Library."

"That will only work if public computers are available without checking in with a student ID. Empty pockets, remember?"

Andrew shrugged. "Let's give it a try."

The walk to the Green Library took twenty minutes, and I was glad I was wearing my comfy and well-worn Chuck Taylors. I was getting a lot of exercise for a woman who was technically sedated in a hospital. As we walked, I looked for differences in the campus. As we walked past the Quad, I could see Memorial Church situated exactly where it should be, resplendent as always with its mosaics and stained glass windows perched above familiar sandstone arches. The flowers planted in the center of the Oval's green grassy fields were still red. In fact, as far as I could tell, nothing seemed different.

The Green Library was also exactly where we expected it to be and was already open. The public internet terminals were right by the information desk, just as expected. I didn't need to flash an ID to gain entry after all. I breathed a huge sigh of relief and tried to contain my nervous urge to continually scan the room. Within minutes, Andrew had completed his search.

"This slice isn't going to help us either," Andrew decided. "Stats look bad here too; I'm going to have Amir reprogram to an even more divergent slice. Time to make a hasty escape."

His probing gaze was tempered by a hint of charm that I hadn't bargained for. Why didn't this ever get any easier? I began to suspect he was intentionally messing with my head.

"What, here?" I stalled.

"If you have a library fetish..."

"Absolutely not!" I hissed. I hurried to the exit before things could get out of hand.

Nerves made me stride quickly across the lush, grassy field outside of the library. It was another block until I reached the Meyer Green. A tranquil park bench tucked beneath a tree would be the perfect place to rest and re-center my breathing. Andrew plopped down on the bench beside me.

"You are making me incredibly nervous," I mumbled through clenched teeth.

"I could help; after all, we're on a schedule here."

I closed my eyes and tried to move my focus from his amused badgering to the sensation of my breath. "Just...give me a minute."

He couldn't even manage to stay silent for sixty seconds.

"Perhaps it's time to do a little boundary testing," Andrew suggested.

"Uh, okay..." I replied, rubbing my temples. "We never did extensive testing on the edge cases to shake out the potential errors in our code. It's not even really finished, but I guess it's never too early to start. But I don't see how we're going to do any debugging here; our code base is hanging out in some other reality."

"You are so literal..." He chuckled, shaking his head.

I could feel my face flush, and I quickly looked away. Was he making fun of me? Was he trying to flirt with me? I felt completely out of my element. He lifted my left hand and carefully traced the outline of the angry welt with his finger. Electric jolts of fission ran up my spine, and I resorted once again to slow, calming breaths.

My mouth went dry. I wondered why I suddenly felt queasy. "You mean you want to test *my* boundaries, then. You probably do this all the time. Seducing women."

His casual shrug answered the question perfectly. "I was just trying to help. We should establish exactly what it takes for you to trigger the exit."

It sounded so logical, yet it was infuriating. And nerve-racking. I stared at him with silent determination. He responded by gently kissing the injury on the back of my hand. I struggled to contain the gasp that completely shattered any hope I had of remaining calm.

I couldn't bear it for another instant; I turned sharply and pulled him close, my fingers tangled in his hair. I wanted him, wanted his embrace, and as he responded once more to my kiss, I found myself again opening my eyes in a hospital bed, hooked up to a dozen wires and sensors in the dim room at Stanford Medical Center.

CHAPTER 21

KATE

September 28

I knew before I even opened my eyes—this time it was different. My hands clutched loose soil; I could detect the scent of the morning sun as it burned the dew from the golden grass. I slowly opened one eye, then the other, and waited for the vertigo to subside. Andrew stood up and brushed the dry brown soil from his jeans, then extended a hand and pulled me up from the patch of dirt and brush I was sprawled upon. When he released my hand from his grasp, I was embarrassed to admit to myself just how dismayed I felt when he withdrew even this simple touch.

"There's no hospital here."

"Roger that, Captain Obvious," Andrew retorted, already heading east through the field toward Campus Drive.

"Now he's cracking jokes," I muttered to myself, hurrying to catch up.

Campus Drive wasn't where it should be. The Cantor Center for the Arts and the Rodin sculptures were not there. Dozens of buildings were missing. Entire *streets* were missing. Stanford of this slice was a much smaller version of the university that I knew. I was relieved when we finally reached Roth Way and could see the familiar green grass of the Oval, the rows of trees along Palm

Drive, and the sandstone arches of the Stanford Quad. My world was shattered again when I saw the car that drove by. Sheathed in iridescent blue paint, the automobile was small, low to the ground, sleek, and aerodynamic. It looked like the unlikely offspring of a forties roadster and a squashed jelly bean. It was elegant and futuristic, and I couldn't stop staring. It literally stopped me in my tracks.

"Is that a concept car some rich Silicon Valley tech baron commissioned?" I murmured.

Andrew, now several steps ahead of me, turned and motioned impatiently.

"Stop staring," he muttered as soon as I was within earshot. "You're supposed to be blending in."

Another beautiful streamlined car passed by, nearly soundless, similar in appearance but with a deep, ruby-red iridescent finish. I tore my eyes away and instead focused on Andrew's retreating form as he moved quickly toward the sandstone arches that guarded the entryway to the university.

We skirted past Memorial Church and cut through the Quad. "Are we headed back to the Green Library?" I asked. The place was still early morning quiet, but we passed a couple of women wearing linen skirts and blouses. Both were sporting thick, wide headbands that shimmered in the morning sun in shifting iridescent hues. They stared at me for a long moment, then looked away. I was instantly uncomfortable and self-conscious.

"We're going to try," he replied, still several steps ahead of me. "Let me do the talking."

The arched facade of the Green Library looked just as I remembered, but the building was missing a huge wing. I walked through the doors hoping to find computers flanking the information desk, but I was disappointed.

"Student ID?" the desk attendant requested. She was dressed conservatively, in a beige button-down blouse with a wide collar.

Holding back her short brown hair was a thick and broad headband, similar to the ones worn by the women we passed on the Quad. It sparkled in iridescent green and violet, like the wings of a dragonfly. She looked up from behind the standing-height wooden desk, examining us from behind her black-rimmed spectacles, and frowned.

"Ve are visitors," Andrew responded, his words thick with an accent that I didn't recognize. He smiled coyly and leaned casually against the counter.

The woman at the desk removed her glasses and beamed at him with a slightly dreamy look in her eyes, but still asked, "Photo ID, please?"

Andrew patted his rear jeans pocket. To my surprise, he produced two pink-tinged IDs that read "FØRERKORT NORGE" in big block letters along the top. His black and white photo graced the top one, and I frowned at the particularly unflattering photo of me on the second. The attendant took another long look at Andrew, then me, and asked, "Where was it you said you were from?"

"Ve are visiting from Nor-vay," Andrew replied, using a singsong cadence that sounded comically fake. At least he had blond hair and blue eyes. Me, Scandinavian? Not likely. I held my breath, certain that the woman behind the desk would see through the ruse.

"Well, that explains the outfits," was the attendant's acerbic reply. She penciled in our fake Norwegian identities on two lines in a large ledger and handed Andrew the cards, waving us in.

"I can't believe that worked," I whispered as we moved deeper into the library in search of a computer. I regarded him through narrowed eyes. "And I thought you said you weren't carrying anything in your pockets."

"Not entirely accurate," he whispered, handing me my fake Norwegian ID. I shoved it into my jeans. "Technology won't come through, but sometimes non-tech items will. Anything too familiar would almost certainly be wrong in other slices, but I was banking on the fact that a Norwegian driver's license is unfamiliar enough anywhere in the States that a fraudulent document from another reality wouldn't be questioned."

I shook my head. What hubris. Lucky for us it worked. "I guess you're a twofer—crackpot visionary and criminal mastermind."

All I got in reply was a quick grin and another impatient gesture.

We walked the entire first floor without locating a single computer.

Andrew paused by the staircase. "There are four more floors; we'll get through this faster if we split up. You take two and three. I'll take four and five. Meet me back here. If you find a terminal, get stats about sea level rise, or CO_2 concentration, or average temperature."

I nodded and we split up.

I walked the entirety of the second, then the third floor without spotting a single piece of technology, which seemed impossible. I wouldn't have been so surprised to find that public computers weren't a thing here, but as far as I could tell, not even the library staff had access to the machines.

I was on my way back to the first floor to meet Andrew when I idly ran my hand over a row of thick volumes. I stopped when I realized I was standing before a shelf housing a row of almanacs. I grabbed a thick volume called *World Almanac and Book of Facts* and flipped through it. On page 1650, I found a list of population by states and was about to continue paging when the figure for California caught my eye. Just a few weeks ago, I'd read an article in the news about how the population of my adopted state had just surpassed the entire population of Canada. Thirtysomething million people. But the almanac put the population of California at a measly 10.68 million. The small size of campus suddenly began to make sense. I tucked the huge book under my arm and hurried toward the stairs.

When I reached the first floor, Andrew was leaning impatiently against a huge cabinet filled with hundreds of tiny drawers. "There aren't any computers—public or otherwise—in this building, as far as I can tell. I think I'm going to need..."

"An almanac?" I suggested, handing him the monstrous volume. I shook out my stiff arm while he hoisted the almanac onto a nearby table and began poring through the index. He rapidly flipped pages, ran his finger down a table of numbers, and looked up with a triumphant grin.

"Atmospheric CO_2 concentration is over one hundred parts per million lower," he reported, stabbing the book with his finger. "I think this slice will do nicely."

I released a huge, involuntary sigh of relief. When my shoulders relaxed, I realized I'd spent the last hour as tense as if I was reliving my Breckinridge Fellowship interview. It was a relief to know that we'd be here for the next couple of days. Perhaps there would be a respite for my conflicted emotions. And maybe the nasty welt on my left hand would finally have time to heal.

"We should take this opportunity to learn a little more about where we are," Andrew suggested. He flipped more pages of the almanac.

"I noticed that the population of California for last year was about a third of what I expected."

"That's odd..." Andrew replied absentmindedly as he continued his search. He paused for a moment and regarded the spine of the volume. "The Dewey decimal system seems alive and well here. We could pore through periodicals, but that could take hours. It might be faster if you find some recent American history. Try looking in nonfiction 970."

"Uh, how do you know that?"

"I know things," he replied, returning to the depths of the

volume.

"What's the call number for astronomy?"

"520," Andrew replied immediately, without looking up.

"North American poetry?"

"811."

"Fairy tales?"

"398.2."

"How on earth do you *do* that?" I sputtered, a little too loudly for a library.

"Eidetic imagery," he replied, turning another page.

I rolled my eyes. "You have a photographic memory. Of course you do."

"It's not so rare. Look it up—153.1," he suggested. "On your way to 970 for American history."

"Infuriating," I mumbled as I set off for the history section.

I curled up in a comfortable, well-worn leather chair and opened up a burgundy leather-bound copy of *America Shall Endure: A History of the United States*. I had just finished the chapter on very familiar-sounding tensions prior to World War I when someone dropped into the adjacent seat.

"Solved the mystery yet?" Andrew inquired.

In response, my stomach let out a loud and embarrassing groan.

"Why am I hungry? Don't I have some sort of nose tube feeding me back at home?"

"You do. You can think of this version of yourself as an instance—a copy made at the time of slicing. So your copy here needs to eat, sleep—all the bodily essentials. And I'm starving, too. Time to find lunch—and someplace to lay low."

"But I haven't learned anything interesting yet."

"Not to worry," Andrew replied. "Just tuck the book in your backpack and we'll be on our way."

"But I don't have a backpack..." I insisted.

Andrew nudged a greenish-gray canvas bag with his foot. My eyes grew wide, and I looked nervously around, but no other students were in sight.

"Come on. No time to waste!" He snatched the book, unfastened the pack, and shoved it inside.

"We're stealing a library book? Using someone else's stolen backpack?"

"You'd better get comfortable with justifiable appropriation," he suggested, rising and shouldering the pack. "In case you haven't noticed, we're hungry, improperly dressed, and eventually in need of a place to sleep. Unless you want to pass yourself off as a homeless Norwegian panhandler?"

"Not really," I sighed. "I suppose next you're going to tell me you're going to hot-wire a car?"

He shook his head. "Too risky—broad daylight, no tools... And you've seen the cars here. Not even close to what we'd find at home. It could take hours."

"I was kidding! Can we please just walk?"

We headed down Palm Drive under the sparse shade of familiar palm trees. Crossing busy El Camino Real was a snap; there was still an overpass, but instead of spanning six lanes of traffic, the artery was just a sleepy two-lane road. As we approached the lower end of downtown, I drew in a sharp breath. Despite the fact that it was lunchtime, the sidewalk wasn't completely overrun with people. Gone were the lines of traffic inching down the street searching for parking. Pedestrians strolled leisurely along the wide sidewalks, the men in linen suits in varying shades of grays and browns, the women in dresses or skirts. I noticed that all the women all wore thick headbands similar to the one worn by the librarian, all in different iridescent hues. Most men wore hats, but those who didn't also sported the same bands. Interesting style choice, I thought. Somewhere nearby, a restaurant was grilling some kind of meat. My stomach rumbled again.

"We're too obvious here," Andrew decided, grabbing my arm and making a sharp left on Emerson Street. The skin where his hand lay felt oddly warm and tingly, and I was relieved when he broke his grasp. I tried to shake off the sensation.

"We need to find a home that's unoccupied," Andrew suggested as we took a left turn on Everett. "It looks like today is trash pickup, so we'll look for a place without trash cans out front. No car in the driveway. Backed up mail or newspapers. Maybe even an unmowed lawn."

He scanned the homes with a critical and practiced eye. Tired and increasingly hungry, I trudged along in his wake.

The streets were quiet, without pedestrians and with only the occasional appearance of one of the gleaming futuristic cars. I followed Andrew as he meandered, turning corners and considering house after house. I noticed that all of the homes were topped with unfamiliar semi-glossy, purple-black roofing tiles. Solar? I wondered how that was economically feasible.

"This one," Andrew suddenly declared, cutting down a narrow driveway that flanked a modest sky-blue Queen Anne Victorian. I noticed four rolled newspapers in a messy pile on the front porch as we headed toward a tidy redwood gate. Andrew pulled the piece of twine dangling from the gate, and it unlatched easily. I followed him through and closed it quietly behind me. He extended his arm, and we both froze, but after a moment, he relaxed.

"No dog," he noted.

"No, but there is a cat." I pointed to a bored-looking furry orange face peering through a nearby window.

Andrew frowned. "Not ideal. There will be someone feeding it." He shrugged and advanced toward the back door.

It took Andrew and his Norwegian ID less than a minute to

defeat the lock on the door. Once inside, I looked about the sunny yellow kitchen. The apron sink and curved white lines of the fridge reminded me of pictures of my grandmother's childhood home from the forties. The fluffy orange cat jumped down from the window and began weaving around my legs and purring. I reached down to pet her, and she rubbed her face on my hand, gazing up at me with half-closed eyes.

"There's plenty of kibble in the cat's bowl," Andrew observed. "We have a little time." He strode to the fridge, pulled open its single large door, and began rummaging around.

"Orange juice," he reported, placing a glass bottle on the counter. It was quickly joined by a hunk of cheese and two rosy apples. My stomach growled again. I gave the cat a final pat and rummaged through the tidy white cabinets. I added a pair of juice glasses, a sleeve of crackers, and a can of tuna to the meager lunch stash.

Andrew sighed as he moved the items to a small white breakfast table near the sunny bay window. He shifted the canvas pack from his shoulder and placed it on the extra chair. "It's not exactly gourmet, but it'll do."

I was ravenous, and the tuna on crackers with cheese tasted fantastic. The cat hopped into my lap and meowed pleadingly, so I fed her a morsel of tuna. She butted her head against my chest and curled up on my lap in a renewed torrent of purrs. Andrew pulled the history book from the pack and began where I left off. In between bites, he turned pages quickly, and I watched his eyes dart about as he skimmed.

In no time the "lunch" was reduced to nothing more than crumbs. Andrew slapped the book shut, startling the cat. He shoved the book volume into the pack as he rose and started for the doorway toward the living room.

"Time to dress like a native," Andrew suggested. "You'll need several changes of clothes. Don't forget toiletries. And see if you can find any of those headbands we've seen everyone wearing."

I could hear him thudding up the stairs. I cleared away the crumbs and the empty containers and found my way to the second story. My new little feline friend followed at my heels.

The staircase, with its curving bannister and carved balustrades, led to a landing with a short hallway flanked by four doors. The one closest to me was a bathroom, old-fashioned with rose-pink tile work and a white pedestal sink. I darted inside and riffled through the shelves and cabinets, gathering items I'd need. At the end of the hall was a double-doored linen closet.

I peeked into the first of the bedroom doors and spied the open closet, unfamiliar clothes strewn on the bed, and Andrew, stripped down to his skivvies. I quickly averted my eyes and took a step back.

"I'll just check these other rooms," I called loudly, hurrying to the second room. It appeared to belong to a young boy who was really into model airplanes.

The third bedroom held more promise. The cat skidded in around the jamb and across the gleaming hardwood floor as I closed the door behind me. The room was tidy and neat, the twin bed dressed in a white eyelet coverlet.

On the white dresser sat a framed photo that showed a pretty girl of perhaps seventeen, sitting on a park bench and holding the hand of a young man. They sat far apart and seemed charmingly shy. I picked up the frame to examine her outfit more closely and was shocked that the perspective changed as I tilted it. I poked the surface of the image and realized that it wasn't paper after all, but its glossy surface was some kind of electronic film. I accidentally swiped my thumb across the bottom and the picture flipped to a close-up of the marmalade cat. I quickly restored the correct image and replaced the photo where I'd found it.

I dug guiltily through the girl's closet until I found the clothes that she was wearing in the photo: a knee-length rose-pink swing skirt with deep pleats and the cream-colored, short-sleeve button-up blouse with the Peter Pan collar. The skirt was a bit on the snug side, but I wiggled in as best as I could.

Embarrassment flushed my cheeks when the first drawer I opened revealed her unmentionables. A tidy bin on the far left contained neat rolls of stockings. I pulled out a pair and was taken aback at their decadent feel. I rubbed one against my cheek.

"What is this fabric? It's even smoother than silk," I murmured to the cat. He sat patently on the floor and watched me with interest. I pulled on the first stocking, past the hem of my skirt and up to my thigh, and then realized that there was no way it was going to stay there.

"You'll need a garter for that," Andrew suggested as he peered in through a four-inch gap in the door that I was certain I had not left ajar.

I nearly jumped out of my skin, belting out a shriek that sent the cat skittering under the bed. I clutched the remaining stocking uselessly to my chest. "Have you no boundaries? A little privacy, please!" I felt my cheeks go crimson. I wondered if his encyclopedic knowledge of obscure women's underwear had anything to do with his eidetic memory. He rolled his eyes but shut the door.

"Hurry up," was his muffled reply. "We can't stay here long."

I ditched the stockings and found a pair of cute brown leather pumps in Mystery Teen's closet that fit well enough. The shoes had a disconcerting heel but were nevertheless surprisingly comfortable. I found a container of hair elastics and wrapped my unruly tresses into a bun. I gathered several more skirts and blouses from the closet and folded them neatly into a pile.

Though I checked every nook and cranny of the room, I was unable to find the ubiquitous headband.

With a shrug, I bid the cowering cat farewell, rolled my old clothes into a ball, and tucked my supplies under my arm, leaving the room as tidy as I'd found it.

A neat pile of currency and a silvery key fob with an unfamiliar logo embossed into the metal rested on the kitchen table next to the backpack. With Andrew nowhere in sight, I decided to take a quick tour of the rest of the house.

The living room was more accurately a sitting room, as there was nothing resembling a television anywhere in sight. The fireplace looked classic Victorian—a tile face surrounded by rich, brown wood carved with floral panels and beadwork. I ran my finger along the heavy cast-iron fireplace doors. They were solid and cold to the touch. The furniture in the room was all art deco— smooth lines and trim brown leather.

Double pocket doors led from the main room into a library and study. Bookshelves lined all four walls and were packed with volumes. All the books were hardbound, which seemed unusual; there wasn't a paperback to be found in the entire room. I vaguely recalled a story my librarian great-aunt told about how paperbacks disrupted the publishing industry in the early 1940s with their low cost and lurid cover printing. Perhaps that never occurred here. I looked over the books and selected a few that looked interesting—one titled *Renewable* in bold green letters, one called *A Compendium of Aviation History*. I also grabbed *Defying Discovery: Milestones in Medicine*. A handsome desk sat in the center of the room. I ran my hand along its polished wood and noticed its smooth, uniform surface. No cables or keyboard trays were evident.

The only corner left unexplored was a small room off the kitchen. It contained a half bath and laundry. As far as I could tell, there wasn't a screen to be found in the entire place. No television, no computers, no tablet devices. Nothing.

The garage was cramped, and boxes were stacked high on shelves on each side, but I managed to squeeze in. I edged past the open vehicle door, which hinged at the back rather than at the front and gave the car the appearance of wings.

Andrew was rummaging around in the small, open hatch at the back of the compact vehicle. I chuckled at his olive-green trousers and ivory aloha shirt patterned in huge green monstera leaves accented with cheery pink hibiscus flowers. Definitely a new look.

He glanced my way with a raised eyebrow. "Decided against the garter?"

"Nice shirt. And quit trying to provoke me. What's the plan?"

Andrew glanced down at the shirt and frowned. "Definitely not my first choice."

He crammed another large, bulky sack into the already bulging cargo area of the car.

"We need someplace inconspicuous to lay low while we do some research. How do you feel about wide-open spaces, starlit skies, and the warm crackle of a fire?"

"It would be great if I were in the Girl Scouts…and I was nine."

He ignored my lack of enthusiasm.

"I'm finished here. Bring the items on the table from the kitchen. And while you're at it, you might as well gather your s'mores supplies," Andrew said, pressing the trunk down firmly and compressing the items within. "Because we are going camping."

We didn't need to have a conversation about which of us was going to drive. The notable thing about the car that we were about to appropriate is that it had no driver's side, because it had no steering wheel. We finally found this slice's technology, and it was on full display in the automotive sector.

I pulled the door closed behind me as I sank into the comfortable tawny leather seat. I fastened the safety belt and handed Andrew the key fob, which attached magnetically to a fob-shaped indentation in the center console. The vehicle's flat-screen display sprang to life. Andrew quickly swiped and tapped, moving through colorful menus.

I rubbed my fingers through the soft pleats of my skirt and kept my eyes trained out the window, in case the pet sitter appeared. My eyes grew wide as it occurred to me that a car this fancy might not be without security features. "Do you think this thing is going to call the cops on us?"

Andrew swiped through more menus. "Not if I can help it. I've been through all of the setting menus and have disabled every security feature I can find." At last, he leaned back into his own seat.

The car slowly but effortlessly navigated itself out of the garage and past the open gate, closing its own garage door. We paused at the end of the driveway, and then the car took a left. I glanced around nervously. I'll admit I was pretty freaked out to be riding in a fully autonomous automobile, but we were moving smoothly with traffic.

"Where are we going?" I asked.

"Ever been to Big Sur?"

"Starving student, remember? I don't go anywhere. What's Big Sur?" I asked, feeling my body tense as the car slowed at the stop sign, then made another left.

"It's the stretch of coastal California south of Carmel. Think seaside cliffs and misty coastline, It's wild, rugged, and even better—virtually unpopulated."

Andrew reached behind my seat and extracted a couple of books. He handed me the American history volume we'd stolen from the library while he cracked open *Renewable*. He nonchalantly flipped pages, ignoring the traffic as it zipped by.

I was unable to stop staring. Not a single passenger in any of the autos was actually driving their car. People napped, read, and held animated conversations. I blushed and turned away from a car containing a couple old enough to be my parents that were unabashedly making out.

"Shouldn't we be doing...something? Something to avert the storm?" I asked.

Andrew didn't bother to look up. "We are doing something. We are staying here unobtrusively so that maybe some of this reality's ecological goodness can leak into ours. This drive is going to take hours. In the meantime, make yourself useful. Read."

I opened *America Shall Endure,* thankful that I'd never suffered from carsickness.

"I should have expected this from a book called *Renewable,*" Andrew muttered.

"What did you find?"

Andrew began to read.

"'During the 1980s, the explosion in machine learning and quantum computing, which had first been discovered in the late fifties, allowed climate scientists to more accurately model and more fully appreciate the effect that rising levels of carbon dioxide would have on the planet. World leaders took the dire warnings of the climatologists seriously, and a plan was put in place to completely ban the burning of fossil fuels worldwide within twenty years.'"

"Oh, wow—they kicked oil almost twenty years ago." It was dizzying to consider. I couldn't quite fathom the tectonic shift in social and political forces that would make this possible.

Andrew's eyes continued to graze the page. "Going renewable meant advancements in fuel cells, solar paint, and electric cars. They even extract significant energy from wave action."

He closed the book and reached for another.

"Oh," I drew out the syllable as the lightbulb flashed over my head. "The pretty paint on all these cars? That must be solar, too." I tapped the car's console screen until I found a graph that showed energy consumption. Even though we'd been on the road for over an hour, the battery gauge still read full. Amazing.

"It's like we've stumbled onto an ecological nirvana," I marveled.

With renewed admiration for this imminently responsible society, I returned to the history book. As I read the first words of the new chapter, my eyes grew wide. I flipped the next page, then a second, and a third.

"You are going to want to hear this," I said. "'In March of 1945, a soldier injured during the successful campaign to retake the Philippine island of Luzon from Japan was transferred to the John Dibble General Hospital in Menlo Park, California. Major Theodore Wilkinson, US Sixth Army, sustained injuries that required the specialized services of reconstructive plastic surgery. Soon after his arrival, Maj. Wilkinson developed symptoms of influenza. Forty-eight hours after he was admitted to Dibble General Hospital, Major Theodore Wilkinson succumbed to progressive respiratory failure.

"'Twenty-four hours later, the first civilian patients were admitted to Palo Alto Hospital with symptoms of flu that had quickly progressed to acute pneumonia. The 'Luzon Flu' epidemic had begun.'"

Andrew rubbed his chin and stared for a moment. "We didn't have a major flu epidemic after World War II."

"Well, they did here. But there's more.

"'A review of the major's history indicated that he belonged to a unit that had encountered a massive die-off of wild ducks as they trudged through a wetlands swamp.

"'Medical professionals now believe that the Luzon Flu strain was a deadly variant of avian influenza that had undergone genetic mutation to become extremely easily transmissible among humans, a process known as antigenic drift. The virus strain was identified as the H5N1 flu virus. Subsequent study of the virus confirmed that its high mortality arises from the hyperproduction of proinflammatory cytokine, also known as 'cytokine storm.'"

Andrew's voice was grim. "They had an outbreak of human-transmissible bird flu."

I skimmed the text. "The outbreak was devastating. Sixty percent of those infected died. By the time the pandemic had extinguished itself in the summer of 1946, over a billion had perished worldwide."

"Well, that explains it," he said. "What if there was no postwar baby boom? No surge of enrollment at Stanford because the soldiers didn't come home—they just died. What if there was no Cold War? No arms race? And a global community of scientists working together instead of hundreds of nations competing? Just look at the technological progress they've made. It's madness. It's brilliant!"

"Here, Kathryn, set up this tent!" Andrew tossed a bulky silver bag from the cargo area of the car toward me. It landed at my feet in a puff of dust.

I sighed and gave the bag a halfhearted kick, surprised at how light it was. I ignored the pack and instead placed my hands on my hips and took in the view. Andrew had chosen well; the little campground was in the middle of nowhere. On a Tuesday night in September, the place was a ghost town, and we'd had our pick of the campsites. Andrew had selected a spot right along the cliff with panoramic views.

I took in the sweeping panorama of the wild coast from the top of the bluff where the campsite lay; nothing was visible for miles except more rocky cliffs meeting breaking waves and then endless, cerulean blue. I found a large, flat boulder and carefully sat, back straight, wind gently caressing my hair. Not a hint of smog marred the horizon. For a long time, I watched the undulating surface of the ocean rise and fall, each swell marking a rhythm, a beautiful visual representation of how meditation made me feel. I closed my eyes and focused my breath, taking pleasure in the cool sea air. With every minute that passed, I could feel the strain draining away; the disorienting stress of multiple far-slice travels began to fade. The retrograde anxiety caused by my newfound petty larceny hobby slowly unwound. The baffling rush of emotion I felt every time Andrew was near floated far from my consciousness. I brought my attention to the sounds, the sea birds and rough waves, and the unbroken whisper of the wind. I was fiercely drawn to this place.

My tranquil nirvana was rudely interrupted.

"Kathryn, can you *please* set up the tent?" Andrew called, still digging around in the trunk of the little vehicle.

I opened my eyes, rose slowly from my perch, and returned to the task. I shot a completely wasted withering glance toward Andrew's back and began foisting out folds of silvery fabric from the bag at my feet.

"I've never pitched a tent in my life," I grumbled. Because you don't really go camping when you awaken every soul around with panicked screams because you've had another nightmare.

As I spread the rustling silver mass, I realized that it was constructed with an intricate pattern of interlocking fabric triangles, and in the center of each was a flexible green insert that resembled a solar panel.

I stretched the tent out along the stubby grass of the campsite into a big, flat circle and shook out the bag. Five metal stakes and a compact, smooth black canister tumbled out, but no other parts or instructions were available.

"Um…" I shouted into the wind. "How do I make it go up?"

"You are a PhD student," Andrew retorted. "Figure it out."

I picked up the canister and examined it. It was the size and shape of an elongated soup can, with no writing of any kind. On the end of the device, I found a short, black, round coupler and a little square indentation. I walked carefully around the tent until I found a nearly hidden flexible plastic hose with a black electrical cable protruding from the back. I attached the hose to the canister, and the electric cable's square black clip fit exactly. Immediately the device began vibrating, and the tent began to rise.

"It's a pump!" I shouted excitedly.

The solar panels on the tent powered the pump, which inflated the entire structure in under a minute. When the pump automatically switched itself off, I was standing next to a fully inflated, seven-foot diameter silver geodesic dome covered in flexible triangular solar panels. The structure swayed a bit in the sea breeze, and I gave it a gentle shove, sure it would blow off across the campground like a giant futuristic tumbleweed, but it stayed put. Just to be completely certain we wouldn't be blown over the cliff in the middle of the night, I attached the stakes, stomping each into the ground.

I surveyed my work with a sense of satisfaction until I was unceremoniously hit square in the back by the flying sleeping bag that Andrew had launched from across the campsite. I turned around to object and just barely caught the second bag.

"The campground host mentioned there's a general store a couple of miles down the road," Andrew called from the back of the car.

Beside him stood an enormous pile of camping gear; I had no idea how he'd managed to fit it all in the little auto.

"Set up or stow the rest, and I'll see if I can find something palatable for dinner. If you see anything that has solar panels on it, make sure to set it out in the sun. And don't go anywhere." Andrew eyed me warily. "I chose the most isolated site possible, so I don't think you'll have any visitors, but be extremely careful until I get back."

Andrew climbed into the car, and it glided silently away down the dirt road. I surveyed the giant pile of gear; with a shrug and a sigh, I began shifting boxes and duffels toward the picnic table.

CHAPTER 22

KATE

September 28

Andrew had returned, bearing groceries. I unfolded from a half-lotus position and stretched, rising slowly and reincorporating myself gingerly back into the world after emerging from deep, tranquil meditation.

"Nine hours," I said, gazing at the sun as it slowly sank toward the horizon where sea met sky. "That's how long we've been gone. I wonder if Ophelia has dissipated yet?"

"We occupied the slice that spawned the storm for well over two days," Andrew replied. "If we want to effect change at home, we should stay as long as possible."

"So, we're just camping out?"

"Yes, we are. And even people who are camping out to save the world need to eat." He rolled up his sleeves. "A little known but important rule of a successful camping trip is to serve at least one truly spectacular dinner," he pronounced.

Andrew extracted a paper-wrapped package, a small block of butter, and a cardboard container of mushrooms. A neon orange silicone tube on the picnic table cleverly unrolled into a two-foot-wide mat topped with a flexible metal disc. The whole contraption was attached to a small box topped with a solar panel.

"What is that thing?" I asked.

"With any luck, it's the camp stove of the future."

Andrew placed a fry pan on the burner and dropped a chunk of butter inside. It began to melt, then sizzle.

He unwrapped the contents of the white paper package and placed two plump, seasoned strip steaks on the griddle. In went the mushrooms and a handful of fresh thyme.

While he cooked, I tossed a bundle of baby arugula and some cherry tomatoes with pine nuts, balsamic vinegar, and olive oil. Andrew transferred the steaks and mushrooms to a pair of blue enamel plates and deglazed the pan with red wine. He drizzled the resulting sauce over the beef, which steamed in the rapidly cooling night air.

I sat at the table in the waning daylight and attacked the meal with the eagerness of a rabid carnivore. The first bite of steak melted in my mouth. The mushrooms were full of earthy flavor, and the sauce was divine. I let out an involuntary groan and quickly scarfed another bite.

"Calm down there," Andrew said, laughing.

"Who knew steak could taste like this?" I mumbled through a mouthful, forgetting all my manners. Did this slice produce the most delicious beef in the known universe? Or was it simply eating outdoors after an exhausting day? In any case, my mother would be appalled with my manners. Unless she tasted this steak.

Andrew added salad to his plate and sipped wine from a tin cup. "Spectacular meal—check."

The meal was finished and the dishes washed; the long, arduous day was growing to a close. As the last vestige of twilight slipped from view, a warm yellow light automatically illuminated the tent, turning it into a cozy beacon. Andrew yawned, and I immediately followed suit. The adrenaline that had powered me through lack of sleep and multiple far-slices had long since drained away, and I was exhausted.

"Tomorrow we'll do more research, but for now, I suggest we get some rest," he said, unfastening the tent's flap and motioning for me to join him inside. After a moment of hesitation, I climbed in and secured the opening behind me.

I surveyed the interior of the tent, which suddenly seemed very small—and intimate. "And our sleeping arrangements are?"

"The sleeping bags are a matching pair, so take your pick."

He unfastened a clasp on the first bag and shook it out, then reached for the second bag and efficiently expanded it as well. The gray fabric crinkled, and the mummy-shaped bags seemed to puff up to an impossibly high loft.

"So we're *both* going to sleep in here?" I asked. My palms felt inexplicably clammy.

"Unless you're planning on sleeping under the stars."

He sat down on the far sleeping bag and pulled off his shoes and socks. I calculated how uncomfortable I'd be if I tried to sleep sitting upright in the autonomous car.

Andrew unbuttoned his shirt and pulled it off, folding it carefully.

"Um, should I step out, or...?" I asked, pointedly examining the underside of the solar panels on the tent's far walls.

"That's not necessary," Andrew replied as he stood up and unzipped his trousers.

"Oh, maybe it is!" I replied uneasily. I fumbled with the zipper of the tent's flap and darted outside.

"Kathryn, come back inside the tent. You're being ridiculous."

"I just need to know, are you completely naked?" I asked apprehensively, my back to the tent.

His exasperated sigh was followed by the sound of a long zip, a pause, and another zip. I was still considering my options when something flapped past my left shoulder. Something birdlike. Then I remembered that birds don't fly at night.

I gritted my teeth. "Oh, it's a bat, I really *hate* bats..." I complained as I fumbled with the tent flap. A second creature hurtled through the air above my head. I glanced nervously over my shoulder as I ducked back inside the tent.

Andrew shifted within the snug confines of his sleeping bag. "A bat," he mumbled.

I rubbed my arms, not completely sure if the goose bumps were a product of the cold night air or my encounter with flying mammals.

I looked from the occupied sleeping bag back to the door of the tent one last time, then realized I had no other option. I slipped off my borrowed leather shoes, unzipped the second sleeping bag, and began to climb in.

"You can't wear your clothes to bed, Kathryn." The tone he used made me feel like an idiot. "These clothes are natural fibers. You'll be a wrinkled mess tomorrow. You'll look like you're homeless."

I was, in fact, homeless at the moment, but he was right...and the point was to blend in. I remembered my street clothes, wadded up in a ball and stuffed somewhere in the back of the car.

"I can sleep in my old clothes." I climbed out of the bag.

"You could..."

Then I remembered the bats and hesitated.

"I don't suppose *you* want to go get them for me?" I asked sheepishly.

"Not especially."

I weighed the options, then sighed.

"Could you at least give me some privacy?"

I was certain I caught the faint tug of a smile at the corner of his eyes as he rolled over to face the tent wall.

As quickly as humanly possible, I slid out of my skirt and pulled off the blouse. I folded both and dived into the sleeping bag, which was surprisingly warm and soft. I snuggled in up to my eyeballs.

With a soft click, the lights were extinguished, and the tent was plunged into darkness. As my eyes tried to adjust, I became hyperaware of the sounds of nature on the other side of the thin fabric—the waves crashing far below, and the sound of the wind in the leaves of the scrubby trees nearby.

Andrew yawned. "Well, day one is under the hood. Forty hours left to go. Good night, Kathryn," he said pleasantly. Did he actually consider me a worthy travel companion? Or maybe it was just blatant exhaustion.

"Good night," I replied, cuddling even farther into the silky fabric. Forty hours left to go.

Within minutes, his breathing became rhythmic and deep.

So much for "no rest for the wicked," I thought.

I lay as still as possible, but sleep wouldn't come. I told myself it was the unfamiliar feel of the ground beneath me. I told myself it was the flapping of tiny wings above the tent. Anything to avoid thinking about the disarmingly attractive man sleeping just two feet away from me. When I closed my eyes and took a deep breath, I was overcome by his scent.

I tried to clear my thoughts, focusing instead on the sensation of my breath, irritated by how uneasy his very presence left me. I had a feeling it was going to be a long, long night.

I open my eyes, and I can't place where I am. It is late; a sliver of a crescent moon hangs high in the sky. And the sound of water. The place feels so familiar. I look around and blink again; I'm startled when I realize that I am back in the courtyard of the Kate whose dreams are a gift. It is reassuring to know I'm someplace safe. I find one of the comfortable teak benches that line her courtyard and sit. I breathe the night air, cool but not cold. I listen to the fountain burbling.

When the arched door leading out of the courtyard opens, I expect the other Kate, but instead it's Andrew, a mug in each hand.

"This is for you," he says as he hands a steaming beverage to me. "She says you're fond of mint tea."

"Thanks," I say, accepting the mug and taking a sip. The tea is hot, barely drinkable, but the clean, fresh scent of mint calms me. It strikes me as odd that that this feels...normal. I wrap my hands around the circumference of the earthenware mug. It is also warm and comforting. He stands, awkwardly. I've never seen him show anything other than complete confidence and composure. This air of uncertainty—it's new, and it's slightly unnerving.

"She said I should come. May I sit?"

I gesture to the end of the bench.

I sip more tea. When I close my eyes, I'm enveloped by the song of crickets chirping and the breeze in the crowns of the towering palm trees. It sounds like home.

"How does she know I'm here? Why did she send you?" I am surprised that I am brave enough to ask.

"I don't know how she knows," he confesses. "She's really...tuned in to the universe, I guess. Or maybe she's just tuned into you. She seemed convinced that talking to me would help you. To be honest, I'm not exactly sure how. She thought it was important. To move you along your journey. On your path."

"It's remarkable that we can have this conversation," I observe, gazing at the night sky. "I was always just a witness to the things I saw in my dreams. I was never a participant."

"You're like her, Kathryn, yet so different. You seem lost. You are capable of far more than you think."

He sounds remarkably sincere. For Andrew. I let that sink in.

"You know, where I come from...you're kind of an ass," I say suddenly.

"You...she...tells me that all the time."

I look up and catch his eye. A wry smile spreads across his face, and he does not look away. There is a measure of humbleness, of vulnerability, of safety that I have never perceived in the Andrew of my reality.

Something about the openness in his gaze offers me clarity, and boldness. "What is it?" I ask. "What is it that brought you together? What binds you to her?"

"I love her. With every molecule of my being," he replies, as if this is simplicity itself.

I sat up sharply and gasped for breath. My heart was pounding, and the sleeping bag fell away from my shoulders, leaving my skin exposed to the chill of the fall coastal air. The temperature had dropped considerably, and I immediately felt the crawl of goose bumps across my arms and up my back. My teeth started chattering, and I quickly pulled up the sleeping bag. I braced myself, waiting for the inevitable echoed physical manifestation of my dream. Waiting for the inevitable migraine. Minutes passed, but neither materialized.

Andrew slept on, completely oblivious to my dreaming or my alarming waking. As quietly as I could, I lowered myself onto the tent floor. I tried in vain to settle back into sleep, but I couldn't shake the sudden feeling of abject and forlorn isolation that descended upon me.

After many miserable minutes, I quietly inched my shrouded feet toward my companion until my sleeping bag made the slightest contact with his. An almost disturbing feeling of relief washed over me, and I was suddenly so very, very tired. With a sigh, I closed my eyes and finally sank into a deep, dreamless slumber.

CHAPTER 23

KATE

September 29

I awoke to the sound of sizzling. Then I smelled it—bacon.

A quick glance confirmed that Andrew had somehow managed to dress and slip out without waking me. I pulled on my skirt and blouse, then unzipped the tent. I stepped outside to a morning that was clear and calm—and fifty degrees. I couldn't help but shiver.

"Grab a jacket from the car," Andrew instructed from his post at the picnic table.

I scurried to the car and dug around the cargo area until I found a warm, cinnamon-colored jacket made of fine, thick wool and buttoned myself into it.

"Coffee?" Andrew asked as I stomped my feet to warm my chilly legs. Damn this reality's insistence on skirts for women! He pointed to an enamel carafe.

"Yes, please," I replied through chattering teeth.

The coffee warmed me from the inside, and the bacon and eggs were hearty and delicious. As the sun ascended over the hills in the east, the temperature began to rise, and I finally stopped shivering.

Andrew dropped *Defying Discovery: Milestones in Medicine* on the table before me. "Time to hit the books."

I drained the last of my coffee and pulled the volume closer. "Sure thing, boss." I found his dog-eared page and started reading.

It was nearly lunchtime before I finally found something interesting.

"Andrew," I asked, eyes still scanning the text. "When were superconducting quantum interference devices invented?"

He looked up and to the left for a second. "SQUIDs? 1964. Why?"

"This book says that a SQUID based on superconducting loops created a sufficiently sensitive magnetometer for MEG to become a viable mechanism to study brain function in the seventies."

He stared at me blankly. "Meg?"

"No, magnetoencephalography. It's a very sensitive brain imaging technique that has only become common in the last several years."

That piqued his interest. Andrew closed his book and rested both elbows on the picnic table. "What else does it say?"

"'Concurrent developments in the rapidly growing field of theoretical computer science in the late 1950s and early 1960s brought the introduction and rapid rise of machine learning—'"

"Deep learning didn't take off until around 2010," he interrupted, rubbing his chin thoughtfully. "But here, machine learning and AI have been on the rise a full fifty years earlier than in our slice?"

I nodded. "And get this—'The development of detection methods for studying the brain coincided with the swift advance of machine learning over the next two decades in a perfect storm of scientific synchronicity. By the late 1980s, researchers were first able to reliably decode signals from the brain.'"

Andrew moved to my side of the picnic table, sitting so close that our elbows touched. I slid the book over.

He continued reading aloud. "'By 1992, the content of a subject's visual thoughts and even dreams could be reliably decoded, saved, and examined. Concurrent studies in reading and written language processing centers resulted in the ability to map the brain's use of text.'"

My mind was flying now, imagining the possibilities. "They can literally read your mind," I gasped. "Their understanding of brain function is light-years ahead of ours."

"That's not all," Andrew added. "Since they can both read and transmit, that means they can also formulate signals that can communicate directly to the brain as well."

I pictured grotesque photos I'd seen where researchers inserted wires directly into the brains of cats. I cringed at the thought. "But how?"

Andrew read further: "'All that changed in 2005 with two startling developments: compact, noncryogenic atomic magnetometers and the advanced photoacoustic imaging of the brain using nanoprobes, pulsed laser, and ultrasound wave detection. These advances made possible a device which could be worn anywhere and was capable of detecting and transmitting a wide range of neurological signals.

"'The device was christened NeuroCereLink Notus. Combined with a neural network housed within a micro-quantum computing device, it became possible to understand and visualize anyone's cognitive state, and also to wirelessly send signals that could induce visual, auditory, and text-based sensations directly in the wearer's brain. With these tools in place, CereLink became the de-facto bridge to networked computing devices worldwide.'"

My palm smacked my forehead as it all fell into place. I turned to Andrew and caught the full force of his intense stare. "Holy hell, the headbands are the CereLink!"

He nodded, and a canny grin spread across his face. "People here don't have computer terminals or computers or mobile phones because they don't need any of those clumsy devices. They just think—their web searches, their messages, even voice-based communication. They just think about what they want to know, and the answer is right there, right inside their head."

"We need to figure out how they're doing it," I insisted. My head spun as I imagined what I could learn about my nightmares if I completely understood every system, every synaptic pathway; it would completely unlock the totality of the neurological workings of my brain.

The gleam in his eye was impossible to miss. "Agreed. The library at UC Berkeley is the perfect place to start."

I spent the first two hours of our trip to Berkeley gawking at the insanely beautiful coastal views. I silently vowed to devote a decent chunk of my next Albaion paycheck to bringing Michelle to this lovely place. When we reached Monterey, we turned inland, and I finally acquiesced to Andrew's insistence that I finish reading *Defying Discovery: Milestones in Medicine*. By the time we reached the university, I was nearly jumping out of my skin in anticipation.

The UC Berkeley campus was vast and bustling. The car circled for fifteen minutes in underground parking before inserting itself into an available space. Based purely on the popularity of its facilities, it would appear that Cal was definitely still among the most elite universities in the world and just as much a powerhouse research institution in this reality as it was in ours.

"Why are we researching this thing instead of, you know, justifiable appropriation?" I asked as we approached the broad, white steps of an enormous, blindingly white neoclassical building.

"It's not just the CereLink. It's the nanoprobes. You need the whole system, and we have no idea how it works, what the risks are, or even how to acquire the probes."

The sweet, musky smell of books hit me the moment we passed through the entry of Doe Library. My footfalls echoed as I struggled to keep up with Andrew.

"How are we going to get what we need?" I whispered.

"The old-fashioned way."

After hours of poring through periodical indexes, we'd found several detailed papers that discussed the inner workings of the strange headbandlike device named CereLink, and another three that discussed the nanoprobes that were required inside the body in order to make the system function.

It was taking me forever to get through just one paper outlining how text is processed in the brain, and how this decoding could be interpreted by the device. I couldn't even comprehend half of it—but I understood enough. Enough, I hoped, to be able to replicate the results myself.

"Fascinating," Andrew murmured as he turned page after page of dense scientific literature.

"Maybe we can figure out some way to try it. Would it work on us, you think?" I scratched my head and wondered if wearing the device was at all uncomfortable.

"It might work...while we're here. But what we really need is to have it work back there."

"At home?" My brows furrowed. "How is that possible?"

"You already know the answer," he replied, eyes intent on the texts.

"Oh, yeah, right. Your wacky-ass memory. You mean you can actually remember all of this? Is it really like a photocopy in your brain?"

He closed one periodical and pulled another journal toward

him. "That's why they call it a photographic memory. Though there's a limit to how much I can recall, and the finer details tend to fade after a while. It's been a very useful gift in my line of work."

I frowned. "Is this the reason you're slice traveling at all? You put me in mortal danger—just so you can steal technology?"

"Keep your voice down," Andrew insisted, breaking his concentration to glance around.

No one was looking, but I found I didn't care if they were.

"Is this how Andric Breckinridge makes all his money?" I didn't even bother to temper the accusation. My chair scraped the hardwood floor loudly as I stood.

Andrew stood and clasped both my arms. "Kathryn," he said calmly. "Please sit down and let me finish this last paper. It won't take long, and I'll explain everything, I promise. Remember, this is not just about Albaion. It's also about you."

I *did* remember that it was also about me. The technology behind CereLink was so far advanced from the imaging, decoding, and encoding technologies that were available to me. And I wanted them, too. I sat in my chair, arms crossed, angry with Andrew for deceiving me but also knowing that I was complicit in his crime. If it even was a crime.

I closed my eyes and tried to focus on my breath. Minutes passed. I spent more time seething than achieving enlightenment.

"Okay, let's go," he whispered, breaking my focus.

I tossed him a dark scowl.

We left the library, but he didn't offer the promised explanation, and I was still too furious to initiate the conversation. We were deep in the maze of underground parking, within spitting distance of the car when I noticed two women approach the vehicle. They wore the ever-present iridescent bands, but they were also wearing navy-blue uniforms. Uniforms with badges.

"Looks like our unwitting hosts have noticed that we borrowed their vehicle," Andrew said, frowning. His face was a mask of pure composure—no indication at all that he was on the run.

"Turn left," he said, intentionally looking away from the parking spot. "And don't look back."

My heart beat faster as I skittered away from the little car. I did my best to suppress my rising panic as I followed his directions, but in the end, I looked back. "I think they're onto us. They're coming this way." My throat constricted. What would they do if the caught us? Would we be thrown in jail? And if they separated us—there would be no way I could extract Andrew from the slice.

Andrew grabbed my hand, and we darted erratically through rows of parked vehicles. Moving faster now, he ducked behind concrete pylons. Over my shoulder, I could see that the policewomen had separated, and while we'd eluded one, the other still had us squarely in her sights.

"She's still following us..." I panted. Thank goodness for the sensible nature of my borrowed shoes.

He nearly yanked my arm from its socket as he darted through a heavy steel door.

"Quickly, down a floor," he instructed, taking the stairs two at a time. He moved with the cadence of a trained athlete. I stumbled behind, trying to keep up.

At the next landing, he shoved open the door and wove through several more rows of cars before he stopped abruptly and tugged me toward a support column. He dropped to his knees and pulled me down with him.

"Why did we go downstairs?" I hissed, swallowing hard. My heart was beating so rapidly that it was making my ears ring. "We need to get out of here!"

He moved his hand over my mouth and shook his head.

I tried to calm my ragged breathing as I listened for the inevitable clang of the steel door. To my profound relief, it never came.

After five unbearably long minutes of waiting, he gestured for me to stand. Incredibly, he was just as poised as ever. I pulled back loose strands of hair with trembling fingers and tried to match his level of self-composure.

We walked the length of the garage calmly, until we reached the access stairs farthest from where we'd parked the car. Three flights up, we burst into the light of day, surrounded by disinterested students but blessedly free of police presence.

We'd narrowly evaded the authorities, but all our supplies had been in the car. There were no extra clothes, no sleeping bags, no books—nothing.

We'd walked over a half mile before my adrenaline tapered off, and then I remembered that I was still infuriated with him. As we approached the edge of campus, Andrew veered abruptly from the sidewalk onto a path that led through a grove of towering eucalyptus trees. As we moved deeper into the park, the sound of traffic died away, and I was enveloped by the fragrance of peppermint and pine and honey. We passed a few students as they hurried by. A bridge traversed a peaceful trickling creek, and as soon as we crossed, Andrew abandoned the path. Late afternoon light sent golden rays dancing through the urban forest, casting long shadows. Great strips of bark peeled from the enormous trunks and littered the forest floor. My shoes crunched over dried bark and leaves, releasing tiny bursts of pungent minty scent.

Andrew stopped abruptly, and I nearly plowed into him.

"Are you ever going to answer my question?" I asked. The fire of my anger had cooled to a dull exasperation.

He turned and fixed those alarmingly blue eyes on me.

"I am in the business of solving problems," he said.

"Which problems, exactly?" I glared at him. "What does that even mean?"

"Of course our stay here was meant to avert a climate crisis.

But we got lucky—we got so much more. If we bring back the knowledge to build that device, along with the understanding of the nanoprobes that allow it to work, we'll blow the doors open on brain imaging research for years to come. Not to mention revolutionizing consumer computing. If we can understand and reproduce the decoding and encoding algorithms that make translation of brain signals possible, then we can leapfrog our current technology by forty or fifty years. Maybe more. And that iridescent solar material that's so ubiquitous here? That solar tech by itself could change how we power our world."

"Yes, I can see how *all* of that will be excellent for Albaion's bottom line," I replied curtly, unable to suppress the cynicism.

"You're right. Investors have short memories and little faith. Albaion is, after all, a public company, and innovation like this could catapult us into the stratosphere."

"So it's all about the money," I said bitterly, looking away.

"It's not all about the money," he insisted. "It's about the science."

He reached out and took my hand, which startled me. My indignation began melting away, and I felt butterflies in the pit of my stomach. I hated how easily he could placate me.

Andrew spoke fervently. "It's about giving you the tools you need to understand your dreams and what they mean. It's about finding tools and technologies to make our world a cleaner, safer, more peaceful place. And it's about understanding how our reality and the multiverse coexist and intersect."

He seemed so sincere. And he was holding my hand. Was he playing me? If he was, it was incredibly hard to resist playing along. What Andrew was doing—what Albaion was doing—felt wrong. But he was right about one thing. I wanted the brain scanning and decoding technology just as much as he did.

I sighed. "You have some big aspirations, Dr. Crackpot Visionary."

I'd never been to Berkeley; its world-class university nestled at the edge of a thriving city was completely new to me. I was unprepared for the sudden transition back to civilization—as soon as we stepped out of the eucalyptus grove, we were plunged immediately into downtown's wide, busy streets.

We had traveled just two blocks when I spotted another uniformed officer advancing down the street on foot. Wordlessly, I grasped Andrew's arm, and he nodded, immediately ducking into the nearest doorway. Landscaped topiary bushes in pots flanked the entrance. We passed through the heavy glass doors below the arched entry into an elegant lobby of the Hotel Peralta.

A dramatic golden chandelier sparkled above, casting a warm glow on the marble floor and ebony pillars of the imposing space. The fine antique table standing in the center of the room supported a three-foot high floral arrangement. Enormous potted palms and other tropical greenery were clustered throughout the expanse.

I kept my eyes trained on the door, certain the officer would follow us in. A minute passed but no law enforcement appeared.

I realized I was still clutching Andrew's arm, and I quickly released my grip, staring strategically at my shoes.

Andrew cleared his throat. "We need a place to stay the night, and a meal would be stellar."

"Can we afford this?" I asked nervously, eyes flicking upward to the chandelier.

"We'll be fine."

"Sleeping in an actual bed *does* sound pretty appealing," I conceded. "How much money did you…borrow?"

"I cleaned out the earthquake survival kit. Our hosts are great planners. They were very well prepared."

"Not anymore," I mumbled.

I waited in an uncomfortably high-backed black leather chair tucked behind the flora while Andrew approached the front desk. He talked to the receptionist for a long time. I noticed that she gave Andrew a sly smile, and she lingered rather longer than necessary as she carefully placed a room key in his hand.

"Only one room left at the inn," he announced, dangling a large brass key. He must have noticed my pained expression. "Don't worry. Two beds."

"Can we just get out of here?" I asked, scanning the lobby for the umpteenth time. "What if the authorities show up?"

"Worrywart," he chided as he advanced toward the elevators.

We rode to the fifth floor and trudged down an empty hallway for what seemed like a mile. Apparently our room was in Timbuktu.

The room was easily three times the size of my bedroom in our dinky apartment and contained the promised two double beds, each topped with a smooth, white cotton coverlet, aligned with geometric precision. The stack of luxurious plush pillows was a welcome sight. Two leather-upholstered chairs with curved backs finished in the same glossy mahogany wood as the headboards flanked a small mahogany table. A large painting of calla lilies, almost luminous in its vibrant use of colors, graced the wall. A cursory glance revealed no television and no telephone anywhere in the room.

It felt immensely strange to have nothing to set down or put away. I sat in one of the curved leather chairs and picked at the cuticle on my thumb. Somehow sharing this room with Andrew felt even more intimate than the close quarters of the tent. Despite my almost visceral longing to lay my head on the cloud of pillows, I was dreading bedtime.

"Do you think it's safe to go home yet?"

Andrew shook his head. "We should stay the duration. We'll exit tomorrow evening." Twenty-four hours left. Then I'd have to... I forced myself not to think about that.

"What do we do for the next twenty-four hours?" I asked, kicking off my shoes and digging my toes into the high loft of the cream-and-coffee patterned rug.

"Room service is on its way. I asked for something quick; she promised sandwiches." Andrew kicked off his loafers and settled back on the bed nearest to me, leaving me perched awkwardly on my chair. "But we're only here until morning. After tonight, we're cleaned out of cash."

"So, we do...what? More breaking and entering? For all we know, we're wanted fugitives."

Andrew rubbed his eyes, the first sign of fatigue I'd noticed. His response was terse. "Don't worry, Kathryn, I'll take care of it."

"Sorry," I mumbled, shrinking into my chair.

He opened his eyes and turned to me, silent for a long minute. I felt myself shrivel even farther under his intense gaze.

"No, I'm sorry," he sighed, sitting up on the edge of the bed facing me. "I didn't mean to be short with you."

I shrugged as if it was no big deal. "I'm exhausted, too."

He sat forward, placing his elbows on his knees and resting his chin on his hands, which brought him still closer to me.

"I asked the receptionist to locate my mother. Unfortunately, just like in every other reality, she's still...gone."

He looked so defeated—and vulnerable. "I'm really sorry," I offered, knowing that this tired phrase never offered any consolation. I was racking my brain to come up with a sensitive reply—how does one conversationally ask the boss about his deceased mother while traipsing about in alternate realities? The etiquette was far from clear. I looked away and tried to think of a useful segue to a less awkward topic.

The knock on the door saved me, but it also caused an instant transformation, like a switch had been thrown in his head. Andrew sprang from the bed and shed his melancholy as if it were a worn sweater. He exchanged light and pleasant banter with the staff, received the tray, and tipped generously.

Andrew uncovered the plates. "Ham and Gruyère panini or prosciutto and artichoke?"

"Gruyère? Sounds fancy."

Andrew looked at me like I was a total cretin. "Swiss cheese."

I reached for the plate. "Hook me up."

Our exile inside the hotel had one upside—it left me plenty of time to meditate. I settled myself onto the thick plush carpet and stretched my stiff legs into a half-lotus, modestly tucking my skirt over my knees.

"Why don't you teach me?" Andrew suggested, dropping to the floor.

"What? How to sit in half-lotus?"

His attempt to draw his feet into his lap was tragically comical.

"No, Kathryn, teach me how to meditate."

I shot him a keen stare; was he mocking my practice? He seemed to sense my reluctance.

"No, really, I mean it. Enlighten me."

"You know that's not how it works, right?"

He cringed as he yanked his foot in a desperate attempt to contort his body into the shape I found so comforting.

"Just stop it right now. Watching you do that is hurting me." I laughed. "Sit comfortably. Take a deep breath."

He rearranged himself and inhaled—held his breath—exhaled.

"Now just breathe normally. And instead of thinking, let your monkey brain settle. Focus all of your concentration on the sensation of your breath—at your nostrils. In your chest. Feel your belly as it rises and falls. And then when you get distracted, do it all over again."

"That's it?" he scoffed.

"It's not as easy as it sounds," I warned him, closing my eyes and relaxing, sinking, feeling my connection to the carpet, to the earth.

"Piece of cake," he mumbled.

I shook my head. Piece of cake, indeed.

CHAPTER 24

KATE

September 30

I kneel on the edge of a wooden platform, splinters digging into my bare knees. Six feet below the platform looms a steel cargo bin, its walls rusted and pockmarked. The pit is easily eight feet wide and fifteen feet long, and it's filled with a jumble of old clothes. As my eyes adjust in the dim light thrown by a nearby flaming torch, I gasp. Among the discarded clothing is a foot. A human foot. Then I see a hand. A forearm. This is not a pile of clothing. It's a pile of bodies.

I gasp and try to stand; my wrists are bound behind me, and the instant I begin to rise, rough hands force me back to the ground. My head pitches forward; I'm in danger of falling into the pit. I regain my balance just in time.

I am at the end of a row of six women, in torn clothing, their hair ragged. The woman beside me weeps silently; I see the stream of tears carving a pathway through the grime on her cheeks. Her face may once have been pretty, but now it is dangerously thin; deep hollows carved below her cheekbones. Her brown eyes are lifeless and sunken. She shivers in the darkness, and I do, too. All of the women are underdressed. It's cold out here, in the night.

I swivel my head, and for the first time, I see them: men in olive-drab trench coats with matching insignia are holding guns. The soldier at the end of the row raises a rifle and aims it at the woman farthest from me. There is a sharp click as he chambers his round, and he takes aim, though there is no chance he will miss at this range. A moment later, the firearm discharges, a deafening roar that echoes through the night. The reverberation of that shot seems like it might never end. My ears begin to ring, a sharp note that permeates my brain. The smell of the gunpowder is acrid and sour. The woman hovers for a moment, then pitches forward onto the top of the heap.

My shoulders clench and I begin to tremble. The guard behind me senses my terror and shoves his foot against my back to hold me in place. My stomach contracts and I swallow hard to keep from retching.

The soldier with the gun moves efficiently down the line, executing each woman with clockwork precision. Click. Pause. Fire. Click. Pause. Fire. When he reaches the woman beside me, she releases an animal keen and, with more speed than I expect, rises to her feet. Before she can turn to face her executioner, she is dead. She falls to the heap below with a thud, and a rank and pungent smell rises from the pile—putrid and with a tinge of sickening sweetness.

I am hyperventilating now, knowing that the soldier stands behind me. I hear the click as the round is chambered, and my psyche cracks wide open. My vision narrows to a tiny point of light. I hear myself release a shrill and earsplitting scream.

"Kathryn, wake up!" he insisted. He held me as I doubled over, my throat raw. I took a ragged, gasping breath; the stink of death still filled my lungs. And then suddenly I was hit full-force with the comforting scent of fresh laundered linen, and of him. My body trembled and my stomach lurched dangerously. The room was completely dark, and for a moment, I couldn't remember where I was.

The room's heating unit clicked, and I flinched and began to tremble. I could feel the press of the rifle at the back of my head. That smell coming off the gun—sulfur with a hint of ammonia— burned my nostrils and my throat constricted.

"Please don't shoot me," I whimpered, tears streaming down my face. "I don't want to die."

Strong arms wrapped around my quaking shoulders, and the sensation of cold metal on flesh evaporated.

"Andrew?" I whispered hoarsely.

"You were screaming," he murmured, smoothing my hair. "And you're hyperventilating. Breathe slowly, from your diaphragm." He cradled my head against his shoulder. I could hear the pounding of his heart in his chest and feel the warmth of his skin. "What happened?"

In a moment, I was instantly jolted to full awareness. I had gone to bed in my underwear to preserve my single wearable set of clothing, and apparently, he had made the same choice. I pulled away, forcing my breath to calm.

"I'm sorry," I stuttered, wiping tears from my cheeks. "It doesn't matter what happened. It's just a nightmare. For me, at least. Someone else's atrocious reality. It's over now."

"My God, Kathryn," he whispered, his hand resting lightly on my shoulder. "I had no idea."

"The meditation should have prevented this. It must be the stress..." My body had gone cold under a thin sheen of sweat, but the skin beneath his hand was on fire. I said a silent prayer of thanks for the darkness. At least he couldn't see the mad flush of my cheeks.

"I'm fine," I insisted, rubbing my temples.

"You're not fine. I think you're suffering from PTSD."

I shifted a hand to the base of my skull and pushed, hard. Despite the darkness, the aura was already faintly visible in my peripheral vision.

"You're about to get an enormous migraine, aren't you?"

"I'll be fine," I reiterated.

His voice was low and measured. "We don't have access to any meds, but there is evidence that therapeutic massage can prevent migraines."

"No, thanks," I replied miserably, pulling the sheets tighter around my shivering body.

"Oh, for God's sake," he muttered, moving closer. "Don't be a baby. I'm a physician, remember?"

I could feel his warm hand as it pressed on my left shoulder. He began kneading the muscle. It was excruciating.

"Ouch!" I whined.

"Sorry," he muttered, decreasing the pressure. He worked the muscle slowly, gently increasing the pressure, until I felt the tension begin to release. Incredibly, the aura began to fade.

"I'm moving to your right shoulder," he announced. He ran his hands lightly over my shoulders, then I felt a distinct pop as my bra was unfastened.

"Hey!" I objected as he brushed the straps from my shoulders. I instinctively clutched the garment to my chest. "What do you think you're doing?"

"Haven't you ever had a massage before? It doesn't work through elastic."

He rested his hands on my shoulders and began to dig in. The pain was nearly unbearable. But then I was faced with a new distraction—I was exquisitely aware that for all practical purposes, I was nearly naked in bed with a man who was also nearly naked. Massaging me. I struggled to banish the thought from my mind.

"Relax!" he demanded.

"Be nice," I winced.

"Nice won't prevent your migraine."

I tried to soften my shoulders as he pressed his forearm along the muscle covering my shoulder blade. I hung my head forward, closed my eyes, and took deep, calming breaths. Then he hit a knot near the edge of my right shoulder blade that caused an audible crunch in my muscle and an explosion of white stars behind my eyelids. For a moment, the pain was piercing, but then it passed. Inexplicably, I found new tears streaming down my cheeks.

"Kathryn, are you okay?" he asked, continuing to probe the spot.

I felt the tension in my shoulder dissipate, only to find my body racked with unexplainable spasms of emotion.

"I don't know what's wrong with me," I blubbered.

"Just relax. You're under incredible pressure, and you're traumatized. It's not uncommon to experience an emotional catharsis during massage," he suggested, sounding precisely like a doctor calming his hysterical patient.

"This is so embarrassing," I sobbed, trying unsuccessfully to pull away. "There is nothing about me that you don't know, and now you're watching me have a nervous breakdown."

Instead of releasing me, Andrew wrapped his arms around my shoulders and pulled me close in a kind of reverse embrace.

"It's because I know everything about you that I'm here," he whispered.

This only made the waterworks worse.

"Kathryn, you can't fall apart right now, or we're in danger of exiting this slice. Lives still depend on us. Concentrate on my words," he instructed calmly, holding me so closely I could feel the vibration of his voice as it rumbled in his chest. "And breathe."

My heart beat fiercely as I struggled to inhale while I wept.

"Trapezius. Subclavius. Subcapularis coracobrachialis."

"Are you reciting anatomy?" I sniffed, trying to rub away the tears. My hand came away wet with salt and snot.

"Shhh. Breathe. I'm a doctor, remember? We go with what we know. Try to concentrate. Brachioradialis. Iliopsoas. Latissimus dorsi."

As I listened to nonsensical medical jargon, cradled securely in the arms of a man I'd met just a week before and who was technically my boss, the absurdity of the situation finally overwhelmed me. I let go of everything, and listened, and sobbed, and let this insane situation be whatever it wanted to be. I relinquished any notion that I was in control of anything and allowed myself to be held until I finally fell into an exhausted slumber.

I could sense the first light of day through my stubbornly closed eyelids, my groggy brain struggling toward consciousness through layers of weighty cotton. I desperately wanted more sleep, but I was intensely irritated by the firm, lumpy pillow.

My eyes snapped open when I realized that the lumpy pillow was Andrew.

He lifted a lock of hair that had fallen across my face and tucked it behind my ear.

"Hi," he murmured, his sleepy voice deep and languid.

"What..." I began. "No, wait. Why am I—in bed with you?"

"Relax, Kathryn, nothing happened."

I peered up through my eyelashes and caught his captivating smile. It all came rushing back to me—the nightmare, the screaming...the massage.

I leaped out of bed as if I'd been stabbed with a red-hot poker.

"Bathroom!" I cried, snatching up my skirt and blouse and

doing my best to cover up as I stumbled to the safety of the en suite. I turned on the shower, left the water cold, and climbed in. I'll admit it was not one of my shorter showers. But in the end, I felt much more composed.

I emerged to find Andrew already dressed. He gestured to a cart stacked with covered plates.

"Breakfast is here, but be quick. We don't have much time."

"Oh?"

I lifted the lid from a plate of rapidly congealing eggs. My stomach rumbled as the aroma hit me full force.

"I had the front desk locate me."

It took a moment for that statement to sink in.

"Oh, you mean the you that belongs to this slice. Wait, wasn't that weird, asking a clerk to look you up?" I asked as I eagerly shoveled a forkful of eggs into my mouth.

There it was again—that piercing stare that always made me feel daft.

"I'm not an idiot—I didn't register with my real name. I registered with the Norwegian driver's license. This hotel knows us as Mr. and Mrs. Lars Jørgensen."

"Mr. and Mrs.?" I choked on my eggs.

Andrew smirked and handed me a napkin.

"The desk clerk was very, very sorry she could not offer me a room with a king bed. Especially in light of the fact that we are newlyweds."

I felt no need to further explore this topic. "So, you exist," I prompted. "And?"

"And I live here. Well, in San Francisco. Which makes the next task much, much easier."

"And what is that?"

"I'm going to make a little withdrawal from my trust fund."

"You're a trust fund baby? If you're independently wealthy,

why do you work for a psychopath like Breckinridge?"

"It's complicated," he replied, shifting his attention to a pile of buttered toast.

The almost imperceptible clench of his jaw was evidence that I'd hit a nerve, so I backed off. Yet if I had a trust fund, I'd move to a tropical beach. Or fund my own lab. Or found my own lab on a tropical beach! I shook my head, a gesture wasted on my companion as his attention was diverted to the leftover bacon on the breakfast cart.

"Whatever," I muttered.

Andrew laid out the plan as we walked south on Shattuck Avenue.

"Wells Fargo has administered my family's accounts since at least the 1930s, and there should be a big branch in a historic building just a few blocks from here."

"What makes you think that the money will still be there?" I mused. "You could be as poor as a pauper in this reality."

"Not likely. My address in this reality is the corner of Green and Fillmore, in Pacific Heights."

"So?"

"In our slice, that neighborhood is home to the founders of Oracle and PayPal, the VP of design for Apple, and a former Speaker of the House."

"Oh. Yeah, you're probably rolling in dough." I thought a minute. "But you only have the ID of Lars Jørgensen. How are you going to convince the bank to hand over your megabucks?"

"Won't that be a most interesting assignment, my dear Miss Moneypenny?"

The modest storefront branch bank I expected was instead a

six-story brick monster that dwarfed the more unassuming buildings surrounding it. The bank's sweeping lobby looked like something out of a bygone era and encompassed the entire first floor. Columns topped by decorative scrolls supported the twelve-foot ceilings. Crown molding was everywhere, and banking associates stood behind turn-of-the-century walnut counters topped with white marble. There wasn't a slab of plexiglass to be seen; apparently armed bank robberies weren't a thing here.

I hesitated as Andrew made his way toward one of the many standing-height counters crisscrossing the expansive space.

"Maybe it would be safer if I hung back here? I'm not very good at this secret agent stuff."

Andrew shook his head. "Definitely not. If this plan goes south, I'll need you nearby to get us out."

I nodded, straightened my skirt, and tried not to look nervous. As Andrew approached the teller, he turned on his thousand-watt smile.

"How may I help you?" she asked pleasantly.

"I'm so sorry to inconvenience you." Andrew's tone was a perfect mixture of humbleness and charisma. "I have an appointment to make a withdrawal from my trust account." He leaned in toward her, and she cocked her head with more interest than I'd expect for your garden-variety financial transaction. Andrew's expression changed, and suddenly he seemed awkward and vulnerable. "I'm afraid someone has made off with my identification…"

"I notice you're without your CereLink," she commented, tapping her own headband device.

"I'm studying Tibetan Buddhism, and removal of all distraction is necessary in order to properly practice dharma." He pressed his palms together at chin level and offered the teller a small bow. It took all the restraint I had to keep from bursting out laughing.

"How very enlightened." She smiled, leaning over the counter and placing her hand lightly on his arm. "Don't worry. I'm sure we can help you access your account, if you don't mind being subjected to a few biometric scans to confirm your identity."

"Not at all." Andrew smiled warmly.

"That's great," the teller gushed. "If you would please meet me in one of the private client rooms at the far end of the lobby, I'll take care of you right away."

"My cousin will join us," Andrew suggested, waving vaguely in my direction as he strode across the room without even a backward glance.

Cousin? I was surprised how much this comment stung.

When we reached the small office, the teller sat behind a heavy, vintage walnut desk, clear of all objects except a large, leather-bound ledger and a black, glossy device no larger than a deck of cards.

Andrew lowered himself into the only available client seat, so I hovered nervously near the door.

The teller stared pointedly at the device, and small yellow lights embedded in its surface illuminated.

She lifted the device and handed it to Andrew. "We'll use the standard fingerprint and retinal scan to confirm your identity. Thumb here"—she indicated the side of the object—"then hold the lens on the back about three inches from your eye."

Andrew did as instructed. The biometric analysis was over in less than a minute.

The teller seemed to stare off into space for a moment, then beamed.

"Perfect! You're authenticated to withdraw any amount you like from your account, Mr. Breckinridge."

Andrew sauntered through the lobby, stuffing a wad of cash equal to two months' of my tuition into his pocket. I trudged three steps behind, glowering. The effort I'd put into gritting my teeth over the last ten minutes was starting to give me jaw muscle fatigue, but I managed to keep silent until we exited the bank.

"Hold up a minute," I demanded, stopping on the marble stairs. Andrew turned, raising an inquiring eyebrow. "Andrew *Breckinridge*?" I shook my head in disbelief. "Your last name is Breckinridge? As in, Andric Breckinridge?"

Andrew's face was flat and expressionless, his eyes cool. "My father."

"Andric Breckinridge is your *father*?"

"Kathryn, please keep your voice down," he insisted, glancing around and reaching for my hand.

"No!" I bellowed. I took three steps backward and wrapped my arms around my chest. "No, no, *no*! You do *not* get to touch me, and you do *not* get to tell me what to do. You lied to me! You let me think that...I don't know what. That you were on my side? That you liked me? *You* are Albaion. You and that cruel, callous, egocentric, evil man. Your *father*? How could you keep that from me?"

"Kathryn, I..."

My stomach contracted into a tight, tense knot, my anger so fierce that my hands began trembling.

"I can't even look at you! I am so angry, I can't even..."

A wave of vertigo flooded over me. In an instant, the worst headache I'd ever felt in my life jackhammered its way into the base of my skull. I closed my eyes and tried desperately to catch my breath. When I opened them, I was staring at the ceiling of an unmarked hospital room at the Stanford Medical Center.

I sat up, struggling with the hospital's warming blanket and a tangle of cables, leads, and tubes snaking from my body. I roughly yanked the electrode cap from my skull by its umbilicus of cables, tossing it to the floor. The erratic movement of my left hand sent the Bug flying; it skittered to a stop beneath Andrew's hospital gurney. My eyes swept the room and settled on the only other person present. Janine sprang from the sofa and hurried to my side.

"Kate, you're back!" She ran her hand over my forehead as I struggled to sit up. Then she glanced at the gurney beside me.

"Why isn't Andrew awake?" she asked, worry furrowing her brow.

I narrowed my eyes.

"He isn't awake because I didn't bring him back," I declared through clenched teeth.

Janine stared at me for a moment, then noted my vital signs. She reached over and depressed the call button, then retrieved the Bug, placing it carefully on the table. Within a minute, Dr. Daniels hurried into the room.

He moved to my side as his eyes played over the array of medical devices monitoring my vitals. Then he peered at Andrew, worry creasing his brow. "Kate, what went wrong? Why hasn't Andrew regained consciousness?"

My eyes were reduced to narrow slits, and my heart was pounding. "Unhook me, now! I am done with this insanity."

"But, Kate…" Janine pleaded.

"*No more!*" I shrieked. The sound of my own voice echoing inside my skull ratcheted the headache from atrocious to excruciating. Janine moved to restrain me.

"Kate, please calm down," she pleaded as she struggled to keep me from tumbling out of the bed. "For heaven's sake, lie still. Your catheter needs to be deflated before we can remove it. And if you pull out your IV, you'll bleed all over the place."

I sank back into the bed and tears streamed down my face.

"Okay," I conceded, covering my eyes with my free hand. It was cold, which felt good, but I began to see the aura, and the pounding in my head strengthened. "The migraine is starting," I whimpered. "It's a really bad one. Is there something you can give me?"

Janine breathed a sigh of relief and nodded, releasing me from her grasp.

Dr. Daniels's solid voice was a calming balm. "IV prochlorperazine, right away. It's likely to make you sleepy, and we'll have to monitor you for side effects for several hours."

"Thanks," I mumbled. Now that the adrenaline surge was draining away, I realized how weary I felt. I tentatively flexed my legs. Every muscle in my body ached.

When Dr. Daniels spoke again, his voice sounded far away. "Kate, a common side effect of this medication is sedation. It should relieve your migraine, but you may sleep for several hours. Can you tell me what happened to you, and why Andrew is still unconscious?"

"I didn't mean to go," I began, wiping a stream of salty tears from my face. I hadn't even noticed that I'd been crying. The pounding in my head made it hard to concentrate. "But I couldn't stand to look at him for another second! Did you know that he's Andrew *Breckinridge*? He's that monster's son!"

Janine hovered nearer. "That is true," she replied patiently.

"He lied to me," I insisted, but the fury that had fueled me was gone. The only sensation that remained was bone-crushing fatigue.

Janine stooped down until she was level with my eyes. She grasped my arm and placed two fingers on my wrist, gauging my pulse.

"I'm terribly concerned for him. The propofol protocol has already proven to be incredibly risky. There's real danger he won't survive if we have to use it. It's likely we'll lose him unless you re-sync into the slice and retrieve him."

"I won't do it," I mumbled. The medication must have already been taking effect; it was impossible to focus.

"I have known Andrew since he was a child," she said, her voice low and even. "He is like a son to me. I can't force you. But please..." Janine didn't even try to hide her desperation.

"That lying bastard can go to hell..." I declared, my words slurred and barely audible. Then the world went black.

The brightness of the early afternoon sun makes me squint, and I wish for a pair of sunglasses. Yet I marvel at the aquamarine sky, the brilliant green fronds of the palm trees rustling in the breeze, the warmth of the sienna-colored terra cotta tiles. I stroll to the fountain in the middle of the courtyard and look down. The bottom of the basin is embedded with glazed sapphire tiles topped with lifelike sculptures of colorful ceramic koi. I had never noticed in the dark. I take a deep breath. I am at the house in Bel Air.

I sit on the teak bench that feels utterly familiar. I listen to the fountain burble and watch as honeybees buzz from flower to flower, their industry a miniature marvel to behold. A green hummingbird with a dazzling ruby throat hovers in midair, drinking nectar from the orange-fluted trumpet of a pineapple sage plant in a pot across from my perch.

It feels like a gift to rest in the warm sun, watching the bees and the birds as they busily complete their tasks. So I sit, for what seems like an hour.

Before when I've visited this place, the other Kate has known. But I am still alone, and so I decide to invite myself into her home.

Is it breaking and entering if I'm invading the house of another version of myself? I let myself in through the white-bordered double doors under the arched entryway. The room I enter is a textbook example of modern design. Contemporary but comfortable, white square-edged sofas surround a fireplace faced in golden travertine. The polished oak floor gleams; large potted plants soften the space. The room is decorated in monochrome and soft beige, except for a trio of large canvases on the wall opposite the fireplace. The three large canvases are simple azure fields punctuated by a few random black dots or an effortless slash of red. I shake my head and wonder if I somehow appreciate modern art in this reality. I doubt it.

I leave the room and wander down a hallway lined with photographs of exotic animals enveloped in lush green forest—a bright yellow bird with a beak black as jet, a three-horned chameleon wearing aqua and saffron stripes, a neon green tree frog perched on a crimson leaf, and a mountain gorilla, staring into the camera lens with an expression as old as time. To my left, a solid maple door stands open. I peer inside at a library with deep leather chairs and floor-to-ceiling bookshelves. A sliding library ladder stands waiting on the far side of the shelves. The two-story arched windows let in the full light of day, but there is no sign of life in the room.

I continue down the hall until I reach the bright, open kitchen—white cabinets, white marble, clean lines. The version of me with a much better haircut is sitting at the high bar of the counter, slurping soup from a carved wooden bowl.

"Hi," she says, setting the bowl down next to a set of polished wooden chopsticks inlaid with turquoise. "Would you like some miso soup?"

"I'm more of a ramen noodles girl myself, but while in Rome..." I reply, settling myself on the adjacent stool. She rises, finds another wooden bowl, and spoons soup from a gleaming stainless stockpot on the commercial-grade stove.

I sip the steaming, salty broth. We sit together quietly, eating soup, for a long time. It is not at all uncomfortable to share this space with her in silence.

I am unsuccessfully attempting to pluck the sole remaining cube of tofu from the bottom of my bowl with my chopsticks when she finally speaks.

"Welcome back. You seem to be getting better at finding me."

"I wish I could say I am doing it on purpose," I admit, finally spearing the gelatinous protein cube with a move I'm sure would bring shame to the entire culture of Japan.

"You may not be doing it consciously," she suggests, "but given the theory of infinite universes, it's highly unlikely you are here by chance."

"Do other Kates show up here too?" I ask. My head spins at the thought of keeping track of multiple versions of myself, each with her own litany of personal problems.

"No," she says, smiling. "So far it's just you. Perhaps this place is a unique beacon for you. Whatever it is, I'm always glad when you visit."

I snort into my soup, feeling sure that can't be true.

She stands up, collects the bowls and chopsticks, and moves gracefully to the sink.

From a high cabinet, she collects mugs and pours tea from an electric kettle.

"I would be pleased to see you if this is a social call, but I suspect that you may have something pressing on your mind. Want to talk?"

I can't tell if we have a special connection because we're the same person, or if she's simply incredibly perceptive. In the end, I decide it hardly matters.

I sigh, staring into the steam rising from my tea. "Under what name do you publish your novels?" I ask.

"My professional name is Kathryn Rathman," she replies.

"And in your nonprofessional life?" I ask.

"Everywhere else, I'm Kate Breckinridge."

I feel a lump in my throat. "And in this reality," I ask carefully, "what does Andrew do? For a living, I mean."

"He started a company called Aegle Bioengineering. He's been toiling

away on the development of a resource-negative and large-scale carbon sequestration technique. To combat global warming."

"What's an 'aegle'?" I ask.

She smiles. "Greek goddess of radiant good health."

I sigh and shake my head. "What is it with the Greek gods..." I mutter. "And his father? What does his company do?" I surprise myself with the level of rancor in my question.

She gives me a puzzled look and pauses for a moment. "Andric Breckinridge has been dead for fifteen years. He suffered a massive heart attack at forty-seven. Isabel divested his holdings soon after his death and has honored his memory by becoming a philanthropic tour de force. I'm curious. Does this have to do with why you're here?"

I frowned. "Are you sure? Where I come from, Andric Breckinridge is alive and well, but he's a vicious megalomaniac. And Andrew..." I feel an unexpected stab of guilt. "Andrew has built a biomedical device that allows him to—well, basically be you, I guess. He uses it to traverse realities." I scowl.

"Ah, I see." She nods. She thinks a minute. "You know, you and I do the same thing. And as you can see"—she pauses, glancing about her sophisticated kitchen—"I have also reaped substantial financial rewards."

My mind reels as I struggle to comprehend this apparent role reversal; in this reality, it's me mining the multiverse for fun and profit. But then I remember one important difference. "When you come back from your visits—do elements of the other realities come with you? To change your world?"

"No, of course not," she insists. "Well, unless you count adding some new fiction. My ego is nowhere near large enough to believe that a couple of stories have changed the course of history."

I knead my forehead with my fingertips and grimace.

"Well, in my reality, the traveling does impact us, in serious and unpredictable ways. What he's doing is making my world worse. And

he's doing it for his father. And if that man isn't pure evil, then I don't know who is."

She took a deep breath. "Are you sure he's doing it for his father?"

I'm unable to contain my irritation. "Who else would he be doing it for?"

She apparently considers this question rhetorical. "And you're here because you're conflicted about his role with his father's company?"

"Well no," I groan, dropping my head and closing my eyes. "I'm here because I'm his ticket out of Alternate Reality Land, and I—I just left him there."

She is silent for a long time. I begin to fidget in my chair.

"What will happen if you don't retrieve him?" she asks, her eyes deadly serious.

"There is good chance he will die."

Her lips are pinched into a thin line. "Then you must retrieve him."

"He lied to me about who is father is!"

Her voice is matter-of-fact. "It doesn't matter who his father is."

"I don't know who he is!" I insist.

"You know exactly who he is. And you know exactly who you are. You must do the right thing. Stop running, Kate. Stop running and embrace what you know."

CHAPTER 25

KATE

September 30

My entire body felt as heavy as a pile of granite boulders. My mouth tasted as if it had been lined with steel wool, but my head was blessedly free of both auras and jackhammers.

I lifted my head and heard the scraping of a chair, and then a cool hand grasped my own.

"You're awake!"

The welcome voice of my sister provided the motivation to finally wrench open my eyes—or to try. They seemed to be glued shut. I raised my free hand and rubbed the crust away.

"Michelle?" My throat was so hoarse. I tried to smile, but my lips cracked painfully. "I'm so glad you're here."

"Let me call Dr. Daniels," she suggested, reaching for the call button.

"No, wait." I struggled to sit up, and Michelle instead reached for the controls to raise my hospital bed into the reclining position. She was wearing her black skirt, black top, and flats. She'd definitely come straight from work.

"I hate to be a baby," I croaked, "but could you bring me some water?"

Michelle smiled, released my hand, and poured a small glass

from a pitcher conveniently resting on the small table between the beds. She glanced furtively at Andrew's unconscious form.

The tepid water tasted amazing.

"Sip it slowly," Michelle suggested. "You haven't eaten anything solid in a long time."

I nodded and handed the cup back to my sister. With another sideways glance at Andrew, she quickly moved around to the chair on the far side of my bed. "He's creeping me out," she complained. "He looks like he's dead."

I could tell that she was holding back a thousand questions, but rather than speak, she slipped her hand back around mine and smiled.

I shook my head and tried to think clearly. "What is the status of Hurricane Ophelia?"

Michelle cocked her head to the side and looked at me like I was crazy.

"You know, the superstorm of the century? Extremely unusual weather pattern? Bearing down on the New York coast? We watched the forecast together on the news."

Michelle laid a hand on my forehead, presumably to check for delirium.

"Katie, are you sure you're all right? There is no hurricane."

I fell back against the bed in relief. One crisis averted. I tried unsuccessfully to clear my throat, and Michelle refilled the glass of water.

"So, Dr. Daniels called me this afternoon." She tried to sound casual, but the concern was easy to detect. "To be honest, I've been worried sick about you but wasn't expecting to hear anything until tomorrow, at the earliest. He explained that you had come out of it, but he hadn't." She nodded at Andrew. "The doctor wouldn't explain what happened."

"That's because he doesn't know what happened," I said, slowly sipping the water.

"So—what happened?"

"This is going to take a while," I sighed. Then I told my sister everything.

When I finished, Michelle stared hard at me.

"My God, Kate—what are you going to do?"

I frowned. "I've convinced myself I'm going to bring him back. Or, at least a better version of myself has convinced me." I motioned to the table between the beds. "But I'll need your help. Can you hand me that damn Bug?"

Michelle grasped the device, gingerly dangling the thing by one of its spindly legs. She dropped it in my lap like it was a dead lizard.

I carefully picked it up and turned it over in my hand. It appeared to be undamaged.

"This stupid IV makes it hard for me to do anything. I'm going to need you to help me position this," I said, holding the Bug as if it was an offering.

"What, right now?" she asked incredulously.

"Yes. It will have retained its programming, and it should activate as soon as it's positioned on my hand."

"Shouldn't I call Amir or Dr. Daniels or—someone?" my sister protested nervously.

I shook my head. "If I wait, I'll change my mind. Probably best to just go in there, find him, and end this irresponsible, ill-advised disaster as quickly as possible."

"Okay…" Michelle agreed doubtfully. She gritted her teeth as she positioned the Bug carefully on the back of my hand. When she released it, she shuddered as if the thing had given her a raging case of the heebie-jeebies.

Then we waited.

"I should be back soo—" I was interrupted by a familiar stab of searing pain.

I knew immediately I'd made a big mistake. Nighttime had already fallen, there was no moon, and I was again in the middle of an undeveloped field, this time enveloped in darkness. There were sharp rocks, and there were spiny weeds, and they were all stabbing my bare bottom.

"Shit!" I yelled. "Shit! Shit! Shit!"

"Hello, Kathryn," a familiar voice rang out from somewhere in the shadows. "Please don't tell me that you sliced here wearing your hospital gown."

I struggled to stand up, feeling the sharp dig of small stones on my tender feet. I cursed the powerful wave of nausea that washed over as I dropped to my bare knees. And then I retched.

"Forgot the anti-nausea too, I see," Andrew called from somewhere in the darkness.

"Would you *please* stop being such a complete and total ass?" I grimaced as another series of dry heaves racked my body.

"I'm going to turn on a flashlight so I can find you."

I sat back on my heels and clutched the back of the hospital gown in a failed attempt at modesty. A brisk gust of wind rustled the dry foliage, and I shivered. A bright point of light appeared thirty feet away and bobbed closer.

"You *did* slice in your gown," he smirked as he swept the light from my chest to my face. I squinted in its bright beam. "Was Amir hammered? He should have realized—"

"Amir wasn't there. Dr. Daniels wasn't there. Janine wasn't there. Your *father* certainly wasn't there." I spat out the word with venom.

For a moment, Andrew seemed taken aback. Then he focused the circle of light on the ground in front of me and began digging around in a large canvas bag. "I brought you some things," he said. He held out his hand, and I reluctantly grasped it, steadying me as I rose from the ground. He passed me a pile of clothing.

"Do you want light or…"

"No. Thank you." My words were clipped, and the field immediately went dark.

I did my best to extract the gravel from my scraped-up knees before pulling on an A-line skirt and a warm, thick sweater. I flung the flimsy hospital gown to the ground.

"I don't suppose you brought any, uh, undergarments?" I was sure my face had flushed and was thankful for the cover of darkness.

The beam of light reappeared, and he handed me the bag. The flashlight clicked off again, and by feel, I located panties, socks, and a pair of comfortable leather oxfords.

"Are you decent?" he asked from somewhere too near for my comfort.

I finished tying the shoelaces. "Sure," I retorted.

The beam reappeared, focused on my shoes.

"You came back," he observed. "Thank you."

"The hurricane is no longer a thing," I snapped. I marched to where Andrew stood and snatched the flashlight, turning it on him. The aloha shirt had been replaced by a long-sleeved button-down in dove-colored cotton paired with well-tailored trousers. But most surprising was the gray band perched on his head, its surface reflecting in purplish-teal iridescence.

My eyes grew as wide as saucers. "Where did you get that thing?"

His hand touched the device. "There's something you need to know about CereLink."

"Did you steal it? Does it even work?" My curiosity immediately won out over my indignation.

"I didn't steal it. And it does work."

I stepped closer and turned the beam on the band. The surface shimmered in the intense light.

"But how? Did you get the nanoprobes? Did it hurt? Where did you even get this device? I've only been gone for—what, maybe five hours? And now you're some kind of cyborg?"

His spoke with exasperation. "You've been gone for seven and a half hours, Kathryn. I'm not a cyborg. And the person who set up my CereLink was me," he explained, plucking the flashlight from my grasp. "In fact, the only reason the device functions at all is because this unit was already paired to the brain patterns of the local version of me—the device normally requires a week of training before it is operational."

"Right. You met yourself. Of course," I reasoned. "I absolutely believe that the version of you that lives here would never willingly walk around wearing aloha shirts. He has a good tailor. He must also have some powerful connections."

"The version of me that lives here doesn't need powerful connections to provide nanoprobes or a CereLink, Kathryn. The version of me that lives here heads the division of the company that *makes* CereLink."

I couldn't keep the accusation from my voice. "And who runs that company?" I asked.

"The company is run by my father."

His jaw muscles were tense. Did he expect me to lose it again? I took a deep, calming breath.

"Andric Breckinridge," I grunted. "I can go halfway across the multiverse, but I can't escape the influence of that heinous man."

"You understand what this means, right? If I can replicate any of this technology in our slice, it means we haven't technically stolen anything."

The irony was, in this case, actually cosmic. I took a moment to consider, and my emotions, so battered from the events of the day, seemed to drain away. I shifted my weight from one foot to the other. Listened to the sounds of the crickets. Swatted at a moth drawn to the beam of the flashlight. I gazed up at the heavens and marveled at the countless points of light twinkling in the vast inky blackness of the night sky.

"So, is it amazing?" I finally asked.

"More than you could ever imagine."

I knew at that instant that I wanted this technology just as much as he did. I reached up, and the tips of my fingers brushed the cool metallic surface of the band.

"I wish there was time to train one for you," he said quietly, "but it's too risky to stay here any longer. Our environmental crisis is resolved, and I'm approaching the end of the sixty-hour window. We must return immediately."

I dropped my hand, still gazing at the device. I wished more than anything to try it on.

"Maybe we can find me in this slice. I'm sure she'd let me borrow her CereLink. We could find her tonight, then head home."

"I'm sorry, Kate," he replied sadly. "I looked for you the moment I put this thing on. You don't exist in this slice. There is no record at all of you, your sister, even your parents."

My chest tightened. Although it was bound to happen sooner or later, news of my family's nonexistence hit me harder than I expected. The invisible band squeezing my heart made me feel physically faint. Or possibly it was my earlier vomit-fest.

In the darkness, Andrew slid his arm around my waist.

"I don't want to stay a minute longer in a world without a Kathryn Rathman," he murmured into my ear. Words that should have made me swoon instead dredged up a morass of confusion. I stepped back and quite literally shone the interrogation light directly on his face.

"What is this thing we're doing? Is it all just an experiment to you? Or maybe it's some kind of testosterone-fueled game? Perhaps you just get a kick out of toying with my emotions."

Andrew fixed his dazzling blue eyes on me and considered his answer carefully.

"I should have recruited you differently. I should have told you about my father."

I should have been angry, but the conversation in Bel Air came rushing back to me. "How did you even get into this? The Bug is *your* baby—why is Andric Breckinridge running the show?"

"Amir and I worked tirelessly on the prototype. And we talked to everybody—literally every venture capitalist and angel investor in the Valley. But let's face it. Slicing is an insane proposition. No one would wait to hear the end of our pitch, let alone invest. In the end, Andric agreed to fund this research. And now we're all reaping the consequences."

I took a deep breath and returned his stare. "I can't be a part of this if I don't know the truth."

"I should have been honest with you about the company, my role there, and about the path down which the Ubiquity project has spiraled. But I promise you, right here, right now, no more secrets, and no more lies."

"No more stabbing," I added.

"No more stabbing," he solemnly agreed, a wry smile playing about his lips.

"But how can I really trust you when I barely know you?" I protested.

He stepped closer again, reached over, and doused the flashlight. When he wrapped his arms around me and pulled me close, I didn't resist. I rested my head against his shoulder. Unexpected waves of warmth pulsed through my body, and my skin tingled beneath my sweater.

His voice was tender. "I think you already know what's in my heart. Can't you tell?"

The question felt dangerous, and I was tempted to redirect, to diffuse the situation with some pithy, snarky comment. But then I remembered the growing number of instances in which the universe had already thrown us together, and I reconsidered. Instead I decided to supply an equally dangerous answer.

"Kissing you is pure, unadulterated bliss," I confessed. "It's consuming my thoughts. *You're* consuming my thoughts. Because of my condition, I've led a somewhat...sheltered life. For all I know, what I feel is nothing more than simple animal lust. So I'll ask you again. What is this thing we're doing?"

"It's not that complicated, Kathryn," he replied, and I could hear it again in the dark, even though I couldn't see it—that smile, tugging at the corners of his eyes. "The thing we're doing is falling in love."

CHAPTER 26

KATE

October 31

Amir bumbled into the team's daily morning stand-up meeting wearing a giant inflatable T. rex costume.

His green-and-gray dinosaur head towered over the assemblage. Every other person in the room was clad in street clothes, unless you counted the spattering of white lab coats. A muffled voice rose over the hum of the small portable pump that filled the costume with air.

"You people are harsh!" Amir grumbled. "C'mon, it's Halloween! Where's the love?"

The sixty-three people crowded tightly into what was previously the Project Ubiquity lab stared at Amir blankly. Only the incredible influence and vast coffers of Andric Breckinridge could have persuaded such a large group of distinguished professionals to assemble so rapidly. Project Satori's technical requirements had quickly swelled the ranks of Albaion, and most of the newcomers didn't appreciate Amir's sense of humor.

"Okay, then, we'll start with the dinosaur in the room. Amir, what's the status of the quantum algorithms?" Andrew asked with a barely concealed grin.

Amir detached his dinosaur head, and his costume deflated.

"My team has verified the secure uplink to the Q-Path 5000-AQ quantum computer. We're ready to start testing your quantum algorithms. Preliminary results should start coming back this afternoon. I really wish we could get one of those babies in-house, though."

"Sorry, but I wasn't able to convince Finance to approve that fifteen million dollar requisition you sent me," Andrew replied wryly. "How about biomaterials?"

Janine spoke up. "We have a video conference call today with our experts at Ohio State University and the US Department of Energy's Brookhaven National Laboratory to finalize the build protocol for the nanoprobes required for Satori. Dr. Ichpujani, our new resident nanotechnologist, suggested the nanoparticles will have the best uptake over the blood-brain barrier if coated with polysorbate-80. The nanoprobes have been tested in mouse models for safety, and we've noted no negative effects."

"Great," he said, nodding. "And as for hardware, here's an update on the detection prototype. My team has completed the integration of the combination atomic magnetometers and the advanced photoacoustic detection equipment. Everything has been moved to the fMRI suite to take advantage of its superior shielding. Measurements indicate the device should be safe for human use, and I'll test that theory later today."

Andrew looked around the room at the collection of luminary technologists, computational neuroscientists, machine learning experts, and bio-nano-mechanics authorities assembled before him. He paused to make eye contact with each member of the group before he spoke.

"I know the pace of this project is brutal, but you've all worked unbelievably hard since the moment you arrived. Together we've come to the precipice of revolutionary technology in record time. I am one hundred percent certain that your efforts here are literally going to change the world. Thank you for trusting me enough to make this journey. Don't lose faith—with your help, I'm confident that success is just over the horizon. Together we'll drive Project Satori to completion. Thank you all. Now let's go make something insanely great!"

I glanced around the room and realized that the face of each and every team member, though already haggard from weeks of toiling round-the-clock, shone like a beacon. It was as though Andrew was projecting some kind of charismatic aura, and we were all basking in it.

And then the moment passed. The team broke into a series of excited side conversations. Andrew grabbed my elbow.

"Kathryn, can I have a word in my office?"

I nodded and followed silently as we snaked through the sterile LED-illuminated halls, my insides churning in furious anticipation. The door of the office had barely swung closed when I reached my arms around his neck and pulled him toward me. His kiss was hungry, and I was swallowed by the peculiar sensation of falling that always ripped through me whenever we were able to manage a few stolen minutes. This moment, just like each one before, never failed to astound me. Within the span of five short weeks, my life had utterly transformed. The huge paycheck, my part in this phenomenal new brain research, and even this relationship—it all seemed too good to be true.

"I dreamed about you last night," I whispered, coming up for air. Even now, after every embrace, I expected to open my eyes someplace else, covered in electrodes.

"Dreamed, or *dreamed*?" he asked, lips on my earlobe.

I involuntarily arched my back as shivers of delight traipsed down my spine.

"The normal kind. I've been adhering strictly to my meditation practice."

"'Love looks not with the eyes, but with the mind,'" he whispered.

I pulled away and gave him a sly smile. "'And therefore is winged Cupid painted blind.' Nice try, but I know that you're ripping off the Bard."

"So you know your Shakespeare..." He reached for my chin and cradled it gently in his hands.

"Michelle played Helena in *A Midsummer Night's Dream* at Shakespeare in the Park last summer." I smiled. "We ran a lot of lines."

The realization that I hadn't seen my sister in weeks weighed on my heart. I really needed to take an afternoon off and get out of this place. And I would; once I finished this phase of my project.

Andrew kissed my nose and released me, and immediately the familiar, dull ache set in. I felt it every time we parted. I knew what he would say. He said it every time.

"We have to be careful," he insisted. "If my father learns about this relationship, he will use it as leverage."

"I know," I sighed. "I'm just as excited as everyone else about the potential for Project Satori. Maybe even more so since I'm the one with the defective brain. But I hate sneaking around. It kills me that I only get to steal a moment or two with you every few days."

"Be patient," he urged. "Once this prototype is up and running, Andric will be distracted publicizing his new triumph and bringing it to full production. He'll be so busy being exalted that he'll hardly notice me."

There was a hint of bitterness hidden under his nonchalance.

"You'd better head back to your office," he suggested. "There are a dozen suits that can badge in here at any time."

"Too bad we can't just pop off to some alternate reality," I replied wistfully.

"Even if Project Ubiquity hadn't been suspended, it would be no use," he pointed out, eyes twinkling. "Because the minute we touched, you'd beam us home anyway."

"True," I lamented. I turned to the door. It was torture to go when every molecule of my being longed to stay.

My new office was a decided step up from my previous workspace in the lab. I didn't have a window, but the recessed lighting had the bright, warm quality of sunlight.

I opened my development environment and compiled yesterday's attempt at implementing the decoding methods for the visual word form region of the brain that I'd read about in the CereLink slice. Instead of success, I stared down a long list of errors.

The thought of the leap we were about to achieve over existing science was exhilarating. I knew it could be done; I had read the papers and I had seen it in action. This made the project a thrilling inevitability rather than a long and frustrating wild goose chase.

The morning flew by. I was so deep in the code that lunchtime didn't even register. The alarm I'd set for three thirty to remind me to eat broke my reverie. I silenced the alarm and ignored my growling stomach. I compiled again, then ran some unit tests, and suddenly, to my surprise and delight, everything appeared to be working.

I committed my code changes and locked my desktop. I picked up the phone on my desk and dialed the four-digit extension to the fMRI suite's control room.

The woman on the other end of the phone was brusque. "Radiology." The background commotion meant something was going on down there.

"Uh, hi, it's Kate. Can I run some tests using the fMRI?"

Even though the huge, expensive machine was installed specifically for me, I was still intimidated every time I asked to use it.

I could hear the din of several conversations in the background and the rustle as she placed her hand over the phone's receiver to reply to a question. "Sorry, Kate. The Satori hardware team is in here with their prototype right now. I don't know how long they'll be. Maybe in an hour?"

"Okay, thanks," I said.

At least this meant I had time for a bite to eat on my way down there. I gathered up the printouts of the sample text I would read during my test and headed out in search of sustenance.

Forty minutes later, I was squeezing into the fMRI suite's control room, already crowded with eleven other people. Through the large plate glass window, I could see three portable server racks arranged in a semicircle around a cluster of white lab coats. As the researchers moved aside, they revealed Andrew seated in a chair, thick inky snakes of cables running from each of the server racks and attached to his huge, black helmet.

I nervously threaded my way through the crowd, past the control station toward Janine.

When I reached her, I kept my voice low. "How's it going?"

"Well, it's a mixed bag," she replied. She looked as worried as I felt. "The safety checks passed, and this morning we switched to the nanoprobes coated in polysorbate-80. No readings. Dr. Ichpujani went back to the drawing board. Fifty minutes ago, Andrew took an intra-nasal dose of the new batch of nanoparticles; this time coated with a different biopolymer derived from crustacean shells called chitosan. They're spinning up the machine for another trial now."

The crackle from the intercom plunged the stuffy room into silence. "Control, we're ready to start the test." The group surrounding Andrew stepped back.

I stood on my tiptoes to try to glimpse the monitors at the front of the room. Amir sat before the console, no longer dressed like a dinosaur.

He spoke into a microphone. "Rock and roll, ladies and gents!"

He unleashed a flurry of keystrokes, and data began scrolling furiously across multiple windows. I itched to get close enough to read the logs onscreen, but the experts huddled around blocked my view.

"Howzit, brah?" Amir spoke into the mic again.

"I feel fine," Andrew's terse reply reverberated over the intercom. "Are you reading anything yet?"

"We're not detecting anything," someone spoke over Amir's shoulder. "I don't understand it. The nanoparticles should be in place by now."

"The diagnostics on all the components checked out," another confirmed. "The hardware all appears to be functioning per design. Something's wrong with the probes."

Amir pressed the mic's activation button. "No bueno. All the gear operation appears legit, but we're not getting the readings we expected."

Andrew sounded strained. "Let it go for another ten minutes."

The tension in the room was thick, all eyes staring at Andrew or over Amir's shoulders at the monitors. Ten minutes passed. Nothing happened.

Amir hit the mic button again. "Sorry, man, nothin'. I'm shuttin' this bad boy down."

Amir pounded on the keyboard again, and the cluster of lab coats inside the fMRI suite congregated around Andrew once more, detaching the helmet as well as a litany of other sensors meant to monitor heart rate, blood pressure, and oxygenation. Everyone except Amir, Janine, and the radiologist shuffled dejectedly out of the control room.

Andrew and Dr. Ichpujani joined us in the control room, as the other white coats wheeled the server racks and the attached cumbersome helmet out of the fMRI room.

"The nanoparticles will work their way out of your system in the next twenty hours or so," Dr. Ichpujani reported.

Andrew ran a hand over his head, and I noticed the gobs of conductive gel matting down his hair. It was painfully obvious we were still light-years away from the elegant technology of CereLink.

Andrew sighed. "Amir, will you run a full diagnostic on the prototype to triple-check that all the hardware systems are fully functioning to spec?" He sounded beyond exhausted.

"You got it, boss." Amir rose from the console. His gray tee read "2B || !2B."

"Does Amir have any real clothes? Or is he singlehandedly keeping the ironic coding T-shirt industry in business?" I asked Janine.

"Don't be a hater, Kate!" Amir winked as he sauntered out of the room in his squeaky flip-flops.

The radiologist, Camilla Herrera, had quickly taken Amir's place at the console. "Kate, I should have the machine up and ready to go in about twenty minutes."

Andrew sighed and turned to Janine. "I'm going to go back over the transcripts. There must be something I'm missing. Those nanoparticles are key; if we can't get them right, this whole thing goes up in smoke."

As if on cue, the door to the control room swung open, and the formidable form of Andric Breckinridge stormed in. I sank back against the wall, and Camilla shrunk down in her seat, but Andrew and Janine held their ground.

"The test of your prototype has failed," he barked.

"We'll rerun again tomorrow, with adjusted parameters," Andrew replied evenly.

"This project is running on borrowed time!" Andric slammed his fist against the console table so forcefully that Camilla jumped.

Andrew kept his preternatural cool. "According to the project plan, we're right on schedule."

Andric's gaze settled on the large, white machine behind the glass window, now performing its start-up sequence. His frigid blue eyes narrowed as he gestured toward the fMRI machine. "Never mind the massive loss we'll take on *that* useless monstrosity!"

Even though it was no CereLink, I was still in awe of the gorgeous seven-Tesla machine just waiting for me beyond the wall.

"Oh, no, we're definitely using that," Andrew and I responded in unison.

I blushed and looked away. Breckinridge gave me a calculated stare.

That was a stupid mistake, I thought. I shifted my gaze downward, excused myself, and slipped into the small side room we reserved for changing into the loose, metal-free clothing we wore for our fMRI test sessions. I lingered for longer than necessary, hopeful that when I emerged, Dr. Breckinridge would have absconded and taken his fury elsewhere.

I emerged from the claustrophobic, jackhammering cacophony of the fMRI machine, and before I even slid the helmet from my head, Camilla was on the microphone.

"Kate, your mobile has been going off like crazy for the last half hour."

I slid off the scanner's bed and hurried into the control room, bypassing the data from the reading trial and immediately heading for the heaped pile of my street clothes, where I found my mobile.

> Michelle: *Hey Kate? Are you there?*
> Michelle: *Kate? I'm really not feeling well. Everything hurts, and I think I have a fever. Can you call me?*
> Michelle: *Oh, man, I just blew chunks all over the restaurant's staff bathroom. Heading home…*

Michelle: *OMG, I can't stop coughing, and I can hardly breathe. Something's seriously wrong.*

Mom: *Kate, can you check on Michelle? She sounds really sick...*

Michelle: *Fever is getting worse; I just checked next door— Mimi is home. She is driving me to the ER. Meet me there?*

Three missed calls: Mom

Voice mail: Mom

Voice mail: Mom

Voice mail: Mom

I bypassed the voice mails and immediately dialed my mother. She picked up on the first ring.

"Oh, thank God, Kathryn! Where are you? Are you at the hospital? How is Michelle?"

"I'm sorry, Mom, but I was at work. I've only just seen the texts..."

"I have no idea what is going on. She won't answer her phone. I tried calling the emergency room desk, and no one will tell me anything."

"Don't worry, I'm sure she'll be fine." I put her on speaker and propped up the phone as I pulled on my clothing. "I'm fifteen minutes away; I'll head over there right now."

Despite my reassurances, I felt as panicked as my mother sounded.

"Camilla, can I borrow your computer for a minute?"

I sat down at her workstation and gathered up the fMRI results, posting them to the server, then launched the Mutt email program on the command line to dash off a quick message.

To: andrew@albaion.com
Subject: fMRI results; OOTO for a while
From: kate@albaion.com

Results for fMRI scans of text reading are on the server in my directory. Code is checked in under my branch <HIEROGLYPH>

Michelle is in the ER, leaving now. Not sure when I'll be back.

-K

I badged into the garage bay, and my access card unlocked the key fob cabinet. Selecting the pickup closest to the exit, I raised the rolling door and gunned the truck across the rutted dirt track, squinting as I headed west, straight into the setting sun.

I had forgotten—it was Halloween. Costumed children crowded the streets everywhere, and traffic slowed to a crawl. Stanford Medical Center was only six miles as the crow flies from the facility hidden in the hills, but it took me nearly an hour to reach it. I ignored my mom's frantic texts, arriving in ever closer intervals.

I parked the dusty pickup in visitors' parking and headed straight to the emergency department check-in desk, which was manned by a harried-looking middle-aged woman in blue scrubs.

"Excuse me? My sister checked in a little over an hour ago? Her name is Michelle Rathman."

I didn't expect the dark look that crossed the woman's face. "May I see your ID please?"

"I'm her sister, Kate. Kate Rathman," I said, handing over my driver's license.

"Please take a seat, Ms. Rathman," the woman suggested, returning my ID and sliding a sheaf of papers over the desk. I realized that the woman refused to look me in the eye and had subtly shifted backward in her chair, as if she wanted to put some distance between us.

"When was the last time you were in contact with your sister?"

A wave of guilt overtook over me. "We've been texting, but we haven't seen one another in almost three weeks. How is she? Can I see her?"

The ER receptionist's body noticeably relaxed, and she gestured to the stack of paperwork. "We are missing admitting paperwork for your sister; please fill out the forms as best you can and return them when you're finished. Someone will be out to speak with you shortly."

I frowned. It was puzzling that she'd given me no information at all about Michelle's condition.

I took a seat and texted my mother that I'd reached the hospital but had no details, and began filling out forms. I had completed only half of the paperwork when my name was called. I approached the desk.

"Kate, I'm Dr. Patel." Short and thin, with closely cropped brown hair and round spectacles, he wore the expected white coat, but he didn't offer to shake my hand. He gestured toward the end of the room. "If you would please follow me?"

I shrugged, dropped my half-completed paperwork with the receptionist, and followed Dr. Patel. "Doctor, no one will tell me what's going on with my sister. Is she okay?"

He gave me a worried glance. "I'd prefer to discuss Michelle's particulars in my office."

I'd barely managed to settle into the seat in front of his desk before the questions started.

"Has your sister recently visited any country in Asia?"

"Uh, no. She doesn't even have a passport. Neither of us has ever been out of the country."

"Does she regularly come in contact commercial fowl, live or dead?"

"You mean like chickens?" I asked incredulously. "No, not unless they're on sale in a freezer pack at the grocery store."

"Does she regularly spend time in environments where she would come in contact with wild aquatic birds?"

"Why are you asking me these questions?" I demanded. "What on earth is wrong with my sister?"

Dr. Patel stared at me. "And the last time you were in contact with her was?"

"I've been working...on assignment. It's been nearly three weeks," I repeated.

"Michelle is quite ill. She's currently in isolation in the intensive care unit..."

"The ICU!" A cold panic sweat broke out on my skin. "How is this possible? She just started feeling sick this afternoon."

"...and since she transported Michelle to the ER, Mimi Wilhardt has been admitted to isolation for observation, until we can determine whether she is infected."

"Wait, my neighbor is infected? With what? What's wrong with Mimi?" I asked in confusion.

"Your sister's rapid influenza diagnostic test was positive," Dr. Patel continued. "I want you to understand, her symptoms are quite severe. Her white blood cell count is very high, which is indicative of bacterial pneumonia. This is a serious complication. She's breathing with the help of a ventilator, and we've started an antiviral neuraminidase inhibitor, which should help bring the viral load down. Right now her fever is extremely high and she is not yet responding to treatment."

"But how?" My voice was weak. "I mean, it's just the flu..."

Dr. Patel's grave look was frightening. "The fever is making her delirious. Her preexisting asthma is contributing to her breathing difficulty. I must be honest with you, Kate. She's at high risk of sepsis, and if that occurs, there is a forty to fifty percent chance that she will not survive. She also has elevated levels of tumor necrosis factor-alpha, which can lead to increased production of other cytokines."

My head was reeling. "A cytokine storm," I mumbled.

Dr. Patel looked at me curiously.

"Is Mimi sick too, then?" I asked.

"No. Not yet, at least. However, due to the severity and rapid progression of your sister's illness, we requested an expedited reverse transcription-PCR assay to determine which flu strain we're dealing with, and the results were...unexpected."

"What do you mean, 'unexpected'?"

"Michelle is infected with the influenza strain H5N1—you might know it as avian flu or bird flu. Normally this strain is not transmissible via human-to-human contact, but your sister has none of the risk factors for contracting this illness. Frankly, we have no idea how she may have come into contact with the virus. Until we understand what we're dealing with, your sister is quarantined under isolation. Out of an abundance of caution, we have quarantined Miss Wilhardt as well."

With every word Dr. Patel spoke, I felt more and more nauseated. H5N1 was not at all unfamiliar to me. H5N1 was burned into my mind—but I remembered it by a different name. I remembered it as the Luzon Flu outbreak of 1942.

"Oh, no..." I gasped. "Michelle threw up at work. At the restaurant!"

Dr. Patel removed his glasses and rubbed his eyes.

"The Centers for Disease Control has been alerted; they are serotyping the sample now to confirm our diagnosis and are also in the process of identifying the staff and restaurant patrons that may have been exposed. My contact at CDC has indicated that over the past twenty-four hours, their colleagues at the World Health Organization have reported seven hundred sixteen suspected avian flu diagnoses. Just over half of the patients have succumbed to their illness, an indication that this strain is significantly more deadly than we've seen in the past. To give you some context, in 2006, the worst year on record for avian flu, just one hundred fifteen cases were detected—in the entire year. Even more dire, the cases are occurring in urban areas, and in countries where it's not culturally common to have close contact with fowl.

"Again, this is out of an abundance of caution. H5N1 has not yet shown human-to-human transmission, but the fact that we have seen a massive uptick in cases in a short period of time, and that we can't explain how your sister contracted the disease is troubling."

The implication was not good. I hoped against hope that I was wrong. "So what do I do now?"

"We've already assembled a team consisting of a critical care specialist, a pulmonary specialist, and an infectious disease specialist. CDC's tests will provide more details on the exact virus subtype we're dealing with." Dr. Patel fixed me in his gaze and spoke in a measured tone. "For now, we watch. And we wait."

CHAPTER 27

KATE

October 31

I found a quiet corner of the ICU family lounge and dialed home.
Mom picked up on the first ring.

"Finally. Kathryn, we have been sitting by this phone for
hours. What on earth is going on?"

"Mom, I need you to sit down. Dad too," I said. Then I relayed
Dr. Patel's diagnosis.

"They won't let you see her?" Mom asked.

"No. They are worried that she's contagious."

"What is her prognosis?"

"I don't know, Mom. There is a whole team of specialists
taking care of her, but no one will tell me anything concrete." I
overheard my mother as she conversed with my father.

"Dad is already on the computer. We'll drive up to Chicago
tonight and take the first flight out of O'Hare tomorrow morning.
We'll be there by lunchtime tomorrow."

My shoulders drooped. I suddenly felt tremendous exhaustion.
Last minute plane fare would cost her a fortune. "Mom, I can send
you the money for your tickets."

Her voice was firm and unwavering. "You'll do no such thing.
My baby is standing on death's door; we'll figure it out." She

promised to send the flight details as soon as she had them.

I ended the call and slumped down in my chair, considering my options. If I had my laptop I could work, but then again Satori was a black project; no way they'd allow the code to be taken outside of the building. My phone vibrated with an incoming text from Andrew.

Andrew: *When will you be back?*
Kate: *Michelle is in ICU, has complications from flu. No ETA for my return*
Andrew: *Anything I can do?*
Kate: *No. No visitors, not even me. While I'm out can you review my code? My branch is called <LUZON>*
Andrew: *I thought your branch was <HIEROGLYPH>*
Kate: *Nope. It's definitely <LUZON>*

Would the reference fly under Andric Breckinridge's radar? I could only hope. In the meantime, what to do? It didn't seem right to leave the hospital with my sister fighting for her life. My phone's battery was running low, and of course I hadn't thought to bring a charger. I put the device in low power mode and fidgeted. I tried flipping through old magazines, but nothing held my attention for more than a few minutes. I needed to calm down; I needed to concentrate. Surely, a little mindfulness could help. I settled into a chair, closed my eyes, and began to focus on my breath.

My head spins; I am suffering from considerable disorientation. Where am I? All around me, I hear the steady droning of traffic, and I detect the faint odor of urine. The air I'm breathing is damp, and I shiver. Whatever I'm sitting on is hard and uncomfortable; it's leaching cold through my jeans. I open my eyes. My heart leaps into my throat. Where am I, and why am I here? I vividly remember that I am supposed to be in the hospital, waiting. Waiting because I can't see my sister, who is deathly ill and in isolation. Waiting for my parents, on an early morning flight they can't afford.

I'm supposed to be in the hospital, but instead I'm sitting on the concrete, on a sidewalk, in the dark night under a streetlight. The signs at the corner of the intersection read Green and Fillmore. Green and Fillmore—why does that sound so familiar? I'm groggy and my reasoning is sluggish, but slowly a realization dawns on me. Is it possible I've managed to dream my way back to the slice that has bequeathed my world with a killer strain of pandemic influenza? Have I inadvertently managed to end up somewhere useful? There is only one way to find out.

I struggle to my feet and take stock of my surroundings. If this is the place, my answer is not far away. I turn slowly around, surveying the nearby homes. Then I spot it—a three-story structure in ivory stucco with entire walls made of glass. Stainless steel. Exposed wooden beams. It stands out, aloof, from the Victorian arches and turrets and scrollwork and finials of the neighboring structures. This modern mansion is where he would choose to live; I am sure of it.

I cross the street, climb the six gray slate stairs to the landing, and knock on the front door. It's made of a single slab of some kind of blond wood and it's very solid. My knuckles hurt and I'm sure the sound won't carry at all. After a moment's search, I find a keypad panel with a call button. I press it and hold. After a moment, I press it again. Press, release. Press, release. Minutes pass. Nothing happens. I fidget, moving my weight from foot to foot, rubbing my bare arms in the chill air. My nerve is about to give out when the intercom suddenly hums.

"What?" a familiar but extremely irate voice explodes from the small speaker.

For a moment I'm paralyzed. If I'm right, I don't exist here. My name means nothing.

"Damn homeless shits, fuck off!" he grumbles.

"Wait!" I shout into the intercom. "I know you gave your CereLink away. Last month."

There is a sharp pop as the speaker is turned off, and I am left despondent.

I'm trying to figure out how to intentionally wake myself up when the door swings open. He stands there in some sort of silky pajama pants—barefoot, shirtless, and with tousled hair, but it's definitely him. The sight of him half-clothed makes my pulse race, and yet I wonder: who answers the door half-naked?

"Who are you?" he barks.

"My name is Kate."

"Get in the house," he orders, standing aside. I scurry through the door, shoulders hunched but relieved to be in from the frigid night air. The foyer is harsh and unwelcoming—polished concrete floors, stark white walls, angular stainless light fixtures.

I follow him through the open space as we reach a room with low-slung, gray, boxy furniture. He drops heavily into a club chair and stares at me with unsmiling eyes. I glance nervously about, unsure where to sit. At a loss, I perch on the edge of the gray sofa. The cushions are very, very hard.

Finally he speaks. "So...Kate. What do you think you know?" The chill in his voice matches the chill of the city, and it's disconcerting. It reminds me of someone. It reminds me of Andric Breckinridge.

"I know your name is Andrew Breckinridge. I know your company makes CereLink. And I know that a month ago, you were visited by yourself. By my Andrew. I know he persuaded you to give him your CereLink and the nanoprobes that support it."

He appraises me with coolness, rubbing his chin with his thumb and forefinger.

"Your Andrew? You must be the sidekick. The return ticket. He didn't mention you were a Jane." I'm unfamiliar with the slang but not with the tone. The slight stings.

A figure appears in the doorway. It's a woman—a thin, statuesque blonde with big eyes and fantastic legs. Her long hair is tousled, and she is wearing a man's long-sleeved dress shirt and nothing more. The top *three buttons are undone. She leans against the doorjamb, cocks her head, and asks, "Baby, who's she?" She is petulant and the slightest of pouts graces her full lips.*

"Cerise, baby, go back to bed. I'll be up soon." The words are innocent but the tone is lascivious.

Cerise looks annoyed but obeys. As she retreats down the hallway, she swings her hips seductively, and he leers at her backside until she is out of sight. My chest aches; it's as if my heart has been stabbed with an ice pick, but I try to push my feelings aside. I need his help; I can't afford to alienate him in any way.

His attention returns to me, and he arches an eyebrow. My shoulders shrink farther as I involuntarily measure myself against the Amazonian princess who has just sauntered out of the room. I feel sorely lacking. But still. I have a job to do.

I take a deep breath and try to compose my thoughts.

"CereLink technology is not the only thing that has come back with us to our reality," I admit. "We had an unexpected hitchhiker: the Luzon Flu. It's a small outbreak now, but it's spreading fast, and none of our antivirals are helping. Please tell me you have some amazingly effective medication or some other kind of treatment that we can use to stop this thing."

He seems wholly uninterested in my plight. "There is no treatment."

"How is that possible?" I lament. "With all the advanced science you have, how is it that you haven't developed any treatment for deadly influenza?"

He drops his chin, stares up at me, and yawns. "We don't need to treat it because no one gets flu anymore. We have a universal vaccine. Influenza hasn't been a concern anywhere in the world for the last twenty-five years."

I know a vaccine can't help my sister; she is already too sick. I wonder if I can actually dream myself into a world where a cure exists. Then I wonder if it's even technically possible to develop an antiviral that will help Michelle. I wonder if she has enough time left for me to try. A feeling of dread begins building in my chest, but I press on.

"How does the universal vaccine work?"

He sighs as if he resents the effort, then rises from his seat. He's gone for a few moments, and when he returns, he's wearing his CereLink. He stares at the ceiling for a moment, then speaks in monotone.

"The surface of influenza virus is covered with protrusions called hemagglutinin molecules. The protrusions make the virus look like a ball covered in lollipops. The hemagglutinin proteins allow the virus to invade our cells. Early vaccinations used a dead or deactivated virus to induce an antibody response; the antibodies generated by the immune system immobilize the virus by attaching to the head of the lollipop. But the vaccine won't work for long because the virus undergoes antigenic shift—it is constantly mutating. The exact configuration of the proteins on the head of the spike changes all the time, which renders your body's antibodies useless. The way to circumvent antigenic shift is to find a target on the virus that doesn't mutate rapidly, or at all. A vaccine of this nature will produce antibodies that can combat any flu variant."

"Okay, that all sounds great," I reply. "But how do we find the target on the virus that doesn't mutate?"

He yawns; it is obvious this topic holds no interest for him. "If I tell you, will it get you the hell out of my living room?"

I get the feeling he is still preoccupied with Cerise. Lips pursed, I manage a single nod.

He sighs, then stares past me with unfocused eyes. For a moment I think he's not going to tell me after all. "Viral neuraminidase. You don't need the whole protein; the gene for this structure codes for four hundred and fifty-three amino acids, and the section from one hundred fifty-three to three hundred seventy-nine are the key to evoking a reasonable antigenic response. And if your dimwit biochemists are still manufacturing vaccines with eggs, then you're screwed. This needs to be a recombinant vaccine produced in bioreactors," he said. "Can we call this visit concluded?"

I hesitate, straining hard to remember the details. "Thanks," I reply nervously, "but I need to ask you one more thing."

He pulls his CereLink from his head impatiently. "You're going to tell me that the prototype for the device he's building isn't working."

I nod.

He shakes his head. "I told him he was going to get hung up on the wetware. What are you using as a coating for the nanoparticles?"

"We've tried polysorbate-80, and we've tried some kind of sugar derived from lobster shells — I think it's called chitosan," I reply, racking my brain for the details.

"Polyethylene glycol grafting?" Andrew asks.

I wish I'd paid closer attention during the morning scrum meetings. "That's PEG, right?"

Andrew's nod was succinct. "Tell him to use PEG-grafted alginate, and this is important: the PEG grafting density must be zero-point-six-five chains per nanometer squared, or it won't work."

"PEG-grafted alginate, zero-point-six-five chains per nanometer squared." I repeat it to myself on a loop, hoping desperately I can remember all of this accurately, long enough to get it home.

"Our deal was that after I installed the CereLink, he would provide the details for how he managed to hack the multiverse. But then he never showed. He was also extremely cagey about the role that you play in the whole enterprise. You're decidedly less sophisticated than I expected. But perhaps you can hold up his end of the bargain."

I resolve not to tell him anything, either. "You said it yourself; I'm just the return ticket. I have no idea how his technology actually works."

I put on my best poker face, but unbidden thoughts about what is necessary to achieve slice exit fill my mind, causing my cheeks to burn. I shrink back into the uncomfortable sofa.

For the first time, his face breaks into a grin — but rather than reassuring me, his expression makes me feel like he is the wolf and I am the henhouse.

"You're blushing. Rather more than a work relationship you have going on, I presume. Unexpected."

The way he looks at me makes my skin crawl. The word repeats inside my head, increasing in its intensity. "No, no, no, no, NO!" And then I am awake.

I jumped into instant alertness, nearly falling out of my chair in the ICU waiting room, intensely irritated but with a completely clear head. I was surprised that I'd fallen asleep while meditating, and my neck was stiff enough to indicate that I had been slumped in my chair for quite some time. I checked my phone and realized that it was not yet even light outside, and quickly thumbed some notes about the scientific details for the nanoparticles and vaccine design I couldn't afford to forget. Risking the last of my battery power, I retrieved the email containing Mom's flight itinerary.

I checked in with the reception desk. The nurse called Dr. Patel, and he brusquely informed me that my sister's condition wasn't improving, and that the team caring for her had started additional antiviral medications. I was still not allowed to see Michelle, and my parents wouldn't arrive for hours; there was nothing more I could do here. But there *was* something I could do if I could muster up some resources. And resources meant heading back to Albaion.

Although it was barely five in the morning, I marched straight to Andrew's office and pounded on the door. It didn't take long for him to let me in. Of course he had started his workday early, or more likely he had worked through the night.

"I just have to say, you can be a real dick," I said.

"Kathryn? What are you talking about? I thought you were at the hospital with your sister. How is Michelle? Are you sure she has Luzon Flu?" He looked exhausted. Definitely an all-nighter.

I glared at him. "I'm not sure. But according to the CDC and the World Health Organization, over the past thirty-six hours there has been a spike in cases of deadly bird flu, in extremely unlikely places. Oh, and PEG-grafted alginate, zero-point-six-five chains per nanometer squared," I said, fuming.

"I don't understand…"

"He said you would overlook the wetware, and that this will fix the problem with the nanoprobes. Write it down; I'm not sure how much longer I can keep all this in my head."

He stared at me, puzzled, then finally his eyes widened with comprehension.

"I don't know how this is possible," he slowly reasoned, "but you must have met Cerise."

I didn't reply.

"Kathryn," he started, rising from his desk, "did you dream? Did you dream your way into the CereLink slice?"

I nodded, and his eyes grew wide.

"Did you do it intentionally? Are you able to direct your dreams now?"

I shook my head.

Exhaustion compounded with confusion was plastered all over his face.

"Kathryn, talk to me," he urged. "Please."

The part of me that was still pissed at the alternate Andrew wanted to storm out of his office. But then again, there was the matter of the vaccine.

"There have been a few times—under stress—where I ended up someplace I needed to be. I didn't try. I can't control it. And if I ever can figure out how to control it, I'm telling you right now—I never want to see that version of you again."

"You know that's not me, right?" His voice held a desperate edge. When he stepped closer to me, I involuntarily leaned away.

"Can you honestly tell me that you're not attracted to her? To women like her? I've seen what you do to literally every single female you come in contact with."

Andrew sighed. "In the interest of complete and total honesty,

I should tell you that I've spent my fair share of time with women like Cerise. Maybe more than my fair share of time. But things change, Kathryn, and people change, too."

In my mind, I imagined a long parade of leggy blondes. "In the interest of total and complete honesty, that doesn't make me feel any better," I sulked. "But since we're sharing, I guess I should tell you that the way he looked at me totally creeped me out."

"But how did he... I don't understand. You talked to him? And he could see you? I thought you had no ability to interact with the environment of your dream. I thought you just had a window."

My jaw set, I stared at him defiantly. "Things change."

The uncomfortable silence between us intensified.

Finally he spoke. "This is a whole new ball game. How long have you had this...ability?"

"It began about five weeks ago."

I wasn't prepared for the hurt expression that arose on his face. It occurred to me that I'd never seen him look so wounded, and my anger faded into gnawing guilt.

"I didn't tell you at first because I didn't trust you, and then later...well, things just started happening so fast. And now there's this new crisis, which reminds me—tell me that some corner of your father's empire makes vaccines. Because that asshat version of you also told me how to manufacture a reliable universal vaccine for influenza."

Andrew frowned, deep in thought.

"There is a biopharmaceutical company in the Albaion portfolio. I can definitely get a message to the chief development officer. Why do you suspect the Luzon Flu?"

"It can't be a coincidence," I insisted. "The samples are with the CDC, so they'll eventually determine whether it's a bird flu strain that can be transmitted between humans. But I'm telling you now—there's no way my sister has been exposed to the avian flu from actual birds."

"There has been some preliminary research that indicated that avian flu should respond well to our existing antiviral treatments," Andrew replied hopefully.

A wave of anguish washed over me as I pictured my sister, pale and delirious, attached to a ventilator. All alone, except for the machines keeping her alive. "So far, nothing is working."

He turned his gaze to the ceiling, cradling his chin in his hands. The longer he sat in stillness, the more amped up I became. He eyed me pointedly. "Even if we can produce this vaccine, you know it can't help Michelle, right?"

It was as if I was riding an emotional roller coaster, and suddenly I was speeding down the big hill, right back into furious.

"Of course I know that!" I snapped. "I'm not an idiot. But if this *is* Luzon Flu, it's going to be lethal, and extremely contagious. And I can't let the death of half the population of this planet happen on my watch."

Andrew nodded. He was almost certainly the only other person who could understand. He simply gazed at me for a long time, with those deep sapphire eyes, now awash in sorrow.

"We have to stop it," he said.

"Of course we do. Hopefully the vaccine can be produced quickly. With any luck, the quarantine will happen fast enough and hold long enough to avert a global disaster."

"I'm not talking about the vaccine."

His words expressed a new sense of quiet determination. In a flash of understanding, I realized he meant all of it; none of this ever should have happened. But for his hubris, my sister would be well. His hubris, and my complicity.

The careening parade of vacillating emotions and lack of sleep was taking its toll, and I could feel myself collapsing under the strain. I slumped into the black leather armchair in the corner of his office, folded myself into a ball, and surrendered to my dismay.

In an instant he was kneeling before me. He took my head in his hands and wiped away my tears with a swipe of his thumb.

"I am a mess," I sniffled.

His smile was wan. "That's understandable."

"The version of you that you might have been... Seeing that broke my heart," I admitted, examining the worn laces of my sneakers.

His pressed his forehead to mine, and I closed my eyes.

"I am sorry," he murmured. "I'm sorry you had to experience that. But have no doubt, Kathryn Rathman, that I am here for you, and with you."

"I can't for the life of me imagine why," I whispered.

He didn't even miss a beat. "Hmmm...yes, why *would* I want to be with a woman who can literally bend reality to her will?"

CHAPTER 28

ANDREW

November 3

The clock was closing in on two in the morning, and he was still at his desk, composing the daily progress report for Project Satori. His eyes were weary; his mind was spent. But a team of sixty-three preeminent experts was counting on him to lead this project. Sixty-three extraordinarily driven scientists and technologists who had accepted extremely lucrative contracts, signed stringent NDAs, and agreed to the very unusual request that they remain sequestered in the compound for the duration of the project. Sixty-three brilliant and extremely motivated specialists who never seemed to sleep. In a moment of irreverence, Amir had nicknamed them the Brain Trust.

She had been right; or, rather, the alternate version of himself had been right. The nanoparticles were the problem. Once they made the adjustments to the particle coating, the Satori device trials became much more interesting. He'd had his head inside the ponderous shell for more hours than he cared to recall, watching video clips of everything under the sun and waiting for the machines to process the signals collected from his brain, but the results were extraordinary.

The prototype and accompanying algorithms were providing copious data. Machine learning specialists had already adapted the deep learning processes previously identified using functional MRI scans to retrain a convolutional neural network to recognize the classification of the images he viewed. The neural net could now name the dolphin or sunset or kiwi bird in the movies he viewed faster than he could shout them out.

Earlier this evening, he'd integrated Kathryn's code for visual text recognition to work with the Satori signal, and he tested it against the gold standard for image reproduction, the Deep Generative Multiview Model. The speed, accuracy, and detail of the algorithms astounded everyone. He scanned printed pages. Each page was decoded as fast as he could sweep his eyes over the letters, and a facsimile appeared on a screen across the room. So much for the eidetic memory, he thought.

No wonder the Brain Trust was unwilling to rest. The advances were coming fast—on the order of days rather than years. Not a single team member doubted that this work would have impact far beyond everyone's wildest imagination.

Now that they had a concept decoder and the functional equivalent of a brain-to-text teletype, the experts were eager to tackle the previously daunting prospect of decoding and reproducing visual images in real time. Which would mean he'd soon be back under the cumbersome helmet. It would also mean he'd have to be careful—very careful—about what was happening in his head.

A distinctive knock startled him just as he hit send on the progress report. Amir let himself in, carrying a broad, wide white porcelain cup on a saucer. He was wearing a gray shirt that read "npm install caffeine," and he looked as exhausted as Andrew felt.

Andrew closed his eyes, relaxed in his chair, and ran a hand through his disheveled hair.

"Your timing couldn't be better," he sighed. "It looks like it's going to be another all-nighter."

Amir placed the coffee on the desk and shook his head. "This is insane, man. I'm just as juiced as anyone about this project, but even I'm beat. And I'm a decade younger than you are."

Andrew reached for the cup and sipped the warm, foamy cappuccino, fighting to keep his eyes from glazing over.

"Eight," he replied. "You're only eight years younger than I am. Let's keep things in perspective here."

"Whatevs, Gramps. You got an eye on the outside world at all?"

"Nope. No time."

"CNN just broke a big-ass story about a deadly bird flu outbreak in Texas. Apparently a cluster of eighty-eight patients were admitted to the hospital in San Antonio in the last twenty-four hours, and forty-seven are already dead."

Andrew closed his eyes, dropping his head into his hands.

"It's definitely getting worse. Every time we fix one disaster, another one pops up in its place. I was hoping it was a fluke. That the virus would surface in a few places and just burn out."

Amir frowned. "So why's it happening now? You said the slice suffered their pandemic in the forties, right?"

Andrew was silent for a long time, then raised his head and stared listlessly at the ceiling. "Honestly, I have no idea. My track record for predicting the effect that slice travel will have on our reality has been abysmal."

"You don't mince words, bro. Guess it was super-sketch to use the multiverse as our dog-food program."

"I'm still optimistic we can contain this before it becomes a pandemic. I received an email from Ebhardt at the biotech subsidiary in Frankfort an hour ago. The samples we delivered from Kathryn's sister and the information about the vaccine target she provided allowed the team to immediately ramp up production on the DNA vaccine. Normally it would take at least ten weeks to get the drug into production, but the CDC and the WHO are already beating down their door. They are optimistic that they could have a viable product in as early as four weeks. Maybe we can get this beast contained before it can do any real damage."

Amir sat heavily in the leather chair and clenched his hands. His normally mirth-filled eyes were dark with worry.

"Michelle didn't deserve this. How's Kate holding up?"

Andrew's look was guarded.

"Her parents are here. I'm sure she's fine."

Amir's expression shifted to exasperation. "Oh, come on. We have been working together for years. I've been sitting right next to you in the same room for, like, sixteen hours a day. Every day. I've known you had a hard-on for Kate since the moment she walked through the door. Plus all those one-on-one meetings? You'd have to be a total bonehead to miss that." Amir gave him a hard stare. "I'm actually a little offended that you didn't trust me enough to tell me."

"I've tried to be discreet. He doesn't know about my…attachment to Kathryn. And he doesn't know that the slice we raided has encoder technology to go along with the decoding that we're developing now."

"But that doesn't matter," Amir argued. "Since there's no way to get back there to pick up the extra tech."

"Well, it turns out that's not completely accurate." Andrew drained the last of the thick, creamy coffee from his cup.

Amir stared, blinking furiously. Suddenly his eyes widened. "It's Kate, right?"

Andrew nodded. "He can't find out."

"Well, you know he won't hear it from me. So, when's our girl coming home?"

The look on Andrew's face made Amir wish he hadn't asked.

"I don't know. I've pulled every string I have to get the foremost medical experts on the west coast on the case, but it's been two days, and Michelle still isn't improving. Kate and her parents have been living at the hospital. Beyond that, I don't know much. She knows it's wise to guard her communications."

Andrew's computer chimed; one of the sixty-three experts needed his attention.

Amir stood, reached over, and nonchalantly retrieved the empty cup and saucer. "You could take a few hours off and go see her."

Andrew's eyes were fixed on the computer screen, and he began typing furiously. "And leave all this?" he replied, his eyes rapidly scanning incoming messages. "Besides, she specifically asked me not to come."

"Well, you're the boss. I'm just saying...it's not always about the work."

"You've met my father, right? It is *always* about Albaion."

Amir shrugged and moved toward the door. "Then I guess I'll get back to it."

With a wry half grin in his eyes, he gave the door a definitive jerk. "Party on, Wayne."

Andrew fought a cynical smile. "Party on, Garth."

Andrew was startled awake when the door to his office slammed violently against the wall. He sat up straight in his office chair, rubbed his dry eyes, and tried to focus. When had he fallen asleep? What time was it?

"Don't you ever knock?" he muttered as Andric Breckinridge marched to the edge of his desk. The man was staring daggers;

Andrew knew whatever came next wouldn't be good.

"You have been withholding information."

"I sent out a status report just a few hours ago. It was very thorough. The project is running ahead of schedule; the trials are going well. You know everything I know."

Breckinridge's eyes narrowed. "What I know is that you neglected to describe the methodology for encoding and broadcasting signals back *into* the brain."

Andrew clenched his jaw and intentionally slowed his breathing. He rapidly ran through a mental list of his actions over the last day. How had information about the encoder found its way to Andric? Or had he simply made the mental leap himself— the logical next step?

"There was a lot of tech that I didn't retrieve. We were only there for two days. And there is only so much I can realistically recall with any level of accuracy. This has always been a factor. The information I did retrieve is incredibly promising. Can't you just be satisfied with what we have?"

Andric waved his hand dismissively. "A minor inconvenience that will soon be irrelevant, as you can wear the device during your future travels. We will observe and record all of your movements and experiences, so this bothersome dependence on your memory will no longer be of concern. A definite advantage. But with only half the function if I cannot direct your actions."

"You know I don't have the ability to re-access a slice. If you want the encoding technology, you're going to have to develop it on your own."

"On the contrary. I'll simply use that little tart you're infatuated with to return and retrieve it."

Andrew was unable to suppress his dazed expression. How could he know? Could it have been Amir? Andrew dismissed the notion immediately, as the more likely explanation dawned upon him.

"You've bugged my office! What kind of cynical bastard spies on his own son?"

"The kind whose intractable offspring turns out to be a disloyal recreant."

The two men stared at one another with mutual smoldering animosity. Andrew clenched his hands so tightly that his fingernails dug deep half-moon indentations on his palms. The oppressive silence stretched on until it was suddenly broken by the vibration of Andrew's phone. Despite his father's scowl, Andrew took a deep, calming breath and answered the call.

"Hello?"

There was a long pause. On the other end of the line, he could hear ragged, uneven breathing.

"Andrew…"

His heart leaped into his throat at the sound of Kathryn's nearly hoarse voice. Something was terribly wrong.

"What is it?" He wanted to say so many things—none of which would be acceptable with his father still fuming in his office.

When she finally spoke, she sounded incredibly small. "She died, Andrew. My sister is dead."

CHAPTER 29

KATE

November 5

The week my sister died, I learned many things—many macabre and horrible things no one should ever have to know. For instance, when someone succumbs to a highly contagious influenza strain, her body must be handled by as few people as possible. Under no circumstances will her ravaged and lifeless corpse be made available for viewing. Not to say goodbye. Not even to her family. The rules say she must be cremated immediately.

When all is said and done, the remains of an adult female weigh only four pounds. Cremains, they call them. When you're transporting cremated human remains via airline they put them in a temporary urn, which is just a fancy name for a small, black plastic box lined with a clear plastic bag. The temporary urn was tall and narrow, and the lid on top opened on a hinge. I couldn't stop thinking of it as a tiny trash can. Another thing I shouldn't have to know.

"I need to take my baby home," my mother insisted.

They had been sequestered in my cramped Palo Alto apartment for days, and they were going stir-crazy.

"You can't take a commercial flight."

Each time I turned on the TV or opened a news site, I was bombarded by images of the seriously ill, hooked up to ventilators and encased in makeshift isolation wards that were little more than cubicles made from heavy plastic sheeting. The number of cases was growing, and so was the death count. Over four thousand deaths attributed to bird flu had now been reported, cropping up in all major cities, with no rhyme or reason to the pattern of the outbreak. Citizens were advised to continue their daily activities, but the b-roll images that accompanied the news stories showed eerily empty scenes of iconic locations: Times Square unpopulated, Disney World empty, Golden Gate Park deserted. The vaccine wouldn't be ready for weeks. The risk was too great.

"We can't sit around here forever," she argued. "We have a farm to run."

"Let me see what I can do."

My parents transported my sister's ashes home on Andric Breckinridge's impeccably appointed private Embraer jet. I saw them off at the generation aviation terminal at San Jose International, where the security was lax enough that I could hug them goodbye on the aircraft. I supposed the rules were different for the obscenely wealthy. Aboard the craft, my empty gaze settled uneasily on my parents. Incongruous in the spacious, creamy custom leather seats, my father sat with his head slumped; my mother curled under the protective arc of his strong arm, ashen and bereft. What was left of my sister rested heavily in my mother's lap, packed inside a plain brown cardboard box. Every time I pictured the small black trash bin inside, a wave of nausea threatened to overtake me.

I sat in my office, staring blankly at the computer, lost in a haze of sleep deprivation. I knew instinctively that if I slept, I would dream; and I couldn't bear the prospect of any more horror. Worse yet, what if I dreamed my way into an existence where my sister still lived? I was certain either experience would break me. I couldn't begin to imagine when I'd regain the focus to touch my code. Not when the world had fallen apart.

I was startled out of my waking stupor by a subtle rap on my door. Andrew let himself in and perched on the edge of my desk.

"Shouldn't you be working?" I mumbled, staring down at my hands.

"I've been working for the last fourteen hours. I think I can spare a few minutes."

"But the flu..."

"I received an update today. They've fast-tracked the vaccine, and thanks to you, production is proceeding more quickly than expected. It's the fastest rollout of a vaccine they've ever achieved. The first doses should be available in just three more weeks."

Three more weeks? That seemed like an eternity. How many more would die?

"Maybe we should slice," I offered, although the thought of another far-slice undertaking made me weak in the knees.

He lifted my left hand and traced invisible whirls around the small scar left by the Bug. "There's no guarantee that we would find a viable treatment. And based on our track record, we stand a real chance of making things even worse."

"But Andric..." I insisted.

"He can wait for an hour." He reached a hand toward me, and I stood and embraced him. He buried his face in my hair, and for just a moment, I closed my eyes. The urge to sleep was powerful, but I forced myself to stay awake. It was a Herculean effort.

I felt a sudden, overwhelming urge to be somewhere— anywhere, but here.

"Take me to my apartment."

"Are you sure?" he asked.

I nodded.

He navigated the pickup to my apartment complex, and I fumbled through my pockets for the key.

I could barely stand the unnerving quiet of the place. I wandered through the rooms, cradling her favorite coffee mug, running my hand over a trashy paperback romance she'd left half read on the table. I expected to be overwhelmed by emotion, but instead I felt its curious absence.

Andrew followed closely as I roamed the small space, my hand absentmindedly lingering over the back of the sofa, a light switch, a doorframe. The emptiness in the apartment echoed the deafening silence in my heart. The vacuum was disconcerting, a hollowness that threatened to swallow me whole.

Andrew hesitated. "Kathryn, maybe this isn't the best idea."

I ignored him. In her room, I held her sweater to my face, and I could still feel the essence of her, clinging to this place. Or maybe it was just me, clinging to her.

Without warning, the grief overwhelmed me. Like a tidal wave, it surged through me and my body was racked with tears. In an instant, his arms surrounded me and I let the wave of blackness overtake me. I sobbed for what seemed like forever, and only an instant; the chasm of loss and longing inside me seemingly endless.

I don't know when my mouth found his, but the hunger I felt was stronger than breathing—stronger than thought, stronger than life itself. I tore at the tiny plastic buttons on his gray Burberry shirt, not caring if I ruined a three-hundred-dollar garment. His hands were on my face, in my hair, under my shirt. I pushed him toward the bed in my sister's room and fell in a heap atop him. In a moment, I had pushed my shirt over my head. I was fumbling frantically with the Italian leather belt at the waist of his well-tailored pants when he sat up abruptly and grasped both my wrists.

"Not like this," he panted in anguish. "Kathryn, you're grieving. If this is just an escape from the pain—"

I suddenly felt the world pitch and roll, followed by the anguished roil of acid in my belly. My hand clamped over my mouth. I lurched off the bed and stumbled toward the bathroom, where I purged the small amount of breakfast I'd managed to coax down that morning. I clutched the edge of the porcelain toilet bowl as if it was my lifeline and wept inconsolably.

He reappeared a moment later, properly clothed and carrying Michelle's sweater. As I slid it on, he gathered me in his arms and shepherded me toward the door. I knew then I could never return. It would be the last time I ever set eyes on the place that my sister and I had called home.

CHAPTER 30

ANDREW

November 20

He was already reclined on the portable hospital bed when she shuffled into Albaion's fMRI suite, wearing a white linen blouse and beige wool skirt that would be perfectly appropriate in the unlikely case that they managed to reach their desired destination.

It was three in the morning and everyone was exhausted, but Kathryn looked particularly awful; her eyes were sunken and vacant, and she moved about in a daze. He was sure she hadn't been sleeping, and logs of her badge activity indicated that she rarely ventured out of her room—not even to the kitchen for meals. Janine assured him she regularly delivered warm broth and mint tea. Kathryn didn't code and she refused to see him. Janine reported that she spent most of her days sitting on her worn cushion, meditating. Waiting for this moment. A moment he was dreading.

Every muscle in his body tensed as the huge CereLink prototype apparatus was carefully positioned over his head. Project Satori staff bumped elbows with the two nurses tasked with attaching the sensors used to monitor vitals for far-slice travel. Through the large windowpane, he could see the ever-present scowl on the face of Andric Breckinridge as he paced in the control room.

Beside him, Kathryn stared blankly as the EKG electrodes to monitor heart rhythm were placed on her chest, arms, and legs. Her expression remained empty as Christopher Daniels gingerly pulled the EEG cap into position over her loose auburn hair. Though she rested only feet away on the second portable bed, he had the uncanny sensation that she was unreachable, miles and miles distant. His hand absentmindedly moved toward his right pocket, but he stopped it with a violent jerk and instead moved it upward until he felt the smooth exterior of the enormous CereLink helmet. He gave the helmet two sharp taps and then flashed a thumbs-up to the control room.

The intercom popped once, then Janine announced, "We're receiving imaging."

As he stared at the fMRI machine, Andrew imagined the impressionistic rendering of the device that would appear on the monitor in the other room, then chuckled ironically to himself as he pictured the visual recursion he was undoubtedly creating with his mental image. Something like the infinity effect in a funhouse, when two parallel mirrors reflect the same image, growing ever more miniscule.

"Andrew, we need you to focus," Janine interrupted. "Can you please concentrate on the text calibration sheet?"

They were calibrating the text transcription. He picked up a white paper card and scanned the paragraph printed upon it—nonsense sentences now familiar after a hundred reads.

The computers would record a video stream of everything he saw, but a secondary computer cluster would also be logging a steady text stream of the taxonomy of everything in his visual field so that it could be searched and cross-referenced later. The object detection would attempt to label everything that passed through his field of vision. The fMRI machine would translate to: hospital, equipment, tool, medical devices, electronics. He glanced at Kathryn. The log would spew: person, adult, woman, clothing. He sighed inwardly at the constellation of taxonomy it would not detect: tenderness and concern. Adoration.

Amir strode into the room carrying a familiar plastic case, flip-flops slapping the floor with each step. He wore a deep maroon T-shirt that spelled out "There's no place like 127.0.0.1" but his characteristic good-natured grin was notably absent.

He deftly unsnapped the latches of the heavy-duty plastic box, extracted a Bug, and positioned it carefully over Andrew's right hand. The second Bug he lifted from the case trailed a long, slender black cable attached to a tiny port in its side. He positioned Kate's device, then unspooled the fragile cable and draped it over her shoulder, snaking it back toward the rack of equipment.

"Okay, lock and load," Amir reported. "Let's clear the room."

Amir, the nurses, and the white-coated Brain Trust cabal shuffled from the room. The heavy door sighed on its pneumatic hinges, and the silence within the heavily shielded room was so complete that even the subtle whirring of the computers in the server racks seemed deafening.

The intercom buzzed again. Breckinridge spoke, revealing his impatience.

"Ms. Rathman, you will begin. As soon as we've detected your REM stage, we will back-sync your device and insert Andrew as well. Determine your whereabouts promptly and return immediately if you have not reached the target destination."

Kathryn's eyes focused for the first time since she'd entered the room; she glowered at the control room window with a look of undeniable hostility.

In the background, through the still-live intercom, Janine spoke tentatively. "They might be more comfortable if I dim the lights..."

"Their comfort is no concern of mine," Breckinridge snapped.

Andrew tried to remember the last time he'd heard his father speak without irritation. Nothing came to mind.

Despite Breckinridge's protest, the lights in the room dimmed smoothly, and Kathryn closed her eyes.

"I want the rest of the details surrounding the CereLink technology," Andric barked. "We must understand how they use it for incoming communication. It's not enough to read the signals. I need to transmit them. I want the technology to make it portable enough to be wearable. And while you're at it, I want the specifications for the solar paint. Read as many white papers and technical works as you can. Remember, it *must* be visual. Read it all. We'll transcribe everything here and sort out the details later. Then get out. I expect this assignment to be completed within twelve hours."

Andrew frowned. He was well aware of the mission requirements. His father had made them abundantly clear—numerous times. No matter that he had explained—more than once—that returning to the CereLink slice ran the risk of accelerating the avian flu pandemic, or possibly contaminating this reality with even more unexpected ill effects.

"Will you please just get off that microphone and let us work?" Andrew muttered through clenched teeth. The intercom pointedly clicked off.

Just feet away, Kathryn rested her head against the slope of the hospital bed and closed her eyes. He could hear her shallow breathing as it became more regular, and he watched as the deep worry lines in her forehead relaxed. Her head, sheathed in electrodes, lolled to one side.

The minutes ticked by in tense silence. Then, without warning, the probe on the Bug violently pierced his skin, pitching him into darkness.

He heard crickets and the tranquil sound of trickling water. When he opened his eyes, he found himself sprawled on the smooth, cool terra-cotta tiles of an outdoor patio. The darkness was gently illuminated by several low landscape lights. Their glow revealed a courtyard surrounded by a white stucco structure with Palladian doors and arched windows. For one disorientating minute, he wondered if he'd landed in a lavish villa in the Spanish countryside.

"I'm over here," Kathryn called from behind him.

He staggered to his feet and ducked around a bushy bird-of-paradise to find her perched pensively on a teak bench facing an impressive cascading fountain.

He focused on her face as he reached into his pocket and palmed the fold of paper. "Are we in the right slice?"

Her dark-rimmed eyes were listless. "I told you, I have no control over where I land. This isn't the CereLink slice. This is another Kate's home in Bel Air. It's kind of...a safe space for me. It's become sort of a homing beacon."

He looked around once more, imagining the soft and dreamy rendition of the graceful arches that his father would see reproduced and recorded on the faraway computer courtesy of the sensors attached to his head. While he was admiring the palm trees flanking the courtyard entrance, he inconspicuously palmed the folded paper from his pocket and passed it to her.

He heard the sound of paper unfolding and intentionally raised his eyes to the heavens, finding familiarity in the constellation Andromeda.

"It's odd," he remarked. "I feel strangely at home here."

"You should," she replied. He wondered if he was imagining the note of tenderness in her voice. "This is your home, too."

The implication of her words became clear, and he smiled. Then he waited. Minutes passed. He heard the soft crinkling of paper as she refolded the letter and slipped it into her skirt pocket.

When she finally spoke, she was guarded. "The outbreak shows no sign of slowing. Thirty thousand infected worldwide. Over half have died. And it's only the beginning of flu season."

He rubbed his face and took a deep breath, but kept his vision trained on the garden. "The vaccine trials are very encouraging, but even if it works perfectly, it will take time to ramp up to full production."

Her voice carried the weight of a thousand regrets. "It won't be quick enough. That virus never should have happened. Too many have already been lost."

"I know," he replied.

"Do you think what you propose will work?"

He refocused his gaze on the fountain. "I think it's the only way."

"Okay," she said. "No promises. But I'll try."

"We need to be careful. Thanks to your code, they can transcribe any text I read, and the visualizations of what I see aren't photorealistic, but they are still detailed enough to be completely recognizable."

"Do they get a transcript of what you hear?" she asked.

"They haven't decoded Broca's area...yet. That means our conversation should still fly under the radar."

"Anything else?"

"Broca's area also controls inner speech, so my thoughts are also private...for now."

Her reply was measured monotone. "Good to know."

"How are you?" he ventured. He intentionally focused his eyes on his hands. "We haven't spoken since..."

She sighed heavily. "Now is not the time for that conversation."

He realized he'd been digging a nail into the cuticle of his left thumb and stared at a minuscule bead of blood as it formed. The courtyard suddenly felt suffocating.

In the face of uncomfortable situations, he'd always fallen back to his work, and this moment was no exception.

"I know you don't have a lot of control over where you emerge, but since you can shift in location, then perhaps landing us inside a library would save some time."

"I'll try."

He knew it was unwise, but every one of her terse responses made him wish he could search her eyes for a spark of additional meaning. Instead he picked invisible dust from his pant leg and looked anywhere except at Kathryn. A warm breeze whispered through the atrium, rustling the flora and scattering droplets from the fountain. Three o'clock in the morning in November still meant temperate nights in southern California.

"Thank you for bringing me to your safe place," he offered.

Her oppressive silence was unnerving. He was relieved when he felt her hand slide over his. Her reply was heavy with fatigue. "I suppose we'd just as well get on with it. Close your eyes; those creeps back at the ranch don't need to see this."

He complied and turned toward her, denying the powerful urge to contemplate the smooth skin of her cheeks, to gaze into her hazel eyes—to ascertain if her actions were mere obligation or if she still felt more. He winced when she placed her cool hand against the curve of his jaw, startled by her touch. Yet his tension dissolved as her lips brushed against his cheek, her breath warm and gentle. For this one moment, the overwhelming avalanche of desire banished the specter of his complicity in all the wrongs he had orchestrated. He surrendered to the urge to pull her toward him, grateful that the Brain Trust had not yet unraveled the secret to   decoding   emotions.

CHAPTER 31

KATE

November 20

It was dark and tranquil in the expansive reading room in Stanford's Green Library because it was three thirty in the morning and the building was utterly deserted. Alone in the shadows, for the first time since Michelle departed, I felt the possibility that there could be a way out of this mess.

I knew I had only minutes alone before they would send Andrew in after me.

I fumbled my way through the darkness until I reached an upholstered chair next to an end table and flipped the switch on a graceful copper and mica Dirk van Erp table lamp. I slipped his note from my skirt pocket and unfolded it on the side table, gently running my hand over the surface of the paper to smooth the creases. He wrote in a neat hand—in block letters that were as precise as if they had been printed by a draftsman. The page was small and the printing was dense. My lips pursed as I reread his carefully chosen words.

Kathryn—

I am so sorry—I can't even begin to apologize for the danger, torment, and sorrow that I have brought into your life.

I know now that you were not trapped in Andric Breckinridge's inescapable grasp by circumstance; you were forced into it by my actions. Perhaps they were equally as perverse as his. I thought I could protect you, but his avarice runs deeper than I ever imagined. You and I and the whole of humanity are nothing more than pawns in his never-ending quest for influence and power. I know that now.

If my father was ever a good or just man, there is no hope of reaching his better angels now.

I know that the directive he has given you is unachievable. Yet I propose a counter-plan. He can monitor me, but he can't control me—not when I'm here, with you. There is one way we can end this. One way that I can set things right. But I need your help.

Everything spun out of control when I created the Bug.

If you have gained any hint of mastery over your ability, do all you can to avoid the CereLink slice. Our presence there runs the risk of worsening the pandemic. Then find us a world where the Bug could never exist. Without it, there is no slicing. Without it, there would be no ecological ruin, no Luzon Flu. Without it, perhaps your sister would have lived.

I know that in this, as in so many things, I am asking too much of you. I also know that of all people, you are perhaps the only one who can succeed.

I remain yours—
Andrew

The clamor at the far end of the room let me know he'd arrived, and I whisked away the note.

"Over here," I called.

"Outstanding!" came his muffled reply. "I've always loved the Bender Reading Room. There are no computers in here, but what do you say we find one and determine where we've landed?"

It took only a few web searches to determine that this slice wasn't going to cut it.

Neither would the next five.

With each attempt that missed the CereLink slice, I'd wake up to the hovering specter of Andric Breckenridge, who grew increasingly enraged. With each attempt that eluded Andrew's requirements, he became ever more determined.

I was simply exhausted, which frankly made slipping into REM sleep easier and easier.

It was just after six a.m. and we were back in the Green Library. I sat at the computer, typing furiously and reading as quickly as I could while Andrew stared out the window at the shifting gray predawn clouds in the early morning sky.

His voice was strained. "Have you found anything yet?"

"Actually," I said, chewing on a nail as I scrolled and scanned. "Nothing. I'm finding nothing. Except—" I stopped, uncertain. Passing him information without alerting the brute squad monitoring his brain was an infuriating conundrum.

He massaged his temples and glanced to the ceiling but avoided looking at me or at the computer. "What?"

"Uh..." I grimaced. "You know what? We're just going to have to go there."

I grabbed a square of scrap paper and a stub of a pencil from the caddy near the computer and scratched out an address.

The sun peeked over the horizon, casting a majestic golden glow on the exquisite dove-gray facade of the nineteenth-century Victorian mansion standing before us.

"My father is going to be furious," Andrew said.

"Then you know this place?" I asked, studying the expansive portico supported by elegant Ionian columns. The graceful balcony that ran the entirety of the second floor protected symmetrical bow windows, flanking a pediment graced with a circle of stained glass depicting a stylized medieval centaur.

"My mother spent twenty years restoring this estate," he murmured, mounting the wide stone steps. At the porch, he lay a hand protectively on a thick white column. "She loved this home, and so did I. He put it on the market the day she died."

I bit my lower lip. If it had been possible to prepare him for what would come next, I would have done it. Instead, I marched to the door and rang the bell.

The petite, trim woman who answered had a tidy graying blonde bob and held a coffee cup in her hands. She had obviously been interrupted in the middle of her breakfast. When she spoke, low and sonorous, she revealed a slight accent that I couldn't quite place.

"Good morning, can I help you?" she inquired, her smile polite but guarded. Then she looked over my shoulder and glimpsed Andrew. Her coffee cup fell to the ground and shattered on the vividly colored checkerboard tiles. She grasped my shoulder tightly for support as her eyes grew round with shock.

Behind me arose a plaintive cry. "Mom?"

In an instant, the woman pushed past me. She threw her arms around Andrew and nearly knocked him off the patio with the intensity of her embrace.

Isabel shepherded us into her elegant, perfectly restored drawing room. Even as we sat, Andrew kept a protective arm around his mother. Isabel leaned into her son, still pale and visibly shaken.

"I don't understand how this is possible," she stammered, for the third time. "You died during a guerrilla raid when I took you on that stupid, selfish trip to Uganda to photograph the silverbacks. I buried you thirteen years ago."

Andrew smiled ruefully. "And I buried you eleven years ago. You succumbed to stomach cancer right after I graduated from Cal."

Isabel took her son's face in her hands and stared intently into his eyes. Her thumbs caressed his cheeks. I squirmed uncomfortably on the satiny, cream-colored cushion. Watching their reunion felt like an intrusion.

"If it's okay with you," I interrupted, "I think I'm going to find the kitchen and make a cup of tea."

"Oh, how rude of me, I can get that..." Isabel insisted, but before she could rise from her seat, I had already excused myself.

I wandered through the hallway and peeked into adjacent rooms, feeling as if I'd been transported back in time to the 1800s. I absentmindedly considered the joy my mother would feel roaming through these beautifully restored rooms, all with appropriate period fixtures and furniture. Thinking about Mom made me think about Michelle, and a jolt of fresh heartbreak struck me like a gut punch. I placed a hand against a doorjamb to steady myself and leaned against the wall. We had found a slice where Andrew never invented the Bug. If he was right—if we stayed here long enough—perhaps it would bend our reality just enough to prevent the Bug from ever existing. I wondered again whether this plan would work; and if it did, what that would mean for him, for me—for all of us.

Isabel prepared homemade chicken orzo soup and turkey

sandwiches for lunch, which we shared outside on the rear veranda, overlooking her picturesque garden landscaped in native plants. I was shocked that such large parcels of land even existed in the middle of urban Silicon Valley. Andrew continued answering her litany of questions—about his life, about his work. About the improbable set of circumstances that brought him back to her. I kept drifting back to the Big Sur coast, imagining how much my sister would have enjoyed the crashing waves against the endless blue horizon when something Isabel said startled me back to attention.

"He *must* be stopped!" she cried vehemently, pounding her fist onto the heavy wrought iron tabletop.

For a moment, I thought, *Who must be stopped?* But in an instant, I knew. Andric Breckinridge. Panic rose like bile in my throat. I shuddered, remembering that he was watching as all of this unfolded.

"Where is he now?" I blurted.

Isabel frowned and shook her head. "Rotting away in prison, I expect," she responded dryly. "After the divorce, there was an investigation into his accounting practices."

I breathed a sigh of relief. In this slice, I wouldn't be subjected to his brooding intimidation.

Isabel's spirited outburst was just the reassurance that Andrew needed. "Our plan was to find a way to prevent the creation of the technology that is causing all this calamity, and I'm sure we've just found it. With your permission, we'd like to stay here for a couple of days."

Isabel's smile was beatific. She took her son's hand between her own and beamed. "My dear—you can stay as long as you like. I'd be content to keep you with me forever!"

CHAPTER 32

ANDRIC

November 21

In the crowded, stuffy fMRI control room, Amir, Janine, and the rest of the bleary-eyed Brain Trust eyed Andric Breckinridge warily.

The initial appearance of his dead wife, rendered as if she had been painted by Renoir, had cast him into uncharacteristic silence. He'd wandered out of the room in a daze and had been absent for nearly an hour.

When he returned, he was more irritable than ever. He impatiently scanned his son's visual log and demanded a transcript of everything Andrew had seen.

When he finished reviewing the data, he was fuming.

"This was *not* the plan. He is supposed to be gathering data about the CereLink. He's not even in the right slice!" Breckinridge snarled.

While most of the staff cowered in the periphery, Janine Mori stood fast.

"We are days away from releasing a vaccine that can halt this budding flu pandemic before it becomes a near-extinction event," she said. "You know he believed returning to that slice would only exacerbate the spread of the virus."

Breckinridge's terrible pause as he glared at Janine seemed to make the very air tremble. His reply was low and threatening.

"I have weighed the risks and deemed them acceptable. He should not defy me."

Janine turned in frustration so he couldn't hear her mutter, "At least someone is willing to stand up for what's right."

Hours passed, and the two bodies in the twilight of the fMRI suite remained comatose.

"There is no choice. We must force his return," Andric insisted.

Janine shook her head. "You know it's too risky."

His cold eyes flashed as he stared down at her. "It's my project, my call."

"She never would have let you go this far," Janine retorted, meeting his icy gaze.

"She has been dead for over a decade. Administer the propofol, now. Or I will relieve you and find someone who will," the CEO demanded.

In the end, Janine relented. She administered the drug to Andrew's IV, and the entire team monitored the readings from the CereLink expectantly.

Thirty minutes passed, then an hour. The images from Andrew's visual cortex degraded, but he did not awaken.

Andric was not deterred. "Increase the dosage!"

To her credit, Janine refused. She pulled Andric aside.

"Andric, I cannot, in good faith, continue to administer this medication to my patient. What you're asking me to do will kill him."

Andric's eyes bulged. "He's destroying everything!"

"He's your son," she reminded him.

Breckinridge's black scowl cast an oppressive pall over the

entire room, but to Janine's immense relief, he did not order the dose again.

At the twelve-hour mark, Janine and the nurses in residence unclothed the two patients and gowned them to make it easier to institute the supportive care regimen of IV drips and feeding tubes and catheters. She carefully folded each garment as it was removed, storing their clothing neatly away in a corner. If she found an errant note in Andrew's pocket, she didn't share that information.

Andric remained in the control room, monitoring his son's unfolding experiences. He ate infrequently and refused to sleep. With each passing hour, his ire only increased.

By morning, Andric had reached the limit of his patience. Before the Brain Trust had arrived, he cornered Amir in the fMRI room and thrust a third Bug against his chest.

"You! You work for my son. You *will* assist me. Sync this device and apply it, immediately."

Amir clutched the Bug and stared at Breckinridge with a look of incomprehension. "Uh, what now? Apply the device to who? And where did you find our backup?"

Fire flashed behind the man's cold blue eyes. "Apply it to me, you imbecile! Since no one else seems able to solve this problem, I will do so myself."

Amir glanced nervously around the room, desperately hoping that Janine would make a miraculous appearance to dissuade his boss from undertaking this lunatic course of action.

"Stop looking about like a ninny," Breckinridge snapped. He waved impatiently at the Bug in Amir's hand. "I know you can sync multiple devices. Just make it work."

Amir shrugged; he attached the device to a console, pulled out the keyboard's retractable tray, and slowly typed a cascade of commands.

Despite the fact that Amir stalled for as long as he could, the synchronization sequence had been completed. Amir unplugged the Bug, which hummed and emitted a triplet of digital beeps.

"Sir, this is a very bad idea," Amir implored, hesitating. "The side effects can be serious, or even lethal. We've never tested you, and sending you to such a divergent slice for your first trial is an unacceptable risk."

"For the love of all that is holy, would you please stop second-guessing me and turn on that blasted device?" Breckinridge hissed.

Amir took a deep breath and shored up his shoulders. Complying could mean he was handing the man a death sentence.

"Sir, I'm sorry, but I can't in good conscience allow you to take this risk."

In one frightening moment, Breckinridge's face contorted into a mask of rage. With astonishing speed, his desiccated, clawlike hand shot forward and snatched the device from Amir's cradled palm and jammed its spindly legs against his right hand. The Bug's sharp probe descended nearly instantaneously.

Amir's eyes grew wide, and for one terrible moment, he was paralyzed in his tracks.

Andric Breckinridge collapsed to the floor, and his eyes rolled back into his skull. His entire body began to writhe and convulse.

"Oh, shit, oh, shit...oh, shit!" Amir stammered. He stared in horror as a slick of white foam oozed from the corner of the man's mouth. Finally shaken from frozen indecision, Amir dashed toward the control room, scrambled for the phone, and punched in the extension for Janine and the medics.

CHAPTER 33

KATE

November 21

My favorite room in Isabel's extraordinary home was the classic Victorian conservatory. The expansive space was filled with lush tropical greenery and orchids of every size, shape, and color in pots, planters, and even on vines dangling from the white-painted rafters. Strategically placed fountains provided peaceful ambience as well as the humidity the tropical plants required.

Comfortable wicker furniture was scattered thoughtfully throughout the room, and I'd appropriated a cushion from the footrest of one of the chairs to serve as my meditation mat. I slowly opened my eyes and contemplated the intricate folds of a nearby purple-and-white spray of flowers. After another marathon multihour session of practice, I reveled in the calm and contentment.

Through the massive panes of glass facing the back garden, I noted the creeping gradient of pale blue-gray—the dawning of another morning. I stretched my stiff arms toward the windows overhead, then turned toward the slightest rustling behind me.

"I'm very sorry, my dear, have I interrupted you?" Isabel asked from the frame of the doorway. She was carrying a pair of steaming mugs; the aroma of mint tea wafted across the room.

I smiled languidly. "Of course not."

She crossed the threshold and moved gracefully through the room, handing me one of the mugs. Isabel settled herself into the nearest wicker armchair. "Sleepless night?"

I nodded. "But on the upside, the meditation can replace most of the sleep...as long as I do it for hours."

"Perhaps I should take up the practice." Isabel chuckled ruefully. "I haven't experienced a full night's sleep in more years than I can recall."

I smiled and sipped the hot tea. Spending time with Andrew's mother had been an eye-opening experience. She was warm, engaging, thoughtful, and gracious—the polar opposite of Andric Breckinridge. I couldn't comprehend how they had ever been a couple. Isabel and Andrew had spent the day in one another's company, leaving me free to read, walk the gardens, practice yoga, and meditate for hours. For the first time since we lost my sister, I felt the beginning tendrils of peace creeping back into my life.

I was considering the beautiful symmetry of a cluster of giant brilliant-pink cymbidium blooms when I heard the doorbell chimes.

Isabel's brow furrowed as she rose from her perch, and the chimes rang again. "So insistent! Who could it be at this early hour?" She placed her mug on the table next to a gilded planter and turned for the door.

Instincts flaring with concern, I padded after her.

As we approached the entryway, the relentless chimes of the bell were punctuated by angry pounding on the door. Isabel reached for the handle.

She eased the door open just a few inches, but the caller flung it inward with enough force to smash the handle into the wall, rattling the stained glass pane in the transom above.

The uncharacteristically disheveled, seething form of Andric

Breckinridge lurched through the opening. He was fearsome at the best of times, but his appearance at this instant was doubly terrifying. His eyes twitched and blinked in random cadence, and his face contorted into an unnatural grimace as he used the back of his hand to wipe away a long stream of foamy spittle from the corner of his grotesque mouth.

Isabel glared at him with a stare of pure venom. I knew this look. It must be a family trait. "Get out of my house!" she screamed, standing her ground.

Breckinridge simply pushed roughly past the slight woman, swatting her away as if she were an inconsequential insect. I drew back against the wall, and he glared daggers at me as he bounded past. He grasped the iron bannister of the dramatic curved staircase and lurched up the stairs, his gait erratic.

For a moment, I was stunned—this shouldn't be possible. It was immediately obvious that the man who had just invaded Isabel's home was not her ex-husband. I broke out in a cold sweat, and a sinking feeling of dread descended upon me. I knew without a doubt that the fury raging up the stairs was our Andric Breckinridge.

He'd reached the landing before I was able to shake myself into action. I scurried up the staircase with Isabel close on my heels. Breckinridge was advancing down the hall, violently throwing open each heavy paneled door he encountered.

"Where is he?" the man thundered.

At the end of the hallway, a bedroom door swung open and revealed Andrew's silhouette.

Breckinridge charged his son. "You *will* leave this place!" he roared. In an instant, both men disappeared into the room. Behind me, Isabel screamed.

I froze, struggling to remain calm as the sound of a scuffle emanated from the room. I knew instinctively that I could not allow fear to overtake me; it would send me back. Which was exactly what Breckinridge wanted, and exactly what Andrew didn't. I forced myself to stop, to inhale. Isabel dashed past me, into the darkened bedroom.

"Stop!" Isabel shrieked. "Take your hands off him!"

"Get off me, woman!" Breckinridge bellowed.

I hovered uselessly in the hallway, trying to calm my mind and body.

"I want you out of here immediately!" Breckinridge demanded.

"Then why didn't you administer the propofol?" Andrew shouted.

"I did!" Breckinridge roared.

There was a dull thud, and then the earsplitting sound of shattering ceramic.

I was still trying to decide what to do when a blurred figure shot abruptly from the room. I found myself pinned to the wall by the strong and surprisingly agile CEO of Albaion.

"You!" he panted, his face just inches from mine.

I could feel the heat from his sour breath. The left half of his face had gone completely slack, as if he had suffered a stroke. His right eye, now red-rimmed and bloodshot, continued to twitch, and the right side of his lips curled into a terrible snarl. I scratched at his gnarled fingers in a futile attempt to break free from his iron grip.

"You are the source of my ruin." His crazed eye narrowed as he drew even closer to me. "I will force you to return us, right now."

I struggled like my life depended on it, but he pressed against me, restraining my movements, while his hands wrapped around my neck like monstrous claws. I was desperate to take a breath, and I kicked at him with all my strength, but he was too close and too strong. Breckinridge's face transformed into an ugly mask of triumph as I gasped and sputtered. He was right; he *was* going to force me to exit this slice, and I just might take him with me, stranding Andrew here alone. If he didn't stop, I was going to die. His fingers tightened around my neck, and the panic I'd fought so hard to contain threatened to overwhelm me. I felt a surge of anger, surgically sharp like the blade of a knife. I couldn't let him win. I couldn't let him force me out. And the only way to do that was to let go—of everything. I closed my eyes and stopped fighting the fear. I allowed my entire body to slump, every muscle relaxed and yielding, and reached deep, deep within my well of inner peace. I waited for the blackness to close in—and then suddenly, I could breathe. I coughed, rubbing my raw neck, and took in great gulps of air. My eyes shot open and I slid down the wall.

Isabel had tackled Andric, and although he grossly outweighed the sprite of a woman, she had somehow managed to pin the struggling man to the ground.

Andrew staggered out of the bedroom, his hand pressed against a gash above his left eye. Blood oozed between his fingers.

"Mom!" he exclaimed. His eyes darted between his mother as she restrained his enraged, writhing father, and me as I rubbed my pulsating neck. I'd never seen him look so bewildered.

"We have to help her," I rasped, lunging toward Andric's struggling body.

Andrew broke out of his stupor and grabbed my wrist.

"No. There is only one way to end this. You must go," he urged.

I stopped in my tracks. "But you said we needed to stay here long enough to uninvent the Bug."

I could swear his piercing blue eyes could see directly to my soul. "I didn't say *we* have to go. I said *you* have to go."

"I won't leave you here!" I didn't even try to disguise my panic. "It's a death sentence!"

For the first time, when I searched his face, instead of inscrutability, I saw sorrow, loss, and unrelenting determination.

In one fluid move, he closed the space between us and his arms were around me.

"I found you because of the Bug and now I'm going to lose you," I insisted, tears streaming down my cheeks. "I won't leave you here…" I whispered, but I could not shut out the overwhelming intensity of the emotions swirling inside.

His voice was low, steady, and resolute. "You must do this," he murmured. My entire body trembled as if I was suffering from hypothermia. And then he let me go.

As the disorientation overtook me and the world began to lose form, the last of his words fell softly on my ear.

"I love you."

I knew I was home even before I opened my eyes. I knew by the sound, and the scent, and the very feel of the air.

I dreaded that first look because I heard the call of birdsong and I smelled the dew evaporating from the grass. Through the grogginess, I could feel the weakness in my limbs and I feared the onset of a massive migraine. Eyes still screwed shut, I pulled myself into a sitting position, shivering slightly in the chill morning air. Small clumps of dry dirt and the razor-sharp seeds of foxtails dug into the palms of my hands, but my knees were protected by my jeans.

For a moment, the disorientation was overwhelming. What was going on? Hadn't I just been wearing a skirt? Where was Albaion's insidious lab?

My eyes shot open, and I struggled unsteadily to my feet. The first golden vestiges of the sun's early morning rays were beginning to shine over the hills behind me as I spun slowly around. Birds, sky, scrubby trees, grasses—there were plenty of these. But no building. I shut my eyes against the vertigo and the mild pounding in my head, and I took a few moments to breathe and to gather my thoughts.

The Albaion building was gone. It had never been here, nor had I ever been unconscious within its walls, clad in an old-fashioned blouse and skirt, traipsing across realities. History was rewriting itself in my brain—I could almost feel the shift within my synapses.

It must have taken me two hours, but I managed the hike out of the hills and onto Stanford's adjacent campus. Dehydrated, famished, and exhausted, I was taken aback by the wave of relief that flooded over me when the building that housed Dr. Daniels's lab came into view. I let myself into the unlocked lobby and found the restrooms, where I lunged toward the water fountain.

It was still early, and I didn't encounter a single soul as I made my way to the second floor. My heart sunk as I realized the door to my office was locked. By reflex, I slid my hand into my right pocket and was amazed to find my key ring—house and office keys ready and waiting.

I let myself into the dark and empty office and rushed to my desk. I dug through the detritus in the top drawer until I found a small bag of roasted almonds, which I tore into with reckless abandon. Then I woke up my workstation, relieved my log-in and password were still active.

I frantically typed in a search for "Albaion Andric Breckinridge" and clicked on the Wikipedia link. The photo of the scowling, defiant man was enough to make my throat constrict. The picture was captioned with the words, *Mug shot of Breckinridge upon his arrest in 2012.*

Andric L. Breckenridge (born February 28, 1949) is an American lawyer, businessman, scientist, and entrepreneur. The son of famed financier and oil magnate Thomas Henry

Breckinridge and grandson of the timber baron James Robert Breckinridge, Breckinridge inherited an enormous estate. He was founder, CEO, and chairman of the Albaion Corporation, which reached a valuation of $110 billion. Breckinridge employed illegal accounting practices to manipulate the debt load of the Albaion balance sheet to drive up its stock price. In addition, Breckinridge utilized shell companies in Luxembourg to bribe foreign officials to win technology contracts, as well as to advance oil contracts that would be advantageous to his personal investing interests. The deception was uncovered in 2011. Breckinridge was indicted and found guilty of eight counts of securities fraud. In addition, his violation of the Foreign Corrupt Practices Act incurred the maximum penalty of $25 million per violation, which resulted in the collapse of Albaion and obliterated his family's personal financial portfolio. He is currently serving an eighty-year sentence at the Federal Correctional Institution in Otisville, New York.

After the first paragraph, I was completely stunned. The ramifications were obvious—no Albaion, no Bug. I quickly called up the CDC's weekly US influenza surveillance report.

Influenza activity in the US has remained uncharacteristically low as we move into December. Influenza A viruses are the most common strain identified. Several influenza activity indicators were lower than normally seen for this time of year. These data indicate that currently circulating viruses have not undergone significant antigenic drift and circulating A(H1N2) viruses are antigenically similar to egg-grown A(H1N2) viruses used for producing the majority of influenza vaccines in the United States.

I breathed a tremendous sigh of relief—not a single word about the Luzon Flu. I scrambled over to Jeff's desk and grabbed the cradle of the only landline phone in our office. I keyed the number for Michelle's mobile phone and waited breathlessly, each ring boring into my brain.

"Hello?" My sister's hoarse greeting indicated I'd woken her. My sister's voice! Jubilation welled up in my chest and I burst into tears.

"Hi, it's me," I sniffed.

"Kate? Did you have a nightmare?" Her voice was thick with sleep, and I could tell she wasn't fully awake. "Why are you calling me at six thirty in the morning? And where are you anyway?"

I smiled as I swiped away the tears with the back of my hand. "I'm just fine. In fact, I'm great! Go back to sleep. I'll be home soon."

"Sometimes you are so weird..." she mumbled, terminating the call.

I bounced on my heels as I carefully replaced the phone in its cradle. My sister was alive! There was no deadly flu, and Albaion didn't own my soul—which must mean that the Bug was never invented.

My elation was short-lived. My chest constricted and I leaned against the desk for support. If the Bug was never invented, was it because Andrew had been killed in Uganda, like he had in Isabel's reality? I scrambled back to the computer for another search. The first item in the list was a recent article in the *New York Times*.

Pioneering Oncologist Falls into Unexplained Coma

MANHATTAN—Dr. Andrew Breckinridge, a rising star in oncological research at Memorial Sloan Kettering who pioneered a lifesaving treatment for stomach cancer, fell into an unexplained coma yesterday. Dr. Breckinridge was speaking at the American Society of Clinical Oncology's annual symposium in Berkeley, California when he collapsed. He was transported to UCSF Medical Center in San Francisco. His mother, Isabel Breckinridge-Hawthorne, released the following statement regarding her son's condition:

Although we have not determined the source of the mysterious illness afflicting my son, doctors and specialists at UCSF are working tirelessly to treat him.

Although best known for his innovative use of nanotechnology to drastically enhance immunotherapy for previously untreatable cancers, Dr. Breckinridge is also the son of entrepreneur Andric Breckinridge, who was convicted of bribery and illegal accounting practices and is currently incarcerated at the Federal Correctional Institution in Otisville, New York. In a mystifying turn of events, officials at the penitentiary confirmed that inmate Breckinridge suffered a massive stroke this morning and is currently unresponsive. He is not expected to recover.

My hand covered my mouth and my pulse raced. Andric Breckinridge suffered a stroke—this morning? Andrew's coma was no coincidence, either.

I called up the Caltrain schedule; I could take the train to San Francisco and I could...I could do what, exactly? I stopped, blinking hard. No one at UCSF would let a random stranger into the ICU. Despite the fact that I had been her houseguest in another slice, Isabel wouldn't recognize me, and if I tried to explain, surely I'd come off as a total lunatic. I'd probably get arrested.

The door of the office swung open. The distinctive staccato

echo of cowboy boots meant I didn't even need to turn around to know that Jeff was also having an early morning.

"Mornin', Sunshine!" he drawled, slapping an opened envelope on my desk. "This here is a letter from the Breckinridge Fellowship committee, and guess who just got funded?" His self-congratulatory grin left no doubt that it certainly wasn't me.

Jeff's broad forehead wrinkled as he took a second look at me. "Hey, darlin', you like you've been chewed up, spit out, and stepped on. I know that losing this grant is hard on you, but..."

Who needed the grant when I had the entirety of the multiverse at my disposal? I raised my hand to silence him and shook my head.

"Fuck off, Jeff."

EPILOGUE

December 22

I sit in half-lotus on a thin cushion in a small, plain room tucked away in the interior of the vast residence in Bel Air. The room has no furniture, and the floor is lined with tatami mats. The walls are painted a pale golden color I have learned is called "La Luna Amarilla." The indirect lighting is warm, soft, and dim. The only decor is a grand oil painting of a lone, windswept cypress perched on a promontory against the backdrop of the sapphire-blue Pacific. I recognize the location—it is the Big Sur coast.

I have been sitting on this cushion for hours. I have confined myself in this room every day for weeks. Every day since I returned to a world without the Bug. Every day that he remains in a coma. This is the thirty-first day.

I throw my hands in frustration, and an odd warble escapes from my throat.

"I can't do this!"

The plump Indian woman sitting beside me opens her eyes languidly and gazes at me with unyielding serenity. Her expression does not waver. She takes a moment to tuck a graying strand of hair behind her ear. She says nothing.

"Gurudevi, this is not working!" I insist. "I can't get to him, no matter how hard I try."

"The great teacher Mata Amritanandamayi says, 'We must remember

that man is not an island, totally isolated and disconnected from others. We are all part of a universal chain, or the universal consciousness.'"

I slump on my cushion and sigh. "Gurudevi, that doesn't help at all."

"She has also taught, 'If you have patience, then you'll also have love. Patience leads to love. If you forcefully open the petals of a bud, you won't be able to enjoy its beauty and fragrance. Only when it blossoms by following its natural course, will the beauty and fragrance of a flower unfold.'"

"But time is the one thing I don't have," I remind her. It is impossible to describe the relief I felt when the sixty-hour mark passed and he was still alive. Although he is trapped in limbo, at least it is no longer due the brain-annihilating circumstance of the Bug. I have no idea how long he'll be able to hold on. Every day that passes is another day that the synapses in Andrew's brain might stop firing. Every day that passes is another day that Isabel might choose to turn off the machines that keep him alive.

"You have no patience, child. Go," she says, waving her smooth, brown hand in a dismissive gesture. "Go and walk in the garden."

I rise from the cushion and quietly leave the room.

When I reach the courtyard, the winter sun is hidden behind ominous gray clouds, but Kate is out despite the dubious weather. She is wrapped in a knobby ivory sweater and is typing on her laptop. She looks up and smiles.

"I see she sent you out to the garden."

I nod.

"I can't tell you how many times she sent me out to the garden." Her compassionate smile hardly dents my frustration. "It took me years to learn how to control this ability. And you've made so much progress— you're here every day, and have been for weeks."

I appreciate her attempt at encouragement, but it doesn't ease my mind. I manage an anemic grin but pace in distraction. Does no one grasp the urgency? I don't have years. Every moment that passes could be his last. Kate closes her laptop.

"Would you like a cup of tea?" she offers.

I sigh once more. What else am I going to do?

"Sure."

While I wait, I sit on the capstones that border the bed of mint. I am absentmindedly pinching its leaves to release the sharp essence when I hear the footfall, and I know it's not the other Kate. I swallow hard and turn around.

"You've been avoiding me," he observes as he hands me the steaming mug of tea.

It's true. I've been studying with Gurudevi for a month in his home, and I haven't seen him once. For the first time I realize that this isn't a coincidence.

"Don't take it personally." I can't bear to look at him, but I can feel his gaze and it pierces my heart. I suddenly feel queasy; I sip the hot mint tea.

He sits patiently beside me on the wall of the garden bed. I stare at my feet. He is too near; I inhale his familiar scent, and the air seems to vibrate with his energy. The nausea intensifies.

I put down the cup of tea. "I'm sorry, I can't..." I object, but as I rise, he grasps my hand and I finally face him. His luminous blue eyes are brimming with concern, and my knees buckle.

He releases me and takes my face in both of his hands. The gesture causes my entire body to flood with radiant warmth. His proximity is unbearable. I close my eyes.

"This isn't right," I protest. "I can't do this to her; she's been so kind to me..."

"She sent me to you. She thinks I can help."

My eyes shoot open.

"I love her and you are her and you are in pain."

"I need to find him," I whisper.

"You need to find him," he earnestly replies.

And then he kisses me.

I blink and he is gone. The entire courtyard is gone, replaced by Isabel's conservatory, festooned with orchids. For a moment, I can't breathe. Then I tear through the house like a woman possessed.

I've exhausted my search through the uninhabited rooms, and in dismay, I reach the huge wraparound veranda at the back of the estate. It overlooks the sweeping green expanse of the wild and dense garden, with its winding path and bushy California native foliage. The clouds are gray in this place too, but here, like me, they begin to weep.

I look up when I hear the crunch of hurried footsteps on the gravel fines of the path.

He rounds the corner of the footpath and stops in his tracks. For a moment, he stands there in astonishment, rain soaking into his dove-gray dress shirt.

My shoulders release in immense and profound relief. A bizarre sense of weightlessness overtakes my entire body. I am not too late.

"Hey," I call with a nod. I swab my cheeks with the sleeve of my sweater. "You're going to ruin that shirt in the rain. What is it, Armani?"

The moment of confusion passes; his face brightens and the spell is broken. He bounds up the walkway and sweeps me up into a soggy embrace. I can't help noticing that his previously lean frame now appears haggard—almost cadaverous.

He pulls back and stares at me in disbelief. In his gaunt face I see boundless relief, but also something else—something harder to pinpoint. He clutches my left hand and examines it carefully. The welt from the Bug has long since healed, replaced by a small, round pink scar.

When he speaks, his weary voice is raspy, and his blue eyes are hollow, but they retain their familiar twinkle. Amusement? Amazement? Or something more?

"You came back."

I shake my head sadly. "I'm sorry to be the bearer of bad news, but I'm afraid you're not going to be able to afford four-hundred-dollar dress shirts on an oncologist's salary."

He looks confused for a moment, then a wan smile spreads over his pale face.

"Especially since your father lost his business and the family fortune years ago when he was indicted for bribery and fraud."

His left eyebrow arches and he cocks his head. "Indeed."

"And Isabel will be ecstatic that you've recovered from your mysterious coma."

His expression transforms into momentary delight, then his countenance darkens.

"You know," he reasons, "this means a significant measure of history has been altered. Without Albaion, without my father, without the Bug—we will never have met. There is a very good chance I will simply wake up from a coma with no memory of any of this. How will I find you?"

"There's no need," I reply with a wink and a shrug. "I finally understand how this relationship works. You get lost, and I find you."

His explosive laugh is genuine—a sound I had feared I'd never hear again. With a tremendous exhale, I realize that all this time, I've been holding my breath.

"What do you say we get out of here?" he suggests earnestly, releasing my hand and slipping his arm around my waist.

Face upturned, I wrap my arms around his neck and pull him close. "I thought you'd never ask."

ABOUT THE AUTHOR

Wendy Devore loves obscure science, complicated emerging technology, and cuddling up with a good book by the fire. She has been known to build websites, edit children's television for PBS, and test software but she's never happier than when she concocts a narrative that will make someone cry. She lives near Lake Tahoe, California with her husband, daughter, and two demanding cats. In her spare time, she enjoys inventing excuses to avoid downhill skiing.